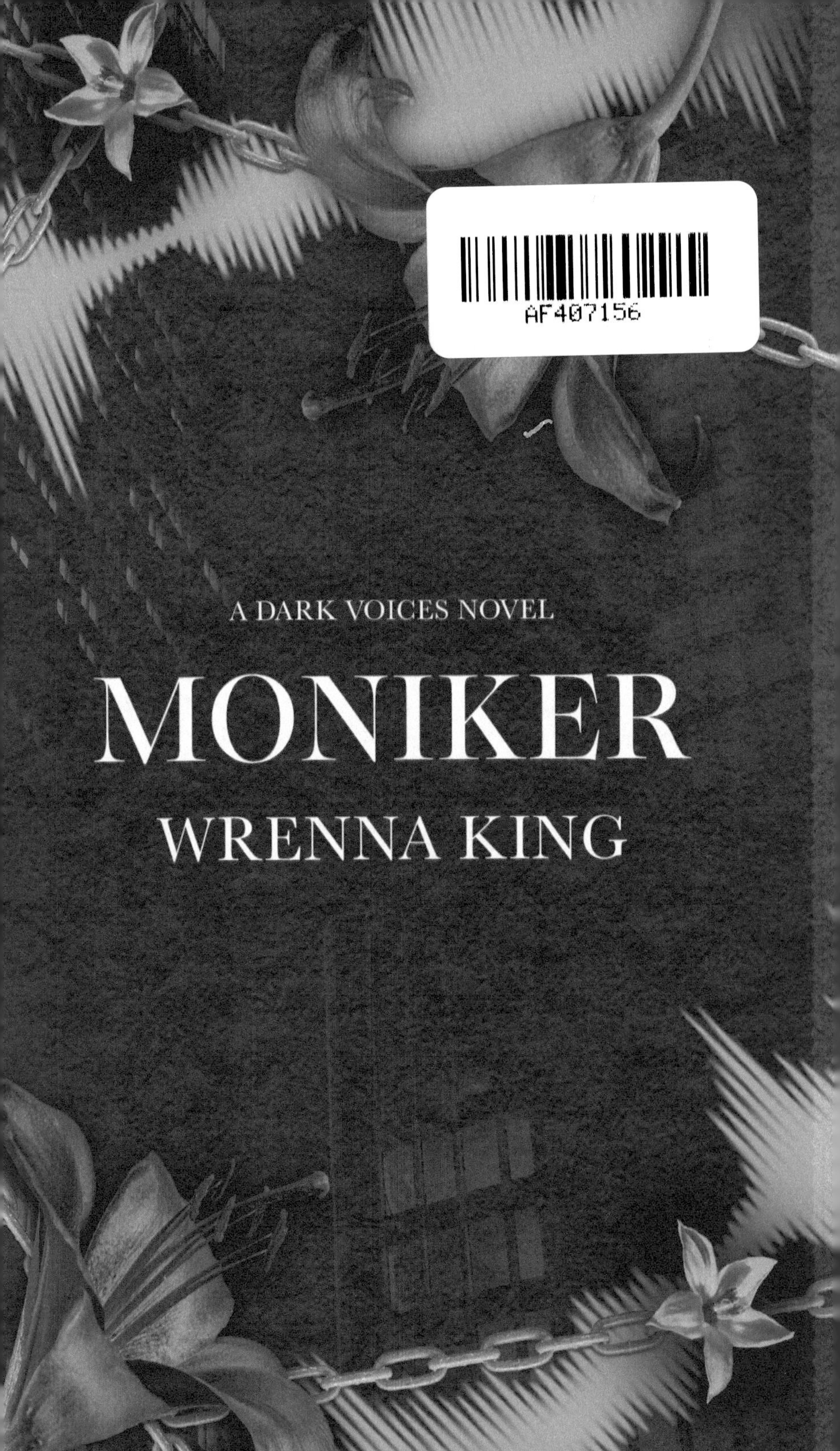

AF407156
A DARK VOICES NOVEL
MONIKER
WRENNA KING

ISBN: 979-8-9935024-0-3 (Ebook)

ISBN: 979-8-9935024-1-0 (Paperback)

Book Cover and Interior Formatting by Disturbed Valkyrie Designs

Illustration by Barnswallow

Editing by Lunar Rose Services

Proofreading by K. Morton Editing Services with Lunar Rose

First Edition 2025

Ink Feather Books, LLC

wrennaking.com

CONTENT NOTE

Moniker contains themes and descriptions of content that may be sensitive to some readers. For a full list of content warnings, please visit wrennaking.com or scan the QR code below. Please do not proceed with this book without consideration for your mental health.

For Mom. I did it. Miss you, everyday.

Medicate Me - Rain City Drive, Dayseeker
When You Say My Name - Chandler Leighton
Drive You Insane - Daniel Di Angelo
over me - Camylio
Please - Omido, Ex Habit
Feel Me Now - If Not For Me
Even When I'm With You - Pierce the Veil
Shame On Me - Catch Your Breath
Outside - breakk.away
i'm yours - Isabel LaRosa
How Villains Are Made - Madalen Duke
Rain - Sleep Token

CHAPTER ONE

RAVEN

I was a terrible daughter.

The thought ran through my mind as I stared out my floor to ceiling glass office windows to the glittering city beyond, disappointment with myself settling in my chest. Traffic was lessening as rush hour faded into a quiet evening. I glanced at the modern black wall clock that read nearly seven, which meant I was due at my parents house for dinner in two minutes. Sighing, I snatched my phone from the other side of my L-shaped desk.

The ringing reverberated through my body, leaving a trail of melancholy in its wake. On the third ring, my mother's eager voice filled my office from the small speaker.

"Hey honey! I just pulled dinner from the oven. Are you almost here?"

I could see her standing with her hip leaned against the counter, the table set perfectly and waiting for a family to be seated around it. The house probably smelled wonderful from whatever she'd made since I would bet money she was the best cook in the city. My mouth watered and stomach growled as I thought of Mom's various casseroles and realized I hadn't eaten since breakfast. Lunch had been taken up by a meeting, and afterward I went back to work without thinking of food.

"Hey Mom. I got caught up at work. I don't think I'm going to be able to make it. I'm really sorry." Staring at the solid wall in front of my desk, I imagined Mom's smile fading as I once again canceled. "I'm still dealing with trying to dig my new client out of the mess they got themselves in. Maybe we can get together next month? This is going to take a while to fix."

Closing my eyes and propping my elbow on the glass, I brought my forehead to rest against my fingers. When Mom spoke again the excitement had drained away, replaced by her normal voice, feigning indifference.

"Oh honey, that's all right. Your dad and I will see you when you're free. You go be great and keep working hard to get that business to the top." Shuffling followed by a *swish* sounded on her end of the line, and I assumed Mom was shaking her head to tell Dad I wasn't going to show. "We love you, honey. Bye bye."

"Love you all too. Bye, Mom."

The beep signaling the end of the call filled my ears, and I scrubbed my hands over my face. Gratitude mixed with a hint of sadness washed through me as I thought of my understanding parents. They loved me unconditionally, and were always supportive of me following my dreams; never counting on the added benefits of my success. When I couldn't make dinner or wasn't able to visit long when I did show up, they never complained.

Tucking my black tresses behind my ear, I looked back to the bright computer screens, the numbers and stock runs beginning to blur. Despite my tiredness and regret, I pushed through, completing additional tasks that would set me up for an easier Friday.

A few hours later I locked the door to my office suite and trudged to the elevators. Once in the concrete behemoth of a car garage attached to my high rise, I pressed my key fob, illuminating my sleek black Lexus parked a dozen feet from the door. The breeze rustled my long locks, and I breathed in the scent of tar that usually lingered in the structure. Adjusting the weight of my purse against my tense shoulder, I was glad I was one of the first in the garage every morning and always had a spot close to the entrance.

When I reached for the car door, chills raised along my skin at the sound of a *clang* in the stairwell on the other side of the garage. My senses went on alert as I turned a three sixty to survey every direction. People occasionally hung out in the garages downtown in my mid-size city, but I usually didn't pay much attention. Tonight felt different; the hair on the back of my neck standing on end. I threw open the car door and hurled myself inside, jamming the locks. If there was someone with ill intentions lurking, little did they know I wasn't the bitch to fuck with.

As soon as the thought crossed my mind, my stomach churned. Doubt crept in the corners of my consciousness, and flashes of a darkened back alley flickered behind my eyes while phantom hands encircled my wrists. My body screamed at the memory of fingers tearing at my clothes and the bruises that marred my skin.

Gripping the steering wheel, I shook the images from my head and stilled my breathing, my usual composure sliding back into place. It had been over a decade. He wasn't here. Still, I plucked the pepper spray from the outer pocket of my purse and whipped the knife from its sheath strapped to my ankle. Gripping the hard leather handle in my palm, I brushed my thumb along the edge of the blade. It was still deadly despite not being sharpened recently. I hadn't ever used the thing, but carried it with me at all times, none-theless.

With my weapons within close reach, I pushed the ignition button and my dash came to life. I buckled my seatbelt and threw the car in reverse. As I sped onto the street, I cursed as my phone's Bluetooth connected, and Zander Kane's voice filled the car. I scrambled to hit the pause button, not in the headspace for an audiobook after the long day I'd had. That morning, I'd been listening to a new release on my way to work, and I must have been really into it because that shit was insanely loud. People at stop lights had probably heard the lascivious narration even though the windows had been up, but I didn't care. I was unapologetic about the books I enjoyed.

Smirking, I drove to my apartment in silence, my body sagging in the seat. The days had run together recently, and the late nights and early mornings were taking a toll. Canceling on Mom and Dad had been the icing on the dejected cake. The hint of sadness in Mom's voice when she talked about missing me forced the weight of my responsibilities to grow heavier. They lived in a suburban town half an hour away from the city, so it wasn't far to travel, but I simply didn't have time.

None of us could complain, though. Not many thirty-two-year-old women owned a rising financial firm, making more money than most ever dreamed of.

The memory of the first time I saw the letters on my door flashed through my mind. Lovelace Financial was proudly displayed on the glass and although it was an uncertain venture at first, the last few years had been a whirlwind. The company had grown to the point where I was able to supplement my parents' income and live the life I had always wanted when I was a kid, not having to worry about food or if the bills would be paid. The only regret was not having more time for the people who mattered most. The only family I had.

My apartment was stale like usual as I hung my keys on their hook by the door. Strolling through the living room, I headed straight to the balcony. I lived a few miles outside of downtown, in a top-floor apartment that had a magnificent view of the city. It wasn't large, but the city was big enough to be successful in. The cost of living was much cheaper than in New York or Chicago, so money went farther, a necessity when supporting two households.

I gazed out at quiet streets and lights dotting the horizon. The sounds of cars and the occasional bark of a dog floated on the breeze. The Thirsty Thursday crowd downtown was out in full force and I was glad I was away from the bars and nightlife. That was something I'd enjoyed for a brief time in college over a decade ago. Focusing on my career and devoting everything I had to the business was enough as I got older.

A career was worse than a spouse with the way it took up every waking moment, and the complications of marriage weren't something I was willing to make time for.

Closing my eyes, I breathed in the late August air. The nights were turning from balmy to bearable, and I relished spending more free time outside when I had it. Not that I had it often. Stepping back through the glass French doors, I made my way to the primary bedroom, my black heels clicking on the tile as I went.

As I moved through the en suite and into the panoramic closet, I shrugged out of the black pinstripe skirt suit, my gaze falling to the monochrome clothing neatly lining the walls. I had never grown out of my goth girl phase from high school and it showed in my style choices. In 2010, everyone wore all black with heavy eye makeup and band tees. I toned back the eyeliner and swapped the T-shirts for suits, but I still kept the general vibe. Most outfits were some variation of black and gray with the occasional white accent.

Once clean and between my sheets in my king bed, I slid my headphones over my ears and grabbed my phone from the nightstand. I pulled up the audiobook from earlier, and Zander's sexy voice filled my ears, transporting me into the spicy scene. It was perfect to finish before bed.

Zander usually did romance, which is how I found him since it was my favorite genre. This story happened to be about a woman who was taken by the mafia and fell in love with the member who worked in secret to free her. Written by one of my favorite authors, the sex scenes were full of angst and perfect for Zander's voice.

"You're mine," Zander said, chills dancing along my skin. "I had no part in your capture, but I'm not sorry they took you. It brought you into my life, and I would let them do it again."

Before I knew it, his velvet voice carried me away to sleep.

CHAPTER TWO

RYAN

HANGING my headphones on their hook, I emerged from the recording booth, exhaustion tugging at my limbs. It was just after five so the neighbors would arrive home soon, dashing any hopes of working for the next few hours. The best time for narration was when people were at work or asleep.

I cracked my neck and padded to the kitchen, my feet protesting the movement. They were aching from standing for hours, and I reminded myself to sit more often while I worked. Standing helped me use the full range of my voice, though, so it was either sore feet or inferior audio.

My phone buzzed on the counter where I'd left it while working as I lifted the glass of water to my lips. Leaving it outside the booth so I wasn't tempted to scroll social media instead of narrating was a necessity. I was easily distracted, and the day had been particularly long since I'd procrastinated with the latest job. The quick deadline because of my delay made me want to put it off even more—not to mention the project wasn't my favorite subgenre of romance to narrate.

Happy contemporary romance usually made the most

money, but my favorites were fantasy and the darker stuff. Those were more exciting to me, although there wasn't anything wrong with the Hallmark stories. They were heart-warming and made people feel good, a much-needed escape from day-to-day life.

I swiped the phone screen, not bothering to look at the caller ID since I already knew who it was. Only one person ever called me. "What's up, Craig?" I answered.

"Hey, Ryan, how's the recording coming along?" My agent's greeting sounded mildly desperate.

Before answering, I took another gulp of water. "It's coming. I just finished a solid session, so I should have everything recorded in the next day or so."

Craig's sigh of relief resonated on the other side of the line. "Great! The requests keep coming in. I think we should ramp up your recording time even more. Let's ride the wave while we have it. You never know when things will plateau and drop off." His voice was accented by the soft tapping of a pen on wood.

"You already have another one for me to start after I finish this one, don't you?"

The tapping stopped. "I sure do. It's one of those spicy dark romances. Your favorite."

I blew out a breath. "At least there's that. If I have to record another cutesy scene in a pumpkin patch or a Christmas tree farm, I'm going to fall asleep. I know people love it, but I need something more exciting. Those are all I've been doing lately," I huffed. "Give me murder, mafia, kinky sex, and all the fucked-up shit."

"Well...there's a catch," Craig said hesitantly.

"Fuck," I said, irritability lacing my voice as I sat the glass on the counter with more force than necessary. "What now?" I asked, aggravation already spreading through me because I knew he was going to say something I wouldn't like.

"The author is indie and fronting the money for a duet."

The beginnings of a headache pulled at my temples as I loosed a sigh and imagined the hassle I could be in for. "Craig, I'm not doing it if I have to record live like the author wanted last month. It's 2024, there's no need for live narration for *chemistry*," I said, adding emphasis to the last word.

"I know, I know. We will try to do it separately and production will splice it together. Since it worked well a few books ago, the author is on board. I talked to her this morning and she said as long as it sounds good she wouldn't need you and your counterpart in person or on a call together. She's dead set on you for her novel, so she agreed when I said you work on your own time."

"Fine," I grunted. "But if it doesn't work, I'm not recording based on someone else's availability. I work when I can, and when the words are flowing. Send me the script, and I'll look it over before I give the green light."

After ending the call, I ran a hand through my russet hair and fell on the couch. I replayed the conversation and contemplated the newest deal. It wasn't that I disliked duet-style narration. It made the most money, but I hated when authors wanted narrators to record live in person or more typically, on a conference call. Everyone loved duet over dual, but what they didn't realize was that it was next to impossible to get two narrators on the same schedule. Not to mention all the work that went into duet and the extra cost.

Catering to other people wasn't something I liked to deal with, and adhering to someone else's schedule was a nightmare. I'd done it frequently when I began my career, but the more popular I became the fewer jobs I took that required me to do things I didn't want to do.

My dislike of being around people was one of the reasons voice work interested me in the first place. I didn't have to deal with feeling like I didn't live up to expectations unless I wanted to seek out reviews on the books I worked on. I'd seen enough of that from my parents, and had no desire to experience that repeatedly so using my voice to make a product was ideal.

It took some time to get the booth set up and all the kinks worked out when I decided I wanted to do voice acting and narration instead of just fucking around on social media. After I signed with Craig and started making a real income, I was thankful I splurged on state of the art recording equipment.

A hint of excitement settled in my chest as I prepared dinner. As long as I could record when I wanted, this project would be fun. I wouldn't have to use my higher female voice so I could enjoy the story more. My curiosity was rampant about the different themes that persisted throughout the darker side of romance that might be in the book, and blood rushed to my cock at the thought. Those novels usually tested the limits of what society deemed acceptable, and I was all for it. I even read books I didn't narrate in the genre in my spare time.

Since I wasn't able to work for a few hours, I decided to see if any of the bros were online. A few hours of video games and streaming would be just what I needed to have a productive night. The more I got done, the faster Craig would ease up on the calls.

"In, in, in, in, in!" I yelled at my computer screen. "Dude, stay behind me. I know he went in here." My heart thudded with anticipation. A few beats passed, and I cautiously stepped around the door frame of the rundown, abandoned house.

Shots rang out, and before I could react, my screen flashed black and a blood-red "dead" appeared.

"Motherfucker! I didn't think the asshole would be right fucking there. Guys, I'm over this shit tonight." My friends' grumbles sounded through my headset, and I quickly clicked out of the game, effectively killing their audio from my stream. "All right, babes," I said to the hundreds of people, most of which I assumed were female, watching me fuck around. "That does it for tonight. Catch you all next time."

Closing all the open tabs, I shut down my gaming computer and plucked my phone from its stand. I hadn't spent a lot of the money I'd earned through narration, but I did splurge for the gaming station that I was seated at in addition to my recording equipment. Complete with three monitors, strips of neon lighting, and a racing wheel, it was the ideal setup.

When I was a kid, video games were a distraction from life and I got back into them a few years ago after college. I'd found that the more I stayed in my room when I was younger, the less I had to hear about how much my father disliked me. Not to mention Mom being indifferent about everything where I was concerned.

The skills from my teenage years came back to me easily as an adult, so I started making content, posting online, and dabbling in streaming. Once my voice acting took off, the streaming got a hefty boost. Most of my current followers were fans that just tuned in to hear my voice. Even without engaging with subscribers directly and not showing my face, they all still tuned in to watch my fuckery.

My thoughts drifted to the beginning of my career as I leaned back in the chair and swiped through my notifications. Eleven months had passed since the fantasy romance I narrated went viral. Before the indie author reached out to me,

I'd gained mild traction with my paid platform and a few audiobooks, but I wasn't successful in narration by any means. My few thousand followers reflected that.

The author found me through social media and loved my voice. She couldn't pay me up front, so we agreed to royalty share. When the fantasy novel and audio released at the same time, they were an instant hit. I knew the performance was the best I'd done, but I wasn't prepared for the insanity that ensued. In a week, agents were busting down my door just like they were for the author. Countless publishers and other indie authors were flooding my inbox with requests for projects, and my subscriptions shot through the roof from fans. I had no idea how to handle it all, but I was fortunate Craig found me. He helped shape me into one of the most popular male voice actors on the market.

I scrolled through the new messages on socials that came in over the few hours I'd been playing and read every one. Some were harmless—just women saying how much they loved my latest audiobook or post. The last book I did dropped a week ago, and it was doing massively well. It was an exciting story since the male character was in the mafia and did some crazy and questionable shit.

Other messages I got weren't so innocent. I received dozens of messages every day and most of them were feral women lusting after me. Turning women into a mess with just my voice always got my dick hard. The power I had without them knowing what I looked like was fuel for countless sessions with my hand.

I rarely interacted with my fans and followers, especially not hooking up with them, but I fantasized about that power more often than not. I couldn't explain why it got me off, but it did. Stepping into a story through narration was the reason I loved my job, but I also relished the attention that came with it. Most likely because it was the first time in my life I wasn't standing in someone else's shadow. Someone who couldn't stand the sight of me.

After clearing the new messages, I switched over to the paid platform where I posted the more 'not safe for work' content. I had gained a hundred new subscribers throughout the week—more than usual. Satisfaction flooded my brain, despite knowing I wouldn't notice the extra money from them. Narration more than padded my bank account, but I still did the erotic content on the side because I enjoyed it.

It was almost nine, so I left the desk and padded through my room to the adjoining bathroom, the tile chilling my bare feet. My apartment didn't reflect my income anymore, but the AC was top notch. The living room and kitchen were one large room in the middle with the bedrooms on either side, one of which was the studio. I was too busy to look for a new place since I was constantly working, but I didn't need much anyway since it was just me. At some point soon, I needed to take some time off and maybe come to terms with a nicer place.

Shrugging out of my T-shirt, I ran a hand through my hair. It was long on top and short on the sides, since I preferred the messy look that running my hands through it gave. Once in the shower, my thoughts strayed back to a particular message I saw that was a reply to a particularly steamy post from last week.

You could read the back of a cereal box to me, and I'd still come just from your voice.

I groaned, lathering my body and trailing my hand south to the hardness between my thighs. The message was from a throwaway account of some person who probably wouldn't follow me on their actual profile. They hid behind an anonymous one because they didn't want their significant others or family knowing they followed a spicy narrator. I thought people should own what they like, but then again, I was the one hiding behind a pseudonym.

After the shower I wondered how I'd gotten to this point. I was pretty much a recluse, working out of my spare bedroom and only leaving the house when necessary. I even had my groceries delivered. Most twenty-five-year-old guys were still in their social phase, always going out with friends or their new wives. But, me? I was at home jerking off to a stranger's message on the internet because I couldn't handle the rejection from an actual person.

Dragging a hand over my face as I walked back to the studio, I sighed at my seemingly pathetic life. Everything was exactly how I wanted it to be, but at the same time, I wondered what it would be like to have people around. The guys I played video games with were in different cities, the only interactions we had being in game and the occasional texts.

Happy would be an overstatement, but I was perfectly content with the way things were. I'd lucked into a pretty cool career, and did whatever the fuck I wanted. Maybe I would have a partner someday, or maybe the occasional hook-up when my hand didn't cut it being the only in person face to face interactions I had. Maybe no one could ever love me since they hadn't before. Regardless, I was just a sloth without a care in the world.

I pushed all thoughts from my mind as I stepped through the cloth curtain, practicing the meditation techniques I used to get in the right headspace for my characters. Booting up the equipment, I stepped from reality into the fictional world the author had created, bringing their characters to life.

The next morning I woke in a daze. I'd stayed up until five when my voice was shot. The blaring phone alarm pierced my temples, and I hated that I couldn't sleep longer. It was late morning, so precious quiet hours I could be working were ticking away. I made a list of everything I had to do that day, one of which was paying bills.

Since I was thinking about finances, I pulled up my bank app next and stared at the massive number glaring on my phone screen. I never really thought about investing my money until Craig mentioned it would be a good idea a few weeks ago. He usually didn't pry, but he chose to offer a rare bit of advice in the moment. His words were hard to hear, but deep down, I knew my popularity might not last forever.

Reluctantly leaving the warm bed, I pulled on a pair of sweats over my tight-fitting boxer briefs. Not bothering with a shirt, I walked into the kitchen and decided it was time to be an adult and figure this shit out. I didn't know how long I would be able to ride the high and eventually, the money might slow down with the demand.

I pressed the button on the coffee maker and did a quick google search for what I was looking for. Tapping the phone number for the first company I saw, I pressed the green call icon. After what seemed like much longer than a usual line would ring, a woman finally answered. "Hello, Lovelace Financial, how may I assist you?"

CHAPTER THREE

RAVEN

"Raven Lovelace speaking," I said into the phone, already exhausted even though it was only eleven a.m. The morning had taken the wind out of my sails, and I still had a long day and night ahead.

What a great way to spend a Friday. The day of the week didn't matter though since I worked all the time, even weekends. After the last few hours, I wanted to crawl into bed with an audiobook and not think about anything except the main characters banging each other into oblivion. The problems continued to pile up, and they showed no signs of stopping. By the time I finished the call, I had another added to a list that was already a mile long.

Pushing back from my desk, I hurried to the coffee machine in the kitchenette. The business suite was small, yet modern and sophisticated. It had three offices and an open space for other workstations should I need them, and it was looking more and more like I would. I tapped my fingers on the countertop and stared into space while the machine whirred, making the fuel I desperately needed to survive the day.

The earthy aroma filled the room, making my mouth water for the blend with a hint of sweetness I kept stocked. I made it halfway back to my office before I was intercepted.

"Hey, Raven, can I have your ear for a minute?" Mia, the junior financial advisor I hired six months ago, called from her office.

Groaning internally, I backed up a step and paused in her doorway. "What's up?"

Her eyes went wide as she took in my disheveled appearance. "Damn, Boss, you look like you didn't sleep at all last night. You did sleep last night, right?" A whisper of worry flashed across her face.

Of course she would mention how awful I looked the moment she saw me. Mia and I had a great relationship, and she was more like a friend than an employee. She and Joanne both were. They were candid and let their personalities show, creating a fun environment while maintaining efficiency.

"I got some, but the holes some of our clients have dug themselves into are wearing on me this morning."

Mia nodded in understanding. "I'm sure they've been giving you hell. I'm right there with you." She sighed. "Joanne has been on the phone nonstop with consults all day, and I think my head is going to spin off my shoulders if I have to do another intake. This stack of files are all new." She gestured to a pile of manilla folders that was at least ten inches thick.

I leaned my hip against the frame and sipped my coffee. "Do you think it's time to hire another person? I think we could all use some help, and a receptionist would be a decent solution. Maybe free you up to work on larger projects, and Joanne to finally run this place."

Mia's eyes brightened and a grin crept onto her face. "I think that would be a good idea, but as always, it's your call. You're the mastermind behind the operation."

My eyes flicked to the clock on the wall of Mia's office. "I think I could actually use a break. I haven't stopped today," I said, blowing out a heavy breath as I dropped into the chair opposite Mia. Sometimes I was so focused on work I forgot to check in with her and Joanne. I made a mental note to be better about that. "How are things with you outside of here? How's your new puppy doing?"

"Oh, he's the cutest little guy ever." Mia's enthusiasm rose further. "I think the house training is starting to take hold, and even Kyle is coming around."

A chill ran down my spine. Mia had talked about her boyfriend before, but the mention of him made me uneasy. I couldn't help but wonder if the days she came in without her usual pep were because of him. Sometimes she let it slip that he needed her home or she couldn't do something because he didn't want her to. As Mia prattled about the puppy, I tried to stay present instead of getting lost in unfounded anxiety on her behalf.

"Anyway, I think his shoe chewing habit is handled since I keep everything put away. Kyle—" Mia was silenced by the ringing of my phone down the hall, and her eyes darted to the doorway. "Do you need to go already?" A frown tugged at her smile.

I moved forward on the edge of the chair. "Yeah, I better get back to it. Next week, we're all going to dinner. I want to treat you and Joanne while it's still just the three of us."

Her smile returned in full force. "That would be so fun!"

Mia spoke again just as I reached the doorway. "Oh! Before you go, the whole reason I called you in here was about the new client I just got off the phone with. I think you might be interested in this one," she said.

I turned back to her, raising a brow. "Oh?" I asked, suddenly a bit more enthusiastic.

"It's another fairly large account we can add to our investment files."

My curiosity piqued, the stock market gears in my head creaking to life. "We haven't gotten a new one of those in a while. Most of our accounts lately have been run of the mill, planning for retirement, upper middle-class types. Give it to me." I took a step back into her office, eager for the details.

"He's a voice actor. Apparently, he got popular really quickly and has hefty funds from it. He said it's possible the amount of jobs he's getting now could taper off in the future if his popularity falls off. So he wants to invest to make money in case that happens."

My jaw slackened as excitement coursed through me. A voice actor? "What kind of voice actor?" I asked, trying to conceal my interest.

"He didn't say, but to be fair I didn't ask." Mia shrugged. "What kind of work does a voice actor do, anyway?"

Heat crept into my cheeks, and I hoped my blush wasn't visible. "Oh, the usual stuff. Kids' TV shows, things like that."

The voice actors I was familiar with did the farthest thing from kids' TV shows.

"Hmm, you think it's someone famous?" A hint of curiosity flashed in her eyes.

I hid my face behind my coffee mug. "It's possible."

"Either way, I set him up for a call with you on Monday," she informed me.

I shook my head. "Call him back and have him come into the office next week instead of a call."

Mia pursed her lips. "I tried. I know you prefer in person meetings with larger clients, but no dice. He said he doesn't like to leave his house."

"Ugh. How can people stay at home all the time? I think I would go crazy," I said.

"No, I think you would go crazy if you couldn't work. Apparently, he works from home. You should try it sometime. There's no need for you to be in the office so much, especially at night and on weekends," Mia retorted.

I rolled my eyes at her. "You're probably right. Maybe, I'll think about it if you'll leave me alone." Mia laughed. "Seriously, though, thanks for checking in. Call on the office calendar?" I asked, stepping into the hall.

"Of course. Already done," she called as I walked away.

"Thank you!" I threw over my shoulder as I sped back to my office. A thousand thoughts ran through my mind. What I hadn't mentioned to Mia was all the voice actors I knew were the ones narrating my romance novels. Especially the steamy ones with insanely hot male voice actors that brought me to my knees with one phrase like Zander Kane. Could I be so fortunate that this client did those? With my luck, he probably did infomercials about some weight loss drug.

I sat down in my expensive silver desk chair and clicked over to the calendar. Most of the time I didn't buy high end things, but the office was an exception. When I brought up Monday's schedule, I spotted the appointment. Ryan Mitchell. That name didn't ring a bell so I opened a new Chrome tab and did a quick Google search.

After half an hour scouring the internet for any mention of a Ryan Mitchell instead of working, I only came up with a news story about a man in Florida who had tried to wrestle an alligator and lost his arm in the process. Those jokes my dad told about "Florida man" rang true, I supposed.

I even checked my audiobook history and searched his name on my various listening apps without success. Maybe this guy really did do acting for animated TV series or something. Or maybe he didn't have an online presence. I would probably never find out since the type of narration he did wasn't information I needed to invest his money.

A tinge of disappointment tugged at the thought, but maybe I could make small talk and bring it up. It would be interesting to talk with someone who narrated books. I flicked my eyes to the taskbar, saw that it was just past noon, and for the first time in months I decided to take a lunch instead of working through it. My usual habit of eating with one hand while typing with the other didn't sound appealing so I popped in my earbuds and walked to the elevator, hitting the button for the ground level.

On the ride down, I opened my phone and clicked play on the audiobook I had left off with last night. Anticipation powered my steps as I exited the building and turned toward the nearby park; Zander Kane's dreamy voice floating through the headphones.

ON MONDAY, the clock clicked over to one, and I grinned while pressing the speaker button on the phone and dialed the number. Excitement had made me giddy for the call all day, and I reminded myself to be professional.

The call connected, and ringing filled the room. After a few moments a voice answered. "Hello?"

My pulse quickened as I skimmed the screen with Mia's notes. "Mr. Mitchell? This is Raven Lovelace with Lovelace Financial. How are you today?" I asked.

Silence stretched across the line, and as I was about to speak again, the voice answered. "Yeah, yes. I'm here."

I stopped dead, my eyes darting to the receiver situated neatly on the desk; the voice sounded extremely familiar.

This was a narrator I'd listened to before. I knew solely

from the few words he'd spoken. Maybe I was going to be lucky after all.

"Ma'am, can you hear me? Ms. Lovelace?"

The voice crashed through my mind, snapping me from my thoughts. I jumped and knocked over the empty water glass on my left. "Fuck!" I yelled as I watched it clatter to the floor in slow motion, but thank god it didn't break.

Shit, shit, shit. This was not going the way it needed to. "Oh my god, Mr. Mitchell, I'm so sorry about that. I just...just knocked over something. My sincere apologies." I rushed to move the conversation forward, hoping he wouldn't say he no longer wanted to hire us. "Um, let's begin. Tell me about yourself."

I waited as he contemplated his answer. Maybe I could segue into asking what kind of voice work he did.

He finally spoke. "I don't really know where to start. I'm a voice actor, and a project I worked on last year went viral, and I've been in high demand ever since."

Project last year. Viral.

"It's impossible," I whispered.

"Uh, what?" Ryan asked.

I fumbled for words. "Oh, um, sorry Mr. Mitchell. Right. I have the profile that Mia put together from the intake call, and I see that you're interested in the investment aspect of our services," I said, trying to get back on track. I had to focus on the task at hand. He confirmed what he was looking for, and as he was speaking my heart skipped.

Zander. Zander Kane.

There was no fucking way. Zander had a book go viral last year. The same one I'd listened to at least three times. Holy fuck. No way was I talking to Zander Kane. His voice had occupied countless hours over the last six months or so. One of my guilty pleasures was scrolling through social media short form videos to get more book recommendations, and that's how I found Zander.

Wait, it was Ryan. There was no mention anywhere online that Zander was an alias, but that had to be the case since I was definitely talking to a guy named Ryan who seemingly had Zander's voice.

Fuck, Raven, pull it together! I shouted internally. Clasping my shaking hands together, I took a few deep breaths. I had to chill the fuck out and get through this call. Reciting my usual spiel to him, I focused on explaining what I knew best.

Fifteen minutes later, I was unsure if I understood what he told me. "So, correct me if I'm mistaken, but you want quick returns on investment? You realize we're talking about the stock market, right?" I asked, assuming he couldn't know much about investing from the conversation thus far.

"Yeah, that's right," he said slowly in a voice that momentarily took my breath away. "I want to invest in case my popularity dies down in the future. Less demand means less income. I want to invest half of my savings to make plenty of money in addition to what I'm currently making."

I almost spit the water Joanne had quietly brought in all over my desk and instead some went down my lungs. "Half?" I sputtered. "You want to invest half of your net worth in high-risk small caps?" I tried to clear my throat while wrapping my head around his words. "That's a substantial amount to invest."

"I have no idea what you mean by high small caps, or whatever you said, but hopefully it works very quickly," he said.

I shook my head, my hair swishing by my ears. "Mr. Mitchell, investments are meant to be invested and then left alone for forty years. Investing in high-risk stocks could make you a lot of money, but it could also lose you money."

"Exactly why I'm not investing it all. Look, Ms..." His voice died away.

"Lovelace," I supplied.

"Right, Ms. Lovelace." The way he said my name so seductively had me shifting uncomfortably in my chair. I would melt into a puddle on the floor if he said it again.

"I'm booked out for a few months, and the requests keep rolling in. I don't see this stopping anytime soon. Even if it did, I still have my other income. I suspect I'll be great for the next five years, but after that, who knows. Are you able to help a guy out?"

Help him out. I might spontaneously combust in the process, but I was good at my job. "Certainly, Mr. Mitchell. I'll put together a portfolio for you, and then we'll schedule another call. Unless you would rather come into the office?" I couldn't help but to ask. I wanted to see the man this voice was attached to.

"Nah, phone call is fine. Thank you, Ms...Lovelace," he said in a sultry voice, and I almost fell from my chair at how hot my name sounded coming from him. "Goodbye."

He ended the call, and I turned to stare out the window, not seeing the buildings or streets outside. I was in trouble. This client was going to be particularly difficult to work with because his voice was so distracting. Eventually, I pulled myself out of my stupor and pushed Ryan Mitchell and Zander Kane from my mind. I had work to do.

A few hours later, I glanced at my reflection in the mirror of the black and white restroom in the office. After the call, the afternoon went to hell, and I looked just as bad. The shorter hair framing my face was wild from tangling my fingers in it when I couldn't concentrate. I could pass for Cousin It instead of my usual Morticia Addams.

Back in my office, I pondered the clock. It was only four on a Monday. Could I get away with leaving? That morning had been productive, a ten out of ten, whereas the afternoon had been a zero since the call.

My thoughts drifted back to Zander, or Ryan. I was definitely going to slip and mistakenly call him Zander at some point. The next call would be after I got his portfolio together. I couldn't get his voice out of my head, and the way he said my name...

I groaned, and put my head on my desk like a teenager trying to catch some sleep in class. "Fuck it," I said into the glass.

Shooting out of the chair, I grabbed my purse, not even bothering to shut down the computer. I hurried past Mia's door to avoid detection, but luckily she was on a call. Once in the lobby I stopped at the chic white reception desk in the middle of the room surrounded by pewter walls. The petite woman with salt and pepper chin length hair looked up from her computer where she had been typing.

"Hey Joanne." I fidgeted with my purse on my arm, shifting uncomfortably on my feet. "I'm going to head home. I'll work from there. Do you have it covered here?" I wasn't going to work at home, especially since I left my briefcase in my office.

The brightest smile lit her face and she clasped her hands together. "You're leaving the office before six? Raven, that's wonderful! You should go home and just relax. No need to work. Everything is going well, and I just sent over the reports you did this morning. I copied you, but a response just came through from the client. They're ecstatic with the numbers," she gushed. "All of your hard work is paying off."

I beamed back at Joanne. "Perfect! I'll see you in the morning. Text me if you need anything."

"Of course," she said as I walked out the door to the elevators.

I pushed the button for the garage and counted my lucky stars that I had found Mia and Joanne. Joanne was the same age as my mom, but she was one of my favorite people. Caring and nurturing to the people she cared about, but when it came to work, she was the baddest bitch around. Polished and refined, but would knock anyone on their ass with her words.

When I started the company, it was just Joanne and I. I convinced her to leave our old financial firm with me to start my own. She said she was ready for something new so I saved up enough money to pay her a decent salary. The managing role had become stagnant for her so she agreed to be the receptionist and secretary until we got on our feet after a few years. With the growth recently, I was happy I could finally hire a replacement for her position out front. I smiled at the thought of her being freed up to run the office and made the decision to post the position on the job sites as soon as possible.

When I got home, I dropped my purse on the kitchen island and gazed around my apartment. I was rarely here during the daylight hours, especially during the week, and the furniture looked a bit out of place in the sunlight. Shaking off the strangeness, I ditched my heels in my bedroom and pulled on a black cashmere lounge set.

I drew the blinds in one of the spare bedrooms I had made into my home office, preferring a darkened vibe over the bright sunlight. After booting up my computer, I went into super sleuth mode. I scrounged the web for any mention of a Ryan Mitchell, a more in-depth search than I did on Friday.

After an hour with fifteen open tabs on both of my monitors, I was still at square one. My computer looked like I was a stalker, which, for this man's voice, I wouldn't say was too far from the truth.

Switching gears, I pulled up social media.

Navigating to the photo and short form video website, I

noted how odd it looked on a computer as opposed to a phone. I typed Zander Kane into the search bar and found what looked to be his account and pulled up the profile. Dozens of black screened videos stared back at me. What? Why would he post blank videos and photos? Then I realized it might just be the thumbnail images.

I pulled up the most recent one posted a week ago and was met with, surprise, a black screen. It wasn't just the video cover photo on his main page. The video itself was blank as well. What the fuck? I stared at the screen as the ten second video replayed over and over.

Fuck. Realization dawned on me. Voice actor. He was a voice actor so it was probably a video of just his voice. I shook my head at my cluelessness and reached for my speakers. Turning up the volume, I exited the video and clicked it again to make sure it started from the beginning.

My heart damn near stopped. Zander's seductive baritone voice filled the room. "Baby girl," he panted. "You do that so well." His breaths came faster, and he moaned, "Your mouth is going to be the death of me."

I rushed to stop the video before it could play again, worried someone might hear even though no neighbors bordered the walls of the room. I sat back in my chair, jaw on the floor at what I'd just heard, heat rushing through my body. Zander's audiobooks were great, but he didn't breathe like that when he narrated spicy scenes in them. It seemed so realistic. My cheeks were on fire and I knew my face looked like a tomato against my usual pale complexion.

Snapping from my thoughts, I grabbed headphones from a drawer, powering them on and connecting them to the desktop. I reached for the mouse and clicked on the next video.

CHAPTER FOUR

RYAN

When I hung up with the financial lady, I pulled up her company website. That fucking voice. It was pure intelligence, even though she seemed a bit flustered in the beginning. As soon as she spoke my cock sprang to life. I worked with quite a few female co-narrators over the last year and had heard their breathy voices in the throes of sexy scenes. None of them made my body pay attention like that woman's timbre. When she accidentally swore I almost groaned into the phone. Throughout the call I only half paid attention, focusing on her voice instead of the boring stuff she was saying about stocks and numbers. My mind drifted to places it shouldn't have gone.

I clicked on the "About" tab, and holy goth baddie. Staring at her photo for much longer than was socially acceptable, my eyes roamed over her obsidian hair that was half pulled back, leaving a few shorter wisps around her face. Her black suit and crisp white blouse fit her perfectly. The thing that drew me in the most, though, was her eyes. They shined like emeralds in a jewelry store. She was as gorgeous as she sounded on the phone, and I found myself wishing I'd met her in person instead of a call.

But then again, I knew this woman was far out of any league I could ever hope to play in.

I finally snapped out of the spell she had on me and realized I was supposed to be working. I began to push away from my desk when I wondered if it could be possible she knew me professionally. I figured it was probably unlikely since I doubted she filled her time with audiobooks or social media.

Her bio said she was the owner of the company, confirming my assumptions, and listed a fuck ton of accolades. She didn't look that old, but I could tell she was at least thirty. Shit, this was getting worse for me, but I wasn't going to complain. Older women were hot as fuck, and my resolve to work ebbed.

Still, I thought there was a possibility she might have heard my voice before. The way she'd been breathless and didn't respond immediately at different points in the call had peaked my interest. Being the fixated person I was, the next three hours were spent looking at my followers on social media to see if they remotely looked like they could be her.

Unfortunately, I didn't find her, but it was probably for the best. If I knew she followed me and was seeing my posts I would've whipped my dick out and fucked myself right then. The thought of that woman listening to my sexy words would have done me in. It would've been enough jerk off material for a week, at least.

When I looked at the time again, it was five. I was out of commission for recording and would be late getting the audio done. What the fuck was I doing? I wasted half my day entranced by someone I'd never met. I hated people, so why was I suddenly unable to think of anything except this woman? Sighing, I hauled my dejected ass to the shower, and then I emailed Craig.

Two minutes after I sent the email my phone rang. "Craig, I literally just told you in the email that I would have it to you tomorrow by noon. An extra four hours won't be the end of the world," I huffed.

"Ryan, earlier you said it would be first thing tomorrow morning since you apparently couldn't record over the weekend," he shrieked. "Everything is due by the end of this week and we still have to go through production. Honestly, what's taking so long with this one? You've not been this far behind schedule in the eleven months I've repped you. Is everything all right?"

"I'm fine. I know I'm overdue. I've been distracted. I'll get it done. Talk to you tomorrow." I tapped the screen to end the call.

Distractions. That was definitely why I hadn't recorded at all this afternoon. I had struggled with finishing this audiobook anyway, but today I procrastinated for an entirely different reason.

The annoyance with Craig still lingered as I went to the fridge for a Redbull. I usually didn't stream on Mondays but I had nothing else to do while I waited for my neighbors to go to bed. Padding back to my desk, I grabbed the gray hoodie draped across the back of a chair on the way. As I sat down my phone lit up. Notifications were usually always on silent since I got so many—except the ringer for calls so Craig wouldn't have an aneurysm. Earlier in the day I'd turned on social media notifications to see how well a new type of video I posted that morning was doing. Deciding to turn them off later, I focused on the computer.

I pulled up the IM and voice messaging app I used with the guys and the phone lit up again a few seconds after it went dark. I navigated to the streaming website and started typing when yet again, the phone lit up. I knew I got a lot of likes, comments, and follows daily, but when the phone kept lighting up, my curiosity flared, and I couldn't stop myself from grabbing it. All of the notifications were from social media so I tapped into the app.

"@finigirl666 started following you."

"@finigirl666 liked your reel."

The last one repeated ten times.

The account was a host of black and white abstract photos, and the profile picture was a monochrome photo of the cropped edge of a mug. Finding nothing of substance, I moved my thumb to the home button after scrolling through the dozen posts, but a flash of color caught my eye near the bottom of the page. I hesitated, homing in on the photo, and tapped to enlarge it. The color that got my attention was a green eye framed by pale skin and a lock of black hair. At first glance it seemed like the picture had been rendered grayscale like the others, but it was in color. The light made the skin appear ashen against jet black hair, and it was one of the most striking photos I'd ever seen.

Could this be her? Was this Raven Lovelace, the lady that was going to turn my world upside down? Intuition told me it was possible.

I worked all night to get the audio finished. Gemstone eyes and vampire pale skin were all I fantasized about instead of gaming until I could record again. It was a struggle to get into the booth and concentrate on the lines when all I could hear in my head was her flustered gasps from the call. The more I thought about it, the more I hoped she recognized my voice.

During the last sex scene I recorded, I gave a little more enthusiasm than I usually did for narration. I caught myself adding in breaths and pants that were usually saved for my paid content. While reading the lines, I thought of her. Running my hands over her body like my character in the book. Making her come with my mouth before thrusting deep inside her. When I played the sound back it was a perfect performance, requiring no redos unlike the morning before. Hopefully, the author would be happy with it.

Finigirl had liked a few more of my reels last night. I deliberately checked my phone around four a.m. to see if anything had happened while I recorded and I was met with a slew of likes around ten, just after I'd locked myself in the studio. I grew hard thinking she might be listening to my videos in bed. I finished the project and sent it to Craig in an email, telling him I was taking a few days off as well.

Over the next three days I mostly played video games while streaming and recorded a ton of new personal content. I was set for the next few weeks for social media and paid subscriptions.

My thumb had just tapped the icon to schedule a post when the phone dinged with a notification. I'd decided to leave the sound on for notifications, always checking them fairly quickly in search of Finigirl, but hadn't gotten any new notifications from the account since Monday. I swiped down to see the notification not from Finigirl, but from the woman herself. Raven Lovelace's name stared back at me from the phone screen.

Heart picking up speed, I quickly opened the email. She wanted to schedule a call to discuss the portfolio she'd put together. I swallowed at the thought of hearing her voice again. Pacing around the apartment, I typed a reply saying that I was available anytime. Her response was almost immediate, saying she would call me in a few hours at three.

I groaned, my blood rushing straight to my dick. I couldn't remember a time I was so gone over a woman I'd talked to on the phone one fucking time. Fuck, I was being absurd.

Scrubbing a hand over my face, I thought back to the last

time I'd gone out to a bar or had a date. I mentally recounted the past few months, coming up with nothing. Surely it hadn't been since my career took off...had it?

Damn, maybe it had, and that was why I was going nuts over this woman. I just needed to get laid and getting laid by her was out of the question. She wasn't the type of woman I would forget easily and I wasn't about to get hung up on someone I couldn't have. Rather, I wouldn't let myself have. She wouldn't give me a second look anyway. A random hookup would do the trick, and I had the whole weekend ahead of me to find a suitable chick who would be down.

I reinstalled the dating apps I had deleted and began swiping. There were hordes of people looking for a quick fuck, which was what the apps mostly consisted of. No one on them wanted lasting relationships, in my experience. The options were endless, but as I began swiping right, my excitement wasn't from the prospect of all the attractive women at my fingertips. It was for the one specific woman who I had a call with that afternoon.

｜｜｜｜｜｜｜｜｜｜｜｜｜｜｜｜｜｜｜｜｜

"Ms. Lovelace. Good to hear from you," I said into the speaker with much more enthusiasm than I intended. I refocused, slipping into the sexy mindset I used when I was Zander without thinking about it.

"Hi, Mr. Mitchell. How are you?"

I clenched a pen in my fist. This time when I heard her voice I imagined that fucking gorgeous face that went with it—and it sounded even better than I remembered. "I'm better now. I hope you have good news for me," I said, as slowly as I could manage.

She swallowed, and her voice came out unsteady. "Oh, uh,

well, it doesn't actually work like that. I just wanted to go over the investment plan I've put together for you so we can get started on Monday. Do you have some time to discuss those?"

"Yes, Miss…" I dropped my voice even lower. "It is Miss isn't it? Or is it Mrs.?" I was taking a risk asking something so personal, but I had to know if she was married. I wouldn't encroach on a marriage. Even flirting was out of the question. Wait, why was I flirting with her? Regardless, if she was seeing someone, I likely wouldn't care, but I drew the line at fucking with marriages. But who was I kidding, I wanted her to be single.

"Uh, yes, it's Miss. Um, about the portfolio. You're going to want to do a mix of investments in small and mid caps, so you don't put all your funds at the highest risk."

So she was single, and it was the best thing I'd heard.

For twenty minutes she droned on about the plans, and I gave the occasional agreement and asked for elaboration a few times. I could listen to her talk about anything for hours.

"Does that sound agreeable?" she asked.

I laced my voice with extra seduction. "If you can make stocks and bonds sound this enticing then I'd hate to be on the opposite side of an argument with you. One sentence and you would have me agreeing with anything you say."

She was silent for a few long moments, and I would've given anything to know the thoughts running through her mind. I finally spoke so she didn't have to, saving her the awkwardness.

"Everything sounds great, *Miss* Lovelace." I chuckled. "You can go ahead and get started next week."

She cleared her throat. "Sure thing. Thank you for your time, Mr. Mitchell."

"I'll talk to you again soon, Raven." I smirked and disconnected the call.

I was more playful with her than I intended, but when I heard her voice again, I couldn't stop myself. I meant to be nothing but business. It turns out I had no self-control. Shaking my head, I shifted back to the task of talking to the ladies I had matched with on the apps. I tried to find one who I could meet that night. Raven Lovelace was far out of my reach, and I refused to embarrass myself by going after her. I had to fuck this woman out of my mind.

CHAPTER FIVE

RAVEN

Mia snapped her fingers in my face, startling me. I glanced over at her standing beside me in the kitchen.

"Can I use the sink? I need to leave soon and you've been standing there staring at the wall for five minutes" she asked.

Nodding, I tapped my smart watch and saw it was already five. "I, yeah, sure. Sorry about that." I grabbed a few paper towels to dry my mug and moved aside.

"Hey, are you doing okay? You seem...distant this week," she asked.

I shrugged as I walked toward the door. "I'm fine," I said over my shoulder, not caring if she heard me or not. Answers to her questions would take longer than I had, so I rushed back to my office.

At my desk with the door firmly closed, I stared unseeing at my screens. Mia wasn't wrong. I had been distant. After my excursions into a certain male narrator's social media on Monday, I vowed to stay off the internet the rest of the week except for work. I couldn't afford distractions. The only thing I had allowed myself was an audiobook. One narrated by Zander Kane of course, but that didn't stop me from daydreaming about his spicier content online.

When I sent the email to Ryan that morning, I was mostly motivated by wanting to hear his voice again. Over the last few days, I told myself Ryan wasn't Zander, and my mind was playing tricks on me. It was just a coincidence, and there was no way they were the same person. After talking to him this afternoon though, I was back in the same headspace as Monday. He had to be Zander.

Since I listened to his more risqué stuff online and the rapt attention I gave to the audiobook all week, it seemed even more likely it was him. He changed his voice a bit from the first call, and it was almost like he was trying to be hot. He came across slow and sultry, igniting my body on fire.

I was so turned on after I spoke with him I almost went to the restroom and got myself off. Almost. My nipples were hard in my bra and wetness coated my thighs. He wasn't going to have that much power over me, though. I would have some fucking self-control and do what I needed to do when I got home—even though it was wrong to get off while thinking about my client.

Sighing, I tried to focus back on work, but I was intrigued that he asked if I was married. Alarm bells should have gone off because clients never asked. It was better if people thought I was married and had a big scary man at home, purely so I didn't have to waste my time with bullshit.

Giving up on work for the moment, I reached down to my knife where it always rested on my ankle. It made boots annoying to deal with, and I used a thigh holster on the rare occasion I wore a skirt, but I was always prepared. Twirling the knife in my agile fingers, concern for my safety usually wasn't a thought. Especially since I had been unbothered for years and was trained to protect myself. I was always in the business of efficiency so letting people think I was married saved the hassle.

The feelings from the garage pulled at my mind. It had felt different, and I couldn't help but wonder if there was a real threat watching. I hadn't been spooked so easily since the aftermath of the horrors I experienced at the hands of trash humans. The light streaming through the windows glinted off my blade and I wondered if I would have to use it sooner rather than later.

When I got home around seven that evening, I couldn't help thinking back to that voice as I showered, taking extra time to pamper myself—luxuriating under the rainfall shower until it ran cold and rubbing my whole body down with soft body butter after. I even put on a calming piano playlist to soothe myself as I tried to relax.

My efforts did nothing to quench the need that Ryan's voice on the phone caused. Between the black sheets of my bed, warmth enveloped me—thawing my bones from the persistent cold that always hardened my body.

Plucking my phone and earbuds off the nightstand, I situated myself in a comfortable position and before I knew it, Zander's voice filled my ears. I'd listened to all his social media posts on Monday, and favorited a few so I could get back to them quickly. After clicking play, I tossed the phone on the bed and slid my free hand over my silk covered body.

Release wasn't something I did often, and I wasn't able to remember the last time I touched myself or used a vibrator. It had been years since I was intimate with another person and I honestly hadn't had the desire. Starting a company and juggling life didn't leave time to think about it.

Quickly realizing I needed more than the short social media clips, I contemplated trying to find a spicy scene from a book he'd narrated. I picked up my phone and scrolled through his profile just to make sure I listened to every video. I was about to switch to my audiobook app when I noticed a link underneath his profile photo of a microphone. I tapped on it and was brought to a list of other links. Most of them were links to his other social media accounts, but two caught my attention.

One was for his professional website and when I tapped the link I was met with all the audiobooks he'd narrated. I searched for an "about" section with no luck so I backtracked to the list and proceeded to the other link I wasn't sure about.

Another profile that looked similar to other social media filled the screen. The same profile photo was there along with a list of pricing tiers. I scrolled through them and my pulse sped up in my chest. I hadn't heard of this site before, but it was some sort of pay to access. The descriptions of the tier benefits caused my imagination to run rampant, the lists arousing me all by themselves.

Without hesitation, I signed up for the most expensive tier with all the available perks. Once I had access, I scrolled through all the posts and could already feel wetness between my legs just from reading the descriptions. There were so many audio clips, I found my mind imagining what he said in them. Sexuality wasn't something I was ashamed of, but I still felt like I was about to do something mischievous. I scrolled to the top and clicked the latest video.

Zander/Ryan's voice began speaking, painting a scene for me. He was talking directly to me, the listener. I was being asked how much I wanted it and I found myself thinking I wanted it very badly. Guilt settled in my stomach like a stone as soon as I had the urge to send my hand south. This was my client. No one would know what I was doing unless I told someone, but I still felt like it was wrong to do this.

Deciding I didn't care, my hand trailed over my nightgown in time with the audio and I brushed my thighs before cupping my pussy.

"Do you like when I whisper my fingertips slowly down your perfect waist, so close to caressing where you want it most but moving away just before I do?"

A moan fell from my lips into the dark room as I listened. "I love teasing you, darling. When you beg me to touch you it makes me so fucking hard for your perfect body." I slipped my fingers into my wetness, moving up and down, my arousal coating my hand. I settled on my clit and circled.

"Be a good girl and be patient for me while I tease. If you're good, you'll get release, all right?"

"Fuck," I groaned aloud. His voice was agony. My pussy was throbbing and I imagined it was his hand between my legs.

"That's it. There's my good girl. See? I told you good girls get rewarded. I'm going to slide my fingers inside your soaked pussy and fuck you so hard you can't think of anything else."

"Yes," I panted. Fuck, this was unlike anything I had ever experienced.

"You're so wet for me, baby. I love it when your mouth whimpers and your pussy weeps. Fuck, you feel so good—gripping me so tight. Yes, baby, use my fingers and come for me. Come all over my hand, baby girl. Give me everything, every bit of your pleasure. I want all of you."

I cried out, my orgasm hitting me like a ton of bricks. I saw stars and colors behind my eyelids as my entire body convulsed. When I finally floated back to Earth, everything was the same as before but different at the same time. I hadn't come that hard in years...maybe ever.

After I cleaned up, I sat in bed with my head in my hands trying to come to terms with the fact that I just got myself off to a voice. No visual stimulation needed. Not to mention it was my client's voice. I hadn't heard of attraction to a voice before, and disbelief that I fucked myself to one ran through me. Was it the anonymity of his appearance? Did not knowing what he looked like make it that much better? Was it just the voice in general that turned me on, or could it be that I was doing something extremely unprofessional?

Coming to the conclusion that it was probably all of the above, I knew it wouldn't be the last time I got myself off to his voice. I settled into bed and as I stared into the darkness, the sexy words replaying themselves in my mind, and I fell asleep imagining him whispering in my ear.

CHAPTER SIX

RYAN

I STARED at the pretty brunette across the table, not understanding how she could talk for half an hour about different paint color combinations, but here we were. After the call with Raven that afternoon, I vowed to purge her from my thoughts. That woman would destroy what little confidence I had gained as a voice actor with her inevitable rejection, and I wasn't going to go backward.

Swiping right on pretty much any attractive girl I saw on the dating app had resulted in countless matches, one of whom was down for dinner on short notice. The same one I was listening to talk incessantly about interior design. I understood she was passionate about her career, but damn, I was about to tap out.

We messaged a bit on the app and agreed to meet at a semi-casual spot not too far from my apartment. I had donned a black button down and slacks that were my usual go to attire for dates despite not going on one for nearly a year. Leaving the top buttons open, I had ran my hand through my hair and called it satisfactory before meeting the lady at the restaurant.

She was my age, very active, clearly social with a seemingly decent personality. A bit too upbeat for my taste, but no one said I was looking for a wife. The opposite actually. She would make do for a hook-up, maybe even a few times. Settling down with someone wasn't in the cards, and that was fine with me. Maybe I hadn't found the right person yet, but more likely, I wasn't the guy women wanted for a long-term partner. Quick fuck, maybe. Getting off to my voice, definitely. Especially women with jet black hair and emerald eyes who had the best of the best in life. Either way, I was content, or I would be, as soon as I worked a certain financial advisor out of my system.

As the dinner dwindled to a close, and my date moved on to furniture placement, my thoughts started to drift. I was staring over her shoulder as she talked when I flicked my eyes down to my phone as it lit up. I swiped it from the table, placing it in my lap, the designer clueless. Excusing myself to the restroom, I stood in the hallway to check the subscription notification.

"@finigirl666 pledged $100 per month."

My cock stirred in my pants. So my "mystery" girl had found my subscription platform. Great. Now, I was never going to get her out of my mind. The only content I posted on there was lewd audio so I knew exactly what she was doing at this very moment. There was no way she subscribed and immediately did something else like vacuum.

My thoughts drifted to Raven and I imagined her spread out on her bed with headphones over her ears. Her hand working feverishly between her legs. I longed to kneel on the bed in front of her and take over with my mouth.

A patron walked by, and I straightened from where I had been leaning against the wall and ran a hand through my messy hair. I shifted my pants and made my way back to the table, paid the bill, and dipped, giving the excuse that I had something come up. I sped through the streets back to my apartment where I bounded through the door. Throwing my keys on the counter, I went to my gaming set-up on the far wall of the living room and turned on the computer.

Tapping my foot while it came to life, I crossed my arms across my chest. I needed confirmation that my Finigirl was Raven, everything else be damned. I had to know if she was fucking herself to my voice. Once up and running I pulled up her social media profile and stared at the photo of her eye. In another tab on my second monitor, I pulled up her company photo. Zooming in so the photo was the same size as the post, I scrutinized every detail of the irises. I was lucky the company photo was high-res.

"I fucking knew it!" I exclaimed to the empty room. A faint blue ring circled the outer edge of the eyes in both images. On the left side of the iris there was also a grain of blue that blended into the green unless zoomed in.

Got her. There's my sneaky girl. There was no question that she knew exactly who I was. It was all too coincidental. Finding my social media after our first call, then subscribing to my paid platform after the second? She knew. She knew her newest client was Zander Kane, and I was bursting at the thought of her listening to my audios while she rubbed her clit and made herself come, following my every direction.

I jumped up from the desk and went through my bedroom and straight into the main bath. My body was begging for free-dom. Flying through the buttons of my shirt, I moved to my belt, not bothering to remove it from the loops as I jerked my zipper down. My slacks slid to the floor along with the black boxer briefs, my cock free from restraint. I was so hard it was almost painful. Turning on the shower, I grabbed a towel from the rack and hung it on the hook.

The hot water was heaven on my skin and I immediately

gripped my length. Green eyes floated in my mind, tears seeping out of the corners as my girl gagged around me. Her long black hair was wrapped around my fist, and fuck, she loved choking on my cock. Goddamn, I hadn't been this hard in ages, and I was already starting to feel the familiar pull in my pelvis.

Raven moved her hand to work in tandem with her mouth, and I was fucking wrecked. I braced my hand against the white tile as I worked myself harder and faster thinking about those full lips on my skin. I gritted my teeth, a low moan tearing from my throat as my release flooded my body, sending wave after wave of pleasure.

"Fuck." I sighed, drawing out the word, and stepped under the showerhead. Water sluiced down my back and over my ass before running down my thighs—the warmth calming me down. My chest heaved, and my legs were unsteady. That was one for the record books. Good thing I didn't have an audience because that was an embarrassingly quick performance. So much for fucking Raven out of my mind—pretty sure I fucked her farther into it.

ılıı||ıı||ı|||ıı||ıııı||ı||ıı||||ıı||ı|ı|ııı|ılıı

THE NEXT MORNING I woke up feeling more rested than I had in years. Usually, it was a bit difficult to get out of bed, but today I got up immediately. After pulling on a pair of sweats, I made myself a simple breakfast of toast and eggs, then settled at my desk. I didn't bother checking my email. Craig could wait until Monday. This weekend I was going to play with a little fox.

The earthy taste filled my mouth, fueling my devious plan. The paid platform populated the screen, and I clicked to the private messaging section that I never used. Searching "fini-girl666," I clicked "message" next to the blank photo. My fingers flew across the keyboard, and I hit send just as my phone rang.

Annoyance flared, and I blindly answered the call. "Dammit, Craig, it's Saturday. What now?"

Except it wasn't Craig on the phone. Instead, a surprised voice said, "Oh, um, hello, Mr. Mitchell, this is—"

I cut her off, staring slack jawed at the computer. "Raven?" I asked in disbelief.

"Yes, this is Raven Lovelace with Lovelace Financial," she answered.

"Fuck, I'm sorry, Raven...uh...Ms. Lovelace." I wracked my brain for an excuse for my rude greeting. "I wasn't expecting a call from you on the weekend. What's up?" I said coolly, hoping she hadn't noticed how rattled I sounded. Had I manifested her calling me with how much I thought about her over the last twelve hours? Maybe the stars were in alignment, and she was thinking about me as much as I was thinking about her.

"I apologize for calling unannounced on a Saturday, but I just had another question before I get started next week." I waited for her to continue. "Do you prefer retail or food service?"

My face scrunched in confusion. "What?" I asked. "I don't, uh, I don't understand what you mean."

A nervous laugh sounded through the speaker. "I just wondered if you had any preference in the type of companies we invest in. There's an array of different ones, and some of our clients have a preference."

This was why she called me? I'd regained my composure by this point, so I turned the charm to eleven. "Why are you working on a Saturday, Raven?" I said in my slow, seductive tone. After knowing she listened to my content, which was very intimate, I presumed to use her first name.

A sharp intake of breath came before she answered. "Oh, you know, owning a business and all. Work doesn't always stop on the weekends when you're the owner of a business."

Another nervous chuckle.

"Hmm. Don't you take a break from the week? Surely you don't work all the time, right?"

"I guess I do work most of the time, yes," she mumbled, her voice a bit quieter. A voice I wanted to hear whimper my name.

I had her now, happy that she divulged that tidbit. "What about the evenings? Do you work then, too?"

I could hear the blush on her pale cheeks. "Oh, I...I do sometimes."

"Do you ever take time for yourself, Raven? Time to do the things you enjoy most?" I wanted her to keep talking. Hearing her voice again so soon was an unexpected treat.

"Sometimes. Not often. There's not enough hours in a day most of the time."

Annoyance pricked my temples. I didn't even know her, and I was already aggravated that she overworked herself. "You really should take a break." My tone switched from alluring to serious. "Working every day isn't healthy. You should do things you enjoy that have nothing to do with work."

She signed. "I'm not sure how this conversation turned to this topic, but uh, I think I have everything I need. I won't take anymore of your time."

"I told you we would speak again soon." I laughed. "Take care of yourself. Until next time, Raven."

CHAPTER SEVEN

RAVEN

Tossing and turning all night with sleep evading me, I finally decided to get up at four a.m. I settled on the couch and listened to almost every audio posted on Zander's paid platform, which dated back almost two years. The farther I went the more I could tell he got better with his acting as time passed. I wondered if he came up with the scripts because those got better too.

After making a meager breakfast of toast, I paced the apartment as the sun rose. I couldn't stop thinking about Zander, or Ryan, or whoever he really was. The obsession was unlike anything I'd experienced, and my brain settled on a really dumb idea. What if I called Ryan? I could come up with an excuse for the accounts so I could hear his voice again.

Before I talked myself out of it, I grabbed my phone and pressed call on his number saved in my email. His voice sounded just like the one I had listened to all morning, and when he said my first name, heat surged between my thighs. As I listened to him say I should work less, I was transported back to his audios that were caring and loving. I couldn't help but imagine what it would be like if he were taking care of me even though I always had to take care of myself.

When I ended the call because I couldn't keep up the ruse any longer, my cheeks were on fire. The excuse I used was ridiculous, but there were, in fact, actual clients that were picky about the types of companies we invested in—but I knew Ryan couldn't care less.

This was getting out of hand. I dropped the phone on the counter and groaned as I rubbed my eyes. Why the fuck had I called him?

I actually hoped I never saw Ryan in person because the embarrassment at how I was acting would be too much. I wouldn't be able to be professional around him, which could get me in trouble. If the Certified Financial Planners Board got wind of unprofessional behavior, I'd be toast.

Glancing at my watch, I decided I'd wasted enough time. It was Saturday so there was a good potential to get a lot of work done. Without so many calls and emails to distract me, I should be able to fly through tasks—one of the reasons I enjoyed working on the weekends.

As I trudged to my office, Ryan's voice sounded in my mind.

You should do things you enjoy that have nothing to do with work.

Looking around the space, I tried to think about anything but that voice. It was the same as the rest of my apartment, clean lines with black furniture and decor. Maybe I should turn it into something more homey, drawing on earth tones or adding some color. Was I getting tired of my usual style, or was I restless from the unusual turn life had taken recently?

With my low-income childhood, I was infatuated with modern design and decor as an adult. It felt expensive, even though I got most of my furniture from IKEA. I was still frugal, but even faux versions of the furniture in the design magazines were enough to satisfy me in a way that I hadn't been when I was younger. My apartment was expensive, but not the things inside it. Guests were none the wiser, not that I ever had guests.

As I sat down and booted up my computer, my thoughts drifted back to Ryan yet again. I wondered how he was in everyday life. What was he like with his friends and family? What were his hobbies and goals? Did he tell jokes or poke fun at those he cared about?

I hadn't thought of a man in this way for years, maybe ever. The last guy was Spencer, and that ended poorly. I didn't have the time or desire for anything other than casual dating, but he was my longest relationship at two years. I was fine being single, and I honestly preferred it since relationships complicated life in general—not to mention work, but I was starting to wonder if I should get back into dating.

Maybe I was just preoccupied with the possibility that Ryan could be Zander. When I listened to the first audiobook he narrated last year, I was mildly obsessed for a hot minute, but nothing like this. That had died away like every other fixation I'd had in the past. Work always crowded in and took over, and hopefully that would be the case this time, too. Unfortunately, I didn't think people simply forgot about him.

Shaking all the thoughts from my mind, I resolved to separate Zander and Ryan. Obsessing over whether they were the same person was counterproductive even though I already knew they were, and in the end, why did it matter? One was business and one was entertainment. I had a job to do for my client, and if he was the voice actor I melted for it had no bearing on my ability to do that job.

My hopes of work went up in flames that afternoon, though, as I kept going back to Zander. I couldn't think about anything except clicking over to the paid website and hitting play on one of the posts. I'd gotten a few things done, but they were housekeeping tasks that didn't amount to much.

Sitting at the kitchen island, I swiped through the notifications on my phone, a missed call from mom, and a host of spam emails. I hadn't allowed myself to check anything since the call earlier. What grabbed my attention was the new message notification I had from the subscription site. Assuming it was an auto-generated message about how if I paid just five more dollars per month I could get some kind of perk, I tapped into the message.

My stomach dropped. It was from Zander's account. Surely it was a generic message thanking me for joining. I just missed it last night since I was clearly absorbed in other matters. He hadn't messaged me specifically, right?

Taking a deep breath, I read the text.

"Hi, finigirl666. With your subscription, you receive a free audio clip. Enjoy." The message ended with a winking emoji followed by a voice clip, and I suddenly couldn't breathe. The room felt like it was a million degrees. I laid the phone on the island and lowered my cheek to the cool marble, letting it seep into my flushed skin.

Zander had thousands of subscribers on the platform. Did he record a personal clip for everyone, or did he have one that was automatically sent? That had to be it. I told myself he had a specific audio that he sent all his paid subscribers. He probably didn't even have to do anything; the website sent it for him.

But I didn't remember this being listed on the page of benefits of subscribing to the account. I raised my head and pressed my thumb to the sensor on the phone screen to unlock it. A quick scroll through the tiers confirmed there was no mention of an extra clip after subscribing. Maybe he just hadn't updated the page recently.

Gathering my courage, I tapped back to the message with anticipation similar to meeting a famous person for the first time. Closing my eyes, I clicked play.

"Hi, finigirl666. Thank you for subscribing to my account. I'm just thinking about your gorgeous eyes, hair, and don't even get me started on that luscious mouth. I can't get you out of my mind. Be a good girl and go click on my most recent post after you get all comfy in your bed. Press play and choose your favorite way to get yourself off. I need you to come hard for me while listening to my voice, baby. Just relax and let the numbers leave your mind for a while. Be my good...fucking... girl."

And with that, I dropped the phone. Staring into outer space, my mind was unable to comprehend what I just heard. My core throbbed, and I was suddenly aware of hard nipples trying to break free from my shirt. Despite getting off the night before, my arousal was intense, like being edged all day from sexting with your lover.

My heart skipped. "Let the numbers leave your mind for a while." The words replayed on loop. I hadn't imagined that right?

I played the clip back three more times to be sure. I wasn't delusional. He'd said those words. How did he know I had a thing for numbers? It was just a lucky guess, right?

Wait, was it possible he knew the account belonged to me? Surely not. I shook my head and read the sentences after the audio that I'd missed earlier.

"For subscribing to the highest tier, you also get a free personalized audio. Send a reply with anything you would like me to say, and I'll record it."

Once again, I was suspicious. How did he have time to record all of this user-specific content? I listened again, and instead of wondering why he did so much for his fans, I followed his directions like the good girl he said I was.

I settled into my soft bed and saw that the last post wasn't the same one from last night, but one posted this morning. I clicked play, and goosebumps raised on my skin.

"This one is for my Finigirl."

"WHAT ABOUT YOU, boss? You seem to be leaving the office earlier these days." Mia asked from across the table. "Did you find a new hobby or something?"

If listening to steamy audio clips counted as a new hobby then yes absolutely. I took a sip of wine. "Oh, I've just been working from home more recently," I answered, trying to stave off any suspicions.

The restaurant buzzed around us. I'd taken Mia and Joanne out to dinner to celebrate the decision to grow the company. We posted our first job today, and when that one was filled, we would post another in a few months. The first task was to firm up a receptionist.

Mia scoffed, flipping her dark blonde hair over her shoulder. "Come on, Raven. You need to do other things aside from work all the time." She threw her hands up. "We worry about you," she said, throwing a glance at Joanne beside her.

"Don't bring me into this," Joanne put her hands in front of her chest. "I agree with you, but Raven is her own person. She knows what works best for her." Joanne was always the wise one.

"I'm fine, ladies. Really. You all are the best staff for caring so much about me, though. A toast."

We raised our glasses, and I smiled at the women in front of me as I cleared my throat. "To expansion and new endeavors," I beamed. "This core team will take the firm to amazing heights. Thank you both for such hard work and dedication to me and my dream. Cheers." Their echoing cheers rang in my ears, and gratitude for them flooded my chest.

"With that, it's time for the old lady to get home," Joanne announced as she scooted her chair back.

"Joanne," Mia whined. "You should stay longer! We're just getting started."

Joanne shook her head. "Nope. Gotta get home to the husband. You girls have fun. I'll see you on Monday."

As she walked away, I grabbed my card to slide to the waiter as he passed by the table. "I must be going, as well. I have some reports to finish up before I go to my parent's house tomorrow."

It wasn't a lie, but I wasn't going until tomorrow evening so I had the majority of the day to work.

"Raven! Not you, too. Come on. Let's go grab a drink at a bar. Kyle's out of town on a business trip, and I can stay out as late as I want." She was almost begging.

I studied her for a moment and felt a stab of sympathy for the woman. She was in her mid-twenties and I wondered why she didn't seem to have any other friends. No person who had a lot of friends would want to spend a Friday night with their boss.

My silver chain smartwatch read eight, and I decided a drink shouldn't take too long. "Fine, one drink. Have you been to the bar down the street? It's the one that's themed like the nineteen-twenties. I've always wanted to stop by but haven't had the time."

Her face lit up. "I haven't, but I would love to go!"

We wrapped up dinner and walked out into the breezy September night, strolling in a bit of awkward silence until we came to a brightly lit gold sign blazing in the darkness. When we slipped inside, my breath caught as we were transported to a different era.

The bar was quaint but extravagant. Every surface was gilded, from the bar top to the high circular tables and even the barstools. Sparkling chandeliers with rectangular jewels lined the center of the establishment, and all of the guests were well-dressed. This was definitely a higher end bar, and I wondered if Mia would have come here if not for me.

We slid onto stools and I ordered a Dark 'N' Stormy while Mia ordered a margarita. Guilt tugged at me. Why had I not gotten to know Mia on a more personal level? She was smart as a tack, and resourceful. So quick and efficient at her job. I was amazed after I hired her and hoped she was around for the long term.

"So how is life outside of work going for you?" I asked, taking a sip after the bartender set our drinks in front of us.

A shadow passed over Mia's face for a beat, then it was gone. "Oh, it's great. The puppy takes up most of my time. I'm so glad I made the leap and got him! What about you?" She narrowed her eyes. "Was there something you didn't want to mention in front of Joanne earlier?"

I looked away from her gaze so she wouldn't see the blush coloring my cheeks. "No, no, I've been working from home more. I'm finally getting out to see the family tomorrow so that will be a bit of a break."

Mia seemed satisfied and glanced around the room, taking in the scene. My watch buzzed with a new text as I lifted my glass. I swiped my phone off the bar, not caring that it was rude to check it in someone's company.

I had been on pins and needles all week. I'd worked to push Zander from my mind and didn't respond to his message, but that hadn't stopped me from listening to all of his new posts and some of the old ones on repeat. He even messaged me mid-week saying his audio offer would expire soon. After the message, I spent more than a few hours with his voice whispering salacious things in my ears. Deep down, I wanted to message him back with a request but I kept repeating *he's my client*, in my head. Every time my phone vibrated with a new message a small part of me hoped it was another one from him.

Slipping the phone in my purse after seeing it was a text from my service provider about some promotion, I glanced up as Mia turned her attention back to me. A question was written on her face, but she hesitated and took a gulp of her drink instead.

Mia's gaze darted to her own phone as it vibrated against the wooden bar. She flipped it over and I glimpsed she was getting a call from her boyfriend. "Shit," she exclaimed, before hitting the side button making the phone go dark.

When her eyes came back to mine, they were haunted. "Raven, I'm sorry. I need to go so I can call Kyle back. I wasn't expecting a call from him tonight since he had a business dinner out of town. He'll be...confused why I'm still out."

I held up my hand, shaking my head. "No need to apologize. Go do what you need to, Mia. I'll see you bright and early on Monday."

Emotion filled the woman's face, her pursed lips turning to an outright frown. I could tell she didn't want to go but didn't have a choice. She nodded. "Thanks, Raven. See you Monday."

She hurried from the bar out onto the street while I decided to enjoy the atmosphere and finish my drink before heading home. The place was cozy, and I resolved to come here again soon. Even if I came alone.

Once my glass was empty, I paid the tab and stepped into the cool night. The breeze had grown chillier than before and my flutter sleeve blouse felt like nothing on my shoulders. The garage was a few streets over from the bar so I wrapped my arms around my middle and enjoyed the fresh air. I hadn't taken many steps this week so the walk was good for me since my block heels were only an inch high and my feet wouldn't suffer.

The sounds and smells of the calm street washed over me. Garlic filled my nose as I walked past the restaurant we went to for dinner, and the low hum of cars on the freeway sounded in the distance. This road was much different than the main street in the opposite direction that would be bustling with college kids and the weekend crowd squeezing into the popular bars.

I'd fallen in love with the city after moving there more than ten years ago. It was smaller than the large city I grew up in, but was still big enough for a successful career. Once I made enough money from working around the clock at my first job, I moved Mom and Dad so they were close by.

As soon as I stepped into the dimly lit ground floor of the garage, dread filled my stomach and my limbs stiffened. I sensed eyes on my back as I fumbled for my keys, goosebumps rising on my skin. My body went on alert as I pushed the button for the elevator. When the doors slid closed and the car moved upward, I blew out a breath. Before the elevator reached the second floor I had my knife under my now untucked blouse.

The doors opened, and I moved my purse in front of my hand while gripping my keys firmly in the other. Chills ran down my spine. Someone was right behind me. I whipped around, drawing the knife, ready to plunge it into flesh.

There was nothing. I turned and sprinted to my car, sweat beading on my brow. Throwing open the driver door, I crashed inside, slamming the lock button as soon as the door closed. I tossed my shit in the passenger seat, knife included, and sat back to catch my breath. I started the car and grabbed my phone from my purse.

Backing out of the spot, I glanced down at my phone to see a text from an unknown number. Through all the commotion, I'd missed the notification on my smartwatch. The screen unlocked after I pressed my thumb to the glass, driving down to the first level. I tapped the icon and slammed my brakes.

"Enjoying your night, baby girl?"

CHAPTER EIGHT

RYAN

My plan backfired. It had been damn near a week, and I hadn't heard from Raven. When I sent her the voice clip I was certain that she would message back with an audio request. She hadn't. I didn't know what was more annoying, the fact that she hadn't responded or that she stopped interacting with my posts on social media altogether. Maybe the voice message was too much for her, or maybe she was just busy.

Of course, she was busy. I knew I shouldn't have read into it, but I couldn't keep my thoughts in check.

Her subscription was still active on the paid platform and would be for the next month until she was autobilled. I wondered if she had unsubscribed after the message, but I wouldn't know until the next payment cycle whether she was charged again.

I bobbed my knee incessantly while sitting on the couch the next Friday. There was another scheme I plotted to get the little minx to talk to me. And by me, I meant Zander. It wasn't going to be as simple as just sending her a message. I had already tried that on the paid site. I kept it simple, just asking for what she wanted in the free clip. When that went unanswered for a few days, I sent another telling her the promotion would expire soon and to send her request as soon as possible. Nothing.

Raven was a successful business woman, not a social media dopamine addict that would fall at my virtual feet. Her minimal online presence indicated she wasn't going to be won over by a personal audio clip and an instant message. I drained the last of my energy drink and glanced at the clock.

Eight p.m. It was late enough she should've been home from the office even though she worked all the time. I tapped the virtual phone app I had installed earlier that afternoon and copied the number Raven called me from on Saturday. It was different from the one she used the first time I had spoken to her, so I was banking on it being her personal cell number.

Pasting the number into the app after I set up a burner phone number, I tapped the text icon.

"Enjoying your night, baby girl?" I pressed send and waited. Patience while hoping she responded wasn't easy, but if she didn't, I had a backup plan. One that involved Zander's voice.

Twenty minutes passed, and I stared at the phone like a fool the entire time, unsure what it was about her that was driving me insane. I knew little about her and had only seen one photo, and yet I was obsessed with the dark-haired woman. It wasn't normal by any means, but I was drawn to her like a moth to a flame. I'd even broken my own rules of not interacting with a follower by sending the audio. What I was doing now was definitely beyond the personal boundaries I'd set for myself as a narrator, but I didn't care in the slightest.

The night I came to the conclusion she was most definitely

Finigirl, my hesitations about pursuing my finance lady were shot to hell. Raven was going to be mine, and she was going to come willingly. What we did after that didn't matter, but I was going to make her want me so badly that she couldn't think of anything else. It was worth the pain that would most certainly come after.

In the past I had tendencies to become obsessed with things, but it never happened with a person before. When I was younger I wouldn't stop playing a game until I beat it, staying awake all night. I was lucky that my parents didn't check on me after I went to "bed," even if they were home.

In college, for the two years I was there, I was consumed by partying and drinking, finally out from under my scrutinous parents' noses. They thought I was attending class and social functions like a gentleman, but I was actually passed out on some dude's couch. Deep down, as a child, I'd harbored hope for my parents to care and finally accept me someday and the drinking was a result of that hope slipping away.

Once I was kicked out of college for missing classes, I had a long conversation with myself and sought therapy to get my shit together. Mom and Dad weren't happy, but they paid for a good therapist, and I appreciated their help in that regard. The straw that broke the camel's back would come later.

I saw the therapist for two years before my parents gave me the boot and stopped paying for it. Without them, I had nothing. No home, no money, no family since my only other relative, my uncle, died in a car crash when I was a child. It was fine with me since I refused to be who they wanted me to be. When I got on my feet and started to earn my own money, I didn't go back to the doctor. I should've gone back considering I was enthralled by the high I get from getting people off with my voice, and now my infatuation with Raven. But I was having too much fun.

Raven was different from any other woman I'd encountered, and I couldn't put my finger on why she was going to ruin me. I just knew that she would. She was clearly attractive, and anyone who didn't think so needed a brain scan. More than that, she was successful and strong. Not to mention she was older and had a corporate goth vibe—weaknesses I didn't know I had until her.

But, there was something else. From the moment I heard her voice, I wanted to play with her. I wanted to make her want all of me, not just my voice. Moving on probably wouldn't be an option even if I could quell my fixation, but I no longer gave a fuck. I knew I wasn't good enough, but she was going to become obsessed with me, too. Then I was going to fuck her until I was branded into her mind and soul, ruining her for anyone else.

A check mark indicating the message had been read appeared, pulling me from reliving my past. My heart woke up in my chest, and anticipation flooded my body. I jumped up and began pacing around my apartment, needing to move.

Five minutes. Ten minutes. Twenty. Still no response. "Come on, baby. You're the worst fucking tease."

At the fifty-minute mark, the three typing dots appeared, and I sat down in my desk chair, focusing on the screen. The dots jumped just like my pulse, and then they disappeared. I groaned at the push and pull she was doing. This woman was a witch weaving a spell on me, and she hadn't even said anything. A minute went by with nothing, and I blew out an exasperated breath.

Then a message appeared. "Who is this?"

Fucking finally. Even if it was a generic response to getting a text from an unknown number.

"Who do you want me to be?" I typed back and hit send.

The flashing dots appeared immediately, and then disappeared again. A few seconds and they were back. Thank fuck.

"I think you have the wrong number."

Come on, babe, take the bait.

I rushed to text back. "I know I have the right one. I'll be anyone you need me to be."

Her response was immediate this time. "Hmm...can you be a serial killer because I need someone to kill this conversation."

A laugh burst from my lungs. My girl had jokes. "Haha, you wound me. I don't think I'll recover from that one."

"Sounds like a you problem."

This woman wasn't doing herself any favors by being sassy. It turned me on that much more. "You're right. It is a me problem. Just like you're a me problem."

The dots disappeared as quickly as they had flashed on the screen. A few minutes ticked by.

"A rando texts me and calls me a problem. Doesn't seem like a conversation I'm interested in."

This was going south, so time to pull out the big guns.

"Fine, enough games. You know I'm Zander, Finigirl."

The text was read immediately. No typing indicator came, and I knew I'd stopped her in her tracks. If she suspected it was Zander on the other end of the line, she couldn't know for sure, but now she did. I assumed I would be left on read for a while so I left the living room in search of a glass of water.

Sliding the phone in my pocket, I grabbed a glass from the cabinet. The water had just begun to pour from the fridge when my sweatpants *dinged*. I forced myself to fill the glass full and take a drink before I checked the message.

"How did you get my number? I'm not in the fucking mood for this shit. I've already felt like I was being watched tonight so this is par for the fucking course."

My blood ran cold. What the fuck? Someone was watching

her? Not that I was opposed to the idea of watching her myself, my cock stirring a bit at the notion, but anger surged to the forefront of my mind at the thought of anyone else watching her.

"Where are you? Are you hurt?" I sent the message without hesitation.

She read the text instantly but didn't start typing. My thumb hovered over the call button, unease churning in my gut. Then a thought popped into my mind. What if she was playing with me too? What if she said those things to get me to call her? I wasn't quite ready to give her my voice live yet so I waited.

She finally started typing. "Are you trying to get me to tell you where I am so you can come murder me or some fucked up shit?"

Annoyance made my rage worse. "Goddammit, tell me you're safe and unharmed or I actually will find you and see for myself."

She responded quickly. "I'm fine. I'm safe. Not that it matters to a famous voice actor."

I released a hard breath. Thank fuck. Suddenly, my weekend was booked full of research. I needed to know more about her, and why she was afraid.

"Good. Next time, answer me when I ask a question. Your safety is no joke."

"Why do you care?" she messaged quickly.

My fingers flew over the letters on the phone. "Because I'm actually a decent person. But if someone were to be followed only to be pushed against a wall and kissed, then I could probably get behind that."

"I don't know whether to say thank you or fuck you."

I smirked at her set up to turn the conversation the direction I wanted. "How about you thank me for fucking you with my voice, and we can call it even."

"<eye roll emoji> I have no idea what you're talking about."

"Don't be coy, Finigirl. Why else would you pay for the highest tier of my content if you weren't getting off to my voice?"

I waited much longer than I wanted for her response.

"What can I say, you have a nice voice."

"Jesus fucking Christ," I said to the silent living room in my apartment. Now we were getting somewhere. She was starting to enjoy this.

Shifting my semi-hard dick in my sweats, I typed a reply. "I think you could use a different word to describe my voice, princess."

"I'm no princess."

"You're right. You're a fucking queen."

"Oh, that was smooth. Seriously, though, how did you get my number?"

The subtle indication that she was going to entertain this had me almost at full attention.

"The paid site. You used this number when you signed up."

She seems to calculate her reply. "I didn't think websites gave personal information."

I knew she would ask. "I have my ways. Now, are we finished with twenty questions?"

"Oh, I'm just getting started."

Fuck me, this woman. She was making this easy. Almost suspiciously easy. She was making it easy to ignore my insecurities, but most women would block a random number immediately, especially one that was sending such suggestive texts. I wasn't expecting that reaction from her. Every person in the world was a bit crazy, but what if my girl was more like me than I thought?

Maybe she had a stranger kink, or maybe she was bored. I didn't know and I didn't care what the reason was as long as she kept texting me long enough to weave my web.

I glanced at the clock, noticing it was fairly early. For me, anyway. I cracked my knuckles and prepared to go as long as she did.

"Hit me with them, then."

CHAPTER NINE

RAVEN

*What the fuck **am I doing?** I asked myself the next morning as I struggled to keep my eyes open, impatiently waiting for coffee to brew. I had a lot of work to do before the afternoon, and being exhausted wasn't going to do me any favors. Once the carafe was full, I poured the biggest mug I had to the brim. Sitting down at the island, I put my head in my hands after taking a gulp of the scalding liquid.

I'd stayed up until the wee hours of the morning texting Zander, and as a result, slept past my usual weekend wake up time of six. An extra hour of sleep was all I allowed myself on the weekends, but today it wasn't enough. I'd slept until eight-thirty and woke up feeling like shit; my sleep schedule royally fucked and an astronomical headache pounding at my temples.

When I got the first text in my car the night before, the eerie feeling from the garage came back full force. I was beginning to question if his silence was finally coming to an end. Was that why I suddenly felt like I was being watched after years of peace?

My palms had been so sweaty the steering wheel slipped more than once as I drove over the speed limit with my knife resting in my lap. It was a good thing I hadn't gotten pulled over because a policeman would have had a lot of questions.

Only after dead bolting myself inside the safety of my apartment did my breathing begin to return to normal. I sat at the island and stared at the text notification, a thousand scenarios running through my mind.

After half an hour, I finally tapped into the message, but the churning in my stomach had me off the stool and pacing. I battled the urge to block the number and switch off my phone completely. Changing my number would be as simple as showing up at the cell store when they opened the next day. If this was the asshole from over all those years ago, blocking would do no good if he already had my number.

But I didn't tap the restrict button, despite my thumb hovering over it for ten minutes straight. I had been in plain sight for over a decade. I wasn't hiding, and I wasn't going to start living in fear now. My panic was replaced by anger as I typed a response. I wasn't a terrified teenager anymore. Maybe this was just some rando fucking with me.

The back and forth texting was maddening, and I was getting more pissed with each text. Whoever the person was, he was facetious. Just as I tapped the screen to block the number, a name flashed across the top in a new notification.

"You know I'm Zander."

"You have got to be shitting me." I said into the quiet room as my blood pressure shot through the roof. If Zander was Ryan then he got my number from my call last weekend. Zander had been the furthest thing from my mind until then. Still, I'd persisted just to see what he would say, but then my annoyance dissipated and I found myself enjoying the back and forth with him. The more I texted the more I couldn't bring myself to stop.

We texted like two teenagers. Arbitrary questions like favorite color and our top travel destinations, not even flirting all that much, though he did ask if flirting was okay in the beginning. The way he seemed interested in me personally had desire raging through my body, and I wanted to flirt with him.

He had piqued my interest, and a giddiness I hadn't felt in a long time coursed through me. It was a bit crazy and extremely unsafe, even though he was my client and I had all his information, but that made it all the more appealing. He could be a serial killer, but he said all the right things. Him being my client only added to the giddiness of texting my favorite voice actor.

There hadn't been a man in my life at all since Spencer. That also meant that I hadn't slept with anyone either. After I broke things off with him, I focused more on my career after deciding I wanted to have my own firm. I had just moved Mom and Dad to my city, and I was determined to have my business running by the time I was thirty. So there hadn't been time for men, and work kept me busy.

My dating history wasn't great anyway. I was independent in relationships and some men couldn't handle that. Lucky me —dating the ones who couldn't. My career taking up most of my time didn't help matters, either.

All the guys in my past were older and pretentious. It was something I didn't notice until I took a hard look at myself after Spencer. They all wanted me to be on their arm as their obedient wife who spoke only when spoken to, and that wasn't me. I was outspoken and did whatever the fuck I wanted to, society's antiquated view of women be damned.

I glanced at my watch and calculated how many hours of work I could get in before I had to get ready to go to the suburbs. I'd vowed a few weeks ago I would make time for dinner with my parents this month, and I was making good on it no matter what. Texting Zander hadn't been on the agenda, but I wasn't going to let it deter me from seeing Mom and Dad.

The computer screen lit up, and I decided I was going to let Zander/Ryan come to me. I opened my email with determination and pushed him from my mind.

After a few solid hours of double-timing work, I got myself ready in some of the most casual clothes I had. Since Mom and Dad came from humble beginnings and humble middles too, they were casual people. Dad didn't own a suit, and Mom never wore dresses or any form of business attire. Which I was comfortable with since that's what I was used to growing up, but over the years my casual clothes had been replaced with pantsuits, skirt suits, and assorted slacks and blouses. I rarely had a casual occasion to go to, so I didn't feel the need to continue buying jeans and T-shirts.

I glanced in the mirror at my reflection and was satisfied with the black skinny jeans and gray tee. Gen Z would never take skinny jeans away from this Millennial. I donned some of my chunkier jewelry that I didn't wear to the office, and out the door I went.

｜｜｜｜｜｜｜｜｜｜｜｜｜｜｜｜｜｜｜｜

"John! Raven's here!" Mom yelled through the house after I walked into the kitchen where she was standing by the stove. Her graying hair was smoothed back into a bun at the nape of her neck, and she was wearing her Kohl's staples, a fitted blouse and jeans that looked like they were from the eighties.

I went to her and put my arms around her small frame. Mom was at least three inches shorter than me, and I was wearing high-heeled boots so I had to bend down a bit to hug her. She held me tight for a beat longer than usual, and I drew back to see that her face was bright with excitement.

My dad walked into the kitchen covered in grease from head to toe like usual. His white T-shirt looked brown, and his jeans had stains covering them. He even had grime on his cheek. Dad was a mechanic and worked on his own projects in his free time. His small income was all that my parents had. They were in their late fifties and Mom had health issues that prevented her from working. I told Dad when they moved here he didn't need to get a job. I would make it work. An expensive car and living in an over-the-top apartment wasn't necessary, but he refused. He said he would work as a mechanic until the day he died. So, I supplemented his income to make sure they had everything they needed.

I looked over to Dad. "I would hug you too, but not with you being disgusting like that," I said, gesturing to his filthy clothes.

He laughed. "Of course, pumpkin. I'm going to go shower while you ladies get your gossip fix."

Mom hurled a dish towel at him. "We do not gossip. We simply discuss current events. Go on, now. Dinner will be ready in half an hour."

I chuckled at their banter, and a pang hit me somewhere deep. Despite all their hardships, they loved each other with a vengeance. Money had been scarce, but love was abundant. The type of love that went beyond a typical suburban family. My parents were ride or die for each other and for me.

I beamed at Mom. The last few years of her not having to worry about money and getting to be a normal older woman warmed my heart. She was active in her little community, and had a ton of friends. Resilient was her middle name. Being from a small town in the deep south and moving to the big city when she was eighteen to get away from an abusive ex wasn't easy. She met Dad after her car broke down one day and the rest was history. Neither of them had college degrees or a lot of parenting when they were kids so as a result they didn't make good financial choices, leaving us in tight spots all throughout my childhood.

That's why I eventually chose to become a financial advisor so I could help other families not make those same mistakes. The pay wasn't bad, either, and with my extensive knowledge of how to make money work, I turned the money I made into a lot more.

I walked over to the sink and began rinsing pots and pans then loading them into the dishwasher. Mom was picky about cooking and usually didn't want help unless it was a holiday so I always did dishes. I wasn't great at cooking anyway, so it worked out.

Mom asked about work, and after I'd filled her in that I posted a job yesterday, I turned to her wiping my hands. "All right, go ahead. I know you're bursting to tell me the latest news from your library ladies."

Her face brightened. "Well, Jessica got a big surprise a few weeks ago. Her daughter, the one who's twenty-one, told her she was getting married. They haven't even met the guy!"

I smiled down at my mom and happily listened to her gush.

An hour later, after finishing Mom's delicious chicken and dumplings, I was stuffed.

"John, do you want seconds?" Mom asked Dad.

"Nope, I'm going to hold out for cake. The less I eat now, the more cake I can eat." He laughed. "It was great as usual, though, honey."

Mom patted his hand and glanced over to me. "I'm assuming a no from you, as well, Raven? Are you staying for cake?"

"When could I ever turn down your Oreo cake, Mom?"

"Good! I was hoping you could stay for a while to visit after dinner."

We cleared away dinner and chatted in the living room for an hour before Mom brought us all dessert that was pure sin. As I was finishing my helping, my watch dinged. After clearing away dishes, I hugged Mom and Dad goodbye and walked out into the quiet neighborhood. Once I was in my car, I opened the text.

It was a photo. I tapped it, making it larger on the screen, and my breath caught, the phone slipping from my hand to the floor. I stared out the windshield into the dark night, swallowing hard, my pulse sending desire to all the right places.

Another ding, and I grabbed the phone like my life depended on it. A text popped up underneath the dim photo of a veined hand adorned with rings on almost every finger resting seductively on a chest in a black button-up dress shirt. "I think this necklace would look great on you, Raven."

CHAPTER TEN

RYAN

My VIRTUAL STALKER skills weren't up to par. I spent all day on Saturday sifting through the obscure depths of the internet to find anything on Raven. During our long texting session last night, I started a spreadsheet of all of the things she told me and added everything I already knew that morning. The cells were filling up with all the information I was finding online.

Talking to Raven and learning things about her had been a dream. I usually hated small talk, but when it came to her, I wanted to know everything. Even obscure things I had never cared about before like if she was early to rise or late to bed. No surprise, she was an early bird.

I cracked my neck after hours in front of the computer and set about making myself a meager dinner. Not in the mood to cook anything extravagant, I threw some fries in the air fryer and a burger in a pan. While I was cutting vegetables for toppings, frustration seeped back into my mind.

There was nothing about Raven from before college. At first I assumed it was because she was a minor during that time, but even my mediocre sleuthing skills could find high school records. Though apparently not Raven's. I found a ton of stuff from her time in college at the local university and her career, though. She was a top performer in her class and a top advisor at the firm she worked at before starting her own. Various awards and accolades were recognized by a slew of professional associations.

I knew my girl was a badass, but I had no idea the extent of her badassery.

My thoughts snagged when I was scrolling through her college records. Raven wasn't a native to the city. She moved from a different state to go to college here. I tried searching other state databases with no luck. There were no Raven Lovelaces in any public school records across the country. Which could have meant she went to private school. Those records were harder to get a hand on.

I couldn't find any relatives, either. If she had gone to private school, surely her family would have had a hefty amount of money lying around. That usually meant that I would've been able to find her parents easily. After all, my own parents were plastered all over the internet with their various charities and fake bullshit.

As I sat down at the round two-top table situated between the kitchen and sofa for dinner, I pushed the annoyance down, focusing instead on the spark of excitement at the last discovery I made. I'd copied all of the information about Raven's company from her website into the spreadsheet when I saw a job listing for her firm. It was an entry level position for a receptionist. An idea immediately formed in my mind, but in order to execute, I needed to come to terms with Raven seeing me in person. I would have a little more fun with her first, though. Possible rejection after she saw what I looked like could wait.

After eating, I padded to the bedroom in search of a black

button-down shirt. I hadn't done laundry for a week, but luckily there was one hanging in the closet. I went over to my dresser and picked over my assorted silver rings. I'd bought them on a whim in college and thankfully had kept them. I was going out on a limb, but being a voice actor for over a year and especially after the last eight months, I had a pretty good handle on what women liked.

I was banking on Raven preferring her stylistic choices in her men, as well. All business, but still dark with an edge. I threw on a chain for good measure and went down the hall to the studio. Slipping into the dark room, I flipped on a lamp in the corner. Just enough light to make out what the photo depicted.

Taking thirst trap photos wasn't my forte since all my accounts were faceless and I hadn't texted a woman in that way in over a year. But after a few tries, I was happy with the result and texted the photo to Raven. She opened it a dozen minutes later but didn't respond. I couldn't help but feel a hint of annoyance with her since I hadn't texted her all day on purpose so she would be eager to talk tonight. I would make sure she knew to respond quickly to me later. I was an impatient fuck and didn't like waiting, especially when I was waiting for her reaction to a sexy photo.

Sliding back into athletic shorts and not bothering with a shirt, I entertained going to bed to set myself up to get a jump on recording the next project tomorrow. I could've started Monday, but it wouldn't have hurt to get some time in since the next week might require errands. About to shut my computer down, I glanced at my phone as a ding filled the room.

A notification from Raven was displayed on the screen.

"That wasn't very nice. I was at my parents' house."

So she had parents and they probably lived in the city or

close by. I tucked that away for later. "Who said I was nice? I think you might like me less if I was nice." I sent the message and then quickly typed another. "I hope the photo was all right with you. I assumed it would be since you gave the green light for flirting." I added a smirk emoji and pressed send.

A text from her came just as I sent the second one. "Fine, you're right." Then another came through. "Yes, it was alright. It's not like it was an unsolicited dick pic. I think you're nicer than you make yourself out to be. Respectable, even."

"You deserve nothing but the utmost respect," I typed back.

"You've only had one texting conversation with me. For all you know, I could be a monster."

"If you're a monster then eat me alive, baby."

The message was seen, but no typing happened. I tamped down my eagerness. *Chill bro, chill.* She didn't have to respond immediately.

After five minutes, I grew anxious that maybe I had gone too far with the last comment. Maybe the endearment was too much too soon, but then the typing dots appeared.

"I have to admit, that line got me."

I grinned as my unease ebbed away and my playfulness returned. "I've had you this whole time."

"Wow, you're cranked up to eleven today."

"I'm always turned to eleven when it comes to you."

The conversation turned from flirty to casual when I asked her about her day. We texted about mundane things, but the conversation was enjoyable. I loved talking to her. After two hours I got antsy and had to move things along. I craved to give her release live instead of from a recording. Moving from my desk to the bedroom, I settled between the sheets and got comfortable.

"You said you were out. I'm assuming you're home now?" I typed.

"Yes, I've been home this whole time. I figured you could wait a bit for a text back."

Heat flared in my chest. "We need to work on that. I don't like to wait."

"I don't remember agreeing to you being my keeper. Besides, I'm not exactly one who goes out on the town late at night."

"I'll let that one slide. I figured so, but was just curious. What are you doing?"

"Just hanging out in the living room, about to go to bed."

"Good, go get in bed." My cock swelled when I imagined her getting in bed in an oversized T-shirt or nothing at all.

"Oh, making demands now, are we?"

"Yes. At some point you'll learn I don't fuck around." I slipped out of my shorts feeling the soft cotton sheets on my bare skin. Something about it made me untamed, or maybe it was just the sexy woman I was texting.

"Are we really doing this?"

I thought about keeping my authoritative tone, but I didn't want to make her uncomfortable. "Only if you want to."

A few minutes ticked by before she responded and my thoughts drifted. I could have called her. After all, it was my voice she craved, but I wanted to draw this out. She might've made the connection that I was her client already; she was a smart woman. But the game of pretending was too good—too hot. We existed in our own little world and once we spoke truths aloud, reality couldn't be ignored.

Her text snapped me out of my daze. "All right. I'm in bed."

She must have been changing. A picture started to form in my mind and I needed more details. "I'm going to be stereotypical for a minute here, but what are you wearing?"

"Omg, really? You're serious?"

"As a heart attack."

"God, how cliche can you get?" The typing dots appeared immediately, and another text came. "A black nightdress."

My cock stiffened. Of course it was black. She was like a dark angel that I was going to bend to my will. "I'm not surprised since you said your favorite color was black last night. I like it. Are you comfortable doing what I say, baby?"

"Fine, why not."

"I don't really like that answer. I need a clear one."

"Okay. I will."

I let out a deep breath. This was it. Her orgasms were going to be mine for the foreseeable future. "Better, but we'll work on it. Caress your body with your free hand."

"Okay."

"Now, linger on your tits, kneading them through the fabric of your dress." I was fully hard thinking about her breasts. I didn't know what they looked like, but I didn't care. They would be perfect no matter what.

"Mm. I'm going to warn you, I'm not very good at this. I don't sext."

"You don't have to do anything. Just respond with yes, no, or an answer if I ask a question. Slip your hand under your nightgown and rub your nipples."

"Yes."

"Tell me how good it feels, baby."

"So fucking good."

"Perfect. I thought it might. You're doing amazing. Imagine how good it would feel if it were me rubbing them, then sucking and licking them with my expert tongue."

"You're good. This is fucking hot."

"Oh, baby, we're just getting started."

I couldn't take it any longer. I gripped my cock, the pressure forcing a moan at the relief. I slowly stroked myself from the base to the tip, balancing the phone in my other hand.

"Move your hand between your legs and slip it into your panties."

"I'm not wearing panties."

"Fuck," I groaned into the room. I was going to burst way too quickly at the thought of the image of her.

"My girl is naughty. Are you wet for me?"

"Yes."

"That's my good girl. Tell me you're soaked. I need you to be soaked."

"Yes. I am."

My head fell back against the headboard when I read her words. Out of all the texts I'd gotten before, that one was the best of all. Raven was drenched because of me. I quickly typed a reply, launching into full send on the conversation.

"Good job, baby. Move your fingers up and down your dripping pussy and then rub that needy clit for me."

CHAPTER ELEVEN

RAVEN

This was crazy. I was sexting a voice actor, who was also my client and getting myself off to it. I hadn't done anything this unhinged for a long time. It felt great. The situation had me so turned on I almost didn't need to touch myself.

I had been wet between my legs since I'd gotten the photo. It was the definition of sexy. A dress shirt, rings, masculine-veined hands. I even spotted a chain around his neck. It was the hottest photo I'd seen, mainly because it was a glimpse of the man behind the voice—and he was talking to *me*.

When he told me to rub my clit, I was done for. I could barely type because my fingers on my pussy were giving me such sweet relief. "It's so good," I texted.

"That's it, baby. Keep going."

I hadn't known someone calling me baby could be so hot. For once, I was enjoying being told what to do. "Yes."

"You're going to wait to come until I say so, all right?" Fuck. I knew this man would be good, from the words I'd heard him say in his content, but this was somehow even better. Probably because he was talking directly to me.

"Okay."

"I prefer 'Yes sir.'"

I giggled. He was also stereotypical, but it aroused me even more. "<eye roll emoji> Yes, sir." I couldn't help adding a bit of facetiousness.

"I might have to spank you for that one."

"You would have to catch me first."

"Fuck, babe. You better be close to coming, because you being a brat is going to make me lose it."

"I'm really close. You can chase me anytime."

"Goddammit, baby. Come for me."

My body had a mind of its own. It was tuned to whatever he said, even in a text message. As soon as I read the words, a tremor built at the base of my spine. My orgasm crashed into me hard, making my legs shake with convulsions. I came for so long I reached a new record.

Once I returned to my body, I took a few minutes to regain my composure and took a quick trip to the bathroom. I searched for my phone in the sheets, which I'd dropped at the height of ecstasy, and unlocked the screen to see three new messages.

"Fuck. Please tell me you came just as hard as I did."

"Baby?"

"Babe, are you all right?"

I quickly typed a reply. "I'm here."

"What happened? Are you okay?"

"Yes, I'm great. I just had to put myself back together."

Twice now he'd seemed concerned about my well-being. He had been a gentleman too, asking for permission to flirt and if I was okay with this. I wasn't sure why he cared, but I wasn't complaining. It was nice to be cared for, a feeling I wasn't used to.

The dots on the screen appeared then stopped like he was hesitant. "Did you finish?"

It's almost as though he was shy now that the haze of lust had dissipated.

"I did. Very..." I sent the text and typed another. "Hard."

I typed yet another message, not caring that I had sent three in quick succession. "Um, thanks? I think?" Awkwardness settled in my chest.

"Good. I couldn't hold out any longer. You're driving me mad."

A rush of unease settled in my stomach, and I questioned my next words. While I enjoyed the illicit act of sexting someone on the internet, this seemed deeper than that. I thought about him nonstop, but was still cautious since he claimed to have gotten my number from the website. Even though he was Ryan, I still didn't know him. I was hesitant, sure, but I was also still human, after all. Somehow I knew he wouldn't try to harm me. Try being the keyword, because try would be as far as he got.

"I want to keep talking to you. Do you want to continue this?"

His reply finally appeared on the screen. "Of course. This isn't a one-time thing, babe. We aren't done yet."

"Good. I'll be pissed if you ghost me."

"I'm too obsessed with you to ghost you."

Heat flooded my body. He clearly didn't know me personally because I, too, became unusually obsessed occasionally.

THE NEXT MORNING, I was insatiable. I woke up with hard nipples and damp thighs. After last night's session I craved more. On a whim, I grabbed my earbuds and phone from the nightstand and tapped into my apps. I went to Zander's account on the subscription app and scrolled through the audio clips.

It was unethical to mix business and pleasure. I knew that. This situation wasn't as bad as a doctor and patient, but it could still fuck with my career if the CFP board found out. Zander's voice was the hottest thing I'd ever heard, and I wasn't going to stop talking to him. If I kept Zander separate from my client, it would be fine. Maybe. If he knew who I was, which he likely did, I could claim innocence that I didn't know he was my client. I tapped on a post and waited for the voice I craved. I'd listened to this one before, but I didn't care. It was still as hot as the first time.

"Welcome home, baby. Did you have a good day?"

I sighed, immediately relaxed by his words.

"Aww, I'm sorry, baby. Come here and let me take care of you. No, no, no, don't pull away. You need to decompress. Here, lie down on the bed."

How this man created a scene with just one-sided spoken conversation was beyond me, but I was here for it.

"That's it, baby. Lie back and relax. I'm just going to caress your body. Does that feel good?"

Moving my hand to my pussy, I rubbed my clit, no teasing needed. I'd been wet when I woke up, but now I was drenched.

"God, baby, you're so fucking beautiful. I can't get enough of you. I can't wait any longer. I've needed to taste you all day. No, lie back. You don't need to do anything at all. I'm just moving to the edge of the bed. Are you ready for me to take care of you with my tongue, gorgeous?"

I was captivated. My arousal was so intense my entire body was throbbing in need of release. It was as if I was in the scene right there with him.

"Fuck, baby, your pussy tastes like heaven. I could eat you all day. This pussy is mine."

The sounds coming through the earbuds weren't cringy. If I hadn't heard the clip for myself I would've assumed they would be awful, but they were the sexiest thing I'd ever heard. The breathing and words said like his mouth was actually on something. How had I never known about this kind of content before?

"Yes, baby. That's it. I want you to come for me. Come on my tongue, baby."

And I did. Right then. When he told me to come my body almost instantly obeyed. I didn't stop the audio, listening to the entire thing replay, and got off a second time.

Later, I had to drag myself from bed, but I finally managed to get going. I had a lazy morning, which was something I didn't do often, but I had errands to run. My Sunday afternoon was going to be busy. After a shower and lunch, I dressed in black athletic attire and pulled on the one pair of running shoes I owned.

As soon as I stepped out of my building goosebumps raised on my neck. The same feeling from the garage was back, and I wondered if I was imagining things. The garage was one thing, but getting the same feeling at home was making me even more anxious. I'd never had feelings like this before in either place.

The day was bright, but my trepidation was a cloud following me as I turned the corner and walked down the street toward the small market I used for my nominal grocery shopping. The thoughts didn't let up no matter how hard I tried to push them from my mind. When I walked into the store, I felt better almost immediately. Running through all the reasons I might feel this way while I shopped, I came up with nothing aside from the obvious. The fucking bastard had found me.

My skin crawled when I left the store and walked toward my apartment. I picked up my pace a bit as my heart thundered in my chest not from the exercise, but from my nervousness. By the time I reached my apartment, I was almost running and was thankful the essentials I needed were scarce this week. Rushing through the lobby, I jammed the up button until the elevator doors opened. The floors ticked away, and as soon as I was in my apartment I locked the door with the dead bolt and put a chair under the knob for good measure.

CHAPTER TWELVE

RYAN

I LEFT my apartment around noon and drove to the outskirts of downtown where residential homes turned into apartment buildings. They were the nicest in the city, and I thought about what it would be like to live in one of them. I could afford it, but I liked where I was on the outskirts. I wasn't quite in the suburbs, but I was away from the hustle of downtown traffic.

Parking my car a few streets away from my destination, I pulled my black hood up over my hair to obscure my face. As I walked along the tree-covered sidewalk, I kept my gaze trained on the ground, trying not to draw attention. Once I found the bus stop, I sat on the bench and pulled out my phone, pretending to be entranced by social media.

Keeping my head bowed, I peered up through my lashes and hair that stuck out from my hood. I took in the apartment building across the street and counted ten floors, paying particular attention to the top level. I saw a large balcony and noted a set of patio chairs and table with nothing else. The terrace was large enough for a full dining table or a set of furniture, but the majority of it sat empty.

The other balconies and windows appeared normal. Various items and personal effects littered the spaces unlike the top floor. Flicking my gaze back up to the top, I saw all the curtains were drawn so there was no possibility of seeing the occupants.

Down the street, a few people milled around, but it was fairly quiet as I watched people come and go for half an hour. I was about to go back to my car when a head of onyx hair emerged from the doors across the street.

Raven was clad in a pair of tight black leggings that hugged every curve on her body and a fitted zip hoodie that was almost just as tight as her pants. My breath caught at the sight of her in person. She was even more gorgeous than I thought she would be.

She wasn't short, but she wasn't what I would consider tall, either. Maybe five-eight or nine. My brain glitched as I took in her curves, every line exaggerated by her fitted clothes. She looked like one of those girls that streamed themselves playing video games, but ten times better. And older. Carrying confidence from years of success, she was the definition of perfection and seeing her in the flesh had confirmed everything I already knew. Even if it was from far away.

A few steps down the street, she stopped in her tracks, looking in every direction. My senses went on full alert. She shrank into herself, and I could tell something was bothering her. I scanned the sidewalks and street, but nothing seemed amiss. Raven started walking again, and I was on my feet before my brain had comprehended what my body was doing.

When I found Raven's home address from my virtual snooping, I decided to take shit full throttle and see what her neighborhood was like. I wasn't planning to see her, or become an actual stalker, but there I was blending into the shadows the best I could as I walked a few yards behind her on the opposite side of the street.

She stepped into a market a few blocks away, and I slid into a small alley, concealing myself so I didn't look suspicious. I looked like a normal guy in jeans and a hoodie, but I didn't know if she had possibly glimpsed me when she came out of her building. She seemed on edge already, and I didn't want to contribute to that.

Leaning against the brick wall, I scrolled my phone, constantly watching out of the corner of my eye. She eventually left the market and once she was far enough away, I slinked from the alley, falling into step behind her again.

When I saw her alarm after she left her apartment, there was no way I wasn't going to make sure she was safe on her trip. Suddenly, her pace quickened, and she broke into a run, her bags swinging on her arms. I let her go, only increasing my steps to a brisk walk, but never losing sight of her until she bolted into her building.

As I walked back to my car, I remembered back to Friday night when I first texted her, the comments flooding back . She thought someone was watching her. Someone other than me might be following her. I wouldn't mind causing her a bit of fear, but in a controlled environment. This was something different entirely.

Rage settled over me again. I was the only person who would be fucking with Raven, and if someone else was, I would find out who.

Later that evening, the phone glared back at me, as I hoped I wasn't making a mistake. Finding out what was going on with Raven was a top priority. I hadn't even met the woman yet, but I would walk through burning embers for her. Maybe something in her past would reveal if she was in danger or if something else was causing her to be on edge. I scrolled through my contacts and tapped on a number I hadn't called in years. I wasn't sure if he would pick up after so long, and the way we left things.

I paced around my apartment while the line connected. Finally, after I had lost count of the rings, he picked up. "What, Ryan?"

I took a deep breath. "Hello to you, too, Dad," I gritted through the receiver.

"Why are you calling? Finally get yourself in a bind, and need a way out?"

I laughed, unable to stifle the sound. "As much as you would like that to be the case, no. That's not why I'm calling. I do need a favor, though."

His huff flamed the anger rising in my chest. "Don't worry, it's a small one. I'm not asking for money, since I've made quite enough on my own. I need your PI's number. Rick is his name, right?"

He scoffed, the sound sending a spear of agitation. "Why? What trouble have you gotten into now?"

I ran my hand through my tousled hair. "That's none of your concern, now is it? Remember how you don't associate with me, your heathen son?"

It was his turn to chuckle. "Why the hell would I give you anything? After the embarrassment you've been, we're lucky we still have any prestige at all. It's a good thing we were able to keep your antics in college from getting out among our contacts."

I conceded a bit even though Dad was full of it since I was already tired of listening to his bullshit. What a surprise, the asshole hadn't changed at all. I softened my tone, trying to get what I needed so I could be finished with the call. "Come on, Dad, it's not asking for much. Your guy is the best. I'll pay for him myself."

"Fine. Only call me again if you changed your ways and want to be a part of this family. Otherwise, you don't get to appear out of nowhere when you need something. No matter how insignificant."

Fat chance of me ever wanting to be part of any family of his. The double beep sounded in my ear, signaling Dad ended the call. I stared at the sunlight streaming through the lone window in the living room behind my desk until a few minutes later when a text with the contact came through. I released a sigh and saved the contact to my phone.

Shit was still the same as it was two years ago when I left without looking back. Dad was still a cocksucker and Mom was likely right there with him. In their eyes, I was a failure and the only thing that would change that would be me agreeing to reform myself publicly in their pretentious social circles. Then I would have to be the perfect gentleman they always hoped for to take over Dad's business. That wasn't happening. Even as a kid I refused to be what they wanted—the ensuing rejection fucking with me my entire life. I would rather be myself though than be anything I was told to be and I didn't give a fuck about the company.

I would call the investigator tomorrow. Right now, I needed to work up the courage for the next few steps of my plan for Raven. She had no idea what was about to come her way, and it was going to change everything.

THE NEXT MORNING I was antsy, and I couldn't focus on work. Every line I narrated was disconnected and lacked any emotion. I was wholeheartedly uninterested in the assigned story, with thoughts of long black hair and soft curves in tight athletic clothes at the forefront of my mind, instead. Raven was becoming a problem.

She haunted my thoughts constantly and after a completely wasted morning with exactly zero minutes of my next project done, I decided to say fuck it. Now that I had seen her in person, even if from a distance, I was a man consumed by lust and need. So I got in my car to drive downtown hoping for maybe another glance.

As soon as I was behind the wheel grief speared me. Probably because I was already in an anxious headspace, but sometimes cars fucked with me after my uncle. He had been the only person in my family that acted like I was worth a damn, and then he died in a car crash.

Not that he was overly affectionate, but he was with Dad at the house a lot and always came to my room to see what I was up to. He didn't have kids of his own so as an adult I wondered if he would have had them if he lived. Based on his interactions with me, I liked to think he would have.

Shaking myself from my memories, I backed the car out of the spot and drove toward the few high rises in the city.

Driving by her building a few times before parking the car, I continued my venture on foot. After a few trips up and down the street, I walked into the lobby of the glass building. It wasn't the tallest in the city, but it was tall enough that anyone who paid rent for a space in it was doing well for themselves.

The entrance was fairly simple, a door with full glass walls flanking it, but inside was a different story. In the center of the room sat a grand wooden desk with gold everywhere. Elevators flanked the desk and by the windows were seating options. An art deco chandelier hung from the ceiling, sparkling like a diamond.

On the wall to the right was a directory of businesses and I quickly searched for Lovelace Financial. Floor thirteen of fifteen. I shook my head, recalling that most buildings didn't have a thirteenth floor because of superstitions. Leave it to my goth queen to find one that did. Before I knew what I was doing I walked to the elevators and pressed the up button. When the doors opened and I was inside, I pressed the button for thirteen. My stomach churned as the elevator climbed upward, and the counter clicked higher.

A *ding* sounded as I reached her floor, and I stepped into a hallway with a business at each end to the left and right. But directly in front of me was hers. The glass doors offered a full view of her reception area, and it was starkly opposite from the vibe in the main lobby. Everything was modern in gray and white with the occasional black accent. It was exactly what I would've expected from her. Professional yet she found a way to integrate darkness.

Before I could poke around anymore, a woman with gray-laced hair came into the lobby from somewhere in the back of the office. Dread coursed through me at being seen. I didn't want to cause a commotion, so I hurried back to the elevators, pressing the down button a few times to get the elevator to hurry up. Thankfully she hadn't noticed me. Once I was back on the ground level, I pushed through the doors onto the bright street and walked to a park a few blocks away to regain control of myself. Being outside for a while would hopefully calm my nerves, and I could get back and do some heavy recording this afternoon and evening, even though I hadn't seen Raven.

The day was beautiful, the sky a bright blue contrasting with the green foliage, and I was actually enjoying being outside. There were quite a few people around since the weather wasn't as hot anymore, which I appreciated. Summer wasn't really my thing, but then again, no season was my thing. Dropping onto one of the various benches lining the paths, I scrolled my phone while the light breeze played with my hair. After only a few minutes a dog barked, and I looked to my left, damn near dropping my phone on the concrete. Raven was walking toward me.

Just before she passed, her gaze met mine, and the world fell away. Nothing mattered except her. She was seeing me, Ryan. Not hearing my voice, not reading words on a phone or computer, but seeing the real me. Of course, she didn't know who I was, but I couldn't help but feel nervous as her gaze stayed locked on mine.

The women I had been with over the years hadn't sparked any kind of feeling, since most were shallow as fuck. When my parents cut me out of their lives, I learned that I liked solitude—the yearning for their attention of my childhood nowhere in sight. Being my own person and never having to hear how someone else thought I should live my life was freeing. The last thing I wanted was to end up with someone who was like my mother and her friends, someone who didn't care about me, anyway. All women weren't like them, but I was still hesitant, my insecurities at the forefront. Getting my pleasure from knowing how many women listened to my audios to get off with the occasional hook up was fine with me.

But that was before Raven. She was different. I was pining after her like a lovesick teenager.

I watched a faint blush creep onto her pale skin, and my trepidation dissipated. She looked away and fumbled in her pocket, drawing out a phone to answer it. Except the phone hadn't been ringing when she took it out.

She hurried past me, and I watched her until she disappeared around a corner in the distance. I stared, unseeing, and replayed the scene in my mind. She was even more stunning up close. She was utter perfection.

I walked back to my car in a daze. All I could see were those gorgeous green eyes staring at me. Raven's face wasn't getting out of my head no matter what I did.

Traffic was light since it was early afternoon so I got home quickly. Hurrying to the studio, I started working on the current job. With renewed enthusiasm, I got a decent amount of content recorded before the noisy evening when people began arriving home from work.

I thought about Raven the entire time, putting us inside the dark romance story. When I paused for the female character's lines, I imagined Raven's voice speaking them since I didn't have to say them myself in duet style. Filling the breaks with her professional yet seductive voice made everything seamless.

Halfway through the story, things got interesting. The main female character, Lena, was asleep in bed when the main male character, Ronan, broke into her house and went into her room. His motivation for following Lena was that she'd broken his heart years before and as he watched, he was falling for her all over again. I took a sip of water, and my voice filled the booth.

"Stay still, Lena. The louder you scream, the more I'll make it hurt." Her eyes grew as round as saucers. Yeah, she knew exactly who I was. That would make this even better.

Suddenly the fight left her completely as she gazed up into my masked face. I knew she was still in love with me after monitoring her texts and calls so I knew she wanted this—wanted me. "I'm going to move my hand and you're not going to make a sound, got it?" She nodded with a whimper.

I released her mouth and of course she disobeyed, but instead of a scream, she whispered, "Ronan."

I slammed her head into the mattress. "I said no talking, Lena." She nodded vigorously in response. "You're going to be silent while I drive you mad with pleasure. You're going to see what you let go of all those years ago. I'm going to fuck you so well you're going to regret leaving me for the rest of your life."

Half an hour later I finished the lengthy scene as I heard a door slam in the apartment above me. Narrating Ronan fucking Lena in the mask while imagining it was me fucking Raven instead had me raging in my pants. I understood why women were obsessed with these books. They were fucking hot, but they were more than that. They were raw and beautiful in a way that easy romances weren't. Real life wasn't a fairy tale, and sometimes the path to your happy ending wasn't always something from a Disney movie.

CHAPTER THIRTEEN

RAVEN

My cheeks were on fire the entire hurried walk back to the office. The guy on the bench in the gray hoodie and jeans was plastered in my mind. He had been perched on a bench in the park with one arm draped over the side and an ankle resting on a knee. My pulse was still fluttering, and not from the brisk pace that I was moving.

He seemed on the taller side from the length of his legs. Dark brown hair that was long on top and mussed like he just raked his hand through it fluttered in the breeze. His clean-shaven jaw looked like it was chiseled from stone, and his skin was as smooth as marble. I didn't think I'd ever called a man beautiful, but he was straight out of a Calvin Klein ad.

I'd stood there like an idiot staring at him, having the strongest urge to run my fingers through his hair and nuzzle close to see what he smelled like. He was younger, not a crease or wrinkle anywhere in sight, maybe only a year or so out of college.

The worst part about the whole thing was that he glanced up right as I stole a glance at him as I walked by. His brown eyes met mine like we were straight out of a rom-com. Holding my gaze, his mouth turned up slightly, and I hadn't been able to look elsewhere.

When I stepped off the elevator and back through the glass door to the office, I wondered what the hell was wrong with me. Men didn't have this effect on me, yet I was daydreaming about Zander constantly and now I was fantasizing about a random guy in the park. I was a successful business woman in her thirties, not a college girl seeing a dude for the first time and instantly having a crush. Maybe my body was just hyper-sensitive to arousal lately. Whatever the case was, it was starting to get on my nerves.

That afternoon the phone rang off the hook until I couldn't take it anymore.

"Goddammit!" I put my head in my hands at my desk trying to ignore it. With a sigh, I picked up the receiver. "Raven Lovelace."

"Hi, Ms. Lovelace, this is Tim with SecureSafe. I was calling about the security system installation you requested."

Relieved that it wasn't another client with a problem, I sighed. "Oh, hi. Yes, I did request two installations."

Shuffling came from the other end of the line. "I see here you needed a business install and a residence install. Are you available for us to send a technician Friday for the business and next Wednesday for the residence?"

After confirming the times with the security company, I laid the phone back in the cradle. It was almost five so I took a break to grab extra clothes from the car. Maybe my comfy sweats would help me get a bit more done before I left. It was the craziest Monday I'd had in awhile and it took a toll on me. Not to mention I was distracted.

Making my way to the elevators, I waved goodbye to Joanne packing her things for the day and pressed the button for the level with the door that led to the garage. The counter ticked, and unease crept back into my mind, still spooked the day before when I'd spent the rest of the afternoon peeking out my apartment blinds and scanning the street for any sign of suspicious activity. I came up with nothing except a raccoon that had successfully breached a trash can across the street. With all of the breaks, I hadn't gotten much done. Which was one of the reasons my day today had been so busy.

Grabbing the clothes, I hurried back into the building. As I waited for the elevator back upstairs, my thoughts shifted to the guy I'd seen in the park that afternoon, and now I couldn't get him out of my head. When I stepped onto the elevator, I let myself daydream. I'd had a rough day and a little fawning wouldn't hurt.

Later that night I trudged out of work after it had already gotten dark. I usually tried to leave no later than sunset, but I was lucky I was leaving as early as I was. I had time for a long bath before bed, but that was about it.

In the garage, the familiar chill ran down my spine. I was used to it by that point, getting the same feeling almost every time I left work. It was usually missing in the mornings when I arrived, even though it was always still dark out. After my awful day, I would've probably let someone take me if they tried. I didn't have the energy to fight back.

Getting into my car, I checked my phone for the first time since the trip to the park this afternoon, and was again met with nothing. I had texted Zander a few times since Saturday but he was leaving me on read. The fucker. I was too old for these stupid games. I threw my phone in my bag and reversed out of my spot.

Rounding the corner to the ground level, I slammed on my breaks. A figure clad in all black was standing in the shadowy turn. My heart galloped in my chest and without looking down, I jabbed the auto lock on the doors.

The hooded shape had the build of a man and he slowly walked toward my car, my headlights illuminating his military style pants. My breaths came in gasps as fear took hold, a fear I hadn't felt in over a decade until a few weeks ago. My phone dinged and I remembered that I had the means to call the police. I scooped up the phone and punched 911.

When I looked back to the figure, he was gone. Of fucking course he was. I looked three hundred and sixty degrees around my car and saw no one around. Had my mind been playing tricks on me because I was so tired?

Wasting no time, I gunned it, tires squealing out of the garage. The barriers were automatic for daily patrons so fortunately I didn't have to stop for a booth. Out on the street, I looked at my phone and tapped the text message I had gotten during the ordeal. What great fucking timing, Zander. Then a thought slid into my mind.

What if Zander, well, Ryan was the one who was watching me? I knew he lived in my city, and he knew my office was in this building. Was he following me?

I shook my head. That couldn't be it, could it? If the guy in the garage was real, he hadn't been texting while he was in front of my car. The text from Zander came through while I was staring at him. Either way, I should stop texting Zander and go about my life. Especially since I knew he was my client. But I couldn't help the pull to text him back. Even if he was trying to scare me, I found myself needing to talk to him. I needed it in my soul, and at that moment, the fear only heightened my desire.

"Hey, baby girl."

Why did that pet name send tingles through my body even

when I was annoyed with him? I typed out my response quickly at a red light, trying to not let my aggravation show.

"What's up? Been a few days. Already onto the next adoring admirer?"

Shit. That was the opposite of nonchalant. I was being pathetic. The guy hadn't texted in two days and I was acting like I'd never talked to a man before. I sped through the streets to my apartment and opened his response after parking the car.

"Oh, you aren't getting rid of me that easily, baby. I was feeling the project I was working on and got it recorded in record time. Nah, I'll be chasing you for the foreseeable future."

Yep, I was an idiot. *He was working.* That thing I should be doing more of instead of daydreaming about voice actors and guys on park benches. Despite my hint of embarrassment, I caught myself smiling down at the phone.

Chase me.

Now, the adrenaline was really flowing.

THE SECURITY TECHNICIAN finished installing the camera over the front door to my apartment the next week with a satisfied smile. I hadn't had any other encounters since the person in the garage over a week ago. If someone was fucking with me or tried to fuck with me further, I would catch them and make them rue the day they set their sights on me. No one could be trusted, and I had to rely on myself for my own protection. I could beg all day, but in the end, the monsters always took what they wanted.

After the tech left, I set about throwing together a salad for an early dinner. I scheduled the install for as late in the day as I could so I could just work the rest of the evening at home.

Working in large chunks of time was better for me. I would get everything I needed finished so I could sit down and work straight through the evening until bed.

My watch vibrated as I cleaned up after my meal. I hadn't talked to Mom and Dad this week, so it was probably one of them.

In the moment I realized, if someone really was out to get me, no one would notice until I didn't show up for work. I'd be dead before anyone even knew I was missing. It would probably be a good idea to talk with Mom every night for a while.

The text was from Zander. We talked a lot over the last week but hadn't gone any further than sexting a few times. A few days ago, he started sending me good morning voice messages, and I blushed at the thought of them.

This text was another image. I sat on a barstool and put the phone back on the island before opening it. Taking a deep breath, I warred within myself if I should keep things going. I was too mesmerized by him and needed to get a grip. Checking my phone constantly to see if he texted wasn't my usual behavior.

Annoyed, I picked up the phone again and opened the text. God fucking dammit. Every time I started to get a clear head about this situation he hit me right where he knew I was weakest. This photo was dark like the other one but he was shirtless. His lower torso filled the frame with black slacks slung low on his hips. His hand was gripping his belt as though he was in the process of removing it.

My body perked up. I studied smooth skin that disappeared beneath the waistband of his pants. Fucking hell, he knew exactly how to play with me in the most agonizing way. His stomach was taut, and my mouth watered at the V that I knew trailed south right to...

The dryer in the laundry room buzzed, scaring the shit out

of me. Fuck, I really needed to pay more attention. I was always accidentally hitting the buzzer switch when I started the dryer.

Bringing my attention back to the screen in my hands, I zoomed in on the photo and took in every detail. The veins in his hand also wound up his arm, and they were on full display. I sighed, wondering what it would feel like to brush my hands along his smooth skin. I snapped out of it and backed out of the conversation. If I kept this up, I would be drooling on the counter.

Another text came through. "Like what you see?"

I typed a response with a smirk. "If by like you mean annoyed with, then yes."

"Annoyed that you're wet from a photo that's very PG-13?"

How did he…Damn it, he was good. I was right back to not caring that I was so enamored with him. "Maybe. I wouldn't be if it was anyone else. Now I need to do something about it."

His response took longer than usual. "Baby, you fucking torture me with your words. Want me to help? I have a little gift for you."

"Ok, I'm listening."

"Good. Listen to this, baby."

A few minutes passed, and a voice message popped up on the screen. Desire wound through me like a vise, threatening to cut off my air supply. He hadn't sent a voice message with sexy words directed at me before, only innocent 'good morning' messages.

I pressed play. "Hey, baby, I need you to agree to do what I say, okay? Text a simple yes back if you agree to be a good girl."

My mouth dropped open, and heat flared in my cheeks. I listened to the clip again and groaned. Why was I so feral over a man's voice? I had a thing for voices, that much was certain, but I had never encountered such an attraction to one as I did with Zander. I didn't even know what he looked like, for fuck's sake.

My phone ringing jolted me from my thoughts. I looked down and "Zander" was written in large font on the screen. He was calling me.

Fuck, fuck, fuck. Panic tore at my chest as I moved from the stool and paced around the counter. I didn't think he planned to call me. I assumed this would be another sexting session. What if I fucked things up by saying something idiotic?

I stopped in my tracks. Why did I care? I never had a confidence issue when it came to men. What made Zander different?

Because you actually like him.

The phone rang and rang and at the last split second before my voicemail picked up, I answered.

"Hello?"

"You all right, baby?" he purred from the other end of the line.

My knees almost gave out. His voice was great in recordings, but nothing compared to hearing it again live. I hadn't talked to Ryan, the client, since I started texting Zander. Ryan. I really did have to separate them in my mind.

"Zander..." I couldn't find any other words to say.

"Yes. Hi, it's me."

"You called me. I didn't expect you to call," I panted.

He chuckled. "I hadn't planned to, but when you didn't text back, I said fuck it."

"Oh..." My voice trailed off into the silence.

"Hopefully, my voice in real life is good for you like the recordings."

I searched my brain for something to say. "Uh, yeah. I've listened to your voice for hours, and it sounds great in person, too." I slapped my hand over my mouth. Oh my god, did I actually just say that? "I mean, I've listened to hours of your audio-books, not hours of your videos on social media." I squeezed my eyes shut. "I'm just going to stop talking now."

His laugh was louder this time. "It's okay, baby, I know you've listened to my sexy content. Want to know a secret?"

"Uh, sure?" I really needed to stop talking like an imbecile.

He breathed heavily into the phone. "Knowing you have listened to my naughty posts makes me so...fucking...hard."

My breath caught. Holy motherfucker. I hadn't ever been this wet in my life, the dampness soaking my thong. I had to sit down on one of the bar stools at the island before I collapsed in a puddle on the floor.

"Are you actually trying to kill me?"

I could hear his wicked smile when he spoke. "Full of questions tonight, baby girl. How about we focus on you instead of me, hmm? Be a good girl and go make yourself comfortable for me, all right?"

Why was I willing to do whatever this man said? I had no idea, but I didn't linger on the question long. "Uh, okay. I'll, uh, go do that while I wait for your text."

His voice turned assertive. "Oh no, baby, we aren't texting for this. I'm going to make you come with my voice in real time, and in return I get to hear every one of your sweet moans."

CHAPTER FOURTEEN

RYAN

Raven squeaked at my words but didn't say anything else. That morning, I had finished recording the pickups for the dark romance from the week before, thankful there were only a few of them since I had been really into the performance. The rest of the afternoon was spent in a novel I started earlier in the week, and the second half of the book had so many sex scenes that beating it alone wasn't working anymore. Especially after imagining Raven in all of those scenes.

When I decided to text her I wasn't planning on calling, only sending voice messages, but when she didn't respond, I panicked. I refused to let her ignore me, so before I knew what I was doing I dialed her number. When she said my pseudonym into the phone I almost came right then. Even though it wasn't my real name, hearing it on her sexy lips had me undone.

Silence stretched across the line, and I wondered if she was going to play along with this. If she didn't, there was a good chance I would drive to her apartment and fuck her senseless. I wasn't sure if she was nervous or intrigued by the call, but I hoped it was a bit of both. I'd learned a lot since I'd been narrating romance novels and was eager to experiment with some of the kinks I'd read. One of which was the hint of apprehension in my girl.

"Babe, are you there?" I asked even though I knew she was still on the line.

She cleared her throat. "Yeah, I'm here."

Shifting on the couch, I adjusted my uncomfortably hard dick. "Good. Now, go to your room."

Soft footsteps sounded in the background almost immediately, and I smiled at her obedience. She was learning.

"All right, I'm in my room," she said.

"Put the phone on speaker and set it on your nightstand."

Her voice became slightly distant. "Okay."

"Take off your clothes and tell me what you're doing as you do it," I commanded.

Her sharp intake of air had my cock aching. I gripped the bulge through my shorts, impatiently waiting for her to begin.

"Fine, fuck it," she said, and I groaned at the filthy word coming out of her mouth. Raven was all professional and hearing her be unprofessional was turning me on so much I squeezed my eyes shut.

"I took off my shirt. Now, I'm undoing my slacks."

"Fuck. You're in business clothes?" I asked, picturing her in the same black dress pants she had been wearing when I saw her in the park last week.

"I am," she answered with a hint of sarcasm.

"I love women in business outfits. You're going to have to send me a photo of them sometime, but right now I need you to keep going, baby." I was careful not to give away that I'd already seen her in some of those outfits.

She hesitated. "I, uh, I'm just in my underwear now."

My cock jumped. This soft side of her was intoxicating.

When we texted she was always challenging, but on the phone she was almost shy. "Tell me what they look like."

"Uh, black lace."

Goddammit, I was going to lose it before she was even naked. No question she would be in black, but lace too? Fuck me. "Take. Them. Off," I gritted into the phone. This woman was driving me insane. I could see nothing but her in barely there lingerie and if I didn't get myself under control I was going to embarrass myself.

"Ok, they're off," she murmured.

"Say it." Silence filled the line again. "Say what you are now that your clothes are gone."

Her whisper was almost inaudible. "I...I'm naked."

I closed my eyes and pulled air in through my nose as slowly as I could manage. I had to regain my composure before I could go any farther. After a few moments, Raven's voice floated into my ear.

"Zander?"

I pinched the bridge of my nose and leaned forward, resting my elbows on my knees. "Give me a second, baby."

"Oh," she breathed. "Are you..."

I blew out a breath. "Yes, babe, I'm having to concentrate on other things right now."

"Right, um..." Her voice trailed off. "Should we talk about the weather?"

"No, I'm fine." I laughed. "Get in bed."

The sheets rustled, and her voice trickled over my skin. "And now?" she asked.

"Oh, eager now, are we? Caress your nipples how you would like me to if I was there."

She gasped. "How do you know I want to imagine it's you?" Her voice turned mocking. There she was, her wicked grin coming through her voice from the other end of the line. Oh, she liked to play. I wondered if she would like the games I wanted to play with her.

"If you didn't, you wouldn't be talking to me right now, baby girl. I promise you that I can outlast you if you want to play, but I think you would rather come instead."

A sharp intake of breath was her only response so I pressed on. "Are you doing it?"

"Mm," she sighed.

"Good, now pinch those perfect nipples," I ordered.

A cry crashed through the phone and I smiled. My girl was great at following directions when she was threatened a little. "Good girl. Keep rubbing your nipple with one hand while you move the other between your legs."

I slipped out of my shorts and boxers, my cock springing free. Gripping the length, I repositioned the phone in my left hand. "Are you wet for me, baby?"

"Y-yes." Her breathy voice made my dick grow even harder. It made sense that Raven would be submissive leaning in the bedroom. Women who were strong leaders in most facets of life were natural subs in private to the partners they trusted. They needed the reprieve from having to make decisions all the time, and I loved that she was obeying so sweetly for me.

"Fuck, baby. Spread your legs wide and tease yourself. Don't touch your clit yet."

Raven whimpered in response, and fuck, I would be dreaming of the sounds she made until the end of time. "Is it good, baby? Say it."

"Yes," she said, louder than the softer voice she had been using. "It's so good."

I started to work my hand up and down my painfully hard cock, trying to stifle my moan so I could hear every noise leaving those perfect lips.

"Dip one finger inside that pretty pussy for me, baby, but imagine it's me filling you up."

"Zander...fuck," she sighed.

My head fell back on the couch at her sounds, and somehow I got even harder. If this was euphoria, I didn't think I'd survive when I finally got my hands on her. "Do you have a toy, baby?" I groaned.

"Y-yes. I have a vibrator."

"Get it."

"It's okay, I don't want to stop."

Annoyance flared in my chest. "Goddammit, get it now."

A small whimper came from her end of the line followed by rustling as she jostled around to do as I said. After a few moments, her breathless tone washed over me.

"I have it."

"I'm tired of playing with you. Turn it on or not, but I want you to ram it hard and deep in that soaked pussy just like I would do with my cock if I were there right now."

Silence stretched across the line. "Do it. Now," I growled. In seconds her moans filled the line again and I ground my teeth together, pumping my cock faster. Our breaths and pants filled the call as we worked ourselves in tandem, a sinful melody of desire.

"Do you want to come, baby?" I asked, my breathing labored. "Tell me how bad you need it."

"I need to come so badly, Zander, please," she begged.

"Goddamn baby. Hearing you ask so nicely is so fucking good. Do it. Rub your aching clit and come for me."

Raven released a loud moan, and within seconds she lost it. This woman did not hold back. She was the loudest I'd ever heard, and we weren't even in the same room. "Fuuuck," I groaned as my release hit me with the force of a hurricane.

Cum coated my hand and thighs while she was still riding her orgasm on the other end of the line.

"Ryan!" she yelled, louder still.

My heart stopped, and I suddenly wished I could melt through the couch and into the floor.

After a few moments she whispered, "Oh, my god." Her voice grew louder and rushed. "Um, yeah, right, thank you. I'll just be going now. Bye." The line went dead.

"Oh, fuck."

SHE KNEW. Fuck, she knew. I watched the coffee drip into my cup from the single serve machine the next morning. I figured she knew, but it was confirmed after she said my real name in the middle of her orgasm. When she hung up the phone immediately, I sat dumbfounded on the couch for longer than I'd like to admit. Just sat there in my mess, staring at the wall and wondering what the hell to do next.

Once I looked down and saw myself still coated in jizz, I snapped out of it and showered. If I hadn't finished work already there would have been no hope of finishing it last night. Unfortunately for me, that also meant I didn't have anything to distract my rampant thoughts since Craig hadn't sent the next job over yet. It had been relatively early and being the night owl I was, sleep was nowhere in sight.

I didn't text her. I thought it would be better to distance myself. Plus, I didn't know what to say anyway. I tried to play video games sans streaming but couldn't stay alive for shit. I even downloaded a new e-book on my phone after finishing the other with no luck. It was probably for the best, since any romance was going to make me think about Raven.

Finally, at two a.m. I went to bed and stared at the ceiling.

Practicing meditation like my therapist had taught me, I actually fell asleep quicker than I thought I would.

And then, awake once again, I had nothing to do except think about the issue at hand.

Everything brought my confidence issues from my fucked-up childhood back to the surface. With people or things I didn't care about, I didn't have any problems. With Raven, I did care for some reason, and Zander was a way for me to be confident with her.

She was perfect. I knew so little about her in the grand scheme of things, but I knew she was perfect. Strong, and the most gorgeous woman I'd ever seen, but the most compelling thing about her was there would be no bullshit with her. Raven was the kind of woman who took exactly what she wanted out of life, and even if she didn't want me, I wanted her.

With renewed determination, I pushed my anxiety down into the pits of hell as I sat at my desk. Twelve hours had been enough to stew in my worry. Raven had already made the connection and continued to text me. If she wanted to end whatever this was, I'd just have to win her over. That thought twisted a knife of dread in my gut.

Picking up my phone, I scrolled through my text message conversations and tapped on 'Dad'. Seeing his name on my screen sent a wave of unease through me. At least I wouldn't have to talk to him again. Next time I needed something I would figure it out on my own.

Tapping on the contact he sent me, I hit the call button. The line rang three times before an older gruff voice answered. "Rick."

I fidgeted with the cord that led to my wireless phone charger. "Hey, Rick. This is Ryan, Steve Mitchell's son. He gave me your number."

"I'm assuming you need something since that's the only

reason I ever hear from Steve. What is it?" His voice oozed annoyance, which wasn't surprising if he thought I was anything like my dad.

"Right, I need a profile on someone. My girlfriend, actually. I think someone might be following her. I want to know if there's a reason why they might be." The lying part of my brain was working full speed. "We just started dating so we are still getting to know each other, but I need to know if she's in danger."

"All right. Is Daddy paying?" he asked.

"No, I'll be paying." That was more satisfying to say than I thought it would be.

"You do know how much I cost, right, kid?" he said coolly. "I'm not cheap since I'm the best PI in the country. I only do work for those that can pay a fair price for the quality of my services."

"Money isn't an issue. Are you available for the job or not?" I retorted.

He chuckled. "Yeah, kid. If you have the money, I'm available. I take half up front and the rest when the job is done. What's her name, address, and business address if you have it?"

I rattled off the info to him and stopped short when I realized I'd forgotten to enter Raven's office address into the spreadsheet, and I couldn't remember the exact building number. "Hang on, let me get it."

I pulled up Google on my computer and typed 'Lovelace Financial' into the search bar. I hit enter and glanced to the right side of the page where the business information was listed. I read the suite number and gave Rick the other information he needed.

"How long do these typically take?" I asked.

"Depends on the other jobs I have going. I have quite a few

right now and some that are high profile. It might take thirty days, but could be sooner. I'll send it over when I can. Have a good one, kid."

The line went dead before I could say anything. I tapped my fingers on the desk, annoyance flaring. It made sense he was an asshole. A nice person wouldn't be able to put up with Dad's shit.

Moving to close out of the webpage, my eyes snagged on the search result below the link to Raven's business website. Reminded of the idea I had thought of before, I decided to set the plan in motion. Especially since she knew who I was. My cock stiffened at the thoughts playing through my mind. I had a hunch my idea would be the perfect scenario to trap my little sable fox.

But the first thing I needed to do was to talk to her. The scenarios in my mind were going to full send, so I needed to check in to see how she was feeling. She suspected Zander and I were one and the same, so let's fucking talk about it. I would wait until the afternoon, though. She was probably busy at work, and I didn't want to take her away from that. In the meantime, I would plot schemes.

At five p.m., once I returned home, I sent a text from the burner number. "Let's talk. Phone call tonight?"

I set the phone on the couch beside me after I made sure the ringer volume was as loud as it would go. *The Dark Knight* played on the TV, and I watched it without paying attention, my mind racing faster than a Formula One car. After an eternity, the phone beeped. I took a deep breath and snatched it off the cushion.

"All right. What time?" was all the text said.

I didn't know how to take that, but I typed a reply. "Whatever works best for you." I refrained from calling her 'baby' even though it was almost a habit at that point.

"I have to work late tonight, so maybe seven? I can talk before I leave the office."

Good. I hoped that also meant she was in the middle of something complicated and had to work late tomorrow, too, even though it was Friday.

"That works." I wanted to add so much more, but I had to be patient.

The only response I got was a like to my last message. Now I just had to keep myself busy for two hours since I already got all the errands I needed to run out of the way this afternoon.

I stared at the TV a while longer before going to the kitchen to make some kind of dinner. Taking time with the preparations, I paid special attention to the knife cuts on the chicken. When I was twelve I'd grown tired of my sitter always ordering take out with the money my parents left her so one day I asked if we could make something ourselves. All the kids at school talked about how their parents or grandparents made meals at home and I wondered what that would be like.

My sitter was a woman in her late fifties who only watched kids in her spare time. She became acquainted with my parents through her rich husband. They hired her when I was a baby, and she was essentially the only mother I had when I was a kid until she passed away when I was fifteen. Cooking wasn't her favorite thing to do, but three years was enough for her to teach me everything she knew. I taught myself the rest.

A pang of grief shot through my chest. I hadn't thought of Sylvia for a long time, but I still missed her. She was the only person aside from my uncle who had anything somewhat nice to say to me. The chicken sizzled when I dropped it into a skillet to sear then grabbed a pot to boil the pasta in. Once the chicken was done, I added the ingredients for a cream sauce to the pan to deglaze. When I sat down to eat at the table, it was six-fifteen.

After I ate I cleaned the kitchen and settled back on the couch since it was the most comfortable place I had in the house besides my bed. It would be a terrible idea to talk to Raven in bed so the couch was the next best option.

The minutes ticked by until the clock on my phone read three minutes past seven. I didn't want to seem overly eager so I didn't call at seven on the nose. Taking a deep breath and pushing my nerves down, I channeled Zander. I picked up my phone and called her from my actual number, the same one she called when she needed to talk to the real me.

Ryan Mitchell.

CHAPTER FIFTEEN

RAVEN

I STARED at the cell phone ringing on my desk; Ryan Mitchell's name was displayed across the screen. This was about to become much more real. Ryan was Zander. I always knew he was, but now it could get complicated.

Last night when I ended the call immediately after my fuck up, I went straight to bed. No work was done, and my day had been all the worse for it. I'd acted like an immature idiot, and the longer I was awake dwelling on it the more embarrassed I would be. At the time, a busier day seemed less painful.

Despite the horrifying ending, the phone sex was hotter than any real sex I'd ever had. I slept like the dead and woke up ready to go at five a.m. When I rolled over and checked my phone, I was worried when I saw I hadn't gotten a text or anything from Zander. As the day dragged on, my nerves were out in full force, and the phone call was the culmination. I could only hope I didn't get fired, or worse, slapped with a disciplinary action if the CFP board found out I'd had a less than professional encounter with a client.

I didn't know what I was going to say or which direction

this was going to go, but sighing, I picked up the phone and swiped the green icon to accept the call.

"Raven Lovelace." I guessed it didn't hurt to be formal. He was technically my client after all.

"Hi, Raven. How was your day?"

His voice swept over me, and the tension instantly left my body. He made me feel so safe and relaxed. Wait, did he just ask me how my day was?

"Um, hi, Mr. Mitchell. It was productive. Yours?" God, I was back to not knowing how to speak like an adult.

"Same," he mused. "All right, now that the awkwardness is out of the way, let's address the elephant in the room."

I laughed nervously at his frankness. "Yeah, I'm a cut to the chase kind of woman."

He chuckled back. "Really? I pegged you as someone who would beat around the bush and take an extremely long time to make a point."

I scoffed at his words. So he was funny, too. Dammit.

"Okay, Mr. Sarcasm. Go ahead with what you wanted to say."

He drew in an audible breath. "Well, it's clear that you connected the dots and figured out who I am."

"Yes. It didn't take me long. You just so happened to call the one financial firm whose owner listens to romance audiobooks. I would know your voice anywhere." Shit, I didn't mean to say that.

A sharp intake of breath came through the speaker. "I'm flattered you knew of my work. I'd be interested to know which book is your favorite." The charm mixed with his seductive tone had to be every woman's dream.

"I didn't used to listen to the other stuff though," I blurted for some godforsaken reason. My cheeks turned red, and I almost groaned.

He laughed. God, his laugh was even sexy. "Maybe not before, but you do now."

"That's neither here nor there." Fuck, this was going sideways. I closed my eyes and followed my gut. "Look, Mr. Mitchell. I'm not sure how or why you figured out my account name, and I admit I crossed a line, but I would very much like to keep your business, which I'm assuming is the reason for your call."

He was quiet after my rush of words. When he finally spoke, goosebumps festered on my skin. "I thought I was the one who was supposed to be talking?" he asked, then continued. "Actually, Raven, I wasn't calling to discuss my accounts at all. I was calling to clear some things up before we move forward."

My jaw slackened. He...what? "I'm not sure I understand, Mr. Mitchell."

"Please don't call me by my last name, Raven. I think we're past that," he said through gritted teeth.

My annoyance flared. "Well, what should I call you then? Ryan? Or do you prefer Zander?"

"Depends on the situation, but for the most part, call me Ryan." Little did he know, I'd probably call him anything he wanted if he asked.

"Fine then, *Ryan*. What can I help you with?" I didn't have time for this, whatever this was.

His voice dropped lower and exuded authority. "You can help me by losing the attitude, first of all."

Despite my irritation, there went the lady bits.

"Take a deep breath, and let your frustration go," he soothed at my silence.

Fuck, this man knew exactly what he was doing, and frankly, I was tired of resisting. I breathed in and out like he said, making the breaths audible so he heard.

"Better now?"

I rolled my eyes. I couldn't help it. "Yes. Now, what can I do for you?"

I could hear his smile through the phone. "I have a proposition for you."

My interest flared, and so did my arousal. "Oh?" I asked.

"I want to continue this, but the reason for my call is to make sure you're on board and to discuss boundaries. I might not be the best person, but I would never force anything on you," he admitted.

Confusion swirled in my mind. On board with what? "What is *this*, exactly?"

"It's whatever you want it to be, Raven. This is going to sound weird, but don't think about it too much. I want to play with you, but I need your consent first."

"Play with me?" I turned my desk chair and stared out the large office windows to the city beyond and realization finally dawned. "Oh...you mean—" I couldn't finish the sentence. It was suddenly hard to breathe. "I don't even know what you look like," I whispered.

"That's the allure isn't it? You hear my voice and imagine whatever you want. You'll see me soon enough, but it's not about any of that. This goes beyond talking to you. Our virtual situation has been fun, but I want to give you pleasure in ways I think you'll enjoy. In person, Raven."

Jesus fucking christ. What was this man doing to me? He had no idea what he was getting himself into. I closed my eyes as a thrill skittered through my body. "Good luck getting around my security cameras." I smirked. "What exactly am I giving you permission to do?"

He chuckled again. "That's the surprise, babe. You won't know how or when, but I could appear at any moment to fuck that sweet pussy of yours. With my fingers, my tongue, or my cock. Maybe all three."

Heat surged between my legs, my body lighting on fire at his frankness. Never had another person caused this reaction from me, but hearing his delicious voice say these things was a drug I was addicted to. Grasping for any semblance of reason, I sputtered, "But you're my client. It's unethical."

"Then you're fired," he said abruptly.

My jaw hit the floor. "What?" I exclaimed. "I thought you just said you weren't going to move your accounts?"

"I said I wasn't calling to talk about my accounts, but if that's your hang up, I'll move them elsewhere."

Groaning, I let my head fall back against the desk chair. He was ruthless and was besting me. But I didn't care. I caved, unable to resist him. "Fine. The accounts can stay, but I need some kind of certainty you are agreeable to keep your money here despite whatever this is or becomes. I'll draft a conflict waiver and put my junior advisor on your file." I paused. "And I need proof that you're safe. I can provide the same, and no worries about pregnancy."

"I figured you might say that. Give me your personal email."

I rattled it off for him and within seconds I had a document with the proof I requested, and I advised I would send mine when I got home.

"No need. I trust you, Raven. Now, as for the other part, I can sign a document if you like. I don't really care what you need me to do, just tell me."

I sighed. "I believe you, I just want to cover all of my bases." I tapped my fingers on my desk. "I just don't understand why you're doing this."

He took a breath. "Sometimes, we don't always understand why we want the things we want."

He hit the nail right on its head, that was for fucking sure. "I see your point."

"Good. I'll whisper all the reasons I'm crazy about you in time. Now, tell me, what are your hard limits?"

The words were out of my mouth before I could stop them. "I don't have any," I said. "Within reason, of course," I rushed to add.

I heard the air hiss from his lungs. "Even more extreme types of play like primal and BDSM?"

My brain glitched on the last one, and all sorts of thoughts formed in my mind. I dared to hope, but he likely preferred the stereotypical gender roles.

"Raven?" His voice pulled me out of my daze.

"Yes. Anything that doesn't involve bodily fluids aside from the usual."

"Fuck, babe. You're gonna be the end of me. It's supposed to be the other way around, you know."

"Yeah, well, I don't play by the rules society tells me to," I stated.

"Damn, maybe we can just skip all of this and get married." he mentioned.

"Oh, not a chance, buddy. You promised pleasure, so now you have a job to do."

His laugh was even sexy. How was that possible? "Don't worry, babe. I always deliver a great performance," he said and then the line beeped, signaling the end of the call.

What the fuck had I just agreed to?

I PULLED into the parking garage at five the next morning, much earlier than normal. Parking in my usual spot, I looked around the car in every direction, scanning the stairwells and darkened corners for anything amiss. Satisfied all was well, I gripped my knife still hidden in my purse and walked to the door to my building. I didn't have the creeps so maybe if Ryan was stalking me, he decided to leave me alone after our conversation the night before.

The morning went by smoothly, and I had more than made up for being behind the day prior. I did enough for three people that morning alone, and Mia noticed.

"You're getting so much done today," she commented as she was pulling her lunch from the fridge. "Even for you, who always does so much already. Did you have three pots of coffee this morning or something?" she asked.

I poured a healthy dose of ranch over the salad I made with leftover veggies from the previous night's dinner. "Nope. Just on it today, I guess." I turned to face her. "How are things going with you?"

"They are…going." She sat down at the small table in the corner of the kitchenette. "Kyle had to leave for work again so it's just me and the puppy. He's gone most of the time even when he's in town so it's not like it's much different than normal." She gathered her sandwich, but before taking a bite she added, "How are the resumes coming?"

I leaned my hip against the counter. "They're going well. I think I'll leave the posting up, but Joanne and I are going through the ones we've received so far this afternoon. I've only glanced at a few, but they seem promising. I'm excited to get Joanne back here with us to manage things. It'll be a huge help to you and I."

Mia nodded. "I'm excited too. It'll be so nice to have another hand around, and it'll be great for the company." She looked down at her plate, and I noticed a hint of a blush creep into her cheeks. "I really love it here, Raven. You're a great boss."

I grabbed my lunch and waved her off. "You flatter me, Mia. I know I'm a lot to work with sometimes, but I'm grateful you're always ready to go like I am. Let's keep up the good work!"

Back in my office, I set my lunch on the open side of my L-desk. Snatching my phone from its stand, I was greeted with no texts as I sat down. Ryan wasn't joking about surprising me. I was antsy, wondering what he had in store when a thought crossed my mind. Ryan said he could appear anytime. I'd been right. He was the one who had been in the garage that night.

That explained my unease in that regard, but this wasn't the type of edge I was used to being on. Always motivated to work was one thing, but always distracted by thoughts of a man was unusual. I had no idea how this was going to go, which was frustrating because I was always ready with a plan for everything.

Parents live in poverty? Oh, hang tight, let me just go get a nice degree, work my ass off, open my own business, and make enough money for all of us.

Become entranced by a guy I knew nothing about, more so than any I'd ever known in the past? I had nothing.

I picked up my phone again and opened the text conversation, the contact still labeled "Zander." Looking back at the two photos he had sent, a rush surged through my body. Though they were the definition of my type, I never dated guys that looked like that. Ones that dressed sort of like me, with the chunky jewelry and all-black clothes. The guys in my past were polished and proper. Suits everyday, dinner out every night at a fancy restaurant. They were all mostly vanilla, too. That wasn't a bad thing, but I wasn't vanilla so the compatibility was always off with them in the bedroom. It was usually the reason things didn't work out after a few times of being with them. Not to mention I didn't fit their picture of wife material. Spencer was the only guy to entertain my desires for more than five minutes. Although, with Zander, well Ryan, I was learning I might like other things. I really needed to stop separating the two. They were the same person.

I closed out of the thread before I started drooling on my desk, still unable to comprehend why he affected me so much. Men hadn't been on my radar since Spencer. I took care of my needs myself when they arose and then moved on without a thought. The desire for a man was nonexistent unless he was a fictional character in a book. Maybe that was it. Maybe I was obsessed with Zander because I had been obsessed with him before Ryan ever called my office.

After I listened to his first audiobook, I was in a chokehold. A woman possessed, I sped through every book he narrated as soon as they were released. It never occurred to me to check his social media to find the other content, but I was glad I found it the way I had.

Shaking my head, I finished my lunch and instead of going back to work, I found myself walking to the elevators instead. I needed a distraction from Ryan. Maybe I would see the hot guy from last week in the park again. I felt a bit guilty because he looked like he was probably just out of college, but oh well. It was common for women in their thirties and forties to be attracted to younger men, and I supposed I was starting to fall into that category. It didn't hurt to look. Anything to get my mind off Zander.

"Hey, Joanne," I said as I walked into our small conference room a few hours later. It served the purpose despite its size. My gaze roamed over the neat piles of paper spread out on the table. "Can you be any more prepared and organized? I think you're slacking a bit."

Joanne chuckled. "I think we have some good prospects here. I also made a spreadsheet with all the candidates as well.

Once we have it narrowed down to the people we want to interview, I'll schedule them for you."

I sat down at the head of the rectangular metal table and pulled a stack of paper in front of me. "Maybe I should just let you do all the interviews. Since you're probably a better judge than I am. Not to mention I hate the thought of sitting through hours of these."

Joanne scoffed. "With all due respect, I don't want to sit through them, either. You're the boss; you get to suffer."

Smiling, I huffed. "I might own the company, but we all know who's boss around here, ma'am. That's why you run the office and I'm hiring someone else to relieve you of the recep-tionist work."

She beamed at me. "That right there is why I came with you. You're a badass, but you motivate those around you to work just as hard as you do. That's a great leader. Trust me, I should know after my many years in the soul-sucking machine that was our old office."

Redness crept up my neck at the compliment. "Well, since I have your approval, I agree I'm doing pretty well." I grinned. "Let's get these out of the way so we can get back to our usual stuff, shall we?"

After two hours, Joanne and I had combed through a hundred resumes and chosen fifteen candidates to interview. The process was arduous, but after sifting through the prospects, I was hopeful we would find a great fit. Skill and experience only went so far. The person we hired also had to fit with our culture and environment. I went through the same process when I hired Mia, and it turned out great.

I pushed back from the table. "Perfect. See if you can get them all in for next week. I'm going to leave the posting up just in case we want to pass on all of these. Hopefully, we have our person in here."

"Absolutely," Joanne said as she gathered the stacks of paper. "Thanks, Raven."

I reached for a stack and Joanne shooed me away. "You get back to work. I'm good here." She winked.

With a nod I left the conference room and trudged back to my office. I had at least four more hours of work until I could head home even though the morning was productive. The meeting with Joanne had taken longer than expected.

I went to the coffee machine in the kitchenette and waited while the brewer filled my mug with magic liquid. I watched the drip mindlessly while my thoughts traveled to Ryan again. A route my mind went down often. Heat pricked my skin as I recalled his words. Almost twenty-four hours later, and I was still giddy. It made me anxious as hell, too, but the butterflies in my stomach were ones I hadn't felt maybe ever.

In my office, I pulled up the accounts I needed to work on, and before I knew it, the light filtering through the windows was dimming. I lost myself to time like usual after putting Ryan out of my mind. Rubbing my bleary eyes, I assumed Joanne and Mia must have left quietly for the weekend without a farewell. They knew once I was in the zone it was best to leave me be, handling all the distractions and closing the office with me being none the wiser. I smiled to myself at the staff I'd been so lucky to find.

I picked up my phone to see a few missed calls that looked like they were spam and a text dated three hours ago. It was from the number Zander texted me from, not Ryan's. A thrill shot through me as I read the words.

"Tonight, I'm Zander. Best be on alert at all times, baby."

My head jerked up and I looked around the office. Was he watching me? I pulled up the new security camera feeds and saw no movement since Mia and Joanne had left. I assumed he was the one spooking me in the garage, but it was still unsettling since I didn't know the guy at all. I only knew his name, profession, and that he had quite a bit of money. But he could still be a bad person.

Despite my concerns I was still on the fuck-it train. The excitement mixed with fear was intoxicating, and I couldn't turn it off. I dropped my phone on the desk and shut down my computer with anticipation, the uncertainty of what was to come fluttering in my chest. When I picked up my purse and started to drop my phone in, the power went out.

CHAPTER SIXTEEN

RYAN

I DROPPED my head in my hands after I tapped the red phone icon to end the call with Craig about the next project. Tonight, I was going to have fun with my girl in person. Finding time to record while playing with my new toy was going to be difficult when I got the script on Monday. The conversation with Raven had gone exactly how I had wanted, and arousal pulsed through my body when I thought about her being on board. This woman was going to be mine if it was the last thing I did. I had a visceral need to possess and claim her, something I'd never felt toward another human.

Running my hand through my wild hair, I recalled my devious plots to give this woman as many orgasms as possible. Some of which she might be begging not to have. Fuck, how I would love to see her beg on the floor with those pouty lips and her usually perfect hair mussed from my hands. With her consent, I was going to fuck her like I didn't have it, and I think she knew that. I wanted her hesitation almost as much as I wanted her pleasure. Raven was smart and cunning, but I was going to best her.

Sporting a semi the whole day, I couldn't contain my excitement and was a ball of anticipation since I had nothing else to focus my attention on. Spending all weekend tormenting the fuck out of my little fox before I got my next job was going to be heaven.

I shot off a text earlier in the afternoon, which Raven still hadn't read. I was banking on her working late as I grabbed my backpack and slinked out the door of my apartment.

Driving downtown in serene silence, a calm settled over me as I channeled the Zander side of myself and pushed reclusive Ryan into a hidden box. Zander was a confident dom who coaxed pleasure from his partners, and tonight I was going to show Raven I was worthy of her submission.

By the time I arrived the light had faded into dusk. I parked my car in the garage connected to Raven's building and donned my black face mask that covered everything except my eyes. Pulling up my hood, I tucked my hair in and pulled it low over my eyes. Raven wouldn't see anything except my outline, but she would hear. She would hear everything.

The fluorescent-lit cement structure attached to Raven's building was ominous. I rode the elevator from the fourth level to the second, the atmosphere adding to the thrill. When I'd scouted the garage while I was out the day before, I thanked my lucky stars there was a concealed door into the building aside from the main entry on the street. Stepping off the garage elevator, I peered around the level as I walked to the entrance and breathed a sigh of relief when the industrial door opened. My lock picking skills were fine for normal locks, but not ones of that caliber.

I contemplated taking the stairs up to Raven's office, but I needed all my stamina for her so I chanced the elevators. Hopefully no one would be around since it was so late. Inside the building, the doors slid open and I pressed the button for thirteen as a hint of unease ran through my gut. I hadn't done anything like this before. Only in the books I narrated, and I wouldn't have done it then without Raven's consent and limits. Since she listened to the same books I narrated, I was taking a small risk that she would like this.

My dick stiffened at the thought of what was going to happen, and I wondered what her reaction to the surprise would be. She would know it was me from the conversation yesterday, but a part of me still hoped she would be at least a bit frightened. Time would tell. I glanced at the blue digital counter as it ticked upward and the doors opened to show Raven's dark and empty office in front of me. Good, her staff was gone.

I hurried to the side where the glass facade became a solid wall, and scouted the office suite. Unsure, I assumed Raven was still in there. If not, I would just pay a visit to her house sooner than intended, which was fine by me. My eyes snagged on the security camera above the office doors. So she wasn't lying about that. I assumed she had them at her apartment too. An idea flitted through my head, but I tucked it away for later.

Walking down the hall in search of the utility room for the floor, I found it nestled just past the stairwell. I tried the handle, and wasn't surprised that it was locked unlike the building door. Reaching into my pocket, I pulled out the lock pick and made quick work of the mechanism. After all, I doubted many people cared about breaking into a utility closet so the security was minimal.

Inside the small room I spotted the electrical panel on the wall to my left and lifted the lid. "Fuck," I groaned. Of course, there was no label for the lights so I had to pull out my phone to search how to read a commercial breaker box. After I was satisfied that I had found the correct switch, I tapped out of the incognito tab and drew in a breath. Squinting my eyes shut in hopes that I didn't set off some kind of alarm or had the wrong switch, I flipped it. The floor went dark out in the hallway and an emergency light came on above my head.

Thank fuck. I left the breaker room and slipped inside Raven's unlocked office suite, making a note to tell her to keep it locked when she was in the office alone, especially after hours. Walking to the left of the reception desk in the middle of the room, I pressed against the wall beside the opening that led down a hallway. With my hood down as far as it would go, I listened for any movement or noise. When nothing came except silence, I peeked around the corner to find everything motionless. Maybe I had missed her.

Tiptoeing down the hall, I muffled the sound of my boots as best I could, in case she hadn't left. The first door on the right was a break room with a kitchen area and a table with a conference room directly across the hall on the left. There was a large area after the break room that had numerous empty desks. I kept moving and passed two more offices on the left and one closed door at the end of the hall on the right. All the other doors were open so my senses heightened. That had to be Raven's office. The offices across the hall didn't make sense as one was empty and the other had a desk adorned in pink decorations. Raven wouldn't have pink in her office.

Flattening myself against the wall, I listened with my ear to the door for at least ten minutes. After hearing nothing, I gently placed my gloved hand on the handle and attempted to turn it. Locked. Rolling my eyes, I pulled my pick out of my pocket and took off my right glove. After a few minutes, I had the door unlocked. My heart leapt in my chest as I turned the handle and the door swung open.

The office was empty. "Fuck," I mumbled under my breath as I stepped inside. I looked around the room for a moment and took in the sleek glass desk and black accents. I smiled to myself at my goth girl's furniture choices. When I went to leave, a voice slithered down my spine from behind me and my blood ran cold.

"Well, who do we have here?" Raven's icy voice asked.

CHAPTER SEVENTEEN

RAVEN

The intruder turned rigid at my words. With his back to me, his fists clenched, and I smiled at catching him at his own game. As soon as the power was cut, a hint of fear had sliced my chest, but it quickly turned to arousal. I'd been on edge since the call the night before. Creeping from my office like a mouse, I locked it on my way out to see how serious he was and hid behind the door in the empty office across the hall.

I listened as he snuck down the hallway, his body barely making a sound. Part of me was nervous that he might be a real trespasser instead of Ryan, but the uncertainty added to the pleasure. I was addicted to the wrongness of being turned on by these circumstances, and when I slipped from behind the door and came up behind him as he breached my office, desire pulsed at the sight of him in front of me.

In the low light streaming in from the large windows, his large form stepped inside my office. Dressed in black from head to toe, his hood was pulled up over his head so I couldn't see even his hair. He was at least six feet tall, but he didn't look overly bulky like the men in the books I listened to. He looked like a normal guy, but the hood and all black got me. Not to mention the uncertainty of the situation itself, and his presence in my office.

He looked around, uttering a curse under his breath at finding the room empty and then stiffened when I spoke. When he turned, the movement played in slow motion, and my breath caught. The open space of the hood was pitch black in the darkness, the light from the city streaming in from behind him. We stared at each other for a long moment, and he commanded the air flowing between us.

Doubt began to creep into my chest like I was in a horror movie as we stood in a standoff. Was this my equivalent of people yelling at the TV screen for the main character to not go in the room where the killer was?

This had to be Ryan. Without the call, maybe I would have acted differently and treated this as a real threat, but deep down I knew it wasn't.

My gaze dropped from the gaping black hole that was this person's face to the gloved fists at his sides. Liquid fire lit me from the inside out as I thought of those gloves running over my skin, caressing me in places that hadn't been touched by another person in years. My body pulsed with need for the stranger in front of me. Even though it was Ryan, he was still technically a stranger despite having already made me come multiple times.

The man moved toward me, and I backed up into the hallway. Each step he took, I mirrored, until I was pressed against the wall, my chest heaving. He stopped an inch in front of my face, and I still couldn't see into his hood. When he tilted his head to the side, I nearly lost my shit. It was both terrifying and hot as fuck at the same time.

When he brought his glove up next to my face, I squeezed my eyes shut on instinct, bracing for an impact. My body was simultaneously telling me to run and to stay to see what he had in store for me. A leather-clad fingertip trailed down my face from my temple to my exposed collarbone, leaving a path of goosebumps in its wake. I opened my eyes to see his head still slanted and looked down at his finger smoothing back and forth.

I glanced back up into the dark expanse as he brought his hand to cup my cheek and I reveled in the cold leather pressed against my skin, my eyes drooping closed again. Before I knew what was happening his body crashed against mine, his hips and chest pinning me to the wall while his hand had moved to wrap around my throat. My eyes flew open and my hands came up to grip his forearm as he squeezed hard enough that I was questioning my sanity, but not enough to cut off my air. I had never been touched this way before, but my body was telling me I'd apparently been missing out while also calling me a lunatic.

His warmth seeped into mine as he nudged my legs apart with his knee and pressed into my core. A whimper escaped my lips as he ran his free hand down my side, and my pussy ached at his touch, longing to be the center of attention.

Bringing his head close to mine, his hood encased the side of my face. Fabric touched my ear, causing me to jerk to the side. Was he wearing a mask of some sort, too?

"Are you scared, Raven?" His muffled whisper dripped down my spine to drench my thighs. A moan left my lungs involuntarily at finally hearing his voice in person.

He rested his free hand on my hip and loosened his grip around my neck. His head moved so the edge of his hood caressed my cheek almost lovingly. As quickly as he was on me he was gone, my body cold without his. I almost cried out at the loss of him.

He gestured to the door of my office, indicating me to enter.

I tried to slow my breathing and walked past him, my eyes never leaving that dark opening I longed to see into. Spinning, I walked backward until my ass hit the edge of my desk. Following my movements with his head, he closed the door behind him and I strained to see into his hood with the dim light from the city outside.

As he came toward me, he held up a hand and circled the air with his finger, motioning for me to sit in my chair behind the desk. Being a defiant woman who doesn't listen, I moved toward him instead.

He stopped at my movement, and I halted a few feet away, not wanting him to retreat. "I want to see you," I pleaded into the charged atmosphere.

He shook his head in response and moved closer, putting his hand out and running his gloved finger from the base of my throat down over my faintly exposed cleavage. Chills bloomed over my body as he leaned in again.

"You'll see me soon enough. Let's play with the mystery while we still can. Tonight, you only get Zander's voice," he breathed, his tone growing lower and demanding. "The chair, Raven."

My body moved on its own accord before my mind could tell it to do so. I backed around the desk and sat on the edge of the chair, swiveling to the right. He took one of the fabric-covered chairs opposite my desk and set it to the side with the back to the windows so he had an unobstructed view of my entire body, bathed in the faint city lights filtering in behind him.

He leaned back, slouching with his knees wide, and rested one arm on the chair while the other came to rest on his crotch. *Fuck.*

"Pull up your skirt," he ordered.

I stared in disbelief. "Here? In my office? Someone could see through the windows," I stuttered.

"You're far enough back that no one will see. If they see anything, it'll be me. Do it," he ground out.

"But—"

His voice came through gritted teeth. "Do. It. Raven."

My hands dropped to the hem at my knees at his punctuated command. A shyness crept over me as eyes I couldn't see watched me slide the tight black fabric to the tops of my thighs.

"Up over your ass."

Averting my gaze from the black hole, I lifted myself off the chair and moved the skirt up to my waist. My cheeks heated at my exposed nylon thong. I clenched my thighs together to hide myself, but also for the much-needed friction. His gaze turned me on, but the modest part of my brain was screaming at me to cover myself.

He did the head tilt again and heat rushed through me, the movement inciting a carnal need that I hadn't felt before.

"Spread your legs."

I throbbed at the direction. Staring straight into the hood, I complied, showing him my black underwear.

"Fuck," he groaned as he sat up on the edge of the chair and rested his forearms on his knees. "Do you like being told what to do, Raven?"

I didn't answer, just looked into the dark hood and wished I could see the man inside even though this was the hottest thing I'd ever experienced.

"You're so defiant. Fighting me the entire way," he crooned. "Lucky for you I like a challenge."

His tone grew harsher. "Answer me when I ask a question, or all this stops." He cocked his head as realization dawned, and he chuckled. "Ah. My girl doesn't like being told what to do. She likes being forced to do it."

He was in front of me before I could blink. How did he move so fast? My chin was yanked hard by his hand, the hood inches above me while another rush of need speared my body. I needed relief soon because this was fucking torture.

"You're going to do exactly what I say, when I say it. You won't like what happens if you don't." His voice was threaded with a smirk on his hidden face. Dropping my chin roughly, he moved back to his perch on the chair.

"Move those sexy panties to the side and touch yourself," he demanded. "You're going to make yourself come to the sound of my voice while I watch."

I moaned at the thought of getting myself off in front of him, this stranger I vaguely knew. This was so fucked up, but I didn't care. He was right. I did want him to make me do it. I wanted to give him the power, something I'd never wanted to do in my life until now.

My hand trailed slowly down my body.

CHAPTER EIGHTEEN

RYAN

Raven's hand moved down her body so seductively I thought I was going to fucking lose it right there in my pants. My cock was almost in pain at the sight of her sitting in that professional desk chair, legs splayed with her pussy only covered by a thin sliver of cloth. I'd never seen a woman so sexy in my life, her eyes hooded with need and her mouth slightly parted, inviting me to taste those full lips.

Adjusting myself in my jeans, I watched her eyes zero in on the movement. When she bit her lip, my pulse raced and if I thought I was doomed before there was no question about it now.

Her hand finally settled to cup her pussy, and I longed to be that hand. Moving up and down over her panties, I ground my teeth together as I tracked her fingers. She pulled her thong to the side and bared everything to me as I watched with rapt attention.

Even in the dim light, she was fucking flawless. Fully clothed, yet she was displaying the most intimate part of herself, and it was driving me wild. The gleam of the city behind me was just enough to show she was glistening with arousal. I momentarily forgot I was supposed to be talking her through it like I knew she wanted even though she hadn't said it.

"Soak your hand in your wetness," I directed.

Without hesitation, her fingers slid over her center before she dipped her middle into her pussy. Pumping a few times, she coated it with arousal. I gripped the arms of the chair to keep from launching myself at her and burying my face in her perfect cunt.

The quick breaths spilling from her lips filled the room, and I cleared my throat. "How wet are you for me, baby?" I asked as her closed eyes fluttered open. A whimper was the only response she gave.

"Use your words, Raven," I growled.

Chest surging, she panted, "I...I'm drenched." Her voice was barely a whisper, but her heavy breaths were powerful.

"Fuck, yes, you are. Good job, baby. Do you want to stroke that needy clit, now?"

Her head fell back against the chair, and a moan tore from her lips. "Y-yes. Please."

"Hearing you beg is going to be the fucking end of me. Do it, baby. Rub your clit for me."

She raised her head back up and stared straight into my soul as she moved her fingers to stroke small circles around her clit. Goddamn, what I wouldn't do to latch my teeth onto it and sink my fingers inside her. That perfect body would be mine eventually. For now, I had to draw this out, this one time with her before she knew what I looked like. Not knowing how she would react to my appearance was in the back of my mind, not to mention I was seven years younger. But no matter how much she gave me, I would always crave more.

She cried out into the empty office. "I'm...I'm close," she heaved. "Fuck, Ryan."

I was on her in an instant, grabbing her hand and pulling it away from her pussy as she protested the loss of stimulation. "No," she whined.

My hood came within centimeters from her face. "I told you I was Zander tonight, didn't I?"

She looked up at me wide eyed and nodded.

"Say it."

"Zander," she whispered.

"Fuck," I groaned, bringing the edges of the hood down around her face so she was in the darkness with me. Moving her hand back between her legs, I pulled back slightly to see her face. I wanted to watch her just as much as I wanted to hear her.

"Make yourself come for me," I said as I let go of her wrist.

"Fuck, Zander. Fuck, I'm going to...oh fuck, I'm coming."

As I watched her lose herself to pleasure, I desperately wanted my hands on her. The orgasm spurred a melody of moans and whimpers that took every ounce of restraint I had. As she quieted, I gripped her chair to try to steady my breathing, but her hard breaths snapped my control.

Bringing my gloved hand to her mouth, I tapped her lips with my fingers. When she opened on instinct I slid the leather in, my voice charged with supremacy. "Suck."

Moaning around the material, her tongue worked through the glove and fuck, this woman's mouth. I couldn't wait to shove my cock into it.

A pop met my ears as I pulled my fingers from her mouth and dropped my hand between her thighs. Raven watched with her beautiful emerald eyes as I pressed the leather into her, drenching it in her need before caressing her sensitive clit.

Eyes rolling back, she was lost to me, mine to command, but I only wanted her release all over my glove.

"One more, baby. Give me one more."

As she groaned at my words, I picked up the pace before sliding my first finger down to her entrance and pushed it in. She wailed at the intrusion, and her walls clenched around me. Bringing my thumb to her clit, I massaged while curling my finger deep inside her.

"Come on my hand, baby," I said.

In seconds she screamed and fell apart for me, her pussy fluttering as she came again. When I finally fucked her, I was in for it. She was a goddess, and I was going to give her endless orgasms.

Opening her eyes after she came back to herself, I left my hand where it was. Her gaze was questioning, but I didn't care. Savoring the feel of her for a few more moments, I reluctantly pulled my hand away and a hiss left her lips at the withdrawal. I drew my mask down, knowing she couldn't see inside the hood, and brought my fingers to my mouth.

She gasped as I licked and sucked every drop of her off them before pulling the mask down and moving my head close to hers. Positioning the hood around her face again, I took her breath into my lungs. Without warning, I crashed my mouth to hers, relishing her sweet lips and making sure she tasted herself on my tongue. Soft and hungry, she completely surrendered, trembling beneath my touch.

I devoured her thoroughly before I drew back and repositioned my mask over my mouth and nose just in case, pulling my hood low again. She stared at me open-mouthed, like she'd forgotten how to move.

"Until next time, gorgeous," I said, rounding the desk and walking to the door. The chair swiveled and she peered at me from behind her monitors, legs still wide open. Smiling under the mask, I slipped out the door, leaving her ruined behind me.

As soon as I got in my car I took my dick out and came in about thirty seconds into tissues I kept in the glove compartment. Double checking there were no other cars on this level, I had half a mind to drive around the garage until I found Raven's car. I would have waited until she came out and then bent her over the hood and fucked her raw like I wanted to in her office. It wouldn't matter if anyone saw us with her skirt hiked up around her waist and me drilling her from behind.

Fuck. I shook my head and tossed the tissues into a plastic shopping bag on the floor in front of the passenger seat. An idea clicked into my mind at the fantasy of finding Raven's car, and I smiled at the opportunity to fuck with her a bit more. Shifting into drive, I backed out of the spot, slowly circling downward until "Level 2" appeared. Spying the door to the building, I noted the cars near it.

I assumed Raven would park near the building entrance and would've laid every cent I had on her being the first to park in the garage each morning. Three cars were parked in the vicinity of the door, two black and one gray. A better stalker would have known what type of car she drove.

As I pulled into a space a few spots down, I was thankful for my tinted windows. With all the spaces on the opposite side empty, I knew I would look suspicious if I backed into one facing the door. Twenty minutes passed on the dashboard clock, and I was wary Raven had left while I was up two levels beating off.

The door opened as I was about to back out, and Raven walked into view looking completely put together. It was like I hadn't made a mess out of her forty-five minutes ago. Even in the terrible garage lighting, she was beautiful. The pencil skirt she wore hugged her delicious curves, and I berated myself for not making her bend over her desk earlier. The urge to see her ass walking in those heels and nothing else had me ready to go again.

She was relaxed, unlike she had been the day I'd followed her from her apartment. That thought lingered in the back of my mind, and I hoped I heard from Rick soon. Something had set my girl on edge, and I was going to find out what it was. I doubted Raven needed to be protected, but maybe she could use someone to help sharpen her claws.

The black Lexus sedan backed out of her spot and turned the corner. I knew the way to her apartment so I let her get a good start. Exiting the garage and turning onto the downtown street, I looked for the silver emblem on the back of her car.

Weaving through traffic until I spotted her, I eased my car into the lane behind her. When she noticed she was being followed, her driving morphed into caution. I tailgated her onto the quiet street she took to throw me off. Detour after detour, she eventually headed the opposite direction of her apartment.

After following her deep into the urban outskirts for thirty minutes, I laughed when she took us into the area of town I lived in. We crept down a dozen side streets before getting back onto the main road again, Raven trying to lose me without luck. Finally, when we were one neighborhood over from mine, she went left and I went right toward my apartment. Deep down, I knew she had discerned I was the one following her, but maybe she still had a hint of fear that a guy —even one who had made her come without knowing what he looked like—was following her. Hopefully, I was getting under her skin, and I smiled at the notion.

"HEY MAN, WHAT'S UP?" I asked when the voice answered the phone on the fifth ring the next afternoon.

"Ryan? What the hell, dude?" Aaron's tone was definitely an annoyed one. "I haven't heard from you in how many fucking years? Nice of you to finally call."

I winced. "Sorry, man. Life, ya know. What's new with you?"

"Not much. Got married, bought a house, got a job, not in that order. The usual. What have you been up to since college?"

I ran my hand through my hair as I paced the apartment. "Nothing eventful," I lied. I had no interest in jumping into the shit that went down after college—rebuilding myself from the drinking only to be torn back down by my asshole father. I definitely didn't want to divulge what I did for a living. Not that I was ashamed of it, I just knew Aaron wouldn't understand.

Aaron and I weren't necessarily friends. We were college roommates before my grades dropped, and I left. The school we had attended was elite, one that had requirements to remain a student. I didn't meet the requirements and only went there because my parents forced me while also paying for it. Aaron also had rich parents, but he didn't lean on them as much as I had. He made a lot of money on the side.

"Figures," he mumbled into the phone. He wasn't always tactful with what came out of his mouth, not that it mattered. We weren't exactly on each other's Christmas card lists.

"Aaron, I need a favor," I said.

Aaron chuckled. "There it is. I knew you didn't just call me to shoot the shit. There's always an ulterior motive with you, Ryan. Some things never change, do they?"

I sighed. "Yeah, I know I asked a lot of favors in college. You covered for me more times than I can count, and I'm grateful for that." I sat down on the couch, ready to plead if I needed to.

"You're the best tech guy around," I continued. "Do you still do your side business?"

"I don't know what you're talking about," he feigned ignorance.

"Come on, Aaron. You made way too much money to have stopped. I can pay you." I gripped the phone tightly.

He sighed. "Fine, I still do odd jobs here and there, but I'm even better now. And more expensive. What do you need?"

Hesitation tugged at me. I knew Aaron, but I didn't know him like I used to. It had been years, and people can change a lot in that amount of time. Even so, he was my only solution to get what I wanted. I had to trust that he was honorable and would do the job, then delete the information. "I need access to security cameras."

"Please tell me they aren't government ones. If so, it's a no go. I learned my lesson with that shit. I'm not going anywhere fucking near a government security system," he conveyed.

I smiled, wondering what the hell he'd gotten himself into. Maybe I would hit him up more often. I'm sure he had some epic stories. "No, they are private cameras," I responded. "One set is at a business and I think one at a residence. They're probably the same brand."

"You think?" he asked. "I'm going to need to know the cameras exist before I can do anything. What city are they in? You better not say they're in a different country, or I'm also out."

I rushed to give him the information while I started pacing again. Shuffling sounded in the background. "Hang on, let me find a fucking pen. My coworkers are vultures."

I waited for a few minutes before he came back on the line. "All right, do you know the brand of the cameras?"

Shit. "Uh, no. I didn't think to take it down. I was pressed for time." Fuck, why hadn't I thought of that? Probably because

I was too focused on the pussy behind the door when I went to Raven's office.

"Well, I need the brand, or else this is impossible since I'm not local," Aaron huffed.

"I can get the brand, no problem. It will just be a few days."

"Ok, what's the name of the company?" he asked.

I cleared my throat. No going back now. "Lovelace Financial," I said and then rattled off Raven's address.

"I'm assuming the business has a website?"

"Yeah," I responded.

"Get me the brand of the cameras. For your sake you need to hope they're cheap and have a back door I can get into. You also need to pray that one of the employees is stupid enough to click a phishing link. If not, well, I'm going to need you to do a lot more work which also means more work for me."

"Let's hope this works, then. Talk to you soon," I said, but the phone beeped before I could finish the sentence. This was precisely why I had no use for Aaron until now.

I laid the phone on my desk and prepared myself for the busy week ahead, the image of onyx hair and emerald eyes never too far away.

CHAPTER NINETEEN

RAVEN

Pissed didn't come close to what I was the morning after Ryan followed me. I knew it was him, but still a small part of me wondered if it was the man who I'd almost let ruin my life. The only thing tamping my anger was the fact he had given me some of the best orgasms I'd ever had. The anonymity of his attire and that I still hadn't met him face to face likely contributed to the intensity of the encounter. Still, following me afterward was annoying.

I grabbed my earbuds off the island after dressing in my most revealing athletic clothes, a low-cut sports bra, and skin-tight bike shorts, in black of course. When I reached for the apartment door, my smartwatch vibrated with an incoming call.

"Fuck." I said into my empty apartment before pulling my phone from the pocket in my shorts and answering. "Hey Mom, what's up?

Shame speared me for being annoyed with the call as soon as I heard Mom's excited voice. "Hey, honey. I wanted to call to see if you wanted to come to an early dinner with me this evening, just us. There's a new locally owned cafe that opened up in town, and I wanted to try it."

I rubbed my hand over my face. "I can't today, Mom. Wait, why aren't you cooking? It's Sunday. You always make Dad meatloaf on Sunday."

Silence stretched over the line before she finally answered. "My legs aren't so great today. I don't think I can stand in the kitchen for too long," she admitted, but quickly changed the subject before I could inquire further. "But I'm fine! I just wanted to see you. I thought we could have a nice little outing and I could bring your dad something home. He's tinkering in the garage today, anyway."

Guilt settled in my chest. I wanted to see Mom, but I had work to do this afternoon, aside from my shit mood. I sighed and shifted to hold the phone with my shoulder. "I wish I could, but with the interviews I have this week, I have to try to work ahead today. My business hours are shot almost every day."

I hadn't told her I scheduled interviews, and her tone perked up when she spoke. "Did you get a lot of applicants?" she asked.

"Yeah, the job market must not be great right now. It's just a receptionist position, but I got a hundred resumes." I sat down on a stool at the island. "I'm thankful I have Joanne to help. There's no way I could have gotten through them all without her. We narrowed it down, and she scheduled interviews this week."

"That's great! I know how important it is to find a good fit. Keep me updated on how they go, okay?"

"All right, I will," I agreed. "I'm going for a run. I'll talk to you later."

"Raven?" Mom asked before I hung up.

"Yeah?"

She drew in a breath. "Is everything else okay? You seem frustrated."

Leave it to Mom to be hyper in tune with me, even through the phone. I sighed. "Yeah, I'm fine, just have some stuff going on."

Mom's voice turned questioning. "Stuff? You would tell me if there was trouble again, right?"

"No, it's nothing like that. I would tell you if it was." I actually wouldn't tell her if some real shit was happening so she wouldn't worry.

I still hadn't mentioned the odd feelings I was getting, or the encounters in the garage. I'm glad I hadn't, now that I was certain they were tied to Ryan. It made sense it was him, so I wasn't worried about it anymore.

"Okay," she said. "I'll let you go. I love you."

"Love you, too, Mom. Bye." I hung up the phone and took a long gulp of water. I stored my phone back in the pocket of my shorts and left the apartment. The elevator ride down to the first floor was slow. It seemed like the doors stopped on every level, which only added to my annoyance. Finally, I walked out into the midday air, thankful it wasn't too chilly, and jogged down the street.

I hoped he was watching. I hoped he saw me in my tight clothes and salivated at the sight. I knew he followed me. Of course, I couldn't be one hundred percent sure, but I was convinced. No matter how hard I had tried to lose him the other night, he was there for what seemed like hours. Finally, his lights had disappeared from behind me. I went home and immediately texted him when I got there that his little trick was funny. He didn't text back so I texted again yesterday morning and asked what game he was playing.

It was naive to text him, and I already knew exactly what he was doing. He bested me this time after my impulsive messages and I could hear the smirk in his voice when he ignored me. I was acting like a lovesick puppy, but after that performance how could I not? It was the best sex I'd ever had, and he only got me off with his voice and hand. Definitely the most erotic situation I'd ever been in.

I turned the corner and ran smack dab into a mountain of a man, his arms reaching out to steady me.

"Oh my god, I'm so sorry," I sputtered. "I wasn't paying attention to where I was going."

I glanced up at the man's face, and my breath caught. His blue eyes shone in the sunlight, and his dusty blonde hair was neatly styled. He looked to be in his fifties. Where had I seen this handsome stranger before? He was wearing a button-down shirt and slacks and was very put together for a Sunday, unless he was a churchgoer. Somehow, I knew that wasn't the case.

He dropped his hands to his sides and slid them into his pockets. "Oh, it's quite all right, ma'am." His gaze flicked down over my body, and I felt very exposed. "You should be more careful. You wouldn't want to hurt yourself."

My skin crawled at his words. They felt threatening, like he would delight in my pain. "Thanks." I dropped my gaze and skirted around his large body, noticing his expensive Gucci loafers. I stole a glance behind me as I picked up my pace. He wasn't hiding the fact that he was watching me, his whole body turned in my direction as he stood unmoving on the sidewalk.

I darted down the next street I came to, escaping the stranger's intense stare. My skin prickled at the thought of him. Shaking my head, I looped back around to my apartment a different way than I had come, not wanting to chance running into the guy again. Once I got home, I locked the knob and turned the deadbolt in place for my peace of mind.

After five hours in my home office, I rubbed my tired eyes and pushed back from my desk after powering down my desktop. Padding to the kitchen in search of something to eat before bed, I settled on baking a chicken breast and vegetables on a sheet pan. I wasn't hungry, but I had to eat something.

I wasn't the cook Mom was. She taught me the basics, but I couldn't do much else. Despite her being the best around, I had never learned her techniques and recipes. I wanted to, but I was too engulfed in doing well in school when I was a teenager. Then shit happened, and my focus shifted to my career after.

The timer on the oven sounded, and I pulled out the food, placing the hot pan on the stove top. I plated and dined quickly at the island. As I was cleaning up, I thought back to Ryan in my office. Heat crept up my body at the thought of his mouth on mine, and I hurried to finish loading the dishwasher. I walked into the primary bath and turned on the waterproof speaker sitting in the corner of the tiled shower. Opening the subscription app, I clicked on the first audio of Zander's that I came across. In the shower, I let the hot water run over my body like Ryan's voice ran through my soul.

"JOANNE, for fuck's sake, how many more?" I asked on Thursday morning after the last candidate I interviewed stepped out of the suite into the hallway.

She scanned her computer. "You have one early this afternoon, and then one at four forty-five. Two more tomorrow and that's it for this round."

I groaned, resting my palms on the side of the grand reception desk. "Wait, four forty-five? That's an odd time. What's up with that?"

Joanne shrugged. "I'm not sure. It's the only time the man had this week. You accepted the meeting. I was about to tell him he needed to make it work during usual hours before you okayed it."

I sighed. "I probably approved it without looking too closely at the time."

"I can reschedule or cancel, no problem. I'm wary of leaving you here with a man at the end of the day, anyway." Her mom mode was kicking in. "I'm going to stay until he leaves."

I shook my head. "No, you most certainly are not. I know you pick up your grandbaby on Thursdays from school. You, ma'am, are leaving per usual."

Joanne beamed at me. "You're right, but I really don't want to leave you alone with him. He could be a bad person. A rapist or a murderer. Can Mia stay?" she wondered, before wincing. "Scratch that, you would be the one protecting her instead of the other way around."

I snickered. "Your true crime podcasts are getting the best of you, Joanne. I'll be fine. I'll have my knife in its holster and my pepper spray in my pocket." I walked around the side of the desk pulling my pant leg up to reveal my ankle black leather boot with the knife resting above it. "You know I'm always prepared for the worst." I grinned with a wink.

"You're ridiculous." She turned back to her computer. Without another glance she added, "and I love it. But I still don't understand your need to carry that thing around all the time."

"Never know when you might be in a pickle." I shrugged.

I walked back to my office and plopped down heavily in the chair. This week was such a wash. My email was overflowing, and my task list was never ending. We needed another employee, but the time lost up front for interviews and training almost wasn't worth it. I could only hope we hired a quick study. I glanced at the clock, seeing there wasn't enough time to start anything before lunch so I went over all the candidates I had interviewed thus far.

The first was an older lady who was probably the sweetest person I had ever met that I had interviewed on Monday. Her hair was a cotton ball on her head and her clothes were right out of the seventies. I would've hired her on the spot, but there was the small dilemma that she didn't know how to use a computer, even though her resume said otherwise. Her last job had been working for an elderly lawyer who didn't believe in computers. How he was able to continue his practice was beyond me.

I met with a young woman on Tuesday who had a degree in accounting and was interested in learning financial planning. She had one of the strongest resumes we got, but when I interviewed her she didn't speak. Her answers were the shortest possible, and it seemed to go beyond nerves. Unfortunately, a receptionist position probably wasn't the best fit, but I spent the last half of the interview going over how to answer questions. I sent her on her way with the advice to keep trying and maybe apply for an assistant position instead, maybe one without a greeting aspect to the job.

The rest of the candidates had been decent, but none of them stood out to me though I could probably get away with hiring one of them. Maybe one of the last people would shape up to be a great fit.

Speeding through lunch, I squeezed in a good hour and a half of work before my two o'clock. I strode into the lobby after Joanne emailed that the next candidate had arrived. I greeted a small woman who looked like she might be mid-twenties, a little younger than Mia, but she was well put together. Dressed in a pencil skirt and silk blouse, I shook her hand and was impressed by her firm grip and eye contact right out of the gate.

Leading us into the conference room, I offered water or coffee which she politely declined. I settled at the head of the table while she perched on the chair nearest the door after we exchanged pleasantries.

"So, Ms. Anderson, what compelled you to apply for the position?"

She had a million-dollar smile. "I hope to work as an advisor or something similar someday and want to get myself into the field. I thought a receptionist position would be a good starting point." Her response was quick, but not artificial like she had over-rehearsed.

I opened the folder with her resume and cut straight to the point. "What do you think you can bring to the table for my company if I hire you?"

That got a pause. Good. I didn't want a robot for a receptionist.

She tucked her hair behind her ear before taking a barely visible deeper breath. "I think I would be a great asset because I also want to learn. This wouldn't just be a job for me. I could go be a receptionist at any business with a front desk, but I want to work here. I researched your firm, and it seems to be one of the best rated in the state."

Damn. This one was legit.

The interview went seamlessly, and before I knew it, thirty minutes had passed. I saw Cassie out after letting her know I would be in touch and turned to Joanne. "She was a good one. I'm excited about her. You said we have three more?"

Joanne shook her head. "Yep."

I nodded. "I don't think we will do any other interviews. Unless I'm blown away by one of the last three, she's it."

Clapping filled the room from behind the desk. Joanne lit

up like a Christmas tree. Being a receptionist slash office manager was hard, and I was ecstatic the firm was doing well enough I could finally get her off the front desk.

I smiled down at her. "I'm going to go try to answer some emails while I wait for the next one. I have half a mind to cancel the rest, but that would be shitty of me."

"Are you absolutely sure you're okay with being alone with the next one?" she called after me.

"Yes, mama bear," I said over my shoulder before disappearing into my office.

No sooner than I had clicked into an email my phone rang. Picking it up without glancing at the caller ID, I grabbed my note pad and pen.

"Raven Lovelace."

"Raven, hello! This is Teresa with the CFP board. How are you doing?"

The pen I was clenching clattered to the desk. Teresa. From the Certified Financial Planners Board. My mind flew in a million different directions searching for a reason someone from the CFP board would be calling me. Aside from the fact that my client dressed as a hooded intruder had talked me through the most intense orgasms I'd had the week before.

A throat cleared on the other end of the line.

"Oh, hi Teresa. I'm well, and you?" I rushed, trying to cover the awkward silence I'd created. The board wouldn't call me unless it was something to do with a violation or a complaint. *Fuck.*

"I'm well, thank you. I was just calling to discuss your last CE submission. In our review of your certificates, it seems there is a duplicate."

A wave of relief crashed over me, and I sank down in my chair. Of course she was calling about my CE reporting.

"I'm assuming this was a clerical error and you have an

additional continuing education credit to submit?" she continued.

"Yes, absolutely. That was likely my oversight. I'll remedy that immediately, and you'll have the additional submission in an email shortly."

As soon as the call ended I searched my certificates, found the error and fired off an email to the board. Once I clicked send I fell back in my chair wiping my forehead. Dammit, I couldn't live on pins and needles being afraid of repercussions. I either needed to commit to this thing with Ryan and stop worrying or I needed to end it.

The rest of the afternoon flew by, and before I knew it, Mia popped her head into my office. "Hey, Raven. I'm headed out a bit early. I need to take the puppy for its next round of shots. I'll see you tomorrow."

I waved my hand at her. "See you tomorrow."

Thirty seconds later, Mia was bounding back down the hall and came to a stop in my doorway, breathing heavily. I looked at her quizzically, raising my eyebrows at her haggard look.

"Raven, holy fucking fuck."

"What's going on?" I asked, starting to wonder if the building was on fire or something.

"The hottest fucking guy is sitting in the lobby right now. Is he a new client? If so, I'm going to need to be the one that calls him every single day from here on out."

I scrunched my face, confusion spreading through my mind. "I don't have any client appointments today. I'm only doing—" Realization dawned. "Oh! That's probably the next candidate." I looked down to see that it was almost time to meet with him.

Mia's eyes bulged. "You're interviewing *him* to work *here?*" she squeaked. "Oh my god, if you hire him I'm going to be so distracted."

I chuckled at her freaking out in my doorway. "Well, I guess that means I can't hire him then, doesn't it? Your efficiency is in luck, because I think I'm going to hire the girl I interviewed this afternoon."

Mia sighed. "Damn. Well fine. I'm jealous you get to sit in the same room as all that hotness for half an hour. Lucky. I'm leaving now. Bye!"

She was a whirlwind, but at least she was fantastic at her job. As she walked back out the door a second time, Joanne's email notification popped up in the bottom corner of my screen. I wondered if the guy was what I would consider attractive. Probably not. I'd seen Mia's boyfriend once when he dropped something off for her, and he was not who I pictured her with. Mia was gorgeous and kind, but he just looked mean.

I rolled back my chair and smoothed my hair, positioning the dark locks perfectly over my shoulders to frame my face. Halfway up the hall I heard Joanne's laughter. Puzzled, I walked into the lobby and stopped dead in my tracks. My stomach fell out of my ass, and my heart pole vaulted from my chest onto the floor. This wasn't a random "hot" guy. Standing at the desk talking up Joanne was the bench guy from the park. I was not getting through this interview unscathed.

CHAPTER TWENTY

RYAN

I was restless all day. It ramped up tenfold as the time inched closer to the interview. The steamy air sat heavy in my lungs as I stepped out of the shower to the vanity and cleaned the foggy surface. Wrapping a white towel around my waist, I leaned over the sink and gripped the edge as my alter ego took over. The mask fell into place, the excitement dissipating. I looked up at my reflection, and Zander stared back at me—all my insecurities vanishing with the fog on the mirror.

Throwing the towel in the laundry, I donned the tightest black boxer briefs I could find. No one would see them tonight, but it didn't hurt to be prepared. The black slacks settled on my hips and I shrugged into a black button down, both of which I had ironed, perfectly creased and crisp.

The pristine silver belt buckle glinted in the mirror as I dried my hair and styled it, long enough on top I needed a bit of gel to hold it in place. I ran my fingers through it and laced the only dress shoes I owned. With the three rings I knew would drive Raven mad nestled on my fingers, I was satisfied. I left the chain necklace in the dish on the dresser, but I would wear it when I visited Raven's house. Whenever that time came.

The bright afternoon sun glared as I walked to my old Honda. My parents didn't spend a lot of money on me since I was their biggest disappointment, but they at least got me a car when I turned eighteen and went to college. It might've been their way of thanking me for at least going to the one they wanted. I hadn't gotten a new one after I started to earn my own money because who was I trying to impress? I lived alone and seduced women with my voice on the internet for a living. I didn't need an expensive car.

The drive downtown was painless since it was mid-afternoon. I had chosen this time on purpose so hopefully Raven's staff would leave before the interview was over. After I parked in the same garage I followed Raven out of last week, I went into the building and rode the elevator to the thirteenth floor. I wondered if Raven would remember me from the park. Her face that day seemed like she wouldn't forget me easily so hopefully, it was a good sign my voice wasn't the only thing about me she liked.

My nerves were nowhere to be found as I stepped off the elevator and walked into the office suite, in daylight this time. I was a few minutes early so instead of sitting in the waiting area, I sidled up to the reception desk. The lady sitting behind it looked up from her computer.

"Hi, I'm Ben Jones. I have an interview with Raven Lovelace." My performance voice was dazzling.

The woman hesitated, almost as if she was stunned for a moment, then beamed. "Oh, yes, I'll let her know. She should be right out."

I flashed a thousand-watt smile. "Thank you, ma'am. And how are you on this lovely day we're having?"

She looked up again and narrowed her eyes. "You trying to get brownie points, young man?"

My laugh rang out into the room as I rested my elbow on the silver surface of the desk. "Maybe," I purred, one side of my mouth upturned. "Do you have some to lend? Maybe put in a good word with the boss for me?"

I didn't have much to gain from this woman since it wasn't like I was going to actually work here, but I wanted her to like me, nonetheless. If I was going to be a part of Raven's life, her employees were going to be people I interacted with sometimes.

"Oh boy, you're going to be trouble, aren't you?" She shook her head as she looked back down at her computer.

Footsteps came down the hall as a woman not much older than me hurried into the room. "Joanne, I'm headed out," she said, looking up from her phone and dropping it into her bag. She froze when her eyes landed on me leaning against the desk.

Her eyes went wide and she looked at the other woman—Joanne, I assumed—before returning her gaze to me. She wasn't shy with her admiration as she took in every detail of me. Finally snapping out of her trance and remembering herself, a blush crept onto her cheeks.

Throwing her hands in the air, she turned back down the hallway. "Oh, I forgot my phone in my office," she said, and disappeared despite having clearly been on her phone when she entered the lobby.

She thundered through the office a few minutes later and hustled out the door without a second glance, and I turned back to Joanne. "She seems like fun."

Joanne laughed. "She's an interesting one, for sure."

My gaze flicked back to the hall, and standing in the center of the entryway was the woman I'd dreamed about for over a month. Dressed in a charcoal pinstripe pantsuit, her straight black hair flowed down over her chest—her very covered chest that had too much fabric on it. Her make-up was minimal, but her eyes were lightly rimmed in black, a look unlike the women I usually went out with. The high-heeled boots peeking out from the hem of her pants could walk all over me.

We locked eyes and drank each other in for longer than was acceptable, but it was as though everything else fell away. It was just us existing in that room, and nothing else mattered. I could look at her until the sun died and bathed the world in ice, never growing tired of mapping every line and curve of her body.

Her pink lips parted slightly, and I ached to taste them again, ached to trail my fingers down the pale skin of her throat. My hand clenched at my side, itching to tangle into her smooth hair. Joanne cleared her throat, and I snapped out of the trance this dark goddess had me in.

I skirted the desk just as Raven walked forward, extending her hand. Her grip was firm and confident, asserting that she was in charge.

"Hi, I'm Raven Lovelace," she greeted, fixing her professional aura back into place.

I smiled wide and nodded, deliberately keeping silent until we were alone. She knew my voice and would recognize it even if I changed it, but hopefully my acting could get me pretty far before she did. This was going to be fun to watch.

She stared at me, waiting for my name, but after a few seconds she turned to walk down the hallway. "Right this way to the conference room."

When she reached the door, she stood to the side and waited for me to enter first. I took a seat at the far end of the short table and Raven did exactly what I wanted by sitting at the opposite end. Resting my hands in my lap, I sat up straight in the chair.

Raven was rigid on the edge of her seat, casting glances in my direction. She slid the folder resting on the table in front of her forward and opened it, pulling out what I assumed was the fake resume I'd sent to her job posting online.

She skimmed the document. "So, Mr. Jones, I'll get straight to the point. Why did you apply for this position?" she asked as she looked up and laid the pages back on the table. She was hot, with her hands clasped in front of her with such a serious look fixed on her features, the definition of a badass corporate woman. My pants grew a little tighter.

When I spoke, my voice was modified from my usual tone and accent. "Well, Ms. Lovelace, I think I would be a great fit to join your team. I'm excellent in customer service, which I assume is the main component of the position." I made sure to emphasize the word service.

I watched closely as my voice settled over her. Her jaw slackened, and her entire body stiffened at my words while she stared at me. It was apparent that she sensed something was off, but didn't know what. Good. I was hoping she wouldn't be quick to assume I would use a fake name. She could know who I was, processing the appearance of the man she'd been playing with. A pang of worry shot through my stomach, but I pushed it down.

Clearly, I had no intention of actually working for her. In this capacity, anyway. This was solely to make her squirm, but I would keep up the ruse as long as I could before I made sure she knew exactly who I was. Leaning back in the chair, I rested my palms on my thighs like I didn't have a care in the world.

"Ma'am?" I asked.

Her jaw snapped shut and she blinked rapidly as a blush tinted her cheeks. "Sorry about that, your voice reminded me of someone for a moment." She looked down at the resume. "So you have three years of receptionist experience with a construction company? Why did you leave that position?"

"I decided to pursue some personal ventures for a while. Now that I have them squared away, I want to come back to working in a corporate setting, which I enjoy." I pulled all that shit straight out of my ass.

Raven tilted her head. "Oh? Were the ventures a small business of some sort?" she questioned.

I held her emerald gaze. "You could say that. I...entertain on the side," I said, daring her to look away.

The longer I stared at her the pinker her cheeks got. She finally looked back down, tucking her shiny strands behind her ear.

"So, um..." She trailed off, her words failing her. Perfect.

I unbuttoned the cuffs of my sleeves and rolled them up, exposing my forearms. Raven's eyes never looked away, and they widened as I leaned forward, resting my arms on the table. Her gaze shot to my hands and the rings on my fingers. Without realizing it, she sucked in a breath and bit her lip. I loved watching her squirm in discomfort.

Desire pulsed through me, and I couldn't stop my words. "Everything okay, Ms. Lovelace? Do I make you nervous?"

CHAPTER TWENTY-ONE

RAVEN

The room was hot—way too hot—like I was going to combust. I wiped my sweaty palms on my pants and glanced back to Ben Jones seated across the table. My senses were on alert with his last question, but I chose to ignore it and only answer the first.

"Yes, I'm fine," I replied.

How did the person I was interviewing have such a similar voice to the one I'd been getting off to for weeks? And those hands. Those hands were adorned with silver bands and delicious veins. Mia was right. Even if I wanted to hire this man, I couldn't. No work would ever get done around here. I expected as much from Mia since she seemed closer to his age, but me? I wasn't sure if it was this specific guy that had me sideways or if I was becoming the next Demi Moore. Is this what happened in women's mid-thirties? We all suddenly foamed at the mouth for younger guys?

But this one, he was everything I didn't know I was attracted to. The rings I liked for sure. No surprise there since I never grew out of my emo phase. But I hadn't ever noticed another man's jaw before except his. It was chiseled from granite, and I longed to trace it with my tongue. The rest of his face was flawless, clean shaven with angles for days. He looked like the guy sorority girls wanted to date. His hair was styled messy, like he just ran his fingers through it so it stood on end. All the guys I had dated in the past had every single lock smoothed in place.

I glanced at his perfect face again and swallowed, trying to form a coherent thought in my scattered brain. "So, uh, do you have any questions for me? I think that's all I have," I rushed, trying to end the interview because men didn't ever have this effect on me, especially ones I didn't know. With this and my recent escapades with Ryan, I had no idea what the hell was happening with my body.

He peered at me under long lashes. "I'm curious what you can do for me, Raven—Ms. Lovelace," he corrected. "If you were to hire me, of course."

The way he said my name sent heat dancing over my skin. I shifted uncomfortably in my seat at the double meaning his tone conveyed. "We have competitive compensation, as well as standard benefits…" My words died in the air between us as he began tracing his lip with his thumb. It was the sexiest thing I'd ever seen, and my core pulsed.

I didn't try to resume rattling off the typical laundry list of benefits employees got. I just stared at the movement, damn near salivating like a fucking animal. He cocked his head to the side.

"Anything else you can do for me, Raven?" he asked as he rose from the chair and walked around the table toward me, my eyes following every step. "I think you have more to offer me than that."

Alarm bells were sounding in my head, but my pussy was the one in fucking control here. I should have been bolting from the room, but I kept my ass planted in the seat as he stopped beside me and crossed his arms. I swiveled the chair and tilted my head up to look at him, his tall body mere inches from mine, and his rich brown eyes searing.

The atmosphere in the room grew heavy, and I suddenly couldn't get enough oxygen in my lungs. He uncrossed his arms and leaned down, bracing his hands on the side of my chair. I looked down at them, and it turns out the veins on his hands trailed up his arms. A rush of heat pooled in my core while a memory lurked at the edge of my mind.

I slowly lifted my eyes to his, his face inches away, and we stared into the depths of each other's souls. I wasn't scared, even though I should have put this guy on his ass and called the cops. It probably wouldn't result in anything though. The police didn't do fuck all the last time I needed them.

He reached his hand up to trace a finger down my cheek, the gesture oddly familiar. My breath hitched at his touch. He had complete control, which didn't sit well with me, no matter how turned on and unafraid I was. The lust-filled haze hadn't clouded my judgment, so I decided to show this guy who he was fucking with.

Leaning forward, I brought my lips so close we were breathing the same air and his eyes dropped to my mouth. Clenching his jaw, he swallowed, and his throat was so delicious I wanted to flick my tongue out to taste him. Reaching my hand down, I moved my leg up at the same time. The fabric of my pants shifted easily and I was able to snatch my knife undetected.

As swift as a falcon, my blade was at his throat, and his eyes grew wide as the metal bit into his flesh. It was a pretty picture to see the silver glint against his flawless skin. One flick to end his existence. The light would drain from his big brown eyes and his lungs would gasp for air he couldn't breathe. The monster in my chest stirred at the thought, but killing him wouldn't be beneficial to the life I built for myself, and slitting his throat would be a waste of his mouth-watering good looks. I decided I'd have a little fun since it seemed he thought he could play with me. Whoever he was.

I curled my lips into a wicked smile. "I can offer you the pleasure of bleeding out on my floor," I hissed, pressing the knife into his skin gently. "You don't know who you're toying with, Mr. Jones, and I think you're in over your head."

I searched his face. I couldn't read him. There was no detection of fear, but his chest was heaving as his breaths came hard. His eyes were alight with something I couldn't place, and a trickle of warning slid down my neck, leaving goosebumps in its wake.

Shifting in the seat, I indicated he needed to move so I could stand up. When he straightened, he backed up one step, and before I was standing at my full height, he dove forward and grabbed my wrists.

My yelp filled the room, and he whirled us around, slamming me into the wall by the closed door. He pressed his body against mine and held my wrists between us, the knife dangerously close to our faces. Both our chests were surging as we stared into each other's eyes. He was a few inches taller than me even with my heeled boots. White hot fire shot through my body as his cedar and citrus scent filled my lungs. He could probably get me to lick his boots wearing that devious cologne.

Moving his right hand to envelop both my wrists, his large fist had no problem securing me. His slender fingers dug into my flesh, and pain bit, but it only heightened my arousal. He moved his free hand to pluck the knife from my grasp with ease, fear nipping the back of my neck as he disarmed me. With the handle nestled in his palm, he brought the blade to my throat.

"You're a stabby one, aren't you?" He smirked as he slid the deadly steel from my earlobe to my collarbone. "I don't think I'm in over my head at all, Raven."

My breath caught. The sensation and his words threatened to send me over the edge.

He moved his lips to the shell of my ear, his breath hot against my skin. "In fact, I could have you on your knees for me in seconds," he whispered, his voice husky. "I've already made you come countless times before. What do you wish to call me today, Raven? Zander, maybe?"

My heart stopped, and the blood drained from my face. "Ryan?" I croaked. Suddenly everything made sense—the rings, the hands, the head tilt.

He pulled back as one side of his mouth crept up into a grin. "You could call me that, too. I'm actually partial to that one." His voice returned to the one I couldn't get out of my mind and his eyes tracked the blade sliding down my neck. "I told you I could show up anytime, baby."

That word. Fuck, I loved how he called me that. If any other man had tried to, I probably would've never spoken to them again. But his voice saying it? It was my undoing.

"I want to taste you so badly I can't fucking stand it," he growled. "But in due time." He stepped away, releasing me, and my body whined at the loss.

I sagged against the wall and rubbed my wrists, faint red marks blooming where his fingers had been. He leaned against the table and crossed one foot in front of the other while twirling the knife. I glanced up, his eyes fixed on me like he was a predator, and I was his prey. Why the hell hadn't I looked at the date of birth in his file? I rose to my full height, my blood boiling.

"So you used a fake name and submitted a phony resume... why exactly? You had no issues just barging in last week." I crossed my arms over my chest. "Why go to the trouble?"

His gaze flicked to my crossed arms, and he cocked a brow when he looked back up. "I thought you might like the gesture," he said. "And I like playing games with you."

He dropped the knife on the table with a *clang*, and I tried to keep from wincing at the sound of metal on the glass. "This is my business, you know. You can't fuck with my company. My personal life and professional life are separate."

He moved his hands to his pockets. "Who said I was fucking with your business? From my vantage point it looks like I'm only fucking with you, babe."

I scoffed and sidestepped the table, gathering the documents into the manilla folder. My arousal had ebbed, replaced with irritation as I walked to the door and pulled it open, looking at him expectantly. "I didn't realize you were so much younger. You can go. I have more work to do."

"Raven," he said on a forced breath, his voice sounding tense. His lips were pressed into a thin line as he stared at the wall, avoiding my gaze. His jaw was clenched, and his body wasn't relaxed anymore.

"Fuck it," he swore, and lunged for me. He slammed the door closed and pushed me against it. I gasped in surprise as he grabbed the folder from my hand and threw it behind him, paper flying and scattering on the floor. He grabbed my hips hard and crashed his body into mine, his lips wasting no time seeking my mouth.

His kiss was forceful and blazing, things I wasn't used to, and in a different time of life, something I didn't like. With him, I would like anything, even the demanding possessiveness. There was no fighting my desire for him, regardless that he could be a decade younger and I could lose my license for having a personal relationship with a client.

His lips were soft yet rigorous, and I realized he was right. He could have me on my knees doing his bidding with a fucking smile on my face as long as he talked to me in that tantalizing voice and kept kissing me like that. CFP Board be damned. I would do anything to keep his mouth on me all night.

The world spun and his lips grew more fervent as he forced his way inside my mouth, a welcome invasion. He explored me like a man starved, and I was lost, lost to the devious flicks of his tongue. Nothing else in the world mattered while he was kissing me.

My body ached as he nudged my legs apart with his knee like before and pressed it between my legs. The pressure at my core made me lightheaded with relief, and his hardness pressed the front of my leg. I groaned into his mouth as his hands slid up my waist and into my blazer. Jerking my tucked blouse from my slacks he reached under my shirt and ghosted his fingers across my abdomen before splaying his hands on my back. His fingers gouged my skin as he nipped my bottom lip.

I cried into him, and he took every sound I made into his body, not letting my moans escape into the room. He turned us and backed me up until the sharp edge of the table pressed into my ass. He moved his hands up, sweeping the jacket down my arms and broke our kiss to spread it out behind me.

Moving back in front of me, his eyes weren't shy as they roamed over my body, leaving a trail of fire in their wake. He reached out and undid the buttons on my shirt one by one, not looking where his fingers worked, but into my eyes, instead. It was like he was committing every detail of my face to memory. A hint of anxiety tugged at me as he undid the last button and my shirt fell open to reveal my black bra beneath. This was actually happening. There would be no going back after this, and as his fingers traced the swells of my breasts, I decided I really didn't care.

CHAPTER TWENTY-TWO

RYAN

There had never been a woman so perfect in the world. That's what Raven was. Utter perfection. Not even supermodels in magazines and actresses on TV screens were as perfect as she was, especially now, looking at me, Ryan, with those emerald eyes. I had perched her on the conference room table, her lips swollen from my assault on her mouth, and she wasn't leaving. She finally had the full package and could have cut our little tirade short for a multitude of reasons. She'd dreamed up the perfect guy in her mind to match my voice, and finally seeing me could have been a disappointment. But she was in front of me, staring at me expectantly and waiting for whatever I would give her.

With her bra and stomach exposed, she looked at me with heavy-lidded eyes and gave me all the confidence I might have lacked before. She wanted this. Not just my voice, but me. I ran my thumb over her collarbone and down to her breasts, eliciting a sigh from her as she dropped her head back, exposing her luscious neck.

Taking the movement as an invitation, I trailed my tongue

from the base of her throat all the way to her chin. She gasped, and I gripped the back of her neck hard, pulling her lips to mine, drunk on her mouth. Nothing else mattered when she was underneath my hands. I'd thought of this moment for weeks, and was growing impatient. I wanted to give her long, drawn out pleasure, but that would have to wait. I needed to taste her body like I needed air, all my former plans thrown out the window.

I reached behind her and flicked her bra clasp open, relief surging at getting it on the first try. If it hadn't come undone so easily, it might have been ripped apart. I needed those tits freed to me.

She shrugged the shirt down her shoulders and flung the bra on the table. My mouth watered at the sight of her pink nipples, hard and waiting for my touch. Her breasts were the ideal size, and when I cupped them in my hands, they fit perfectly. Like she was made for me.

Her skin was flushed, pink splotches painting her chest like artwork. Diving back to her mouth, I palmed her breasts hard and she arched into me. Reluctantly leaving her lips, I kissed my way down her neck and over her chest to her nipple.

When I clasped my mouth onto the sensitive peak, I was rewarded with a moan that made my dick throb.

"Ryan."

Fuck, there was no sweeter sound than my name on her lips, and I sighed against her at the thought of her moaning around my cock down her throat.

I peppered kisses to her other breast and gave it the same attention. Flicking my tongue over her again and again, I reached up to do the same motion with the pad of my thumb on the other side. Her pants filled the small room, and I reveled in the sound.

As I lifted my head after releasing her from my mouth,

Raven stared straight into my eyes. The women I'd been with in the past had been shy when they were intimate, always looking away or closing their eyes. But Raven trained her emeralds on my every movement. She watched, breathing fast as I unbuttoned her pants.

"Next time, wear a skirt. This would be much easier," I grunted, working the annoying zipper down.

She threw her head back and laughed, a sound so intoxicating I vowed to coax it from her as much as possible. Along with all the other sexy sounds she made.

"I've never laughed when my pants were being taken off, but surprisingly, it didn't kill the mood," she said when her chuckles subsided.

I grinned down at her then stole a kiss from her lips before shoving her backward. Lust clouded her eyes as her elbows landed on the table. She wasn't laughing anymore, and soon she would be screaming.

"Lift your hips," I commanded as I braced her boots on the sides of my thighs and hooked my fingers into her waistband. Her heels dug into me as she hoisted her ass off the table and I slid her slacks off.

Taking a knee, I worked the wide leg fabric over her shoes because those slutty boots were staying on. She raised back up on her hands and looked down at me, bared except for a piece of silk. I crawled my hands up her legs and kissed in their wake until my head was level with her pussy.

"You are every bit the queen I said you were, baby. On your throne with me on my knees before you," I purred against the skin of her inner thigh, dropping kisses between words. "I'm forever yours to command."

Her lips parted, and I didn't take my eyes off her as I grabbed her ankles and placed her legs on my shoulders. With her knees bent, her legs fell to the side, opening her body fully to me.

"Don't you dare move your feet off me. Don't try to keep your weight off me, either. I want you to dig your heels into my back as you come. Got it?" I demanded.

She bit her lip, but I didn't wait for a response. I moved her panties to the side and she gasped as air hit her sensitive flesh. She glistened in the fluorescent light and I salivated at the feast before me.

"Fuck, baby, you're exquisite," I said, lowering my mouth to her. She was ecstasy on my tongue, and I lapped every bit of arousal from between her thighs, my breath hot on her skin. The room filled with her moans as I teased her with short flicks. She writhed on the table, eyes locked on me.

"Ryan, please," she choked. "I need more."

Her plea was my undoing. I latched onto her clit and sucked the life out of her. Her moans took on a higher pitch, and she wove her hand into my hair, fisting the strands. My skin burned from the sharpness of her heels pressing into my back, but the pain had my cock growing even harder. It was a good thing I'd come twice already today in case I couldn't hold myself back once I saw her. Good planning on my part, since I'd never be able to hold myself back from her.

Reaching my arm up around her thigh, I offered my fingers to her. "Suck," I said around her clit.

She didn't hesitate. Taking my middle and ring fingers into her mouth, she swirled her tongue, coating them with her saliva. When I jerked them away, she whimpered and I almost came at the sweet sound.

Sliding my middle finger into her pussy, I curled it forward in a way that had her walls clenching around me with a vengeance. I glanced up at her, and she was still watching every move I made, mouth fully open. Her eyes blazed as I slid in another finger so slowly she grew impatient.

"All of it. I need all of it," she panted.

"Beg for it. Beg me to let you come." My voice was gruff. "Tell me how much you want to come on my hand and tongue."

Her body grew still, and she pierced me with those green eyes. "I don't just *want* to come all over you. I *need* to come all over you," she deadpanned.

"Fuckkk," I groaned before ramming my fingers all the way inside her and crashing my mouth back to her pussy. She didn't need to beg. She had cast a fucking spell on me, and now I was hers. I was fucking hers.

She jerked beneath me and cried as she came, her walls convulsing around my fingers and her boots biting into my back even deeper. I locked onto her clit, lapping and sucking her through her orgasm. When her fingers slackened in my hair and the aftershocks eased, I pulled away, withdrawing my hand that was drenched in her wetness. I brought it to my mouth while still kneeling between her legs and sucked every digit dry.

I sprang up and slammed my mouth to hers, a gasp of shock escaping her as I placed my hand on the small of her back. She circled her arms around my neck and dove into the kiss, tasting the sweet sex coating my tongue. A loud blaring caused us to jump apart like we had been caught in the act like teenagers. Raven looked at her ringing phone, a puzzled expression on her face before realization dawned.

"Fuck!" Raven yelled as she smoothed a hand down over her hair. "Goddammit, you have to go."

Grabbing her bra and fixing it in place, I stared in confusion as she hopped off the table and shoved her leg into her pants, struggling to get the boot through the fabric. When they were finally situated back on her hips, she pulled on her blouse and fumbled with the buttons, hands shaking.

I stepped to her, grabbing her hands and bringing them up to my mouth, where I planted a kiss on each. She watched as I released them and moved mine expertly down her shirt, fastening each tiny closure.

She blew out a breath, and turned to grab her jacket once I finished, and groaned. "Well, this is fucking ruined," she said as she grabbed the material she'd soaked off the table. I looked at her expectantly as she glanced at her watch. "You weren't my last appointment of the day. I had a very important call scheduled exactly five minutes ago."

"Why do you have calls scheduled so late?" I asked, annoyance swirling in my chest as she snatched her phone and hustled to the door.

"Work doesn't stop at five when you have a business to run."

Reluctantly, I followed her out into the hallway, and she didn't give a second glance before she hurried to her office.

"You can see yourself out!" she called as the door slammed behind her.

Standing in the hall staring after her, my dick hard in my pants, I had to clench my fist to keep from barging into her office and bending her over her desk. Fuck her phone call. I wanted to teach her she couldn't barge out on me, but I would bide my time. In the end, I didn't want to cause her to lose business, so she was lucky her work was the reason she left me hanging. Still, I didn't forget so easily, and she didn't know what I had in store for her. I was a rabid dog on the loose now that I had finally tasted her, and she was never going to be rid of me.

After I walked to the door and it swung closed behind me, I glanced up at the camera to the right of the glass. The bright red light glared, almost mocking. I took note of the brand etched across the top of the device and pulled out my phone, quickly texting the name to Aaron. The elevator doors parted and I pressed the silver circle labeled "Garage".

My pocket buzzed as I entered the structure, swiping *accept* on the call.

"Rick," I answered. "Nice to hear from you." I tried to keep the frustration out of my voice, but a touch leaked in.

I had been patiently waiting for the file on Raven for a week, and my stomach vibrated with anticipation before Rick dashed my excitement, sending it down the drain.

"I have much bigger things to deal with than this, kid. Be glad I got it done within a week," he snapped, his gruff voice cracking like a whip through the phone. I could only assume people did whatever this dude said.

I pulled the door of my car open, Rick's tone adding to my sour mood. "Can you send the file directly to my email?"

He shuffled the phone, and the speaker scraped against something unseen, causing a harsh swiping to hound my ear. "I can, but you aren't going to be happy with the results. Your lady there is hiding something. I only found the same information that you said you did. She didn't really exist before college."

I stopped cold, my hand frozen in midair above the shifter. "What do you mean she didn't exist?"

"I mean exactly what I said," Rick huffed. "There are no records of Raven Lovelace prior to her acceptance into college. No birth records, elementary, or high school records, nothing. The only thing I found was the city and state she came from on her college application. I looked everywhere in that city and found nothing."

I scrubbed my hand over my face. "She had to exist somewhere. Could she be from a different country?" I questioned.

Something wasn't right. I could feel it in my gut that there was more to this than just the simple explanation that she wasn't born in the U.S.

"Maybe, but it will cost you to find out. Poking around in foreign records isn't easy."

"What city?" I asked.

Rick said the name and kept speaking, "There's a myriad of potential reasons why I didn't find everything with the normal search, but digging deeper won't be cheap."

"Do whatever you need to. I don't care how much it costs," I said, running my free hand through my hair. "I want the full file, but send me what you have."

"Don't expect it anytime soon. I have other shit to do," Rick grunted, and the line went dead.

I dropped the phone in the cup holder and leaned my head against the seat. What the fuck was going on? Rick was one of the best PIs in the country. He had ways, probably illegal ways, of getting information. I knew from the price tag that his "normal" search was much more thorough than any typical investigator's methods, so if he couldn't find information it had to mean something was off. He would've looked in the right places so that only led to one conclusion. Raven's past was buried.

I thought about the city he mentioned, and I remembered Dad's company had a location there. He and Uncle Jeff visited often even though it wasn't the office they worked out of. I had always wanted to go with them when I was kid, hoping to finally be enough for Dad—but of course, I was always dismissed. Shaking out of my thoughts, I started the car.

"What are you hiding, Raven?" I sighed into the silence and the empty garage around me.

CHAPTER TWENTY-THREE

RAVEN

"THANK YOU, Mr. Lopez. I appreciate the opportunity to work with you. We'll get started first thing next week. You have a good evening."

I hung up the phone and blew out a sigh of relief that my being late for the call hadn't fucked up my shot with a huge client. At first, it had been hard to focus on finance with my thighs still soaked and my nipples aching to be touched, but Lopez had been easy to impress. He was a sweet older gentleman who reminded me of Dad. Needless to say after drawing the comparison to my father, my feral body calmed the hell down.

I went to the restroom and smirked at my disheveled appearance staring back at me in the mirror. I looked like I had fought a bear with my wild hair and smeared makeup. After righting myself, I braced my hands on either side of the sink. What the hell was I doing? Having sex on my conference room table with my fucking client hours after a call from the board? It was something out of one of my romance novels. It didn't happen in real life without consequences, right?

Plus, he was probably nearly a decade younger than me. He had to be twenty-three or four. Maybe he was in his late twenties and just looked younger. That was a possibility, but I needed to ask him. A part of me felt it was wrong to look in his file so that's why I hadn't before. I brought my hands up to my face and pushed my palms into my forehead, where a headache was beginning to stir.

Even if he was older, he was still my client. I really needed him to sign the conflict waiver. Maybe if I disclosed the relationship or whatever the hell this was to the board they would overlook it. I could outline all the steps I was taking to keep things ethical.

I groaned at the possibility they might not see it that way and went back to my office to grab my purse and phone. The whole way home I thought about Ryan and the mind-shattering orgasm he'd given me. Sure, the sexting and phone sex had been great, and even the one I had given myself while he watched was more intense than I'd ever had. But Ryan between my legs, looking up at me like he would do anything I asked? Earth-shattering. Everything about him was impeccable. His voice, his purposefully messy hair, those fucking hands and that mouth.

I needed to stop this foray before I was too far gone...too addicted to stop, but I was already lost to him. I had thrown caution to the wind time after time when he could easily ruin me, and I didn't ever lose control like that. I didn't take risks. I couldn't, for the sake of my career, my own livelihood, and my parents. If I lost everything, they would, too.

My apartment was cold and uninviting when I walked in the door. Nothing about it made it into a home and I was hit with the realization that aside from work and my tiny family, I didn't have much. There were minimal personal touches in the space except stylistic furniture choices, and a tinge of regret and longing for someone else's things in the rooms pricked my chest as I ate dinner and eventually went to bed.

Nightmares plagued my sleep, and I woke up multiple times in a cold sweat, gasping for breath. I was back in the alley, the darkness closing in around me as footsteps sounded in the distance. There was no way out. Every direction I turned ended in a brick wall. My breaths became haggard, and I felt for a weapon, coming up with nothing.

The footsteps came closer, and it became clear there was more than one set. As the sounds grew louder, I jammed my arms over my head, a scream tearing from my lungs. Harsh laughs joined the hurried steps, and I dropped to my knees, tears streaming down my face.

The dreamscape shifted, and I was held against a wall of a body, my wrists pinned at my sides. He held me to him while a distorted man stepped in front of me and dragged a thumb across my cheek.

I woke myself up groaning in terror. My neck was so tense that my head was drawn back, and my hands were clenched into fists. I tried to relax my body as I lay in the dark, but ants were crawling on my skin. I had to move.

In the kitchen, I got a glass of water, the cool liquid soothing my scratchy throat. As I set the glass on the counter, the skin on the back of my neck tingled as if I was being watched. I looked around the dark apartment, the only light streaming from the water station on the fridge and saw nothing wrong in the shadowy corners. I was being ridiculous. My uneasiness was because of the bad dreams.

Rubbing my forehead, I took the glass to the sink and started to walk back down the hall when movement in my periphery snapped my head to the left. In the dark I saw nothing, but just to be sure I headed to the light switch on the opposite wall.

As I reached for it, something caught my hair and pulled me backward into a hard chest. I cried out into the darkness and a gloved hand slapped over my mouth, muffling my screams. My pulse shot through the roof as my arms were pinned, and my natural responses kicked in. I was a fighting kind of woman, so even though the intruder had caged my arms, I kicked my leg backward, hoping to catch balls with my foot.

Based on the build, I assumed they were a man, but he wasn't caught off guard by my tactics. My leg went between his and in a quick heave, he lifted me up off my feet and pitched me forward. The floor slammed into my knees, and my cry into his hand was nearly silent. He came to the ground with me and my nails clawed at the fabric covering his arm.

He jerked my head back into him and something cold and metal was threaded around my neck. My heart skipped, and I stopped struggling, knowing that he probably had a weapon, and I was defenseless. He pulled the chain taught, the links biting into my skin. I sobbed, tears streaming down my face, and chanted *please* over and over underneath the glove.

Not that my attacker would listen. He was my worst fears of the last decade materialized. He was the eyes watching from the shadows, always lurking, always watching and waiting. This was it. I'd managed to live peacefully and unbothered, but I'd always feared he would come after me for what I did. He'd finally caught me, and I was finally going to meet the fate I'd evaded all those years ago.

He wrenched my head to the side and his hot breath danced across my neck. He was really going to take this all the way back to that night and play out the whole thing. As his lips brushed against my skin, my body betrayed me as chills skated down my spine. He kissed his way up to my ear, his warmth lighting me on fire with rage.

"I think I like you in this position, baby, on your knees with a pretty necklace around your throat."

The words knocked me sideways, and I went still and silent. A wave of disbelief crashed over me, drenching my anger as relief followed closely behind. What the actual fuck?

I reached up, tugging his hand off my mouth, and he let me. "Ryan?" I choked. "What the fuck are you doing?" As the words left my lips I slid my fingers beneath the chain around my neck and tried to loosen it.

"Uh uh, baby," he said, as he pulled the chain tighter. "It's Zander tonight. You're going to make up for lost time earlier," he taunted. "As your punishment, you're going to suck my cock and I'm going to watch, all while I have your pretty little throat at my mercy."

Heat rushed between my legs, pooling in my core. My chest heaved again, but for a completely different reason than before. My nipples pushed against the black satin of my sleep dress as Zander traced my collar bone with his thumb, an action he seemed to love doing. Having his chain around my neck and his rough hands manipulating my body into the position he wanted was something I hadn't dreamed I would like. But knowing it was him behind me was everything I didn't know I wanted.

"How did you get in?" I panted as he moved his hands to my breasts and palmed me through the slick fabric.

"You said no limits, baby. So I threw a cloth over your camera and picked your lock." His chuckle was somehow erotic. "The funny thing about locks is they're only there to make people feel better. If someone wants in, they will find a way to get in. It's actually not that difficult."

My mind was in a lust-filled haze, only mildly registering his words. His hands traveled down my stomach, grasping my thigh with one and cupping my pussy with the other. His knees were on both sides of my hips and he pressed his hard length into my ass.

"Fuck," I moaned.

He had somehow secured the chain around my neck and the ends trailed down my back, the coldness soothing my hot skin.

"Turn around," he ordered, dropping his gloved hands from my body.

I scooted on my knees until I was facing him. Kneeling on the floor together, we stared at each other in the darkness. His hair stuck out from under his black hood and his face was barely visible. Fuck, he was hot like this, too. Earlier in my office, he was mouthwatering in his business casual attire. Now, he was wearing a hoodie and dark jeans, looking like he was ready to hurt me in the best way. He had put my pleasure first this afternoon, but now he was ready to take everything he needed from me whether I wanted it or not. The thought of being used that way made my pussy throb.

We crashed into one another with the force of a gunshot. Zander claimed my mouth, his tongue lapping every part he could reach, and I drowned in him. His heady smell of cedar and citrus, the same one from the office, filled my senses, and I groaned into him. Our hands tore at our clothing and while I was unsuccessful at removing his hoodie, my dress was ripped down the middle before I knew he had even reached for it.

When he pulled away, I ached for his lips. He kept his eyes locked on my face for an eternity, like he was deliberately not looking at my body on display for him. His jaw clenched and nostrils flared, tension written on his features. I dropped my gaze to the fisted gloves at his sides, and my mouth watered at the thought of them whispering down my body.

I flicked my gaze back to his face, and he finally let his eyes fall. He heaved in a breath as he took in my generous breasts and pink nipples. His head tipped forward as his gaze trailed lower over my soft stomach. When he landed on the V between my thighs, his breath rushed out as he ducked his head to the side.

"You're going to be the fucking death of me. I keep saying it like it's a revelation, but I should accept you're my undoing," he panted. His voice was different. I hadn't heard it this deep and gravely before. Even his sexy audios on his website weren't like this.

In a flash he was on his feet and in front of me, snatching the chain from where it rested between my shoulder blades. He crouched, his other hand grabbing my hair and yanking my head back so I was staring into his eyes.

"Are you going to cooperate with me, Raven?"

I just looked up at him, and when I didn't answer, he gave the chain a yank. I whimpered and began nodding frantically.

"I need you to use your words, baby," he snarled, the endearment adding a hint of sweetness. "Tell me you're going to obey me or tell me to stop."

My voice came out in a whisper. "I'm going to obey you."

"Say my name."

"Ry—" The chain dug into my neck harder before I could finish.

He brought his face so close to mine that our noses almost touched. "I told you before what you were to call me. Don't tell me you already forgot. You're not off to a great start."

"Zander."

One side of his mouth curled at my response. "That's right, baby."

He took me in a fiery kiss before he let go of my hair and rose back to his full height, his hood falling, hair wild. Peering up at him through my lashes, I watched his free hand unbuckle his belt. He ripped it free from the loops across his body, the leather snapping in the silent room. The act was so arousing it wouldn't have taken much at that point to make me come.

The chain clasp had slipped around to the front of my neck, the metal loop biting into my throat. I was his vassal, and I was aroused by it. He shouldn't have this power over me, but the thought kept repeating in my mind. I was never in a vulnerable position with anyone, especially a man, but he was different. For some reason I didn't understand, I wanted to submit to him. I wanted to give him my body in a way I hadn't given it to anyone else. Not demanding he remove the chain from my neck when I realized who he was proved that.

Zander backed away a few steps and with a yank of the chain I lurched forward, my hands hitting the hardwood. A wicked grin spread across his face, and the dim light from the kitchen rendered the scene sinister as he held the chain tethered to my neck. He tilted his head to the side, the gesture becoming one of my favorites, and looked at me expectantly. "Crawl."

The way he said the word had me reeling with desire. The number of times he'd gotten me so close to orgasm with just his words was insane. I wasn't an untouched woman, but my pussy was acting like I was. His voice and the way he used it was my undoing.

I moved forward on my hands and knees toward him, gazing up at him as I inched closer. The chain dragged on the floor like some perverse prison scene. Even so, the man I was crawling to made me want to do this. He was making me obey, but I wanted every second of it.

"Up on your knees," he said when I reached him.

I automatically bowed my head, some primal sense of submission surfacing without a thought. He gripped my chin with his thumb and forefinger, the leather rough against my skin, and tugged my face upward to meet his gaze.

"Take me out."

A breath whooshed from my chest. I'd wanted more this afternoon before I had to rush out, wanting to drop to my knees and suck him dry. Now I was going to get the chance. My stomach fluttered with the anticipation of seeing and tasting the most sinful part of him.

Reaching up, I undid his jeans, pulling them low on his hips. They were tight so they stayed where I left them. I shoved his boxers down, and his cock was free of restraint. From what I could see in the faint light, he looked delicious.

Taking his length in my hand, I stroked from base to tip, not needing further direction. Feeling his veins beneath my touch, I heard a hiss of breath through his teeth as I moved. Shifting my head forward, I flicked my tongue, barely touching his skin. I teased his length and head, not closing my lips around him on purpose, eliciting a deep groan from his lungs. The sounds I was forcing from him flooded my body with desire.

When I finally closed my lips around his glistening cock, he jerked the chain and I fell forward, taking every inch of him all the way to the base. He was slightly larger than average, and I gagged when he hit the back of my throat. The harsh movement brought tears to my eyes as I grabbed his hips and gasped for air.

"You're so beautiful when you're choking around my cock, baby." As the words left his lips, Zander withdrew and thrust in again getting the same reaction. "Work me, baby. Show me what that mouth can do."

Doing exactly that, I was a woman possessed by a feral desire to own his orgasm. I needed it to be all mine. I sucked and licked like my life depended on it because in this moment, it did. He could take away my oxygen in a second and there would be nothing I could do as the world faded to black.

He wouldn't, though. Somehow I knew I was safe with him, and it allowed me to lose myself in obeying his commands.

"Fuck, baby, that slutty mouth is flawless. I'm…so fucking…close," he said through gritted teeth and then put his hand on my head. "Stop. Hold still."

He tore his gloves off and threw them to the ground before he slid his hands into my hair on either side of my head. Fisting my strands, he thrust his hips, taking complete control of my body.

No man had ever fucked my face, especially like this, but it unleashed a demon inside me that clawed Zander's exposed thighs. The world spun out, and I lost all sense of time and reality. Only Zander and I existed, and I didn't want it to end.

"Fuck, Raven," Zander groaned as he heaved into my mouth one last time and spilled down my throat. I swallowed every last drop like I was an animal searching for water in a desert.

The sound of his release was ecstasy to me. His heavy breaths and throaty moans had me crying in protest as he pulled away, my body wanting to keep his connected to mine.

I looked down at the floor. It felt like the natural thing to do in the moment when Zander took a knee in front of me. He placed his hand under my chin, tipping my face upward, still holding the chain as he moved from my chin to between my legs.

"I was initially going to come here, make you suck me off, then leave." He drew his fingers through my wetness and grinned. "But I can't leave my baby girl wanting. I knew this pussy would be wet for me after that performance. You looked so aroused taking my cum down your throat that I had to touch you. I'll always need to touch you, Raven."

I drew in a quick breath as he found my clit and expertly

stroked in the most perfect way. I was coming in seconds as I looked into his dark eyes. My moans turned to cries, and tears streamed down my face as I rode out the wave. The cries turned to sobs as Zander withdrew his hand, and his seductive grin fell into a look of concern.

"Raven, what's wrong? Why are you crying?" I covered my face with my hands to hide my tears. "Did I hurt you?"

I shook my head as he reached up and pulled the chain free from the loop, dropping it to the floor with a thud. He grabbed my wrists and drew my hands away, searching for answers in my tear-soaked skin.

"Talk to me, baby," he asked, his voice tinged with alarm as he wiped the tears from my cheeks. "I couldn't stand it if I upset you and went too far. Tell me I didn't go too far."

I shook my head, my voice hoarse and unsteady when I whispered, "Stay with me? I don't want to be alone anymore."

CHAPTER TWENTY-FOUR

RYAN

I took Raven's face in my hands and pulled her into my chest. She cried softly into my hoodie as I looped an arm around her shoulders and stroked her hair. She was vulnerable, and I suspected she didn't show this side of herself to anyone. Hell, she might even hide these feelings from herself.

I wasn't sure what brought her to this state, but I'd learned in the past that sex makes emotions surface that are usually tamped as far down as we can shove them. Carnal sex brings it out even more. Raven was a strong woman, and submitting to me the way she did had probably released pent-up feelings.

As she cried in the dark against me, I didn't want to take her emotions away. I wanted her to feel everything so she could work through it, but I wanted to help her. I wanted to be someone she could show her weaknesses to without fear of appearing weak. She was anything but weak.

Her sobs turned to sniffles and I stood, pulling her up off the floor with me. The whispered words had ripped open my chest, and though my plan hadn't involved staying the night, I hadn't wanted to leave even before she asked me to stay. I walked us through the massive living room and down a hall that had a handful of doors on either side. Assuming the main bedroom was the last one, I shuffled us in and closed the door. It was dark, but I could tell by the almost nonexistent light from streetlights outside the curtained window that I chose the right one.

I walked to the side of the large bed and flicked on the lamp, the soft warmth filling the room. Everything was adorned in black which I wasn't surprised by. The sheets, the drapes, and decor on the light gray walls were all the same shade of onyx, but it was tasteful. It wasn't over the top, which could have easily been the case with this theme. I liked it.

When I looked back to where I left Raven, she was gone. My gaze traveled to the ensuite bathroom with light spilling from underneath the door. I wasn't going to let her isolate herself now that the post-sex haze was fading. If she didn't want to be alone before, she wasn't going to change her mind once she regained her composure.

Moving to the door, I knocked but she didn't answer. "Raven, I'm coming in whether you want me to or not. You have five seconds before I do. And don't try to lock me out because we both know that won't stop me." My poor attempt at humor probably didn't make her laugh but it was worth a shot.

"One. Two. Three." Right before I said four, the door opened.

A plush white robe, the ones you see in hotels and movies, covered her body. The useless dress she'd been wearing was still ripped to shreds on the floor somewhere. She looked up at me with blank eyes for a moment before walking back to the sink.

I moved behind her as she ran a damp cloth over her face,

but I didn't touch her. I wanted to spin her around, take her into my arms and never let go, but I kept my hands at my sides.

"Tell me what you need." Gone was the dominant Zander, and in his place was me, Ryan, who just wanted to make her smile.

Raven sighed and turned around, crossing her arms over her chest like she was embarrassed. "I don't need you to stay. I'm better now. I don't know why I said that out there," she murmured as she averted her gaze.

I shook my head. "I'm staying. I technically just broke into your house." I chuckled. "Then I defiled that pretty mouth, and after all of that you asked me to stay." I moved close enough that our bodies were touching and grinned down at her. "Baby, I'm staying."

Loosing a breath, she finally looked at me. "Fine."

"I didn't scare you, did I?" I said as I reached up to tuck her hair behind her ear.

She leaned into the touch and closed her eyes. Cupping her cheek with my palm, I smoothed my thumb across her soft skin.

"Yes, but I wasn't scared anymore when I knew it was you. I didn't know I would like something like that, but I did."

I kissed her forehead. "Why aren't you scared of me, Raven? Most people would be scared."

Her green eyes glinted, tears pooling in their depths, as she stared into my soul. "There are worse monsters in the world, Ryan. I know a monster when I see one."

The blow of her words landed in my chest, and I almost stepped back reflexively. Instead, I hauled her into my arms, hoping her body against mine would quell the burning inside me. "What happened to you?" I whispered.

I didn't know what or who happened to her, but I wanted to hunt down her monsters. I wanted to strangle the life from their lungs. Someone or multiple someones had hurt her, and they deserved to suffer for it.

We stood in silence as the minutes ticked by. Raven in my arms was the most natural thing I'd ever felt, and I wasn't ever letting her go. When she finally drew back and looked at me again, the tears that threatened were gone. She gazed up at me with a face devoid of emotion, like she was indifferent.

"It doesn't matter. I'm fine. It was a long time ago, and I've moved on."

Clearly, she hadn't moved on, but instead of pressing, I steered her into the bedroom. She crawled into bed without hesitation, the robe parting slightly around her breasts as she did, and my mouth watered at the hint of them.

I pulled the duvet up over her and situated myself atop the covers with my back against the wall. Settling on a pillow, she gazed up at me.

"You can sleep, too," she breathed as her eyes roamed over my clothes.

Finding her hand underneath the sheets, I entwined my fingers with hers. "I'm making sure no other men break into your house to give you orgasms. That's my job now."

She giggled, the sound a sweet song drifting into the room. I leaned down to kiss her cheek, and soon her breathing evened out as I watched over her.

I JERKED AWAKE, disoriented and unsure of my surroundings. I glanced around the unfamiliar room, trying to right myself. A whimper came from beside me and I glanced over to see Raven on her back with her brows creased and her eyes squeezed shut.

I must have dozed off while she slept. I only meant to stay

for an hour or so before creeping out to make sure the rest of my plan for her was in place. Breaking into her house was only the beginning.

Scooting back, I brought myself flat against the wall after having slumped down in an uncomfortable position in my slumber. Raven cried out, her breaths coming in pants and tears leaking from her eyes. I hustled to my feet and pulled back the covers, sliding in beside her. I hated that my clothes were between us so I pulled my hoodie and T-shirt over my head and threw them to the floor.

Pulling her into my arms, I rolled her onto her side to face me and held her head to my chest. "Raven, baby, it's just a dream," I soothed, loud enough to bring her out of sleep, but quiet enough to not startle her.

Her breathing began to return to normal and she shifted in my arms, bringing her hands up to my bare chest. Her nails dug into my flesh, but I didn't care. I would rather her cause me pain if it took hers away.

She moved her head back, and I glanced down, meeting her eyes. I smoothed the hair that was plastered to her face away and wiped her tears like I had a few hours before. She was beautiful even with tear-stained cheeks and hair mussed from sleep—looking at me with emotions written on her face that I couldn't decipher.

"Are you all right?" I asked, and as soon as the words left me, her tears welled up again.

She shook her head and buried her face back into my chest. "He came after me. In my dreams," she sputtered. "I was into what happened earlier, but before I knew it was you I thought he found me."

I pulled back and searched her face. "Who found you? Raven, tell me what happened."

Sighing, she sat up in bed, pulling her robe back into place after it had fallen off one shoulder. She dropped her head in her hands like she was ashamed. "When I was eighteen, I was sexually assaulted. Before I decided to go to college to pursue finance," she admitted, wiping her eyes. She glanced over at me and must have seen the rage plastered on my face because she rushed to add, "The guy wasn't able to go all the way before they were dealt with and the other one just held me for him. I wasn't raped, but he touched me."

That didn't help. Just the thought of someone touching her without her explicit consent prior made my blood boil. I would have never done the things I had with her if I hadn't known her boundaries beforehand.

I gritted my teeth. "You can tell me as much or as little as you want, but I have to know one thing. Are you still in danger from them?" I asked. I was terrified of her answer given that she was nervous someone was following her, but if she was being threatened I was going to lose my shit if anyone came near her.

"No. The guy that did the most is dead now. His friend who held me down ran away before the cops came." She clasped her hands in her lap. "He's still out there, and he threatened me before he left, but I haven't seen or heard from him since."

She peered out into the room, her voice dropping to a whisper. "I sometimes dream that he finds me. My therapist said it can happen for decades after the event."

Realization hit me like a ton of bricks. Raven thought I was him earlier. I dropped my head into my hands and balled my fists in my hair. "Fuck!"

I couldn't bear to look at her. I'd done too much, went too far. I brought all of that back for her. Her soft touch caressed my arm. "Ryan."

I lifted her hand from my arm, bringing it up to my lips. "Raven, I'm so sorry. I—"

She put a finger to my lips. "I know what you're thinking. Stop. You didn't know and honestly, once I knew it was you, I was ready to do anything you told me to. You make me want to submit in a way I've never wanted to before."

"I'm supposed to be the one comforting you right now, you know?"

She smirked. "Yeah, well, it's in my nature to be the composed one." She shifted closer, moving so she was nestled into my shoulder, staring out into the room. "But with you, I feel like maybe I don't have to be."

My heart squeezed like a vise in my chest, and even though I was already obsessed with this woman, the night solidified the idea that I was beginning to feel something more than that.

CHAPTER TWENTY-FIVE

RAVEN

Sunlight streamed into the bedroom as I rolled over and stretched. Sunlight. I never stayed in bed after sunrise unless I was sick. What day was it? Then everything smacked me in the face. Ryan.

He had broken into my apartment and then I asked him to stay with me. I bolted up and glanced around the room, thankfully not seeing any trace of him. He must've left before I woke up. Heat rushed to my cheeks as I thought of how awkward I would've been if he had still been there. I groaned. I was never going to be able to talk to him again, or I'd die from embarrassment.

Rubbing my eyes, I padded to the bathroom where I stopped dead, the memories from the night before floating back one by one. I had told him. Not everything, but I'd told him about the one thing I didn't tell anyone. Mom and Dad knew most of it, but they were forbidden to bring it up unless I did.

Another realization barreled into me. Work. Fuck! I was late. So late. I ran to the nightstand and grabbed my phone, seeing that the clock read seven fifty-five. When I turned the phone over, there was a sticky note on the screen.

"Open my texts before you freak out."

Too late. Already there, buddy. I tore the note off the phone and saw new message notifications from Ryan and Joanne. Ignoring the thread with Ryan, I tapped the message from Joanne.

Instead of asking where I was, her text read, "Oh no! I hope you feel better!"

What?

My eyes flicked up to the message before hers. That asshole.

Switching into the convo with Ryan, my blood was boiling. There were a slew of voice messages from six a.m.

I hit play on the earliest message and the voice I couldn't get enough of drifted from the speaker. "Take a deep breath. I know you're probably panicking right now. I texted Joanne from your phone and said you weren't feeling well, and that you would call her later this morning after you got some more sleep."

How did that fucker get into my phone? He must have used my fingerprint to unlock it while I slept. More frustration crept up my spine, but his message continued on and I found it hard to be anything but obsessed with that voice.

"You're going to call Joanne and tell her you're staying in bed today. Do it now then listen to my next voice message."

Fuck this guy. I had too much shit to do at work to not go. I didn't care if he made me feel some type of way last night by staying with me and holding me after a nightmare. I scrolled and tapped the next message.

"I know you didn't call. Seriously, Raven, call her. I have a plan for your day that doesn't involve working. Give me this. I know you probably haven't taken a day off in a long time or ever. So fucking call. Now. In case you did call before listening to this, that's my good girl. I know you didn't, though."

I blew out a breath. This guy. I threw the phone on the bed and paced the room with my hand on my hip, mentally ticking through all the things I needed to get done at work before the weekend.

The Lopez account needed to be finalized for early next week. I guessed it could wait until tomorrow or Monday at the latest. Then I had all of the doc review for Mia to do as I always did on Friday. Fuck, and I needed to email the woman I actually wanted to hire for the receptionist position. What was her name? Anderson?

I scrubbed my hands down my face. Had it really only been yesterday that I interviewed her? It seemed like ages ago. My mind flicked to the last interview I'd had the day before. Ben Jones. I laughed. Ryan must love to come up with names for himself. I wondered if he had alter egos as well.

Stopping by the bed, I threw my hands up. "Fuck it."

Grabbing the phone, I opened the contact and tapped Joanne's name from the Favorites list.

"Raven!" she chirped after she picked up. "Are you all right? You must be really sick if you're staying home."

I cleared my throat trying to sound like it was scratchy. "Yeah, Joanne. I...woke up not feeling so well last night. I'm not sure what's going on, but I think I should stay home. I don't want to get anyone else sick." I tugged at the hem of the robe I still wore. "I'll try to work remotely later. Tell Mia to go ahead and see what she can do with the Lopez account and have her email what she manages at the end of the day."

"Sure thing. Are you sure you're okay?" A hint of suspicion tinged Joanne's words.

"Yes, yes I'm fine. Promise you'll text or call if you need anything." It would be just like her to try to not bother me, but this was the first weekday I hadn't gone into the office since I started the company.

"Of course, Raven. I hope you feel better!"

Her genuine care for me had me smiling to myself. "Oh, wait! As your first act of being office manager, can you call the lady I liked from yesterday? I'll email her at some point, but I'd like for you to informally offer her the job. If she verbally accepts, cancel the other interviews and if not, reschedule."

"Yep, can do. I know you liked her. Oh! Monday, I need all the details on Mr. Hot Stuff."

My cheeks burn. "Joanne! He's younger than your son!" I squeaked.

She laughed. "Oh, honey, age doesn't matter. When you're my age, the young studs remind us of the good days. Anyhow, I'll let you get back to resting. Don't worry about the office, okay?"

I scoffed. "You know I will. Talk to you later."

I ended the call and tapped back into Ryan's messages, clicking play on the third one.

"All right, now, if you didn't do as I asked and you are getting ready for work right now, I'm going to have to punish you. Not to mention you'll miss out on the great day I have planned. If you actually did as I asked, go into the kitchen."

Punish me? I had to admit, I liked the dom in him, but maybe we needed to level the playing field soon. It's all about balance after all, right?

I shook my head and shoved my feet into my slippers, heading toward the door. As soon as I stepped into the hallway, my nose went on alert at the delicious smell permeating the apartment. My stomach growled, and it was like I stepped right into a bakery. In the kitchen, I was greeted with a note.

"Breakfast is in the oven. French toast muffins. Sit down and take your time eating. I assume you always rush through meals so today, you're going to enjoy them. After breakfast, listen to the next voice message."

He made me breakfast? My mind glitched at the thought that the person who broke into my apartment to fuck my face had cuddled me the rest of the night and then whipped up breakfast for me. Maybe he had bought the muffins at the store?

The smell intensified when I pulled open the oven and my mouth watered. The muffins definitely weren't store bought because they were in my muffin tin. They looked like something from a high-end restaurant. The tops were golden brown and instead of typical liners, they were in little parchment paper squares with the corners sticking up. That's probably all I had for him to use to make them, although it actually looked fancier.

I pulled the pan out of the oven with a dish towel and sat it atop the glass top stove. As I moved to reach for the cabinet that held the plates, I saw one had already been placed on the countertop with a fork resting in the center. Now he was just showing off. I wondered what else he had done while I slept. I trudged over to the coffee machine and lifted the lid. I preferred a typical coffee maker to the espresso and single serve ones, and when I looked into the stainless-steel water tank, it was filled to the top. I knew the grounds would be resting in the basket as well, but I checked anyway. Sure enough, all I needed to do was press 'Brew'.

The aroma of coffee mixing with the cinnamon was a dream. I situated myself at the island with my breakfast and did as I was told. Usually, everything in my soul would be screaming at me to rebel, but today, all was quiet.

I took a bite of the muffin, the flavors exploding on my tongue and groaned into the empty kitchen. It was the best thing I'd ever tasted. Great, he could cook too. Shaking my head, I pulled up his texts and hit play on the last voice message.

"I'm so proud of you, baby. I know you're probably struggling with this, but I'm proud of you for taking some time for yourself, even if I had to push you a little."

I tapped pause as warmth spread through me at the words. My parents always made sure I knew they were proud of me, but it felt different coming from him. Water pooled in my eyes, and I fought to keep it from spilling over. I thought I didn't need anyone else except Mom and Dad, but now I was starting to realize maybe I wanted someone else. Specifically, I wanted this sweet and mysterious man who kept surprising me.

"Go into your room and get ready for the day. You can do as much or as little as you want. This is about you. If you want to go the whole nine, do it. If you want to do nothing, that's also fine. You're perfect either way. Just dress in casual, everyday clothes. No pantsuits. Text me when you're finished.

My mind kicked into overdrive. What was wrong with me? I was ditching work, doing exactly what a man I barely knew said, and I was going to keep doing it. He was right. I never took time for myself and maybe it was time I started. Maybe there was more to life than work and calculating every single decision I made. Throwing caution to the wind, I finished breakfast and got myself ready in jeans and a lightweight plum sweater. With no makeup and my hair down, I actually felt comfortable.

I grabbed my phone and texted Ryan.

"All right, I'm dressed and ready."

A voice message came through a few minutes later.

"As much as I would like for you to not be dressed, good. Grab your keys."

THE SUN GLARED off the windshield right into my eyes as I drove along the street toward the address Ryan had texted me. I didn't recognize it, and he forbade me from Googling it. I almost did anyway, but I decided to just go with it, something I was doing more of lately.

I plugged it into my GPS and was enjoying the drive. I wasn't in a rush, and the traffic was flowing easily since it was late morning. I couldn't remember a day when I wasn't hurrying around to get as much done as possible. Taking my time was proving to be quite nice, and I had a flutter of excitement at not knowing what to expect from the day.

When I pulled into a shopping center, I looked around for suite 705. When I found it, I was met with a used book and music store.

A smile tugged at my mouth, as the elder emo side of me jumped for joy. I was transported to my teenage years when I would spend whole Saturdays in the music store down the street from our house listening to music. I didn't have the money to buy all the newest CDs or an iPod like the kids at school so I listened in the store. It was my favorite use of my free time aside from curling up with a book at the library. Having access to a music *and* bookstore in one place would have been my best dream come true.

I picked up my phone and clicked play on the latest voice message that came through while I was driving.

"I'm going on a lot of whims today, but I'm betting you like music. I know you like books, so I luckily don't have to guess at that one. I like the spot, so I thought you might, too. It's one of the few places I leave the house to go. They have a nice area to read and a fairly large selection of old and new novels. I'll be here when you're finished. No rush. You have as long as you'd like, babe."

Staring at my phone like it was going to grow legs and walk away, I wondered how Ryan knew me so well. We had texted about mundane things, but I didn't divulge as much as he seemed to know. I hadn't told him about my childhood, or—

A chill ran through my bones. No, it couldn't be possible, right? Ryan couldn't have found anything about my past. It was a different time, a different place, and I had distanced myself from the situation, and there was no way anything was linked to me. I hired private investigators under a guise to be sure once I had made enough money to spare on the expense.

Taking a few deep breaths to steady myself, I pushed the worry from my mind. I was going to enjoy the day Ryan had planned for me and not question it. I was finally beginning to realize that I did deserve some me time every now and then, and it would start with going into that store and enjoying my afternoon.

Three hours later, my stomach grumbled, the muffin from that morning long forgotten. I browsed the aisles of music, then moved to the books section, plucking one from the shelves and settling into a soft chair by the window. The book was old and the faded cover had drawn me in. It had been well-read and loved by someone. I hadn't heard of the author or title before, but it was in the romance section so I knew I'd enjoy it.

I hadn't realized how much time had passed before my body yelled at me for food. Paying for the book, I stepped outside, searching the strip mall for anything to satiate my hunger until I could have a proper meal that evening. I still had no idea what the evening held for me, but it was likely a safe bet that food would be involved.

A shiver ran down my spine, and the familiar feeling of

being watched was back. The same one I got in the garage. I smiled to myself as I thought of Ryan sitting in a car at the edge of the lot somewhere watching my every move.

After a quick sandwich from the deli on the corner, I settled back into my car and texted Ryan.

"All right, what now?"

I tapped the steering wheel as I waited for the response that came a few minutes later in the form of another voice message, Ryan's sensual tone filling the car.

"Goddamn, Raven, I'm going insane for you. I can't stop thinking about that mouth and what you can do with it. Fuck."

The voice message ended, and heat flooded through my body. The way his words were laced with desire had me clenching my thighs together. His voice was always sexy, but he could flip a switch and make your panties wet with one fucking sentence. No wonder he was so successful in his career.

Another message popped up, and I tapped play.

"Sorry, I had to take a sec. I'm a little on edge after last night. Go back to your apartment and run a hot bath. Text me when you're in it."

A few minutes passed, and when no more messages came, I started my car. Forty minutes later I turned the hot water on in my excessively large tub and adjusted the temperature until it was only mildly scalding. I placed my phone in the basket fixed to the front of the tile to the left and dropped my robe. Once comfortable, I grabbed my phone and hooked my finger in the ring on the back.

"I'm in the bath."

When the text was sent and the tub was full, I rested my head on the rolled-up towel at my neck. Hot steam filled my lungs and I was as light as a cloud.

My phone buzzed in my hand jolting me back to reality. Of course, he was calling.

"Hello," my voice cut into the quiet room.

"Hey, baby. Having a good day?"

I drew in a breath before answering. Could he get any better? "I am. It's been a great day. Thank you, Ryan. I really appreciate all the effort. It wasn't necessary, but I'm grateful all the same."

He chuckled, but when he spoke, his voice was serious. "I'd run through fire for you, Raven. Convincing you to have a day of self-care is the least I can do."

My stomach fluttered. Was this what people meant when they said they got butterflies? I shouldn't be getting butterflies for Ryan. He broke into my apartment, for fuck's sake, and I knew he was following me around. But at the same time, I should've stopped being delusional. Everything he had done turned me on more than anything ever had.

Ryan's voice floated into my thoughts. "Are you all right, baby?"

I cleared my throat. "Yes, I'm fine. Wonderful, actually."

"Good. You've been such a good girl for me today. Now, it's time we begin with your rewards. Here is how the rest of the afternoon is going to go. After your bath, you're going to get dressed for a date. Wear a formal dress. Do your makeup or not. I don't give a fuck because you don't need it. Wear your hair however you want. It'll be beautiful regardless." He dropped his voice and I could hear his smirk on the other end of the line. "But first, you're going to get yourself off to my voice, while I relish your whimpers."

And that's exactly what we did.

CHAPTER TWENTY-SIX

RYAN

THE BEEP from the microwave sliced through my brain like a knife through butter. I had pulled all-nighters before while working, but today, my body wasn't cooperating.

I opened the door and pulled out the lukewarm coffee. I could have made a fresh cup after this one went cold while I was on the phone with Raven, but even that was more effort than I had energy for.

The past twenty-four hours were a pipedream and were the best of my life. As soon as she was in a deep sleep after the nightmare woke her up, I set about her apartment to see what sort of breakfast I could round up with the ingredients she already had. The original plan was to pay her a little visit then leave. I was already going to take her to dinner, but once she showed her vulnerable side, my brain re-wired itself. It was clear she needed a break, so I wanted to plan a whole day for her. She worked too much.

The only sleep I had was the short nap I had gotten at her place since I went straight to the studio to record after leaving. Craig had sent the next project early and with a deadline. The production timeline had moved up and if I didn't get started right away I would miss it. I could cancel the date, but I wasn't going to sleep until I wined and dined Raven, and finally felt her soft body around mine. Pounding coffee would have to suffice until I could pound her instead.

Leaning against the counter, I ran a hand through my hair. I had a few hours until I was supposed to meet her, but my dick was screaming at me to go to her apartment and bury myself deep inside her. The night before was glorious, but I craved more. I would always crave more from her. Her moans as she came to the sound of my voice in the bath were playing through my mind on repeat.

A part of me was surprised when she texted that morning saying she was actually going to take the day off. I didn't know which route she would take, assuming she would probably go to work, but Raven seemed to be enjoying being told what to do for once. My suspicions that she longed for someone else to make decisions for her seemed spot on. Some of the women I had been with were leaders, but they didn't want to lead in the bedroom. I took a chance Raven would be similar, desiring authority from a partner.

It was becoming clear this was more than physical attraction with Raven. At first—after I got over my issues surrounding possible rejection—I thought I might be satiated after having her, but there was always a thought in the back of my mind that knew that wasn't the case. Even before I met her, Raven had infiltrated my very being, and I hadn't seen anything except her since.

Last night when I was holding her solidified that. I didn't think I'd ever been in love, and I wasn't sure what love looked like in a healthy situation. But what is love if it's not thinking of a person every waking moment and going to the ends of the earth for them? Maybe that's infatuation and obsession, but isn't that how most relationships begin? All the books and stories I've narrated are exactly that—obsession that grows into love.

Of course, books weren't real life, but the unconditional love the characters always had for each other was what everyone wanted, right? Each person had a different story, but overall the desired result was the same. A person who would stand beside their partner and support them even if the world was on fire. I'd found the woman I wanted to be that person for. Even if I was shattered in the process, one hour with her would be better than none.

I downed the rest of the coffee and sat the plain white mug in the sink. In the living room, I got in a quick workout of push-ups and other cardio I didn't need equipment for. After I was a sweaty mess, I showered and dressed in the only suit I owned. It wasn't designer, but it was nice enough. Hopefully nice enough for the woman who had everything. I was all in for her, and I figured she preferred a well-dressed man as opposed to a slouch in sweatpants and a hoodie.

That was the reason I was taking Raven to the nicest restaurant in the city. I wanted to show her that I could be refined like my parents had always wanted me to be. For Raven, I'd be anything she wanted. No ordinary guy would suffice for this perfect woman, so I pulled out all the stops. Luckily, the restaurant was within walking distance of the place I wanted to meet her.

After driving downtown and parking, I counted the paces from Raven's office to the park when we first laid eyes on each other. By the time I settled on the same bench I was sitting on that day, I saw the limo was close on the company's app. Within a few minutes, Raven sent a text.

"Why am I at my office?"

I smiled at her questioning everything. I quickly typed the

number of paces and turns she needed to take that would bring her to me. When the limo arrived at her apartment, she lost her shit, saying it was ridiculous and that she could drive herself. She was practical while still living comfortably. I liked that about her since I didn't like to spend money, either.

My nerves kicked in, so I scrolled mindlessly through my social media profiles that I neglected recently. The comments on older posts of people asking where I was distracted me from my sweaty palms. I no longer cared as much about driving my followers mad with my voice. I only cared about driving her mad. I still loved my career, but Raven was at the forefront.

The click of heels on the paved pathway drew my attention. I glanced up and damn near stopped breathing. She stood a few feet away, and for a moment, I was paralyzed by the sight of her. She was wearing a long-sleeved black evening dress that came to a halt mid-calf, and her hair was in a half bun with the rest flowing over her shoulders. The dress hugged every curve of her body, and I was at a loss for words, my dick hardening at the thoughts running through my head. She was my own personal goth queen, and I wanted to skip dinner and go straight to dessert.

Her lips curved into a smile, and I snapped out of the trance she put me in. Picking my jaw up off the ground, I jumped to my feet and closed the distance between us. When I held out my palm, she brought her hand up in offering. I grasped her delicate fingers and dropped a featherlight kiss on her soft skin.

"Raven," I breathed. "You are the most beautiful woman to ever walk the earth. I'm in awe of you." Her blush was apparent even in the darkness. "Do you remember this spot? You probably don't since you were in the middle of your work-day, but it'll always be special to me."

Her voice came in a whisper. "I remember."

My heart skipped. "You remember seeing me here?"

"Of course, I do," she scoffed.

I beamed down at the gorgeous woman I would have on my arm for the evening. "Obviously, this might be a bit forward of me, considering everything that's already happened between us, but, may I?" I tilted my head toward her so she understood what I was asking.

She gave a slight nod, and I rested my hands on her perfect hips and ducked to take her mouth with mine. She tasted like heaven.

Like she was mine.

It was torture to pull away, but I wanted to make the reservation since we wouldn't be guaranteed a table if we missed it. She peered up at me with heavy-lidded eyes. "As much as I would like to have you for dinner, we're going to be late if we don't go now." I laughed.

"Why delay? We can go back to my apartment right now, and you can have me all night." She crossed her arms over her chest.

I groaned and turned away from her, biting my fist. After I did a few math equations in my head, I turned back to her. "You're going to have to stop talking that way, or I'm going to do exactly that, woman. You, in that dress, with that mouth? I'm already on edge as it is." I jerked her to me, pressing my groin against hers so she could feel me. She drew in a sharp breath.

"Be a good girl, and let me take you on a proper date, all right?" I growled in her ear. "Let me treat you how you deserve to be treated. I want nothing more than to take you back to your apartment and fuck you until you can't remember your name, but no matter how much of a slut you are for me in private, out here you're worth the entire world. Understand?"

Her chest heaved against mine as she bobbed her head in agreement, her voice absent at my words.

"Good."

Releasing her, I offered my arm. With a smile she took it, and we began walking the few blocks to the restaurant. A comfortable silence stretched between us, and I never wanted to lose the feeling.

As we strolled through the trees, Raven rested her hand on my elbow, drawing her body close to mine.

"How old are you, Ryan?" she asked.

I hoped my answer wouldn't be a deal breaker for her. "Twenty-five. You?"

"Thirty-two. Is that all right with you?" There was a hint of unease in her voice.

I lifted her hand for a kiss. "None of that matters to me, darling. As long as it doesn't matter to you."

"It doesn't. At first I was nervous, but it was silly." The sounds of the city enveloped us until Raven spoke again. "Tell me something about you that no one else knows," she purred as we stepped onto the sidewalk at an intersection.

I gazed down at her, and in the bright streetlamps, I could see that she had foregone her usual heavy eye makeup for a more subtle look. My pulse quickened at seeing her like this. It probably wasn't something she did often, but her feeling comfortable enough with me to venture outside her comfort zone made me long for her even more.

We crossed the street when the walk sign appeared. "That's not too difficult. I'm sort of a recluse so not a lot of people know much about me. You know more about me than most people."

She glanced over at me as we walked along in the mild breeze. "I'm interested to know even more," she murmured.

My stomach flipped, and I couldn't help the smile that

crept onto my face. I pondered my answer before continuing, deciding to leave the heavy stuff for later. "When we were texting the first night, I wasn't honest. You asked my favorite food, and I lied. It's not tacos, although they are second. Not a soul on the planet knows that my favorite food is actually Oreos."

Raven abruptly came to a halt on the sidewalk in front of a bank.

"There's no fucking way." She stared at me like I had just grown a second head.

I tilted my head. "What?"

She shook her head vigorously. "There's no way your favorite food is Oreos."

"And why not?" I said, reaching out my hand to her.

She slid her fingers into mine and we were moving once again.

"First of all, you made a culinary masterpiece with those muffins. I thought I was going to get off when I tasted them. They were pure fucking sin." She chuckled. "I've deduced you can at least bake if not also cook, so you have to have a more refined palette than Oreos."

I cocked an eyebrow in her direction. "People can like Oreos, and like more complex flavors, ma'am. Are you the gate-keeper on who's allowed to like junk food?"

This got a full-on laugh. "No, but still. Second point, Oreos are the favorites of five-year-olds. No adult who's had steak, pasta, or literally any food would think, 'Hmm, I'd like to eat an Oreo instead of all the other amazing things there are to eat in the world.'"

"Go ahead, keep telling me how ridiculous I am. I can take it." I winked.

Her next words were a whisper, and I could only make out "mine."

"What did you say?" I asked in confusion.

Raven sighed and turned to me. "How can Oreos be your favorite when they are also *my* favorite?" Her cheeks flushed at the confession.

I blinked at her, not believing my ears. "They're your favorite, too?" I asked incredulously. "There's no way that you, Ms. Proper Business Lady who probably eats lobster for dinner everyday, likes to eat Oreos at all, let alone prefer them to something like crème brûlée."

She scoffed and began walking again, this time leaving me behind. "Now who's gatekeeping," she muttered.

I hurried to catch up to her, sensing a shift in her mood. "Hey, Raven, wait. I didn't mean anything by that." Dread filled my chest at the thought of ruining the night for her. I couldn't fuck this up. Not now.

She glanced at me from the corner of her eye, her head barely turning as she matched her pace to mine, then gave a small laugh. "It's all right, I'm great. Now, where are you taking me?"

"RYAN, this is way too much. You didn't have to do all of this," Raven peered around the balcony, the glittering fairy lights glinting in her green eyes. "It must have cost a fortune to rent out the entire veranda." She turned to me, her eyes piercing. "This is the most expensive restaurant in the city. We could have easily ordered pizza at my apartment."

I stared at her, unsure why she was making a big deal about the gesture. Surely the men she was used to did things like this for her all the time. She knew I could afford it, so why was she being modest?

"Come on, babe, don't hurt my pride. I wanted to make an impression. It is our first date, after all." I winked.

Raven strode across the concrete like a dark angel coming to claim my soul. When she reached me she traced a finger over the collar of my shirt then down the lapel of my jacket. Her voice dropped an octave. "What about the impression you made when you pretended to interview at my office, and instead fucked me with your tongue on my conference room table until I screamed?" I sucked in air as she leaned in and brought her lips to my ear. Her breath was hot against my skin, and her filthy words were an electric current through my body. "Or what about the impression made when you broke into my apartment and slipped your chain around my neck and fucked my face? You didn't seem to be concerned with impressions then."

She smirked and stepped back, leaving me desperate for her. She was a vixen, and I wanted to chase her.

Regaining my composure, I smirked right back. "Maybe that was the intended impression."

I stepped forward and reached for her luscious hips, pulling her back to me. "Maybe..." I whispered into her hair, after her body crashed into mine. "Maybe I wanted to show you more of who I am and what I like. You might be a queen, but you're mine. I do what I want with things that are mine."

She gasped as I released her and moved toward the lone table. "Shall we?" I said, looking at her stunned form standing a few feet away. "I have many other plans for you tonight, so let's begin the finale to your day, darling."

CHAPTER
TWENTY-SEVEN

RAVEN

"I'll have the roast chicken breast with the sauteed vegetables," I said, closing the menu and placing it on the side of the table in front of the waiter.

Ryan looked up at me from the leather-bound list he held, his features curious. His eyes speared into me like I had ordered cow balls or something. The waiter cleared his throat.

"For you, sir?" he asked.

Ryan's gaze never left me as he flipped the menu closed and handed it to the waiter. "The Wagyu filet mignon. Medium. Grilled asparagus. Thank you."

My cheeks flushed as I looked up and gave the waiter a small smile. Ryan's gaze was still on me when I looked back to him, but it was more quizzical. He leaned back in his chair with his elbow resting on the arm, and his fingers framing his face. His posture was like a high-class billionaire trying to size up his competition and his delicious suit only added to the persona.

"You ordered one of the least expensive items on the menu. You fussed over the limo and restaurant. Why, Raven?"

A thousand excuses flashed through my mind as I looked down at my hands in my lap. He was observant. I needed something believable, but after a minute of trying to arrange the words in my head, I decided I didn't want to use a made-up excuse with him.

"It's heavy. You sure you want the nitty gritty of my past so soon?"

Ryan moved forward putting his forearms on the table and steepling his fingers. "Raven, I want all of you. Every detail of your past, good or bad. I want to know everything about you from the important to the mundane. Nothing is too soon for us."

He leaned back again and I downed the rest of my wine. Taking a deep breath, I told him about my childhood.

"I lived in poverty all my life. From the time I was born to the time I began working at my first firm." His jaw tightened like he was fighting to keep quiet, but I continued anyway. "I don't mean poor in the sense that we didn't have nice things. Sometimes the bills took all the money and we only had basic food to eat. There were weeks when I didn't have protein or vegetables; only bread and rice."

I looked away from his searing eyes out to the city beyond the terrace. The memories I tried to keep out flashed through my mind and the old hurt seeped into my bones. I took a deep breath, steadying my voice.

"It took a long time to get out of the hole once I was making good money with my career. I had college debt, but I also had my parents' debt. I decided when I graduated college and had a job waiting for me that I was going to help Mom and Dad, too. When I finally made it, I brought them with me." My voice cracked despite my efforts. "I had to become the best in the business so I could ensure I could support two households. My parents tried their best, and they loved me. Love didn't buy food, though."

I turned back to him. "So to answer your question, it's a habit. I still live a frugal lifestyle when it comes to food. I have a nice apartment, a nice car, and I've spent money on nice work clothes. I don't hesitate at buying other things I need or want —within reason—but food is different to me."

Ryan considered me for what seemed like an hour before he finally spoke. "Phenomenal," he said.

"What?"

"I said, you're phenomenal. I knew it already, but now I'm certain." One corner of his mouth twitched up in his half smile that I was beginning to be infatuated with. "I can't think of anyone else who is as mesmerizing as you. Although, I don't know that many people." He laughed.

I gave a tight smile and he reached for my hand over the table, giving it a squeeze. "Raven, what you're doing for your parents is amazing. Most people wouldn't. You continue to fascinate me the more I learn."

The waiter stopped by to pour more wine for me and water for Ryan as he released me. When we were alone again he said, "Tell me more about your childhood. Where did you grow up? Where did you go to high school?"

My stomach dropped. I knew it was a possibility that he would ask more about my former life once I brought it up. I couldn't tell him everything even though something deep inside pulled me to do exactly that, but I couldn't. Not now, or maybe ever, so it was best to steer clear of the subject until I came up with something to tell him.

I swirled the wine in my glass and changed the subject. "That's enough about my past. Why don't we hear about yours now?" I offered.

He shifted uncomfortably, the first sign I'd seen that there was more to him I didn't know. He was more than a hot voice and body that could send me into the clouds. I wanted to know everything about him, too.

"I promise it's boring."

I shifted my face to the serious demeanor I used at work. "I could listen to you read an instruction manual, and I wouldn't get bored. Your voice is what I want to listen to when I fall asleep at night and when I wake up in the morning. I didn't know I had an attraction to voices until you, but here we are... or maybe I just have a thing for *your* voice."

Ryan looked as though he was about to jump over the table and fuck me right there on the terrace. "That would be called a voice kink, darling."

My face heated. "Oh, there's a name for it. Well, at least I'm not the only person who has it." I broke into a smile, and my tone turned playful. "Come on, I want to know more about you. You know some of the gritty details of my life, so it's only fair you give me some, too."

He ran a hand through his hair and the movement made me want to replicate it with my own. I wanted to feel his silky strands flowing through my fingertips, but even more I wanted to hear the sounds he would make when I fisted my hand and pulled.

He finally looked back at me. "Fine," he sighed. "My childhood was opposite from yours. My parents...they are well off, and I had everything I wanted when I was a kid. Except their love."

My breath hitched, and I had the urge to go around the table and wrap him in my arms. "Why didn't they love you?" My voice was a whisper as I almost didn't want to know the answer. No reason was good enough for a parent to not love their child.

He fixed his gaze on me. "They never should have had children. They only care about their money and appearance. When I was old enough to contribute to that appearance, I wasn't the proper son they could parade around to their friends. I was barely average in school and just wanted to play video games in my spare time. I didn't want to play an instrument or sport." He sighed and looked away. "They couldn't exactly brag about my Call of Duty high score to their rich friends at society events."

My heart broke for him. A childhood without parents' love was unfathomable to me. My parents loved me more than anything, and I found myself wishing that little boy had what I had, even though my family had nothing but our love.

"Ryan," I breathed. "I'm so sorry you went through that. I guess things still aren't well with your parents?" I didn't want to pry, but I held out hope that maybe somehow he had mended the relationships. He quickly squashed that hope.

"Things only got worse as I got older. I'm not on speaking terms with them," he murmured before his voice grew louder. "I'm just thankful they didn't have any other children. I was enough of a disappointment that they wouldn't risk the chance of two failed attempts at a kid they couldn't make more money off of."

The conversation shifted when the waiter came up to the table and sat our plates in front of us before making sure we were settled and skittering off. The food smelled amazing, and I couldn't help the twinge of jealousy at Ryan's perfect-looking steak. My chicken also looked exceptional, and I couldn't wait to dig in. Ryan's gaze lingered as I took a bite.

"Oh fuck me, this is terrific," I said with my mouth full and completely forgetting my manners. I slapped my hand over my mouth as I finished chewing and began to apologize, but I burst out with laughter instead.

Ryan's fork was suspended halfway to his mouth and his

jaw was practically on the table. I stifled a giggle as his trance was broken, and he shook his head. "You continue to surprise me, Raven."

"What, are you used to dating women who shyly poke at their food and only take a few bites? There's nothing wrong with that, but a childhood of food insecurity makes a woman who eats." I took another bite, taking my time chewing as Ryan watched my every move. "I try to stay healthy and I lean toward cheaper options, but I eat to make sure my body is nourished. Even if it's difficult with work sometimes."

"Good. That's one less thing I have to worry about when it comes to you. I already worry about your safety, and that you work too much, but it's nice to know I don't have to worry about you skipping meals or anything. You're going to need all your strength when you're with me, babe."

My skin sparked as he continued through his steak, unfazed at what his words did to me. I had never met a man who could make me blush like Ryan. But then again, I hadn't ever met a man like him, period. He was acting proper through the meal, but his mouth was anything but proper. None of the men in my past would've ever spoken so freely and filthy. I loved it, but he didn't need to worry about me.

"I can take care of myself. I have for a long time."

The rest of the meal passed in companionable silence as we enjoyed our food. It was exceptional, which was to be expected from the most opulent restaurant in the city. Our conversation flowed easily afterward, and it was like we had known each other for years. Every now and then, I would catch Ryan's eyes fixed on me above his glass, and the way he looked at me made me feel like the most beautiful woman in the world, like I was the only one he could see. The lust was there, but something else pulled at me. I wasn't sure what it was, but it was more than just wanting to jump his bones, even though I definitely wanted that.

The realization that I hadn't thought about work the entire evening so far slammed into me. Work was always in the back of my mind, but tonight, I hadn't thought about it once, even after taking the day off. I looked into Ryan's eyes and it was that moment I knew he was different. This was different.

He pushed his plate away. "Dessert?" he asked.

I smirked. "I had something other than food in mind for dessert."

He laughed. "Isn't that supposed to be my cliché line?"

"Not if I get to it first." I winked.

"Well, in that case, let's get going, or else I might bend you over this table and make you scream so loud the whole city hears."

And with that, my panties were ruined.

｜｜｜｜｜｜｜｜｜｜｜｜｜｜｜｜｜｜｜｜｜｜

We walked to Ryan's car parked in the garage connected to my building, enjoying the crisp October chill as the sounds of the city played a song around us. The whir of the interstate in the distance, a steady rhythm for the melody of the engines driving on the street while sirens and the occasional horn were the bridge.

We rounded the corner of the foot entrance to the garage, and suddenly Ryan slammed his body into mine, crushing me into the wall of the stairwell. My back collided with the concrete, and I looked into Ryan's eyes in confusion. Gone was the nice guy that took me to a fancy restaurant and held open doors for me. The eyes staring back at me were the ones I looked into from my knees in my apartment last night. They were hungry, and I was dinner.

He grabbed the back of my neck with one hand and placed his other behind my head before crashing his lips to mine. My head hit the concrete from the impact of his mouth, but Ryan's hand cushioned the hit. He kissed me like the world was ending. Only when his hands began to rove my body did I remember we were in a public parking garage where anyone could walk by.

I shoved at his shoulders, and he reluctantly pulled back, coming to the same conclusion I had. He didn't bother to wait for the elevator, pulling me up the stairs and as soon as we hit the first landing, he was on me again. I was like a horny teenager, but it was freeing in a way I hadn't allowed myself to be in a long time.

When we finally managed to step from the stairwell, the familiar feeling of eyes watching me trickled down my spine. A moment of panic coursed through me. Why was I having the sensation of being watched when the person who had been watching me was beside me? I must have subconsciously associated the feeling with the garage since it was where I usually felt the eyes.

I shrugged off the unease as Ryan opened the passenger door, and I slid into his car. I watched him hurry around the front and into the driver's seat where he rested his forehead on the steering wheel. Worry tugged at me.

"Are you okay—"

I reached for him, but he grabbed my wrist in mid-air, catching me by surprise and halting my words.

"If you touch me right now we're not going to make it out of this garage," he growled without lifting his head.

I grinned as he let go and placed my hand in my lap. "Noted. Let's go. I'm losing my patience too."

He drew in a heavy breath before sitting upright and putting the car in drive. As we drove toward my apartment, my desires turned back to their usual pattern. The closer we got to my bed the more I had to hold my thighs together.

"I need to ask you something," I blurted before I could think better of it.

Ryan was stoic as he drove, seemingly somewhere other than in the car with me. He finally answered, "Sure."

His monotone made me question if I should proceed, but I had to know. I couldn't hold myself back any longer with him. "You know my limits. I want to know yours."

I held my breath as my words hung in the air of the car.

"When it comes to you, I don't have any aside from the far out there stuff. The ones you would have to search the pits of the internet to find."

I released the air from my lungs. "I think I know what you mean. Should we have safe words just in case?" I wanted to make sure we both had an out. "I'm...I'm not sure I'll be able to control myself with you."

He slanted a glance my way. "If you would like."

I hadn't ever been self-conscious in a discussion about sex before, but I was now. I stared at my hands in my lap, suddenly afraid I might go too far or somehow mess this up. Tonight, I decided I didn't just want a fling with Ryan.

"How about we make it simple and use 'limit'? If either of us feels like it's too much we say it without hesitation." Worry tinged my voice, and it was clear Ryan could hear it since he reached for my hand.

"I don't think I'll ever use it, but we have it just in case." He gave my hand a squeeze as he pulled into a parking spot at my apartment.

I sighed in relief, hoping I didn't turn out to be too much for him.

CHAPTER
TWENTY-EIGHT

RYAN

I WAS SO COOKED. With every new thing I learned about Raven, I was pulled in farther. She was a fucking black hole, and there's no escaping her. Not only was she a successful, badass businesswoman, but she also supported her parents. I could hardly keep my cool during dinner while she was talking about them and everything she was doing for them. 'Stick to the plan, Ryan,' was on a loop in my brain.

When I listened to the details she shared about her childhood, I wanted to break something. Rage coursed through me for what she'd been through, but Raven didn't need a raving lunatic at that moment. She was simply answering my question, which I had stupidly asked. I had no idea her experiences as a kid influenced her spending habits as an adult, which were not too dissimilar from mine.

Glad she was vulnerable with me, I still itched to learn why everything about her up until college was scrubbed from public records. Guilt nagged for having Rick look deeper into her past. I should've let her tell me on her own. But if there was a chance it would reveal who was following her, I would do it ten times over.

Raven was intoxicating, and the last few hours with her had tested me in ways I didn't think I would be tested. Being in her presence caused a myriad of emotions to run through my body, and as we took the elevator up to the top floor of the building to her apartment, I balled my fists at my sides so hard my knuckles were white. If I touched her, I wouldn't make it inside. I would've fucked her right there in the elevator and not given a damn who saw.

The elevator dinged, and I clenched my jaw as she fumbled with her keys. I couldn't hold back anymore. I yanked the keys from her hand and swiftly opened the lock. Before Raven knew what was happening, we were inside the foyer, and I was pushing her to the right toward the dining table. I jerked her handbag from her arm and tossed it to the floor. Claiming her mouth, I fumbled with my suit jacket buttons and wrenched it off my shoulders to follow the bag.

Raven reached her hands around to the back of her dress, and I broke the kiss to spin her to face the table. Placing my hand between her shoulder blades, I pushed her face down on the ebony wood. She gasped in surprise, and air hissed through her teeth as I yanked the zipper down her back, revealing the thinnest black lace bra and thong I'd ever seen. I was salivating at the spot where the zipper ended just above her ass at the small of her back. Good fucking god, I couldn't wait to see her without so much fucking material hiding her body from me.

"Up," I commanded, taking a step back.

She wasted no time hauling herself to stand while holding the dress in place. I gritted my teeth. She was doing that on purpose. "Take. It. Off," I snarled. "Now."

Her lips curled into a mischievous smile as she slid her arms out of the sleeves and let the dress fall.

My dick almost burst out of my pants at the sight of her. The lace was useless as I could see every inch of her body. My gaze trailed up from where the dress pooled on the ground, taking in her luscious thighs and hips that gave way to her perfect stomach. Her nipples were swollen to points and she sank her teeth into her bottom lip as my eyes drank in her body.

I stepped back to her, coaxing her lip free with my tongue. My hands wandered over her shoulders to her tits and I caressed the taut skin with my fingertips. She moaned into my mouth, and I dropped my hands to her round ass, desperate to squeeze it as hard as I could.

Pulling my mouth away, I peered down at her. She was the most gorgeous woman I had ever seen, and she was mine. She might not know it yet, but she was.

"Take off my clothes," I rasped.

Reaching for the buttons of my shirt, she carefully unbuttoned them. With each movement I ached, my whole body thrumming with feverish need for her. When she got to the buttons above my stomach I swatted her hands away and yanked the shirt over my head. Wrapping my fingers around her throat, I pulled her to me, my lips unable to go without her any longer.

"Ryan," she squeaked as I tightened my grip on her airway.

"What, baby?" I asked when she didn't continue. "Use your words."

She gasped, looking up at me with hooded eyes. I was so turned on by the effect my voice had on her. When I used my Zander voice, she melted like butter beneath my fingers.

"I...I need you," she panted.

Smirking, I dug my fingers into the side of her neck even harder. "Need me to what, baby?" I whispered.

She squeezed her eyes closed. "I need you to fuck me. Right. Fucking. Now," she said through tense jaws.

"My pleasure."

Flicking the clasp of her bra, I ripped it away from her perfect breasts, and moved my free hand down her stomach. Sliding into her panties and between her legs, I found exactly what I wanted. Another moan sounded from deep within her chest and jolted through me like lightning. "Take my cock out so I can sink into this perfect pussy that's already soaked for me."

Raven moved like the wind to my belt and wrenched the leather free from the buckle. She made quick work of the zipper, shoving my slacks and boxers down my thighs to the floor. Sitting back on her heels, she admired my hardness. She cautiously ran her hand over me all while she chewed her bottom lip. It was like I was a rare luxury and she was mesmerized at the sight of me.

I dropped my head back at her touch, a groan sounding in the quiet room. No other woman had made me feel like this, but Raven had me damn near exploding with just her fucking hand. I looked down at her, marveling at how a creature of this world could be so transcendental. She was a witch, and I was gladly under her fucking spell.

Unable to hold back, I pushed her hand away just as the pressure began to build at the base of my spine. The edging was torture, but I refused to come anywhere except inside her.

Dragging Raven up by her elbows, I led her down the hall to her bedroom. I wanted to bend her over the table and fuck her into oblivion, but the first time I pushed inside her was going to be in a bed where she would be comfortable. We weren't fucking teenagers, no matter how we were crazy for each other, and I didn't want her to be distracted by discomfort. She was going to focus on nothing except my cock stretching her so deliciously.

In her room, I whirled her in front of me and backed her up until her legs met the bed, pushing her down onto the soft mattress. I crawled over her, using my teeth to pull her panties down her thighs. When I moved back up her body, I drank in her mouth like I was dying of thirst. Realizing I had forgotten a very important item in my pants that were still in the dining room, I untangled my tongue from hers, and she whimpered when I pulled away.

"One second, babe. I'll be right back."

She dug her nails into my back, the bite of pain deliciously shooting through my skin. "No. I told you before," she panted. "We're good. Please fuck me, Ryan."

Fuck. The thought of pounding her bare unleashed an animal deep inside me. I searched her eyes. "Are you sure? I don't need—"

Her eyes bore into me. "If you don't shut the fuck up, I swear I'm going to tie your ass to the bed and take what I want," she threatened, her tone no longer playful.

My mouth dropped open at her outburst, and for a moment I had no response. The image of her riding me flitted through my mind and I silently promised she would be doing that before that night was over.

The corner of my mouth turned up into a smile. "You're so needy for my cock, aren't you, baby?" The fire left her as she nodded and crumpled beneath me.

I notched myself at her slick entrance and pushed in just an inch before slamming all the way to the hilt. She screamed at the invasion and wound her fingers into my hair as I pulled out painfully slowly. She felt fucking spectacular, her body fitting perfectly with mine. If there was a heaven, she was it.

My hips thrust hard before picking up my pace. I reached between our bodies and circled my thumb over her sensitive clit.

"Oh fuck, Ryan. Fuck."

Her moans and breaths were music to my ears. I lost myself in her words and cries, the sounds giving pure euphoria. Time didn't matter in the supernova of our connected bodies. "You're fucking perfect, Raven," I whispered into her hair. "So fucking perfect. You take my cock like it was made for you." I quickened my ministrations with my thumb as my orgasm began to build.

"I'm going to—" she groaned.

"Yes, baby, let it out. Let go with me."

Her face tensed with pleasure. "Keep talking."

I smiled, wondering how I got so lucky that my girl had a voice kink.

"That's it. Come on my cock. Grip me so tight with your sweet pussy that I can't help but unleash inside you."

I rocked my hips into her with an upward motion, searching for the spot that would send her over the edge. "You're mine, Raven. This pussy and all its orgasms belong to me now. Give it to me, baby. Give me all of you. I need your release more than fucking anything."

"Yes! Fuck, Ryan!" she screamed.

I didn't know if she was agreeing that she was mine or if she was lost in her lust, but it didn't matter. Raven was mine, either way. As her pussy fluttered and pulsed around my cock with her release, I spilled into her. All the pent-up emotion from the last month left my body, and I was lightheaded with ecstasy. I marked her with every last drop before sliding free and collapsing on the bed.

I pulled her close, a sudden wave of exhaustion crashing over me. The lack of sleep was finally becoming too much.

Raven nuzzled her face into my neck, and I breathed in her honey-scented hair.

"Are you tired?" I asked, fighting the sleep that was desperately clawing at me just like Raven had moments before.

"Yeah, but I need to go shower before I can sleep well. I can't go to bed with your cum dripping down my thighs." She giggled.

"You totally could, or I could clean you up with my tongue." I smirked.

"You look like you're about to crash," she threw back.

"All right," I said, propping up on an elbow. "Let's go shower."

She pushed me back down. "No, it's okay. You had a long night last night. I won't be long."

I started to protest, but she put a finger to my lips, which I promptly kissed and took into my mouth to suck. She pulled her hand away and crawled out of bed. When she disappeared into the ensuite I marveled at how she knew I needed sleep without me telling her. As sleep pulled me under, I let myself imagine my life like this all the time. Raven and I doing everyday things together, me having dinner waiting for her when she got home from the office, falling asleep with her in my arms. I let myself dream about that life because I wanted it to be my reality.

···||||·|·||||··||··|··||·|||·||||||·||·||·|··||·|||·

WHERE WAS I? I swam my way into consciousness, fighting through confusion. I felt like I had been hit by a truck and had slept for days. I couldn't remember what happened before I went to sleep. Finally, I wrenched one eye open and surveyed the room around me.

I wasn't in my apartment. This room was adorned in black.

My pulse raced at the unfamiliar surroundings, but then the events of the day came rushing back. I was at Raven's, and I'd fallen asleep while she showered. I glimpsed the clock on the nightstand and realized I had been asleep for a few hours.

The bed was cold around me. I tried to reach my arm out in search of Raven, but I couldn't move. I whipped my head up. What the fuck?

My wrists were cuffed to the bed. I pulled at the restraints, but they didn't budge. I looked at my feet, noting I was still naked, and they were cuffed, too. In my bleary state, I was disoriented, and panic tugged at me. I had no idea what was going on and my fight or flight response caused my heart to kick my ribs like it was trying to break free of my chest.

"Raven?" I called, trying to keep my voice even. The dark room was foreboding and I was alone. My thoughts traveled to the possibility that she had a stalker. Had they taken her and tied me up to delay me coming after her? How the fuck did I manage to sleep through being restrained to a fucking bed?

I pulled at the cuffs as hard as I could, but the wood didn't give. I tried to roll over and get better leverage, but my feet kept me from moving.

"Fuck!" I yelled out into the empty room.

Fear stabbed through me like a blunt knife. How the fuck did this happen? Raven was right here with me, and someone had taken her. I was right here and couldn't manage to protect her. Goddammit, I was a fucking idiot.

I kept pulling on the restraints when footsteps sounded out in the apartment. Were they still here? Maybe I still had a chance to get to her before whoever it was took her away from me. I tried working my wrist through the cuff, but it was too tight. My chest was going to burst if I didn't get the fuck out of there.

Movement in my periphery caught my attention, and I

stilled, looking to the door as it slowly swung open. A hooded figure clad in a long robe stepped over the threshold and I swallowed. Great, they were back to off me before they left with her. Too stunned to speak, I followed the person's movements as they glided to the bed and reached out a gloved hand.

The leather was strange on my skin as they trailed fingertips up my exposed body, from my hip, along my stomach, to my chest. My lungs heaved as I squeezed my eyes shut, recalling Raven's beautiful face. If I was going to die, I wanted her face to be the last thing I saw.

"Well, well, look what I caught in my snare. A new toy to play with," a sweet voice giggled.

My eyes shot open and my cock stirred at the voice I had come to crave, an entirely different feeling flooding my body, replacing the fear that filled me before. "Raven?"

"No. You'll call me queen. Ma'am and mistress are acceptable as well. You're not the only one who's multifaceted, my darling."

Taken aback, my mouth hung agape while I was laid out naked before her. What the hell was going on? Why was Raven dressed like that, and why the fuck had she tied me up? Reality slapped me in the face, and my cock began to swell.

I'd gotten it all wrong. Raven wasn't a submissive in bed. I assumed she, like a lot of other strong women, wanted to relinquish control in that vulnerable part of her life, but I couldn't have been farther from the truth. Raven might have played sub for me, and I didn't know her motivation behind that, but my sweet Raven was a domme. And I was cuffed to her bed, completely at her mercy. Fuck. This wasn't on my bingo card.

CHAPTER
TWENTY-NINE

RAVEN

Me in my element with Ryan cuffed to my bed? The hottest vision I'd ever laid eyes on. Moisture coated my thighs as I ran my glove up and down his stomach. Once he realized it was me in the shroud, he'd gone silent and completely still except for his heaving chest. My gaze was drawn to his hardening cock. Hope flared in me, and I implored him to not shut me down. If he did, though, I would accept it because I didn't want whatever this was to end.

"You remember the safe word, my prince?"

Ryan's eyes snapped back into focus on my faceless hood. He swallowed hard, his throat bobbing with the movement.

"If at any time you wish to stop, use the word, and I'll stop immediately."

I moved forward and cupped his face with my leather clad hand. His jaw clenched, and I sweetened my words. "No questions. If you don't want this, it's all right. I'm not going anywhere."

He closed his eyes, but when he opened them, they were

clear. "You're not going to tell me what's going to happen, are you?" he asked.

"No, darling. Not even a bit," I cooed. "I'm sure you can hazard a guess, but the surprise is the best part of this."

"Why didn't you tell me? Surely, that would have been something to discuss before restraining me to your bed?" It was more of a question than a statement.

I stood up to my full height, which neared six feet with my heels, and squeezed my fists at my sides to keep myself from punishing him for that. He was going to be a brat. "Questions later. Are you going to use the safe word? Make your decision now," I said through gritted teeth.

He didn't hesitate. "No."

I tilted my head, not unlike the way Ryan always did. "No, what? I need words, love."

His lips parted slightly at the endearment. I knew exactly what he was thinking, and I was thinking it, too, but I shoved that into a box to sort out later.

"No, I'm not using the safe word," he finally said.

Smiling beneath the hood, I reached my glove out to touch him again, running my fingers dangerously close to his hard cock. Ryan drew in a sharp breath that sent shivers all over my body. "Good. Now, usually your questions would have earned you a punishment, but I'm feeling generous so you get a pass." I snapped my head to look at his face. "But moving forward, you're to behave, understood?"

"Yes."

My hand shot out and fisted his hair, pulling slightly. "Yes, what?"

A groan escaped him at the sudden bite of pain, and satisfaction flooded me. My guy was a bit of a masochist after all. "Yes, ma'am."

"That's what I thought."

I untangled my fingers from his soft strands and stepped back from the bed so he had to crane his neck to see me. Slowly removing my hood, I fixed my eyes on Ryan, taking in my feast like a hungry tiger. He was glorious. His pale skin gleamed in the dim light from the window and I noticed a sheen of sweat on his chest despite the mild temperature in the room.

Sliding the gloves from my hands, I slowly unfastened the robe, letting it fall from my body to rest on the floor.

"Fuck me." Ryan groaned as his eyes roved over me.

My face was painted with heavy cat eyes, and much more makeup than I ever wore. A studded collar adorned my throat while leather straps with gleaming silver buckles crisscrossed my chest and back over a red bra covered in thin black lace.

I watched his gaze drop lower to the lace garter belt and matching thong before finally settling on the fishnet stockings and onyx pumps. He looked stunned, as if I was a goddess. None of the others had ever looked at me like that, and I reveled in his stare. I twirled for him and moved my body seductively, his moans telling me he was feeling exactly what I wanted him to feel.

After I sauntered back to the bed, I hoisted myself over him, settling my pussy on his stomach. I worked my hips as I flicked the clasp of my bra open and shrugged out of it, pulling it free from the chest straps and dropping it on the floor. Caressing my breasts, I put on a seductive show for him. Ryan watched longingly as I pushed them together and squeezed. My nipples were hard as rocks under my fingertips and my head fell back at the relief of my touch.

"Raven, please," Ryan choked.

My head snapped up. "Did I say you could speak?"

"N-no," he sputtered.

I brought my face within an inch of his and sweetened my voice. "Tsk tsk. You'll speak only when spoken to my pet,"

Digging my nails into his shoulder drew a whimper that made my core pulse. "I told you what you'll refer to me as tonight, like you always say to me. I get to have multiple names as well, darling. Understood?"

He nodded, and I relented, but not before dragging my nails over his collarbone.

"Ah, fuck," he said through gritted teeth. Bright red marks marred his perfect skin and I smirked.

"You're going to have difficulty listening to directions, aren't you, baby?" I reached around behind me and grabbed his hard length. "But you like the pain so you're going to keep speaking even when I say not to."

"Yes," he groaned.

Turning myself around to sit on him in reverse, I shoved my ass into his face as I spit on his cock and jerked him fiercely. As I pumped, he was a blundering mess of moans behind me, and when the muscles in his thighs tensed under my free hand, I stopped.

"Baby, uh, Mistress, please. Please don't stop."

I sat up with my ass still pressed into him, and my clothed pussy grinding into his chest. "I changed my mind. You can speak so long as you're begging. Fuck, I love hearing you beg."

Grinding my clit into him a few more times, I crawled over the side of the bed, edging myself just like I was edging him. I ran my fingers from his chest to his toes, and his head fell back on the pillow. Fuck he was so hot like this. Jumbled and disheveled, begging for me to let him come.

I crossed my arms underneath my breasts and watched him writhe as his eyes squeezed shut. He was much more into this than other men I'd played with, and it turned me on so much I almost threw the whole idea out the window and rode him right then. I had to be patient, though. I wanted this ever since the beginning and now he was finally mine to bend.

After his breathing slowed, I moved back to the bed and brushed his hair from his face. He looked at me like I was the only woman in the world with his heavy-lidded eyes, and something curled deep in my chest. "You're such a good boy for me," I said, caressing his cheek. "And good boys get rewarded just like good girls."

I climbed over his legs and went to work on his cock with my mouth. He was hard and smooth as I licked every inch of him. I could suck him for hours and never get tired of it. When I took him all the way into the back of my throat, a growl tore from his chest, and I cupped his balls. When he tensed I smiled around him before pulling my head back.

"Not yet, my prince."

He cried out at my retreat, the beautiful sound bounding out into the room. "Please, baby, please," he gasped.

"Uh, uh," I tsked.

Crawling up his body like a cat, I looked into his eyes and decided I wanted a little more pain. I dropped my mouth to his taut nipple and circled my tongue. He moaned, and I reached up to tease the other with my fingers. Just as he was enjoying the sensations, I pinched with my hand while bringing my teeth down, biting and pinching his sensitive nipples at the same time.

He bellowed at the lance of pain. "Goddammit!"

I soothed the hurt with my tongue over both peaks, giving a few extra licks to bring him back to pleasure. When I looked up, tears seeped over the sides of his face into his hair. I took his face in my hands.

"Are you all right, baby?" I asked, worry constricting in my chest. Had I been too much? "Use the safe word if I need to stop." My voice was laced with trepidation.

He looked at me with his beautiful brown eyes, his jaw a hard line. "No."

A smile curled my lips, as I bent down to lick the moisture away. Reaching up, I grabbed his wrists where the cuffs bit into his skin.

"I'm going to uncuff you, but you're going to do exactly what I say, yes?" I asked.

He nodded, and I flicked the cuffs open, rubbing his tender flesh. I moved off the bed and down to his feet, where I undid those cuffs, as well. He raised his head to look at me as I backed up, my body even with the far edge of the nightstand.

I snapped my fingers before resting my hands on my hips. "On your knees."

Ryan scrambled from the bed and knelt on the floor at my feet. He was flawless, and he naturally lowered his head instead of looking up at me. I let him stay like that as I took in the smooth curves of his shoulders and back, down over his firm ass. My mouth watered at the thought of taking a bite out of that ass.

Threading a hand through his hair, I pushed him lower to the floor. "Swear your loyalty to me, my prince."

He reached out to me, his hands hovering over my legs. "May I, ma'am?" he asked cautiously.

"Yes, you may."

He ran his hands agonizingly from my thighs to the tops of my heels, and my eyes fell closed at his touch.

"May I speak, mistress?"

"Fuck," I groaned. That voice was my undoing. "Yes," I hissed.

"I'm yours to command, my queen," he professed. "Any wish you can dream up would be my pleasure to fulfill. I'll kneel before you and do your bidding until my last breath."

Oh my fucking god. My eyes shot open, and I looked down at him just in time to see his lips drop a kiss on the top of my glossy black pumps. I was supposed to be the one in control here, but he had me almost dropping to my knees with him.

Steadying my breathing, I placed a finger under his chin and lifted his face upward to meet my gaze. He blinked up at me, waiting for instruction like the good sub he was. "Beg to taste me," I commanded.

He sucked in a breath. "Please let me taste your sweet pussy, mistress. I'll die if I don't right now."

I hoisted a leg up on the end table and pulled the thin fabric of my thong to the side, not caring if my heels scratched the wood. "Yes."

He dove into me, his fingers gouging into my ass as he drilled his tongue into my soaked cunt. I shrieked at his invasion, finally allowing myself to feel good, too, as I rode his face.

His mouth was everywhere, and when he focused on my clit, latching on with his lips, I almost lost it. I yanked his head back by his hair just before I fell over the edge. He was dripping with me, and I was captivated by the exquisite mess that he was.

I bent down and licked myself off him as he groaned into my mouth. "On your back," I demanded.

Ryan situated himself on the floor of the bedroom and I tore my thong down my legs. I squatted over him, his cock positioned at my entrance. "Hands up."

He lifted them to me and I grabbed his wrists, slamming them into the floor above his head as I sank down on his length. He groaned at the movement and finally being inside me. I admired the way the muscles in his chest were pulled rigid with his wrists secured by my hands.

I rolled my hips, our breaths becoming synchronous. His eyes were fixed on my bouncing tits as I picked up my pace and angled my body so his dick hit the perfect spot inside me that would shoot me into oblivion.

"Come with me, darling," I begged. "Fall with me."

"Fuck, fuck, Raven!" he whimpered.

He released inside me, coating my walls just as I crested and stars dotted my vision. I rode out my orgasm and collapsed on top of him, my pussy rippling with aftershocks.

We were a heaving jumble of tangled limbs on the floor and I was utterly spent, too tired to move.

"Now," Ryan mustered. "Time for me to take care of my queen. Your turn to be commanded."

I protested as he lifted me off his cock, pulling us both to our feet. "Shh," he said.

A squeal tore from me as he crouched and hoisted me onto his back like I was a monkey. "Put me down, I'm heavy."

He carried me to the bathroom. "Hush. I'm going to bathe us and then we're going to bed and not moving for at least twelve hours."

I stifled a giggle as he set me on the tile, pulling me to him and kissing me until I forgot everything except for him.

CHAPTER THIRTY

RYAN

A WARM GLOW of sunlight cascaded over the monochrome of the room. I hugged Raven tighter against my chest, my dick hard against her ass, and buried my face into her dark locks. Once we finally went to sleep the night before, I slept like the dead.

My hand caressed her stomach, back and forth, as I mentally recounted the events of the previous twelve hours. Being submissive wasn't something I ever thought about doing, but for Raven, I was quickly learning I would do anything. I would drag my dick through glass if she asked me to.

When I got used to the idea, I enjoyed it. Raven was a fucking goddess and I was hers to play with. It was hot, not only the sex, but surrendering to her was enthralling. I had never given someone complete control before and it was a release I didn't know I needed. I wondered if Raven felt the same way when I had been dominant with her. I doubted she had been submissive with many others if any and I made a note to ask.

My kisses down her back and shoulders combined with the

movement of my hand over her thighs stirred her awake. She stretched and pressed further back into me, eliciting a groan from my lungs.

"You had better stop moving your ass or I'm going to bend you over and spank it until it's red with my handprints."

She chuckled and rolled over to face me. "What if I tie you up again and spank yours instead?"

I kissed her mouth hard. "We'll discuss that fun topic later, *my queen.*"

"Fine. Until then I think I'd like some action with all this talking." She bit my lip playfully.

I reached between her legs and cupped her pussy. "Be careful what you wish for, baby," I threatened before hauling her up on all fours. "Ass up, and face in the pillow. Arch that pretty back for me while I have breakfast."

WE SAT down to my second breakfast of the day an hour later, and Raven groaned around her first bite before I could lift my fork.

"Good?" I asked.

"That's a dumb question, but I'll humor you. It's not just good, it's delightful." She hurried to take another bite of the hash I had made while she tried to help. "I might just take you hostage so you can be my live-in chef."

I chuckled. "If I'm going to be your chef, we need to stock your kitchen with more than the basics. Be thankful you had potatoes and eggs since there's no breakfast meat to be found in here." I gestured around the open kitchen with my fork. It was a dream to cook in. Raven had it equipped with fine appliances I assumed didn't get much use.

"You don't want chicken for breakfast?" she teased.

"No, I'll pass, but thank you for the offer. The only time chicken is good for breakfast is when it's deep fried, and as much as I'd like to see you covered in flour, I'll save that for another day."

"I wouldn't be covered in flour, you're the one who's the messy chef. I'm certain you would have the entire kitchen covered in it like you had potato peels everywhere."

I sent her a glare. "Cooking is an involved process. I can't be worried about cleaning up while I'm cooking. I have to focus on the food."

"Well, it's a good thing I'm great at cleaning up since I never learned much when it comes to cooking. Mom is the best chef, but when I was a kid, she had to make quick meals, and I always had my nose in a book." Her gaze drifted to a spot above my shoulder as she recalled her turbulent childhood. "I wasn't interested in anything other than books and music. When I moved out and went to college, she taught me the basics like baked chicken and vegetables. Enough to feed myself. Over the years, work never lent free time to devote to hobbies."

Silence stretched between us, and I wondered how her relationship with her parents survived everything they'd been through. I decided on what I thought was a safe question. "Do you see your parents often?"

She sighed. "No. I moved them here from the big city, but work keeps me from getting to the suburbs as much as I'd like. I try to see them at least once a month." She looked down at the table, and I could tell she wasn't happy with that. "I make sure they have everything they need, but I'm not a great daughter in other ways. I cancel on them all the time for work, and I know it bothers them. Especially Mom."

My heart squeezed. "I'm sure she understands," I said, trying to comfort her in some way.

Raven pushed the last bites of food around on the gray plate. "Yeah. She has all kinds of things she does in her little neighborhood, and Dad stays busy in his garage, but..." Her words died away as a tear escaped down her cheek.

My chair scraped the floor as I moved around the dining table to pull Raven into my arms. "You're a fantastic daughter and your parents know that. I'm sorry, I didn't mean to upset you."

She buried her face into my chest for a few moments. "It's all right," she said, looking up at me with clouded eyes. "I just wish I could see them more."

I kissed the top of her head. "Only you can decide what the solution is there, but in the meantime, the only tears *I* want to be responsible for are the ones running down your cheeks as I fuck your face."

She shoved me away with a push to my chest. "You're an ingrate." She laughed. "You don't think about anything else, do you?"

"Not since I heard your voice, no." I smirked. "You're not the only one with a voice kink."

She stilled, letting my words sink in. Her eyes gleamed, and it struck me that Raven might not have many things that were just for her. Maybe I could be just for her.

"Who said I have a voice kink?' she asked, sitting back down on the wooden chair, crossing her legs like the empress she was.

I leaned against the table, crossing my arms over my chest. "I did, '*Finigirl*'. Oh, and you also agreed last night."

Raven's jaw slackened, before her lips formed a hard line as she tried to suppress a laugh. "You know what, shut up." Her face turned curious. "Actually, you never told me how you figured it out. That I'm Finigirl."

"I might not be a professional stalker like the men in the

books I narrate, but I'm not too bad at figuring things out." I braced my arms on the side of her chair and leaned down until my face hovered over hers. "No one else has your emerald eyes. They were the first thing I noticed in your business photo, and when I saw your social media after you followed me, I would have known that shade of green anywhere."

She drew her bottom lip into her mouth, and the simple movement made me wild. She cocked her head. "Do you do this with all your followers and fans then? Do you stalk them and break into their homes, too?"

I could tell there was some sincerity to her question, so I reached my hand up to grip her throat. "Only if they're you," I rumbled as I dipped my head to capture that perfect lip she loved to bite.

She sighed into my mouth, subsiding her worries to me. When I broke the kiss she whimpered, and fuck me, if it was the last sound I heard before I died, I would die happy. I sat back down and turned my tone serious to quell her concerns.

"I don't talk to people personally unless it's regarding a job, and even then, it's all usually handled by my agent. In the beginning, I did everything myself, but now I don't have to. So I don't."

She tucked her hair behind her ear. "So why do you do it, then?" she asked. "Why do you do the paid stuff and social media posts, aside from the audiobooks?"

I sighed. I guessed we were going all the way there. My gut told me that it wouldn't make her run, but it was still early on. I knew Raven was understanding and open-minded, but I still had a nagging worry about being vulnerable.

Taking a deep breath, I launched into the story. "That's how it all started for me. Social media. Back in college, I dicked around with my friends, streaming ourselves playing video games online. People kept telling me that my voice was soothing, and then women started messaging me."

Raven's lips parted slightly, and the trepidation in my gut intensified, but I kept going. "I'm sure you can imagine the things they were saying. That my voice was attractive and such. One of them mentioned she would love to hear me say some lascivious things like her favorite book characters. I was single at the time with no desire for a serious relationship, so I came up with my pseudonym and made profiles on social media. The paid content came after I had a decent following. I learned I could make money off my voice, so why not? I didn't have much, so it made sense."

"Wait. I thought you said your parents were wealthy?" she asked.

I couldn't look her in the face while I told her, but it was a better alternative to what I thought I was going to have to tell her. Picking up the dishes, I walked back to the kitchen to clean up. Just as I thought she would be, Raven was close on my heels.

"I struggled with drinking and got kicked out of the Ivy League school my parents paid for because I never went to class. I moved back home, and they paid for a therapist to get me through that."

The cold water from the sink was grounding as I turned it on to rinse the dishes. When I opened the dishwasher, Raven came up beside me and took the plate from my hands, depositing it in the rack.

"So that's why you ordered water at the restaurant." She gave me a reassuring smile, and we set a routine of me rinsing and her placing it in the organizing rack.

"Like I said last night, my parents always wanted me to be their poster boy. Their only kid had to be one they could parade around in front of their friends and eventually take over Dad's Fortune 500 consulting company. Much to their dismay, I wasn't that kid."

She gave me a sideways glance and kept transferring the dishes I handed her. "Once I got sober, I told them I wasn't going to be that. I remember the night I broke." My gaze drifted, unseeing the gray backsplash as I was transported back in time. "Dad had been pushing me all week to talk about the company. That night at dinner, being his usual asshole self, he berated me for taking so long to overcome my addiction. The look on Mom's face when I yelled back at him is still clear as if it were yesterday. I hadn't ever raised my voice to either of them. When they talked at me, I just ignored them and went to my room. But this time, I couldn't hold back anymore."

Coming back to reality, I dried my hands on a dishtowel, watching the movement with intensity so I could avoid her eyes. "I packed my shit and left everything. I only had enough to get on a plane to a random city and get an apartment. So, I ended up here."

We stood like that for a moment, me at the sink and Raven leaning against the dishwasher. She probably thought I was a fucking idiot for leaving so much money behind when she couldn't even buy a damn book when she was a kid. She moved in my periphery and placed her hand on my arm. When I turned to her, there was nothing but compassion and understanding in her eyes.

When she took me into her arms, I breathed a sigh that felt like a release of all the emotions I still held on to about my so-called family.

The next thing she said surprised me since the conversation had completely gone down a different path. "So you did the voice acting just for money?"

My stomach dropped. I thought I'd gotten out of telling her by focusing on my parents.

"No, I didn't just do it for the money." I turned away, walking to the end of the island, running my hands through my hair before lacing my fingers together around the back of my neck. "I did it for the pleasure of it all, too," I murmured into the silence, my pounding heart the only sound in my ears.

"It began with the posts on social media, but then it grew to include the books," I continued. Throwing caution to the wind, I faced her. "I get off on it, Raven. Knowing people are turned on by my voice, it ignites something in me that nothing else ever has." I paused before adding, "Nothing until you."

She pursed her lips, looking away, and I waited for her to tell me to get the fuck out of her apartment.

When her eyes came back to mine, exasperation was etched into her face. I blew out a breath and closed my eyes, waiting for the last nail in the coffin. Fuck. I shouldn't have told her. I shouldn't—

Her voice drifted across the space separating us, but there were no undertones of anger or frustration. Just her usual perfect voice. "Ryan," she whispered. "I'm the last person to kink shame."

My eyes snapped open and she was looking at me with the same fire she usually had in her eyes. "For fuck's sake, I was turned on by you breaking in here and putting me on my knees." She gestured to the door. "The only thing that would've made it better was if you were wearing a Ghostface mask or something."

A growl tore from my throat, and I lunged at her, colliding my body into hers. She lost her balance, but I was there to catch her. Sighing relief into her mouth, I claimed her lips with passion, vulnerability, and something else altogether. She tasted like acceptance and understanding, and my tongue claimed every morsel she gave me. She hadn't run away when I told her the one thing I thought I could never tell anyone. One of the things that kept me from relationships because I knew I couldn't give it up. She didn't push me out or tell me to leave. She met me with her own ferociousness and depravity.

Finally breaking the kiss, I hauled her back to the bedroom where I showed her exactly how depraved I could be.

CHAPTER THIRTY-ONE

RAVEN

"ONLY one more week left up here!" I exclaimed to Joanne as I dropped off documents at reception to be mailed. "Are you excited to finally be the badass manager that's going to keep us all in line?"

Joanne looked up from her computer and her eyes sparkled with excitement. "What are you talking about? I keep you all in line already."

"You have a point." I chuckled. "Your second official task, should you choose to accept it, will be to get Cassie's new hire paperwork done and get her in the system."

Joanne swiveled her chair toward me and crossed her arms over her chest. "If I didn't already have the documents ready for Cassie to sign when she starts, I wouldn't be your office manager, now would I?"

"Someone is sassy today. I love it. Don't ever change."

With a wink, I turned toward the hall before Joanne said my name and I looked back.

Her face had morphed into concern, and she lowered her voice. "Are you going to talk to Mia?"

I sighed. "Yes, I'll talk to her this afternoon."

As I walked back to my office, I added that conversation to the long list of things I had to do before the end of the day and shook my head at the cliche of having an HR meeting on Friday. The week had been a whirlwind of catching up after my impromptu day off and subsequent weekend of debauchery with Ryan. I had gotten some work done from home, but nowhere near as much as usual, and it didn't help matters that he had crawled under my desk while I worked.

A smile crept onto my face at the memory as I sat down at my desk. He'd been skimming the script for his current job on the couch in my office while I ran numbers and reviewed files. I was in the middle of running checks when my chair was pulled backward.

"Hey! What are you doing?" I squealed.

Ryan smiled a wicked grin. "Nothing you don't want me to do, boss," he said before kneeling between my chair and the legs of the wood.

I watched with curiosity as he maneuvered himself into the small space and laughed at how funny he looked. If the desk wasn't a modern one without drawers he wouldn't have fit. Even so, he had to crouch to avoid banging his head.

My laughter died as he pulled the chair back into position with a swift jerk. "Lift your hips, baby."

I would do anything he said when he used the Zander voice on me. Gripping the arms of the chair, I lifted my ass off the seat as he pulled my leggings down my body.

"Get back to work, boss," he growled as he pushed my knees apart.

My computer dinged with an incoming email, and I was startled out of my daydream. I glanced at the clock in the taskbar. Fuck. I still had three hours before I could meet him.

Ryan spent the majority of the weekend at my apartment,

but we hadn't talked much since. I was buried under a mountain of accounts, and he neglected his own job to occupy the underside of my desk. He said he would have to pull some all-nighters to finish the book he was working on, and I admitted to myself it was probably for the better that we kept our distance. I still had a business to run, even if all I wanted to do was cuff him to my bed and never let him leave.

I was enamored with him. It turned out I liked to be both dominant and submissive, a true switch. I wasn't sure that would be the case with anyone else, but it was with him. Relinquishing control was easy since he always had my best interests in mind. Above all, he was safe, and I could finally let go.

An email notification with Mia's name flashed in the corner of my screen as I clicked back into my database. A pang of sympathy pierced my chest. Since she'd rushed out of the bar a few weeks ago, she had been more subdued than usual. More often than not, Mia always lit up the room.

This week was different all together. She had been in her office with the door closed all day, every day, and she hadn't said more than a few words to Joanne or me. A few times when I walked past her door, I thought I heard her crying softly. I assumed whatever was bothering her would probably pass, but as the week wore on, it was clear that it was serious, and I suspected it involved her boyfriend.

A few hours later I knocked on Mia's door and was met with silence that stretched longer than normal. "Mia?" I called.

Her voice was barely audible. "Come in."

I pushed open the door and was taken aback by folders scattered everywhere. "Whoa, what happened?"

Mia didn't look away from her computer. "I couldn't find a file. I had to go back through everything I did last month, and I haven't cleaned it up yet." Her voice was gruff, like she had been crying, but it was laced with anger and frustration that gave off a menacing aura.

Walking further into the room, I closed the door behind me with a click. "I'm sure you'll get to it when you can," I said as I perched on the arm of the chair opposite her desk. "Is everything all right?"

"It's fine. I got a head start on things for next week, and you'll have the reports by the end of the day on Monday."

I sucked in a breath. "Mia, you know that's not what I meant. I know work is fine. You are a killer at your job. What's going on? You have been distant and unlike yourself this week. Joanne and I have both noticed. We want to make sure you're okay."

She looked down at her fingers resting on the keyboard. "I'm sorry. I...I have issues going on at home. I won't let it interfere with my performance." She lowered her voice to the smallest whisper. "Please don't fire me."

My heart shattered for her even though I didn't know what she was dealing with. No one ever knew what others were going through deep down, and I knew that feeling all too well. I recognized the isolating behavior and the change in demeanor among the host of other indications. Standing, I moved across the small room to stand as close as I could with the desk between us.

"Mia, I'm not going to fire you. I just said you are the best at your job. Now, I'm going from boss to friend, okay? I don't know what's going on, and you don't have to tell me, but please know that I'm here for you. My door's always open regardless of whether it's about work or not." I flattened my palms on the hardwood next to her keyboard. "I've been through some shit, too. I may look put together, but we all struggle. It took a long time for me to get where I am and to be okay."

A lone tear slid down her cheek as she slowly moved her hand to cover mine. "Thank you," she whispered before pulling back.

I tapped the desk in quick succession before moving to the door. "All right, now let's close out the day right. I have a date to prepare for and you have a fucking mess to clean up, ma'am."

I looked back from the doorway, and her jaw had slackened. "Wait, a date? Raven!" she squealed, but with a wink I closed the door behind me.

꧁꧂

"I want to see your recording set up," I said to Ryan over breakfast the next morning.

He paused mid-chew. "Why?" His face had turned from playful to perplexed at my question. I wondered what made him think I wouldn't be interested in his craft.

We spent all night tangled in each other after I got home from the office, but we had done very little talking unless you counted all the coaxing each other to release. I was disappointed when he said he had to work and wouldn't be able to spend Saturday with me, so I tossed around ideas and finally landed on the perfect solution. One screen would work, and since I'd gotten enough done through the week, I didn't think I would fall too far behind.

I forked the last bite of my eggs into my mouth. Ryan decided to make a simple breakfast so he could leave quickly. "Reason number one is I want to see you work. For no other reason so I can drool from the sideline while I watch," I said casually. The fork clinked against my plate as I got up and moved behind Ryan's barstool.

I ran my hands over his shoulders and down his chest,

dropping a kiss to his neck and bringing my lips close to his ear. "Reason number two is that since you have to go record and can't play with me all day, I'm going to bring my laptop and come with you."

He reached up to grab my wrists. "Better watch it, baby. Keep saying things like that and I might fall in love."

I squealed in surprise as he whirled me around and into his lap. "Ryan! We're going to break the chair!"

He nestled his face into my neck, and his breath warmed my skin. "I'll buy you a new one," he purred as he ghosted kisses along my collarbone.

My giggles bounced off the kitchen cabinets and filled the open space with an unfamiliar brightness, something the dull walls hadn't seen before.

I kissed his cheek and set to clearing the dishes from the island. He didn't get up to help, instead just watched me as I worked. I stole glances at him, blushing every time I looked up and saw him still staring. His face was a mask of stillness, concealing any thoughts that were playing in his mind. As I finished the task, his mouth curled into a grin as he rose from the stool and caught me by the waist, pressing a kiss to my forehead.

"I'd be honored if you came with me, babe."

An hour later, we walked into Ryan's minimal apartment in the suburbs, and I smirked as soon as I took in the small, but open galley-style space. I wasn't surprised at the lack of decor as I looked around. Ryan was a typical bachelor in his twenties when it came to the furnishings. A tiny two-person table sat in the middle of the kitchen and beyond it, the living room boasted a couch, an end table, and a TV stand. I rolled my eyes at the monstrous gaming computer setup that took up the other half of the living room along the far wall.

I moved toward the desk, taking in every detail of the

room. "This is pretty impressive. I didn't know you were this serious about gaming." Running my fingers over the keys, I accidentally pressed one. The click was loud and caught me off guard. "Even a mechanical keyboard?"

Ryan glanced at me from where he dropped his keys on the ivory counter. "I've played most of my life. It was my escape when I was a kid. I had the best system, but when I moved here, I only had a basic PC. I bought that baby when my career took off. I haven't really bought much else"—he gestured around the room—"as you can see."

He leaned against the counter and crossed his arms over his chest, a position that sent currents of electricity through my body.

"You know there are people that can make the design choices for you if it's not something you want to deal with, right?" I joined him in the kitchen. "Most men don't care, but you have the money now, so why not?"

He studied me for longer than usual before sighing and pulling open the fridge. "I don't need nice things."

Realization hit me like a ton of bricks. My mouth fell open as Ryan handed me a bottle of water. The coldness trickled from my hand, up my arm, and settled in my chest. Fuck, I was so inconsiderate.

I dropped my voice to a whisper and my eyes to the floor because I was too embarrassed to look at him. "I'm sorry, I didn't think before I spoke. That was inconsiderate of me. It makes sense now why you haven't decorated."

A whoosh of air sounded beside me as Ryan came to rest his forehead on my shoulder. "It's alright. I still have shit to work through, but I'm getting there."

I sighed. "Having nice things won't make you like them, though." He squeezed me a bit tighter at that. "God, you must think me insufferable," I groaned.

Ryan lifted his head and tilted my face to his. "No. You're allowed to want expensive things. This is a me issue. Not you. You're perfect. It's not like you're out here living in a mansion with a butler and a chef on staff." He laughed. "Even if you were, I wouldn't care. You're you, and I like you the way you are."

My mood brightened, and my mouth turned mischievous. "Can I pay you to be my chef? The catch is, your uniform is an apron. *Only* an apron."

Ryan's laugh boomed, and I wanted to bathe in the sound. He pulled me into his arms. "You wouldn't have to pay me to be your naked chef."

With a kiss on my cheek he moved around me, walking backward toward a door to the left. The smirk on his face had me desperately hoping that was the door to his bedroom so I could taste it. Throwing him a wicked grin of my own, I followed him as he turned the knob and flicked on the lights.

My lewd thoughts were dashed but quickly replaced with curiosity as I stepped into Ryan's studio. A small sofa and table lined the wall, but the majority of the room was taken up by black room dividers.

"This is where the magic happens," Ryan said. "In the beginning, I only had curtains hung in here, but once things started taking off, I boxed in the space." He pulled back the cloth panel situated between the wall and the divider that served as the door and stepped through the small opening.

Inside the cramped studio, the walls were lined with foam and a long desk spanned the majority of the wall except for a small section in front of me. Ryan moved a chair back to stand in front of a laptop and other unfamiliar devices perched atop the beige wood to the left. I stepped forward and studied the microphone attached to a large metal stand that had various hinges.

"What's this for?" I asked, running a finger over the fabric of the circular attachment in front of the mic.

"That's a pop filter. It reduces the popping sounds that happen when you speak certain letters."

"That matters?" A hint of embarrassment heated my cheeks at my cluelessness.

"It does. It can cause the track to be choppy, and I personally find it very annoying when listening to audio that hasn't been recorded with one." Ryan moved to the mic stand and demonstrated how it moved. "I can adjust this so I can narrate while standing up or sitting down. If I'm sitting, I just put my laptop, which I read from, on the desk here or if I'm standing, I use the podium," he explained as he indicated a tall wooden platform to our right.

My gaze snagged on a small rectangular device with a ball of fluff attached to the end sitting on the desk. "What's that thing?"

"That's a handheld mic I use to record my social media content. I don't get into the whole setup for that stuff." His features turned seductive. "I also use it to record the little voice message you like so much."

I laughed, heat rising into my cheeks. "I haven't ever given much thought to what goes into narration. From the looks of all this stuff, it seems much more complex than I thought."

He chuckled and shifted his focus to a box with a bunch of knobs and dials. "You're right. It does require more than people think. I control everything with the audio interface here. This is the connection between the microphone and my computer. Volume, output, and a lot of other technical stuff here."

My lips parted at how knowledgeable he was. The tone of his voice as he talked showed it was more than just a job to him, whether he would admit that or not.

I listened intently as he continued. "I don't do a lot of final mastering anymore except for my social media content. All of my narration and voice over jobs are handled through my agent who gets everything finalized by a production company for the customers. I used to do it all, though. It takes a lot of time to master, and having a company do it frees me up for more raw recording."

Glancing at him sideways, I pretended to keep looking at the switches. "Do you think you will do this long term?"

The more time I spent with him, the more I wanted to know every detail of his life. I wanted to know his goals and plans, because I was drawn to him in a way that I couldn't explain. My soul yearned for his and I realized I was more than addicted. I wanted to meld our spirits until it was impossible to know where I ended and he began.

"I want to do it as long as I keep getting work. Aside from the pleasure aspect I get from it, I enjoy the flexibility with my schedule and the varied day to day. Every book and project are different."

Silence settled over us in the small space, and I wondered what else Ryan might want in the future. I decided long ago that I was fine being alone in life. My work was my spouse, but I wondered what something different might look like.

Ryan's job and kinks didn't bother me. I wasn't so anti-quated that I cared if he looked at other women or even got off to them. My apprehension stemmed from the fact that he might not want anything serious. Even after the short time I had known him, I knew in my gut this wasn't just going to be a fling for me. What was it going to be for him?

Ryan ran his hands through his hair and sighed, a bit of awkwardness creeping in the air. "I better get to it. Do you want to chill on the couch or in the living room?"

I shrugged off the weird feelings. "Can I watch at some

point? I want to see you work your voice sorcery that makes women come apart at your words."

"Sure. I do have to warn you though, you'll be bored in no time."

I grinned. "Oh, I highly doubt that, sir. I don't think bored is anything I'll ever be when I'm with you. Plus, how many people get to say they have watched their favorite narrator at work *in the flesh*?"

He laughed and pulled me into his arms. "And speaking of flesh..." I flicked my tongue across his cheek. "Yours tastes divine, and once you're finished working, I think I need a meal of Zander. Especially after his voice gets my pussy all worked up."

"Spoken like my sexy little voice slut." He bent his head to kiss me and whispered against my lips. "Maybe I'll find a sexy scene in my script to record while you watch. I want those panties ruined."

I nipped his lip with my teeth and pulled back. "Maybe I *should* work in the living room. Otherwise, neither of us will get anything done."

"You're not wrong." He chuckled. "Go set up out there, and I'll come get you when I get to a good scene."

With a peck on his cheek, I reluctantly trudged out of the room in search of my laptop.

AFTER THREE HOURS of not so efficient work, my curiosity got the better of me. I sat my laptop on the couch and crept to Ryan's studio. Turning the knob as quietly as possible, I slipped into the room. Ryan's voice was muffled from the foam, but it seemed like he was really into whatever scene he was working on. I moved to the makeshift curtain door and opened it wide enough for my ear to have no barrier from that intoxicating voice.

Time escaped me as I leaned against the wall, listening to Ryan work. It was as if I was in the story with him. I closed my eyes and let the scenes play out in my head, thankful this was dual style narration so I could hear the female's lines, too. Even Ryan's feminine voice did things to me.

My heart leapt when the story shifted, and his voice turned emotional. I listened as he declared his love to the female character and held my breath as he pleaded for her to love him back. A tear ran down my cheek, and I knew. I knew I wanted that same affection from him.

I brushed the tear away and pushed off the wall, padding back to the living room. Back on the sofa, I pulled my knees up to my chest and decided I was going to tell Ryan everything; I would lay my spirit bare for him to decide if I might be worthy of his love. If he could even love me at all after he saw the monster caged deep inside.

CHAPTER
THIRTY-TWO

RYAN

"Can I ask you something?" Raven asked as she nuzzled into my chest after I fucked her senseless all over my apartment when I was finished recording. I'd gotten to a sex scene in the script and I pulled her into the studio. What began as her listening, turned to hands exploring and before I knew it I was playing a game of trying to narrate with my fingers inside her.

I pulled her shoulders in tighter and wrapped my other arm around her back to cup her perfect heart-shaped ass. "You never have to ask permission to ask me something, baby. Ask away."

She blew out a breath. "We never really discussed the other night." She hesitated. "After our date."

"The one where you made me a whimpering mess?" I chuckled, my skin heating as I remembered kneeling at Raven's feet.

Raven groaned. "Yeah, that's the one."

I trailed mindless strokes up and down the small of her back. "What about it?"

Her voice turned to a whisper, suddenly unsure of herself. "Did you...did you like it?"

"The way I came for you wasn't an indication?" I moved my hand to tip her chin up to me. "Of course I did, baby. It was fucking hot."

The corners of her eyes pulled tight as she grinned. "Really? So you're into it?"

I nodded and she dropped a kiss on my chest. "In my opinion, BDSM looks different for everyone," she said. "Being a domme is my typical role with partners, but only in the bedroom. I don't always do it, either. Sometimes it's just sex, nothing too wild, but every so often it's something I need."

"Raven—"

"Shh, let me finish. I didn't want to tell you because I wanted the thrill of surprise. You said you didn't have many limits, and I made sure to designate a safe word first. I would never create an unsafe space for you."

I cut off her words with my lips, savoring every inch of her mouth. When I pulled away her eyes were clouded with need. I could have her again if I wanted.

"Listen, that wasn't something I've done before, and if I'm honest, I wasn't expecting it. I thought you might be more submissive because you're so dominant in every other facet, but I was wrong. Regardless of my experience, I would submit to you any time you wanted because I trust you." When I brushed the hair from her face, something shifted in my chest. "I like to be dominant too, though. I guess I like both. Is that okay with you?"

"The truth?" she said as she buried her face against my skin.

I kissed the top of her head. "Always the truth with me, baby."

She took a deep breath. "I haven't ever submitted to

anyone, either. Not like I did with you the first night. When I realized it was you and not him, I wanted to let go. I felt safe enough to let go. I'm sorry I cried after. Everything hit me at once, but like I told you before, I liked it. I like being both ways with you."

"Don't you ever fucking apologize for being emotional or vulnerable with me." I gripped her neck and forced her head back, staring into her eyes. "If someone can't handle you at your weakest, they don't deserve you at your strongest. I want all of you. Your tears, your smiles, your laughs, your whimpers." I chuckled, rubbing my nose against hers. The mood lifted and she smiled.

She settled back against me, the silence stretching between us. Her steady breaths on my chest was the only sound, a perfect white noise for just existing with her.

Suddenly, she spoke and snapped me out of my daze. "Do you like Halloween?"

"I don't dislike it. I'm indifferent, I guess. My parents never played up holidays so I don't have the same attraction to them as other people."

Her head snapped up. "Wait, are you saying you never went trick-or-treating as a kid?"

"Nope. I got into shit when I was in college on Halloween, but honestly, the day didn't matter. I got into shit most days when I was in college."

She raised up to sit beside me in the bed, the sheet falling away from her body. Her breasts were still red from my hands and mouth, and a nudge of satisfaction stirred between my legs despite the multiple times I'd already come for her.

"I'm devastated you didn't get to experience the best day of the year like a normal kid. I love everything about Halloween. From handing out candy at my parents' house to staying up late watching old slasher films." The tempo of her words increased with excitement. "Since I opened my office, I've always done a big, themed display the week before. The first year I did Frankenstein and built the monster himself..."

She was so fascinating with her animated rambling that I fell into a trance, her stories about her decorations drenching me like a rainstorm. Her lips moved quickly, and she gestured with her hands, and I lost the ability to speak. I was captivated by her, this beautiful creature that was enthralled by something so simple as Halloween decorations.

"Are you listening to me?" Raven snapped.

I reached for her, tugging her back down to my chest. "Of course. I would listen to you ramble all day, baby. Inject that shit into my veins," I said as I kissed her forehead.

She chuckled. "Sorry, I get excited about Halloween."

My laugh boomed off the walls. "You? My goth queen, excited over Halloween? Surely not."

"Hey!" she said as she nudged her knee into my thigh. "If you don't behave like a good peasant, the queen might not consider your company worthwhile any longer."

Before she could blink, I flipped her onto her back and hovered above her. Her squeal of surprise swelled my cock.

"Could a peasant coax a sound such as that one from a queen?" I lowered my head and nipped her bottom lip before pulling back. "I think not," I whispered and devoured her mouth thoroughly.

When I came up for air, she was heaving. "Even though I'm not well-versed in all things spooky, I can still think of a few things I'd like to do with you on All Hallows Eve. Maybe some hunting and masks would be ripe for the occasion."

Her pupils dilated, the emerald only a sliver around the black, and she fervently nodded. "Please," she whimpered.

I rolled back to the bed and cuddled her back into my side. "Your wish is my command, my love."

Her breath hitched, and my heart stopped. Fuck. I didn't mean to say that. Just then my phone rang on the nightstand, and I lunged for it, thankful someone decided to bail me out. "Aaron" was displayed on the screen.

"I need to take this, babe." I swung to the side of the bed, sliding my thumb to answer the call. "Hey, man. Give me a sec."

I put the phone on the nightstand while I slid into sweats. "All right. What's up?" I asked as I walked out of the room and closed the door behind me.

"I'm in the camera system. One of the employees clicked the link yesterday, and I hacked into the feed today. I'm gonna send a link to an app for you to download, then login credentials. You should be able to see and hear everything, in addition to controlling the rotation features."

"Thanks, Aaron, I owe you. Send me the costs, and I'll send the money."

"No sweat."

The phone beeped, signaling the end of the call, and I laid my phone on the counter. Trepidation hung in my chest. I was going to have to talk to Raven about what this thing between us was. I was attached, and if she didn't feel the same, it would be better to end it now. I was going to be hung up on her, regardless, but it would suck worse the longer this went on. Saying I was addicted to her was an understatement. Hell, I might not leave her alone even if she told me to.

The phone rang on the counter again, and "Dad" flashed on the screen. Fuck answering that. I wasn't going to be subject to whatever bullshit Dad had to say right now. He rarely called me, but it was a Saturday night, and he was likely too far into the whiskey. He always liked to berate me when he was three sheets to the wind when I was a kid. Every now and then over the years of being shunned, he would get drunk and call to tear into my ass.

I silenced the ringer and turned to the cabinet for a glass. The bedroom door creaked open and Raven stepped out, fully dressed.

"Hey, I'm going to head out. I've got to run to the grocery store on my way home, and I need to get some chores done before I go have lunch with Mom tomorrow."

My stomach dropped as she came to give me a hug and kissed me on the cheek. She hadn't mentioned meeting her mom. I assumed she would crash here tonight or we would go back to her place. Thoughts ran rampant through my mind. Had I spooked her with what I said? Was she running away because this was, in fact, just something casual to her?

I hurried around the counter and caught her arm as she was halfway to the door. "Raven, wait."

She turned, looking at me with her gemstone eyes and that was it. That was the moment I decided I was going to do whatever it took to keep her. Even if she didn't want a relationship, it was better than a life without her.

A lock of hair had fallen in her face so I reached up to brush it away, my fingers ghosting along her cheek. "Are you okay?"

Her green eyes bore into me like the winds of a cyclone. I held my breath, ice water sluicing down my spine and heart pounding in my chest.

"Raven, I...I didn't mean—"

She reached her hand up to cup my cheek, cutting my words short. "I'm fine, Ryan. Don't overthink, all right?"

I let out the breath, the hiss between my teeth filling the space between us.

"I'll text you later, and maybe we could have dinner tomorrow before another busy week?" she asked.

I ducked my head and sucked her bottom lip into my mouth in response. "Be safe, all right?"

She donned a wicked grin. "Don't worry. Anyone who fucks with me will have it coming to them. I bite back."

I brought my lips close to her ear and whispered, "Promise?"

THE APP FINISHED DOWNLOADING, and I tapped the blue magnifying glass icon. After entering the login details Aaron had sent me, two camera feeds filled the screen.

I couldn't quell my curiosity, and needed to test the cameras anyway, so as soon as Raven left, I downloaded the app. Tapping into each feed, I rotated the camera using the arrow controls and everything seemed to be responding adequately. The green night vision effect had an eerie feel to it, but both the outside of Raven's apartment door and her office were dark and undisturbed. There was also a feature that allowed me to go back in time since it seemed the cameras recorded instead of just being a live feed.

This was full send stalker mode, but was it actually stalking if the person I was watching had just been in my bed, and I was simply doing it to make sure she was safe? The question lingered in my mind, and now that I'd gotten to know Raven, guilt tugged at me for watching her. That guilt was dashed when she walked into the frame of the apartment camera.

As I watched her fumble with her keys and disappear inside, I suddenly didn't care what was wrong or right when it came to her. It didn't matter in the beginning when I craved her so badly I couldn't stop myself, and it didn't matter now that I was falling for her. The aching feeling in my chest when I thought about her was there from the beginning. Maybe it was an obsession at first, but it grew into something different. I knew from the moment I heard her voice that she was different.

I had to stop myself from grabbing my keys and driving to her apartment to tell her exactly that. She said not to overthink it earlier, but the fear of fucking this up lingered. I couldn't lose her, no matter how much I wanted to make sure she knew she was mine. I would give her the space and whatever time she needed, but she was fucking mine and had been all this time.

CHAPTER THIRTY-THREE

RAVEN

"All right, what's his name?" Mom asked over lunch the next day.

I blinked up at her, dumbfounded. "What do you mean? Whose name?"

She set her fork on her plate and dabbed her mouth with her napkin. "I know my daughter. You've met someone."

Chewing the bite of salad I'd just taken thoroughly, I contemplated the best answer. I swallowed, sighing at the inevitable vulnerability I came here for in the first place. "I never said there was someone"—I looked to the side of the sunny cafe patio—"but yeah, I have."

Mom knew when my flings turned into exclusive dating situations over the years, but I had never shared a lot of details. The main reason being I never got too deep into the feelings with any of them. With so much weight on her shoulders, I never wanted to place more worry on her.

When I looked back at her, there were a myriad of emotions in her eyes, concern being the most prominent. "Have you done your research?"

I looked down at my fingers fidgeting with the napkin in my lap. "I don't have to," I said, my breath hissing through my teeth. "He's my client."

Looking up through my lashes, I saw Mom lean back in her chair. "Oh, this is going to be good. Go on, give me the 411."

A laugh burst from my chest at her words. "Mom, no one says that anymore."

She scoffed. "Well, I don't keep up with all the new words the young people use. Now, spill the beans."

"You're my best friend, but you're also still my Mom, so you don't get everything," I chuckled. "I was initially worried about the client aspect, but I trust him. He offered to move his accounts to a different firm."

Her face morphed from playful to serious. "You don't think there could be any ethical repercussions?" she asked.

I shook my head. "I trust him. Plus, I've thought a lot about it, and I've decided to let Mia run lead on his file. I'm not going to be involved, and I'm going to make the CFP board aware of the situation. I can create a firewall if necessary."

"I trust you in your decisions, especially for your business. You're smart and will do the right thing, whatever that needs to be." Mom shifted from a look of seriousness to a playful one. "Now, tell me everything else! I want all the details about him. What's his name? How old is he? What does he do? If he's your client, then he's a businessman, right? Does he own a company?" Mom rambled when she was excited.

"Geez, Mom, slow down," I suggested. "I'll tell you *almost* everything."

She looked like she was going to come across the table and shake the words out of me if I didn't hurry up. I took a deep breath.

"No, he doesn't own his own company. He's a voice actor."

Mom's gasp rang out across the patio. "A voice actor? Please tell me you don't mean commercials."

Puzzled, I thought back over the conversations I had with Ryan. "I'm not sure if he's done commercials before, but that's not what he does for the most part."

A clap came next as Mom clasped her hands to her chest.

"What's gotten into you?" I asked.

She dropped her voice to a whisper. "Does he do those naughty books?"

"Mom!" I yelped. "What do you mean, naughty books? How do you know about those?"

"Oh, honey, I wasn't born yesterday," she scoffed. "You know we're more open with each other than that."

"I know that, and I also know you're aware those books exist, but how did you know about the audio?" I stopped in my tracks. "Mom, you haven't."

A blush crept over her cheeks. "Just because I'm older doesn't mean I'm boring, dear daughter."

"Touche. Well." I dropped my face into my hands. "Yes. He...does those."

"Hmm," she pondered. "I wonder if I know him."

I jerked my head up. "No. Absolutely not. You're not allowed to ever know his pseudonym. Ever."

"Oh come on, Raven. That's not fair, now is it?"

"It's more than fair. You get to know him by his real name, Ryan." I huffed.

"Fine. It's not like names matter to me anyway, now, do they?" It was more of a statement than a question.

"Regardless, there's something else." I sighed.

She cocked her head. "What would that be, then?"

Deep down, I knew Mom wouldn't judge me for who I dated or how I lived my life, but telling someone else about Ryan was challenging. I was afraid the excitement would drain from Mom's eyes when she learned about his age. She'd watched the aftermath of someone older taking advantage of a younger person all those years ago. Watching me go through the aftermath of assault was one of the hardest things she'd been through and I knew what it did to her. I would never take advantage of anyone, but I didn't want her to have any reservations.

"He's twenty-five."

"And? Why does that matter?"

I jerked my eyes to her face. "He's a lot younger than me. You don't think that's an issue?"

"If he wasn't a mature guy I know you wouldn't have given him a second look, honey," she said.

"Yeah, you're right, but after everything we went through, I just want to make the right decision, you know?"

Mom leaned forward and took my hands in hers. "Listen, Raven. I think you haven't let yourself get too comfortable with someone because of all the things you suffered. You've poured yourself into your career for the last decade, and I think it might be time to do some other things. I'm so proud of you for everything you've done for yourself and us. The firm is in a good spot. I know you like to work, but, honey, you're allowed to have a life outside of it."

I looked up at Mom with tears in my eyes. "I just don't want to mess anything up for us, Mom. You're right, I'm afraid of getting close to someone and getting hurt, but that's why I wanted to talk to you. I've realized I want to try with him, even though I've only known him for a short time."

"Well, if you already know that then why do you need my opinion? I'm sure he's wonderful. You deserve everything, Raven. You've given so much, and now it's time for you to take back from life."

My chest tightened with love and adoration for the woman

in front of me. She was my best friend and the reason I was the person I had become. Before I went to college, I ran to her when I needed advice or help. I took on more of a leadership role in the family once I began my career. Maybe it was time I let go and listened to her again.

I looked out at the quiet street beside the cafe. It wasn't just Mom. My heart was telling me the same thing she was.

"Fucking hell," I muttered, the sound fading quickly in the empty parking garage. I picked up the fallen Halloween decorations, trying to juggle them in my arms. I'd already made three trips to my office with various pumpkins, bags of cobwebs, and most importantly the foam panels for the grand display.

With the last of the supplies somewhat secure, I hit my key fob to lock the car and walked toward the building door. The sun had yet to peek over the horizon, so the only light was fluorescent. I took a few steps when a bang sounded on the other side of the garage in the stairwell.

I jumped, but then smirked when I assumed it was Ryan fucking with me. I hadn't mentioned his little spying on me in the garage and outside my apartment, but I knew it was him. Someday, I was going to be the one to spy on him and catch him in the act. Today wasn't that day though. I had way too much to do to worry about him and why he was up at the ass crack of dawn in my garage. Halloween was this week, so I needed to get the office decorated. I hurried toward the door with my bags and disappeared inside, putting together the list of tasks I needed to do that morning so my afternoon could be spent turning the office into a spooky wonderland. Too bad I couldn't leave it that way all year.

The afternoon came faster than I had hoped, but as I put together the foam board coffin I made, I couldn't quell the excitement in my stomach.

"Are you passing out candy this year?" I asked Joanne as she hung sticky synthetic cobwebs around the front of the reception desk.

"Of course. I get so much joy from all the little ones running around in their cute costumes. Their excitement is contagious, and the best part is when my grandbaby stops by. Are you going to your parents' like usual?"

Grabbing the glue gun, I ran a bead along the length of a panel. "Yep, I wouldn't miss it. Their neighborhood is perfect for trick-or-treating. My apartment building, not so much." I pressed the foam board to the sturdier cardboard I had cut for the back. I discovered I needed something that would be strong enough to keep the coffin upright when I was crafting everything at home.

"Shit. Mia, will you hold the other end of the panel? I don't think there's enough pressure to make it stick."

Mia rushed over and secured the other end of the foam to the cardboard. "This really is an epic idea, Raven. I'm not creative enough to come up with building a coffin like this. You really do love Halloween."

I laughed. "Yeah, it's my thing. This year I wanted to pull out all the stops. Dracula is my favorite classic novel. Contrary to popular belief, vamps were cool before Twilight."

Cassie snickered from the corner where she was adding the finishing touches on a table with red goblets and decanters of fake blood. "What, you don't like vampires that sparkle?" she asked.

"I actually liked Twilight when I was a teen. I was Team Edward all the way, but Count Dracula is, and always will be, the OG. If I were Mina Harker, I wouldn't want to be rescued." I stood up and grabbed the last piece of black foam board as laughs sounded throughout the room.

"I just know of Twilight from my mom," Cassie said.

I froze, the glue gun poised in mid-air. realization slamming into me. "Wow, I feel old now."

Joanne laughed and moved to sift through the remaining decorations. "You all are young enough to be my daughters. Who's really the old one?"

"Fair point." I sighed.

Our banter continued until all the decorations were hung. Once the coffin sat for an hour, the main attraction was ready to be put into place. Mia and I hauled it into an upright position and set it in the corner amongst two tables. The black lace tablecloths added the perfect touch to the various goblets and decanters of liquid I had dyed to look like blood sitting atop them.

After draping cobwebs in the corner of the coffin, I tacked purple fairy lights along the top of the inside. The coffin was as tall as I was, and as I dimmed the lights, Mia powered on the flickering candelabras. The room was transformed into a vampire's dungeon.

"It's perfect!" I said, clapping my hands and twirling in a circle. "Thank you all for helping. This is going to be a fun week."

My watch buzzed, signaling an incoming text. I plucked it from my pocket and saw a message from Ryan.

"How's the decorating going? I can't wait to fuck you senseless in Dracula's lair."

A blush crept over my cheeks, and I couldn't help smiling as I typed a response.

"That doesn't seem like a business text. You never smile when typing emails on your phone."

I jumped as Mia's voice sounded closer than I thought, and

I shielded my phone from her eyes, her expression morphing into one of suspicion.

"Raven! Are you texting a guy? Your cheeks are so red!"

I stammered, and Joanne smirked from behind the desk. "Uh oh. I thought I heard something before I left during the last day of interviews. When you were meeting with that young, handsome guy." She waggled her eyebrows, while Mia and Cassie gasped.

"Joanne!' I exclaimed. "That would be extremely unprofessional."

She crossed her arms, suspicion painting her features. I blew out a breath. "Fine. You all win. Yes, I'm texting a guy."

Mia looked like she was going to burst from excitement. "Is it the hot one? The one that I ran back to your office about? Oh my god, I would lick him from head to toe."

"Mia!" Joanne scolded.

I was used to Mia's bluntness, but the thought of Ryan with anyone else made my blood boil. Obviously, Mia wasn't serious, but the ping of jealousy confirmed how far I had fallen for him.

"All right, all right," I said, putting my hands in the air in surrender. "Yes, it's the guy from the interview, but..." My voice trailed off.

I hadn't decided until then I was going to tell them the full story, but since they were a part of my team they would likely find out in the future, anyway, so I bit the bullet.

"I have to come clean. That guy used a fake name for the interview. I already knew him, but I didn't know what he looked like. He was playing a prank on me."

"Did you meet him on a dating app?" Cassie chimed in.

I looked at my feet, a hint of shame settling over me. I knew they wouldn't judge, but I was still anxious. "No. That guy... he's our client. The voice actor, Ryan Mitchell.'

Mia squealed; Cassie looked confused; and Joanne's mouth fell open in shock.

"Wait. You have a thing with the voice actor?" Mia asked after she stopped the banshee noises.

I nodded my head as the reception area phone rang, giving me an out. Joanne hurried to answer it, but not before giving me a look that said she would be paying me a visit later.

I helped Mia and Cassie clean up, and five minutes after I sat back down at my desk, Joanne slipped into my office and closed the door. She dropped into a chair and studied me as I typed an email.

Once I finished, I swiveled toward her. "Go ahead. Scold me for fraternizing with a client." I looked down at the documents stacked neatly on my desk while I waited for her to tell me I was making a mistake.

Instead, she laughed. I jerked my head up in bewilderment.

"Raven, I'm not here to criticize. I've known you for years and I know you would never do anything to jeopardize this company. I know you have a plan for the situation, which I'm assuming is to let Mia handle his account and put a firewall in place."

I gaped at her. "How did you—"

Her lips pulled into a warm smile. "Honey, I know you. I also know that shit like this happens, and you aren't the first to sleep with a client. You are sleeping with him, right?"

Heat surged to my cheeks again, a frequent occurrence as of late. "Yes." My voice was so small I wondered if she heard me.

"Good," she replied.

"Good? What do you mean good?" I asked.

She sat forward in the chair and pierced me with her intense eyes. "You needed to get laid."

"You're not wrong." I laughed. "I was going to tell everyone once I established what the relationship looks like with him. At first it was just playing around, but now, I've fallen for him."

"Fallen for him as in you love him?"

I chewed on her words before nodding. I hadn't admitted it to myself, but hearing them aloud, there wasn't a doubt in my mind.

"It all happened quickly, but I do. It started when he contacted us to handle his assets a few months ago."

"I'm happy for you, dear. This is from a friend, not an employee. You deserve happiness in this part of life in addition to your successful career. It doesn't have to always be about work, you know."

I glanced out the windows to the city beyond where people were beginning their evening commutes, a sense of determination settling over me. "I'm starting to realize that. I haven't allowed myself anything else. After shitty experiences, I shifted my focus to college and my career, determined to give Mom and Dad everything they could ever want after what they got me through. I wasn't going to be a woman who fell and stayed down so I picked myself up and did whatever it took to have the future I wanted. Maybe it's time for something more."

Joanne stood, placing her hand on the doorknob. "I'm proud of you, Raven. You're one of the strongest people I know."

She slipped from the room, and I grabbed my phone, tapping the call button by Ryan's name.

CHAPTER
THIRTY-FOUR

RYAN

I walked out of the Halloween store with more nonsense than I thought I would end up with. Tonight was the night that I'd been looking forward to for weeks since Raven mentioned wanting to play on her favorite holiday. As usual, I procrastinated until the last minute, but luckily I found what I needed.

Halloween was a day I'd never paid much attention to. I ignored all the kids in my private school when I heard them talking about trick-or-treating for candy or dressing up in costumes. When I went to college, the only thing I cared about were the Halloween parties that gave me an excuse to drink the night away.

Raven's fascination with the spooky time of year was the cutest thing I'd ever seen. I wasn't surprised, since it was her whole vibe, but it was adorable nonetheless. I picked up a simple black Anubis mask, opting for something unique as opposed to the typical slasher villain masks. She had mentioned she liked those, but I wanted to do something different. Something she hadn't come across before.

As I settled into my car and pulled out of the parking lot,

my phone rang. Rick's name was displayed on the screen, and I quickly tapped the answer button on the steering wheel.

"Hey, Rick," I greeted. "Did you finally get the info?" I was beginning to think he had ghosted me.

Rick's flustered voice boomed through the car speakers. "Ryan. Ryan, I found everything." He sounded like he was trying to steady his rapid breathing. "There's things you don't know."

I slowed to a stop in an intersection, my pulse kicking into overdrive. "Slow down, what do you mean? Of course there are things I don't know about Raven. That's why I hired you."

After Raven told me briefly about her past, I assumed Rick would find that she had been assaulted, but I wanted to know more. I wanted to know who was still out there and a threat to her. I still felt guilty for hiring Rick at all. I should have let Raven tell me when she was ready, but I couldn't fathom something happening to her. Especially now.

Static came through the line like he was shifting the phone. "No, there are other things you don't know, Ryan. Things that could land me in danger. Not only because I found them, but because I'm telling you."

"What do you mean? Rick, what did you find?" Worry churned in my gut as I stared ahead at the red traffic light. Had Rick found her attacker? I picked my phone up from the cup holder and minimized the call to check the cameras while Rick continued.

"Your girl was attacked not long after she turned eighteen. Because of the severity of the case, they treated her as a minor, which is why I didn't find it before. The court records were sealed, but there's other reasons why there's no record of her before college that I don't have time to get into right now."

I released a breath as the light turned green. "I knew she was assaulted, but I didn't know she was so young."

My heart broke for her, yet I was astounded she had overcome the traumatic encounter at such a young age.

"That's not the worst of it, Ryan." Rick's voice had slowed to normal, but it was still dripping with trepidation. "I'm going to send you the court documents and everything else I found. You're going to see things in there that are going to change your life. I'm disappearing. You won't hear from me again, and neither will anyone else."

Confusion clouded my mind, as I sped toward my apartment, anxious to see what the files contained. "What do you mean? What could Raven have to do with you?"

"Nothing directly, but I have to protect myself. Once you see the file, I'm sure things are going to happen. I won't have any tie to me whatsoever with this," he pressed.

"Fine. I'll wire the rest of the money to you as soon as I get home." Frustration laced my words as anger overtook all other emotions. Anger at not getting the full story from Rick directly, anger that something was about to happen whether I wanted it to or not.

Rick's voice cut into my thoughts. "Don't worry about the money. I don't want another link to me."

"Whatever you want, dude."

"Ryan, one more thing," he added. "Be careful. Don't do anything rash after you see the file. You have to understand that there are people in the world who are so powerful they can get away with anything. Even murder."

The line went dead. What the actual fuck? Murder? What did murder have to do with this?

"Fuck!" I yelled into the car as I banged my fist on the steering wheel. A thousand thoughts raced through my brain. I tapped Raven's name on my phone, hovering over the call button. Hesitating, I decided I couldn't let her know I was upset. I had to be calm. Taking a few deep breaths, I steadied my voice and ringing filled the car speakers.

"This is a pleasant surprise." Her sweet but authoritative voice immediately stilled my nerves. She was okay.

"Hey, baby. How's work?"

"Hang on, let me shut my door." I heard her heels click across the tile of her office and my thoughts strayed to her bent over her desk in only those heels. I would lie down and let her walk all over me with those fucking heels.

"All right." I heard the door close and the squeak of leather as she sat down. "It's going okay. I'll admit, I'm a bit distracted." Her voice turned seductive and my cock stirred even with the other things on my mind. Raven had been so busy this week that I hadn't seen her since Sunday.

"Distracted? I wonder why?" I drawled.

She laughed. "You know exactly why. I would much rather be on my knees with you down my throat than analyzing stocks right now."

"Fuck, Raven," I said on a sigh. When that intelligent mouth turned feral I was instantly hard, not even thinking about what she could do with it.

I sighed. "Baby, I might not be able to wait until tonight if you keep talking like that. You'll have to send the ladies home so I can fuck you on every surface of that office."

Raven's sensual tone flowed through the speakers. "Ah ah, I have work to do. You're going to be a good boy and wait until tonight to claim your prize. I may be the hunted, but only when I say."

I groaned. "You're going to make me come in my pants in my fucking car. I've had blue balls all week, and now you're whipping out the good boy? That's so unfair, babe."

"When did I ever say I play fair, Mr. Mitchell?" I could see the smirk on her face.

"Fine. I cave. You win. I'm almost to my apartment, and I have activities to prepare for."

Her tone changed back to playful. "Victory! You really are the perfect man, letting me win all the time. I'm the luckiest lady in the world. I can't wait for what's in store tonight."

I pulled the car into a parking spot. "You're in for it, baby. I'll talk to you later."

"Bye, Ryan."

"Raven, wait." Apprehension was winding its way back into my chest after her distraction.

"Yeah?" she asked.

I sighed. "Please be careful, okay?"

"Always, babe. Bye."

The phone beeped, and I gathered the shopping bags, bounding out of my car and to my apartment. Once inside, I threw everything on the counter and raced to my computer. While it was booting up, I tapped my fingers on the desk.

Unease swirled in my gut at what I was about to see. Something wasn't right. Rick's call was so strange, and I wondered what I could see in these files that would change my life? Did Rick know how far I had fallen for Raven? Was there something that was going to change my mind about wanting to be with her?

I shook my head. No matter what was in the files, I was in this with her. I planned to tell her tonight that I wanted to be exclusive. I knew she wasn't seeing anyone else, and I was going to make sure she knew this was more to me than sex.

My email inbox loaded on the computer screen and the first message was from an unknown address. The message was blank except for an unfamiliar attachment. After navigating the encryption, the files began to download.

All too quickly and too slowly at the same time, the download completed. The file explorer window jumped on the screen, listing a dozen folders. I clicked into the first one and the first document was a police report.

Pushing away from the desk, I paced the living room. Once I saw this, there was no going back—no undoing once I read Raven's legal documents. Shame surged through me at the thought of the intrusion, but the part of me that was in love with her nagged that I had to do it. I had to see what was going on.

I stopped in my tracks. I loved her. I loved this powerful woman and I would do anything for her. I would stop at nothing to keep her safe. Fear slammed into me, and I knew, I just fucking knew that she was in danger.

I flew back to the computer and pulled up the police report. My heart stopped as I read the words in the boxes and the narrative below. Confusion clouded my brain and realization stabbed me right in the fucking heart. Staring back at me from the screen wasn't Raven's name. It was a name I didn't recognize, Leah Williams, and to my horror, typed halfway down the page, was Uncle Jeff's name in glaring letters.

CHAPTER THIRTY-FIVE

RAVEN

"What are you supposed to be?" I asked Dad as he strode into the living room of my parents' house. "You look like you're about to go to a hoedown."

He was dressed in a flannel button-down shirt and jeans with a cowboy hat on. His usual attire was cargo pants and a white T-shirt with a work shirt unbuttoned over the top. It was the typical uniform of a mechanic.

"Your mom dug this hat out of the closet and said I should be a bull rider. You know she always picks me something to wear on Halloween even though the candy is your thing."

Mom strode in from the kitchen in a straight black wig and abstractly patterned dress that swept the floor when she walked. "I always wanted to date a bull rider when I was growing up. They were so handsome. I couldn't get enough of them."

Dad rolled his eyes. "Alright, Cher. Maybe you should replace me with a bull rider all year instead of just on Halloween."

Mom threw a candy bar at him which he promptly reached

up and caught out of the air before it hit his head. "I'm sure you can ride better than any cowboy, dear."

"Oh gross, you two. Please stop. Pretend you still have to be PG around me even though I'm thirty-two."

Leaving them to their lewd conversation, I walked down the hall to the half bath to check that my costume was perfect. Trick-or-treating would begin soon. Closing the door, I looked in the mirror and wiped a smudge of eyeliner from underneath my eye. I'd laid it on thick that morning for work, and I was happy with how it had held up. I smoothed my hands down my long-sleeved black dress that was cut low. My black hair was draped down my back, not too dissimilar from mom's wig, and my lips were painted a deep crimson. I looked like a vampire Morticia Addams when I added my teeth. I walked back out into the living room with Mom and Dad just as the doorbell rang.

After two hours and three large bowls of candy, I fell on the couch. The visitors had been nonstop the entire time, and I was beat. I loved the kids, though. There were so many unique costumes, and even Dad had greeted a few. Mom handed me a plate with a slice of chocolate cake.

"I also wrapped up a piece for you to take to that new boyfriend of yours," Mom said. Dad immediately perked up.

"Mom!" I scolded just as Dad quirked an eyebrow in my direction.

"Boyfriend?" he asked as I buried my head in my hands.

"Mom, you have such a big mouth."

She scoffed. "Honey, after our lunch a few weeks ago, I figured it was safe to mention it. You seemed pretty smitten."

"Smitten?" Dad asked.

"I was going to tell him when I had the conversation with Ryan," I groaned.

Mom walked back into the kitchen for Dad's slice. "You

should get a move on it, dear," she said when she came back into the living room.

"Out with it, pumpkin," Dad said as he forked a bit of cake into his mouth. "Tell me all about him."

I gave Dad the basic rundown and waited for him to say something. I wasn't sure what his reaction would be since I hadn't mentioned many of the guys I'd dated.

"Pumpkin, you'll always be my little girl, and I will always want to protect you, but you deserve someone if that's something you want. I'm sure he's great."

Mom chimed in. "Can we meet him? I want to meet the man who's managed to warm my daughter's cold heart."

"Mom!" I gasped. "You are on it tonight. Dad, good luck with her." I stood and walked into the kitchen.

"I like it when she's feisty."

I made a gagging sound as their muffled laughter filtered into the kitchen behind me. As I rinsed my dishes, anticipation danced in my chest at the thought of my plans for the rest of the evening. I never let a man be in control in any fashion before Ryan. Needless to say, my fantasy of being fucked by a masked man on Halloween wasn't one I ever thought would come true. I didn't think I would be able to relinquish control in the moment because of my PTSD.

Ryan was different. I trusted him from the moment I knew he was the stranger playing with me. He would never harm me, and I was finally beginning to believe that my attacker wasn't ever going to find me again. I knew it was Ryan who watched me from the shadows, and a part of me was comforted by that. He was watching me because he cared.

I finished up in the kitchen and said goodbye to Mom and Dad. Checking my phone when I got into my car, there was still no text from Ryan. I wasn't expecting one, but I was hopeful he had some kind of taunting in store for me, or at least a spooky message. A hint of disappointment pricked at my chest as I drove to my office, where we'd already decided he would find me.

Pulling into the garage, my hair stood on end as soon as I got out of the car. Ryan was probably already watching me. I checked my watch and noticed it was still half an hour before he was supposed to be here. Maybe he was going to surprise me early.

The garage was dimmer than usual, a few of the fluorescent lights having burned out since that morning. As I walked to the door to the building, a huge raven landed on the concrete ledge and croaked, as if in warning. I tried to shake off the eerie feeling as I pulled open the heavy door.

This was part of the game. The thrill of Ryan showing up and claiming me. This feeling was supposed to be exciting, but as I unlocked the door and stepped into the vampiric reception area, I began to wonder if this was a good idea.

I walked to my office and dropped my bag onto the floor behind the desk. I usually put it in a drawer, but I decided to leave it within reach. Powering on my computer, I went through emails while I waited on Ryan. Even at eight-thirty on a weeknight with plans, I was still working. I couldn't turn it off.

The minutes ticked by. The time Ryan was supposed to arrive came and went. After half an hour passed, I shut everything down and reached for my phone to call him. The sound of the glass door out front opening and closing caught my attention as I hovered over the call button. My mouth pulled into a devious smile as my heart began to race.

Heavy footsteps grew closer, and as the handle to my office door turned, desire flooded between my thighs. The door swung open, and my arousal turned to terror.

"Hi, Raven—or should I say, Leah?"

CHAPTER
THIRTY-SIX

RYAN

The toilet flush reverberated in my ears after I threw up for the second time that afternoon. I leaned back from my knees and sat on the bathroom floor, pressing my cheek against the cool tile wall. I had only gotten through the police files. There were still more documents Rick had sent over, but after reading Raven's testimony of what happened, I ran for the bathroom, everything I'd eaten that day making a gruesome return.

Blood rushed in my ears as I hauled my ass off the floor and to the shower. Steam clouded the room after I turned on the water as hot as I could stand it. Maybe I could burn the images from my mind. Right before I stepped into the scalding water, I double checked the security camera feed. There had been nothing out of the ordinary in either location since I'd talked to Raven. At least she was safe.

The water sluiced down my back and loosened some of the tension in my shoulders. I focused on steadying my breaths as the horror of the words I'd read played back through my mind.

My uncle. Jeffrey Mitchell. The uncle that I thought died in a car crash when I was eleven had actually died at the hands of the woman I was in love with. The uncle who was the only person in my family who seemed to actually care about me as a child. The uncle I had missed ever since he died.

When I read the file I couldn't believe it. Couldn't believe that he tried to hurt Raven. He hid his demons better than Dad who didn't give a fuck who saw. And Raven. My Raven was confident and didn't take shit, but she was a killer?

Not that he didn't deserve it after what he tried to do to her, though.

My heart cracked further as I thought back to Raven's words all those years ago, transcribed and then sealed away and never read again. Except they had been read. By me. I didn't regret it, though. I ached for everything she had been through, and finding out it was at the hands of the one person I admired tore through my chest like fire.

The scent of cedar and vanilla filled the shower as I lathered my hair, my stomach still churning. Reading the recount of what happened painted the sequence of events perfectly in my mind. Raven's love of books must have also rendered her a storyteller. The words she told the police depicted the scene as though it were in a book, but was it the truth? The police didn't believe her. She wasn't arrested for a crime since she had bruises all over her body and didn't have a record. They had no evidence the murder was premeditated.

She said she'd been walking downtown in the large city I assumed she grew up in—the same one on her college application—when she was attacked. Two men, one of whom was Jeff, began following her, and once she turned onto a less populated street, they grabbed her.

She fought, though. She fought them with everything she had as the unknown man held her for my uncle. Just before the point of no return, Raven said she mustered every ounce of strength she had and kicked the guy restraining her in the balls. She lunged at Jeff, grabbing the knife she noticed at his belt. Before he knew what was happening, she buried the blade to the hilt in his chest. She said she didn't think twice before yanking it free and dragging the sharp edge across his throat, spraying my uncle's blood all over her body.

Realization dawned on me. That's why Raven carried a knife. She'd pulled a knife on me during the interview. At the time, I had been intrigued by it, but I had written it off as Raven just being careful. Alone in an office with a strange man would warrant having a weapon, but another thought nagged at me.

Why was Raven so quick to play with me while I was Zander? She should've blocked my number when I texted her since there was clearly someone still out there. If she was as scared as she acted, she wouldn't have entertained me at all.

Shaking the water from my hair, not knowing what to believe, I stepped from the shower and couldn't help but wonder about the second man. Was he someone I knew? He was with my uncle, so there was a possibility he ran in my father's circle.

As Jeff bled out on the street, the other man told Raven she would never sleep in comfort again, because he would always be watching and waiting for the perfect time to strike. Then he disappeared. She said she hadn't heard from him since, but in my gut I knew he was following her the night she thought it was me. I wouldn't be able to sleep until I knew who he was and made sure he never bothered her again.

I reached for my phone on the vanity and swiped it open to the camera app that was still pulled up. Everything was still fine, but I wasn't sure what I was going to do.

I didn't know if I could follow through with the Halloween plans. Telling Raven I knew what happened was the only viable option, but then I would inevitably have to tell her about Rick. I was under no assumption that if I told her she would stay, and would have a restraining order in place before I could blink. I wouldn't blame her. I'd invaded her privacy, but even when I hired Rick I knew I would stop at nothing to ensure she was safe.

That was before. Before I'd fallen for her and before I found out she killed Jeff. At first, I thought this would be a sex thing, but I quickly realized it was never going to be only that. I'd never planned to settle down with anyone in my life, but then Raven stepped all over those plans with her black stilettos. Now, she'd thrown a wrench into those plans too.

THE MINUTES TICKED BY. The time I was supposed to show up at Raven's office grew closer. Yet, I hadn't left the couch. After my shower I sat down and couldn't muster the strength or will to read the rest of the files Rick sent. I'd wasted hours staring at the camera feeds and rolling my thoughts around in my head, warring with myself over what I was going to do.

I watched Raven leave her office to go to her parents' to hand out candy, and nervously waited for her to return. I didn't text her. I couldn't trust myself to not spill everything as soon as I saw her name displayed on my phone screen. I told myself over and over that tonight was just like any other night. Raven had years of Halloweens since that night and nothing happened. Tonight was no different despite my newfound knowledge. She was fine.

I glanced back to the phone as Raven stepped into the camera's view at her office. I released a heavy breath, and my hands shook with relief at visible confirmation of her safety. Although, maybe she didn't need anyone else to protect her.

The phone vibrated in my hand as the camera feed disappeared, and the incoming call screen replaced it.

Mom was written above the answer and decline icons.

Panic tore through me. Mom hadn't called me in years. Why would she be calling now? I let the vibrations continue until the last minute when I finally decided to answer. I swiped the screen and tapped the speaker button.

"Hello?" I said in barely a whisper.

Silence stretched between the lines for a few seconds before Mom finally answered in a choked voice. "Ryan."

I immediately knew something was wrong. I hadn't heard her speak in that tone often. Unease washed over me at what was going to be the second hysterical call I'd gotten in one day. "Why are you calling? What's going on?"

"Ryan. It's your father. I'm so sorry," her voice cracked.

Did he finally die or something? I shook my head in disappointment at that being the first thought to run through my mind at her words. "What about him?"

"He..." A sob cut off her voice.

"Just tell me what's going on, Mom." I sighed.

She sniffled and drew in a breath. "Ryan, your father is on his way to you."

My stomach dropped. What the fuck?

"Why? What the hell does he want with me? He made it crystal clear that he wanted nothing to do with me years ago."

"I know. It's not anything good. I'm not involved in your father's private dealings, Ryan," she admitted. "I'm just his wife. It's my job to sit by the pool while he works and to look pretty on his arm at social events. I just wanted to warn you. He wasn't happy when he left this morning, and I've been sick with worry all day."

My blood boiled in my veins. "He left this morning, and you're just now telling me? It's eight o'clock at night. He's probably already here." Rage tinted my vision at her audacity. "Why bother, Mom? You never bothered when he hurt me before. Why the hell are you bothering to give me a head's up now? You don't give a fuck about me."

"Ryan, I'm scared!" she yelled. "It's no excuse, but I've always been terrified of your father. If he finds out I made this call, things won't be good for me. I acted how he told me to so I could protect you. As long as everything was smooth between him and me, he didn't really care what you did when you were a child."

The anger ebbed a fraction. "What do you mean?"

"I did what I had to do to make sure you weren't in his line of sight. That meant ignoring you myself. I hated it every day, and I wanted to die, but I kept going because of you. When you were struggling and came back from college, the help we gave you was because I begged and pleaded with your father until he gave in," she admitted. "When you got upset and left, there wasn't anything I could do to convince him to keep paying for your therapy. I tried. He forbade me to give you a cent or anything else because you were the one walking out on him. Not the other way around."

The guilt punched me in the stomach. "Mom..." My voice trailed off. I didn't have words. My brain wasn't processing what I was hearing.

"You don't have to say anything, Ryan. I don't even care if you hate me for it. I did what I had to. You're successful, and I'm proud of you. That doesn't matter right now, though. I have no idea what he's going to do. He got a call this morning and lost it. He wouldn't go into any detail with me, but I overheard him say something about coming to find you."

Mom started to cry again, and the desire to comfort her overwhelmed me. "Mom, it's all right. I'll be fine. I can protect myself from him. You don't have to worry about me. You just need to be safe yourself, all right?"

"Okay. I'm so sorry. I'm sorry for everything."

"We will talk about it later, maybe. Right now, I've got some other stuff going on. I've gotta go, but I'll call you when I can."

Her agreement came in a whisper. "And Mom, call me if he does something to you."

She assured me she would, and I ended the call. I was almost half an hour late to meet Raven. I jumped up from the couch and tapped into the security feed as I grabbed my keys.

I stopped short of the doorknob, the keys clanging to the floor. My heart skipped as I stared at the phone screen. "Fuck!" I yelled to the empty apartment, loud enough to be heard outside in the parking lot.

I watched in horror as a man walked into the camera's view and went right into Raven's office.

CHAPTER
THIRTY-SEVEN

RAVEN

The hairs on the back of my neck stood on end, and my blood ran cold. That voice knew my former name. The name that had haunted my dreams for over a decade. No one knew me by that name except my parents—and him.

When he stepped through the doorway, my stomach dropped even further. Blue eyes glared at me from beneath perfect dusty blonde hair. He was the man I'd run into on the street last month. He looked familiar then, too, and I realized I had been glimpsing him for months. I never thought anything out of the ordinary, but the truth hit me like a ton of bricks. Ryan hadn't been the one following me. It was him, my initial fears confirmed.

He looked around my office. "You have been a busy woman since the last time we properly spoke. From a scared little girl to a successful entrepreneur. I'm impressed."

I was frozen in my chair, my mind replaying how it felt as he held me underneath my arms against a brick building while his friend touched my body. I kept my face composed, as badly as I wanted to vomit.

"You do know who I am, don't you?" he asked, his eyes fixed on my face.

I didn't answer. I needed to be calculated with my words and try to delay and distract until I knew how to get out of this mess.

"Now, Leah, you know I'm the one that got away," he scoffed. His large frame shifted and he moved to sit in one of the chairs opposite my desk. He placed one ankle on a knee, his expensive shoes shining in the fluorescent light. "I told you I'd be watching, didn't I?"

Years of training my mind slid away. My rage and fear were replaced with the calmness I'd had in the aftermath of killing his buddy. I'd worked tirelessly to tamp down the monster lurking inside me that took pleasure in what I had done, but now, I let her roam free.

I laughed, the sound indifferent and deep, filling the room. "Yeah, watching your friend die at my hands must have really traumatized you. I assumed you would have shown up long before now." I leaned back in my chair into a relaxed position. "Did you finally work through your issues in therapy, or did it just take fourteen years for you to finally grow some balls and come back for me?"

His mouth crept into a sadistic smile. "She's still a cunt bitch, I see." His laugh clanged through my bones. "Lovely, my dear."

"You surely didn't think I was going to be a cowering mess in the corner waiting for you to show up again, right?" I jeered as I gestured around the room. "Look at what I've built. I should actually be thanking you and your homeboy. You lit a fire under my ass. Thank you for that."

His smile faltered the tiniest bit, almost as if I imagined it before it was back in place. "Speaking of thanking each other, I should be thanking you." He leaned to his right, resting his elbow on the chair. "I was angry at first. Angry that you killed my only brother. Then, as the years went by, I understood you did me a favor. I would've had to kill him eventually, anyway, to take over my family's company. So, actually, thank you, Leah. You took that burden from me, and I'm forever grateful."

A maniacal cackle tore from my chest. "I killed your brother? Oh, even fucking better. I'm honored, truly."

"He always was a hotheaded imbecile." The man looked so relaxed, like this was a friendly business conversation. "He saw you somewhere while visiting one of our offices and decided he wanted you. Admittedly, I was an idiot for entertaining him, especially while I was so...inebriated."

I listened, the new information coating the back of my throat with ash.

"I was pretty reckless back then. The run-in with you wasn't the only time I'd escaped death, or worse, prison." His eyes had been wandering, but now they rested back on me. "If you have enough money, though, anything is on the table."

Venom coated my words. "I didn't need money to over-power you and slit your brother's throat, did I?"

He laughed. "See, that's my point. If I hadn't listened to my fool brother, you wouldn't have gotten away from me, girl. I was so drunk and high from the purest drugs and top shelf alcohol I could barely stand, and that's the only reason you stood a chance against me."

He sat up straight, steepled his hands in front of his chest, and flashed the brightest smile I'd ever seen, searing straight through me with his cold blue eyes. "But you know what? I'm not high right now, Leah."

Every time he said my birth name, chills slid down my spine.

He looked around the room as if he were pondering his

next words. I saw the moment he landed on what he was going to say next as he flicked his gaze back to me before standing.

"You know, I almost left you alone," he said as he stalked to my desk and dragged his fingers over the glass surface. "All these years passed and while I always kept an eye on you, even in person sometimes, the anger had left me. Like I said, I was thankful for you taking care of a future problem I didn't realize I would need to deal with at the time."

He walked around my desk so slowly I had to fight to keep my body in my chair as I tracked his movements and swiveled my chair as he went. He stopped at the side and put his hands in his pockets.

"Then something interesting happened. Something I wasn't expecting that enraged me all over again."

I crossed my arms over my chest, the desk no longer a barrier between us. "Let me guess, the big bad wolf got pissed when I decided to pave my own path with my firm. When I decided to make a name for myself in the town I fled to because of you."

His laugh boomed throughout the room. "Leah, you're still that naive little girl you were back then. You have no idea what you had in your grasp. It's a shame, honestly. For any other man, it would've been the ultimate reverse card for you if you had known. I'm not most men though."

The monster in my chest stopped pacing and glared at him. I regretted not wearing my knife on me like usual, but if I was quick enough, I could snatch it from my purse on the ground at my feet.

The man, whose name I still didn't know, walked closer. He brushed the hair off my shoulder, his fingers trailing the exposed skin at my collarbone. I held my breath as the monster screeched.

The air moved as he brought his lips to my ear. "How does

it feel when my son is this close to you? How does it feel when he hunts you and watches you just like his father? How does it feel when he fucks you, Leah?"

My body went numb, and my brain emptied. Every ounce of feeling and humanity left within my body drained away. Raven no longer existed. The monster within took over, and I thought of nothing except the years of pain I suffered at the hands of others. I shed my skin like a snake and replaced it with unadulterated malice.

He chuckled, his voice rumbling off my neck, the derisive tone from before replaced with ire. "I'm going to show you how a real man fucks, Leah. How a savage plays with his food before he devours it, before he rips it to shreds beneath his teeth. You aren't escaping this time, bitch. When I'm done with you, not a trace of your body will remain. The legendary Raven Lovelace, disappearing without a trace."

A crash boomed at the front door, and the man whipped a knife to my throat. Glass shattered, and Ryan's voice roared through the office. "Raven!"

He thundered down the hall and froze when he reached the doorway, taking in the scene before him. Utter shock fixed his features, but the monster didn't care.

"Oh, son, how nice of you to join us." The man's voice grew mocking again. "I was just asking Leah what it felt like to be stalked by the son of the very man who's been her shadow for years."

CHAPTER THIRTY-EIGHT

RYAN

Disbelief stunned me as I saw my father with a knife to Raven's throat. Confusion swirled in my mind as he looked at me expectantly.

"Well?" he asked.

I shook my head as I stepped farther into the room, trying to steady my thoughts and I realized he had asked a question. My voice was unsteady when I spoke. "Wh-what?"

He sighed in annoyance. "Ever the disappointment. I asked if you wanted to watch what I'm going to do to your little girl-friend here. I don't mind an audience. I might even let you take a turn before I snap her neck."

Bile rose in the back of my throat, and nausea almost took me to my knees. I couldn't think, couldn't move, couldn't breathe. I was rooted to the spot, my mind unable to figure out what was happening or what to do.

Dad stood to his full height and twirled the knife in his hand. Raven flinched away, her hand shooting to the spot where the knife had been. Dad began pacing around the room.

"Actually, I changed my mind. You, my darling girl," his

gaze slid to Raven, "You're going to do me another favor. Just like all those years ago. You," a hysterical laugh tore from his throat, "are going to take care of this worthless piece of shit my wife birthed. He was next after I finished with you, anyway."

Another favor? All those years ago? My brain wasn't computing what he meant, then everything clicked. Dad was the other man. He was the one who got away after holding Raven for my uncle to rape her, and now he was back to get his revenge.

Raven finally looked at me. Her eyes were hard and nothing like I'd ever seen before. She showed no ounce of fear, and my heart kicked my ribs. Her eyes told me I wasn't leaving this office. Not with her or any other way. The only thing I could do was try to stall the inevitable.

"What do you mean, favor?" I whispered.

Dad rolled his eyes. "You're so goddamn slow. Always have been. Such a little pain in my ass. I wish I'd gotten rid of you when you were a kid." He twirled the knife in his hand. "All those years ago, your little girlfriend here killed your uncle. Your own flesh and blood. You already knew that though, didn't you? Our pal Rick has been busy uncovering everything I worked so hard to hide."

The gears started turning, and everything began to make sense.

"I was going to kill Jeff eventually. I just hadn't realized it yet. Our girl went ahead and took care of it for me. A little earlier than necessary, but it likely saved me a hell of a lot of trouble."

I looked back to Raven, and her face was stone as she listened to Dad ramble. I didn't care what happened to me as long as she was safe. She was telling the truth to the police and my grief for Jeff was replaced with acceptance. I resolved to do whatever I had to for her to get out of here. Even if that meant giving my life for her. Without her, life wasn't worth shit, anyway.

Dad moved to stand behind her chair. "Are you angry with him, Leah? You've killed before. Want to do it again? It would be quite poetic to inflict your wrath on him, wouldn't it? Your last act of vengeance."

He placed a hand on the chair back and made a show of flipping the knife in the air and catching it by the blade, holding the handle in front of Raven's chest. She stared at it for what seemed like an hour before wrapping her black-tipped fingers around the hilt.

"Go on, darling. Do as you wish. I'm in no hurry. I've got all night," he said, urging her to stand as he moved to the side of the room. Almost like a referee in a cage match. "It's not like his intentions with you were pure, anyway. After all, he did hire a private investigator to find every detail about the past you wanted kept hidden. That's why you changed your name after all, isn't it?"

Raven's face transformed into a mask of anger, her lips pursing into a thin line.

"He is my son though, no matter how unfortunate. I'm sure I transferred some of my deviant ways when I pumped his mother full of the seed that created him."

I bit the inside of my cheek to keep from lunging at him, to stop him from spewing lies and bullshit that was making her hate me. Finally, I spoke in the steadiest voice I could muster. "Raven. Listen to me. I need you to understand—"

My words were cut off as Raven shot from her chair and charged around the desk, the force of her body crashing mine into the wall. Her free arm came up and she pressed her forearm into my throat. Her face was rage, and I knew she was going to release her wrath on me and everything else in her way. She was smart, but I hoped she could outsmart Dad and get away.

She looked at me with those dead eyes as the minutes ticked by. When she spoke, her voice was a low rasp, a sound that penetrated my chest and wrapped my heart in a vise. "You don't get to speak. I trusted you, and you betrayed me," she spat.

I didn't move, my heart breaking into a thousand pieces.

"You're his son. I let my guard down once. For one person, and it was for my attacker's fucking son? I bet your pathetic sob story about your childhood was all a ruse to make me care for you, wasn't it?" She was shaking with rage, and I knew it was a matter of time before the blade in her hand sliced across my throat.

I willed my eyes to tell her none of this was true. None of the things she was saying were what I intended. I willed them to show the love I had for her, even now as she was about to snuff the life from my body.

"You think you're big shit, don't you, motherfucker?" Her voice turned mocking. "Oh, what if I make the girl my father went after years ago fall for me? Wouldn't that be the ultimate fuck you to him? Well, guess what?" She brought her face within an inch of mine. "I'm no fucking girl, and I'm no fucking game."

She flicked her eyes to my father where he stood watching then brought the knife to my throat. A tear slid out of the corner of my eye. I couldn't go without saying it. Saying those words that had been in my heart for a while. I needed her to know. She had to know.

"Raven," I choked. "You've made me the happiest I've ever been. I didn't think anyone was capable of loving me, but you did. It's okay. Everything is okay, and you're going to get out of this. Please be happy. Be happy for me, baby. I love you."

Tears streamed down my face for her. Even with a blade poised to stop my breaths, I loved her with every shred of my soul. Dying a thousand deaths would have been painless if they were all for her.

I grabbed the wrist that held the knife. "Do it."

Her eyes flashed, and moisture welled in her beautiful emeralds. The sharp steel tip pressed into my skin and blood trickled down my neck. Before I could blink, the warmth of her body was gone, and she dove sideways at my father, pouncing on him like a cat.

She was a blur as she tackled him to the ground, catching him by surprise. He didn't register her movement quickly enough to fight, and my brain didn't have time to tell me to move before she whipped the edge of the knife across his throat, red spraying the walls. Gurgling came from Dad's throat as he fell to the floor, and my senses finally kicked in. I walked the few steps to where Dad's body lay in a sea of blood. His eyes stared into the void, and his chest was unmoving.

Raven hurried to move herself off him, chest heaving as she stood at his feet. I slowly lifted my eyes to her, the knife hanging from one hand at her side. Her face and chest were coated in crimson splatters, while her nostrils flared. She stared at him, her pupils blown out so much only a sliver of green remained. Stunned, I watched as she spat on my father's body, unable to believe what the fuck just happened.

Every emotion possible flooded my body and I became lightheaded. I moved toward Raven, but she backed away. "Don't touch me," was all she said before she disappeared through the door, leaving me with a dead body. My father's dead body. I swayed on my feet and dove from the room and into the office across the hall where I dry heaved until spots dotted my vision.

CHAPTER

THIRTY-NINE

RAVEN

I GRIPPED the edge of the sink and watched the water run clear in the basin. Moments before, the white marble had been stained red. I turned the water off and stared up at my now clean face in the mirror.

I'd scrubbed the demon's blood from my body furiously, the task the only thing on my mind. Since that was finished, I was left with nothing to do now except try to tame the monster that stared back at me.

Closing my eyes, I slowed my breathing and focused on calming my pulse. Ryan's tear-stained face floated behind my eyelids. A mix of emotions flooded me as I replayed the events. Hurt slashed my chest that he was the son and nephew of my attackers. Unease rested in my stomach that he'd hired a private investigator. The strongest emotion of all was the devastation wrapped around my heart as I heard him say he loved me over and over in my mind.

He likely didn't love me anymore. I'd killed his father. No matter if he hated him or not, he couldn't love the person who killed one of his parents. I didn't regret it, though. I enjoyed every fucking second. Killing him had lifted a weight from my shoulders that had been there for fourteen years, and I'd known if this day ever came I would be happy.

I just didn't expect the anguish that came along with it.

I was never going to hurt Ryan. I loved him, and I knew he didn't fall for me solely to fuck with his father. His actions had proved he didn't know about me before. Still, I had to convince everyone I was going to do it, including myself. It was the only way I could attempt to get us out of the situation, even though it was going to cost me the only man I'd ever loved.

Sighing, I looked in the mirror for an undetermined amount of time before leaving the restroom. Walking back into the vampire den that was the reception space, I spotted Ryan sitting on a chair in the darkened room. His head was in his hands, and he didn't look up as I walked past what used to be the glass door scattered everywhere.

Glass crunched as I moved across the room and stood in front of him. "Nice job with destroying my door." I rested my hand on his shoulder and he didn't move. Anxiety laced through my body at my poor attempt at humor. "Ryan," I muttered. "Ryan, are you all right? Are you hurt?"

When he finally raised his eyes to mine, they were damp with emotion. He studied me for what could have been hours. "What now?" he asked.

I blew out a heavy breath, looking back to the shattered door. "I'll call the police. You'll have to stay and give a statement."

He nodded his head and stared off in the distance at nothing as I walked back to my office for my phone. I knew better than to push him. He was going to need time to process everything just like I was going to. Once I reached the doorway, I looked at the dead man that had haunted me for years. He'd helped create the man I loved. What a fucked-up way the universe came back to bite me in the ass.

Hours passed as the police, coroner, and investigators did their jobs. They released Ryan a few hours in, but I was stuck there until nearly three in the morning answering their questions. I had to go to the police station the next day with the security camera footage and answer even more questions.

By the time I walked into the garage, I was dead on my feet. A small part of me expected Ryan to be waiting in his car parked beside mine, but when I pushed open the door to the parking garage he wasn't. I shouldn't have been surprised. The woman he was fucking killed his father. Why would he be anywhere near me?

The foreboding feeling I used to get in the garage wasn't there. I immediately knew I wasn't being watched anymore. As I got into my car, a knife of misery dipped in relief twisted in my gut, slashing apart everything inside me. Relief that I was hopefully safe from the devil himself, and I didn't have to wonder if he was coming for me anymore. Misery because the man I wanted to come after me never would again.

I cried. I cried for everything I had gained and lost, but mostly I cried for the woman who would never have to worry about that man again. I cried for Ryan's mother. No matter how terrible she was; there had to be abuse there. I cried for Ryan, not only because I might not ever hear from him again, but because he was also rid of his demon father. I believed the things he told me about him, even though Ryan hadn't been completely honest with me.

When I stopped crying enough to see out the windshield, I started the car. Backing out of my spot, I wiped my eyes and drove toward my lonely apartment.

A WEEK. It had been over a week since I killed my sort-of boyfriend's father who assaulted me when I was eighteen. I had to close the office and get everyone on remote work for the clean-up and new door installation. I was sure they weren't complaining, but being at home all the time was driving me insane.

I glanced at the clock and decided five thirty was fine to call it a day, especially on a Friday. I couldn't take it anymore. I had to get the fuck out of the apartment. Before I shut down my computer, I clicked open a new tab and pulled up Ryan's socials.

Still nothing. He hadn't posted anything since before Halloween. I missed him, but at this point, I just wanted to make sure he was all right. It wouldn't hurt if I drove by his apartment right? Just to see if he was there.

I changed from my lounge clothes and grabbed my keys from the counter. Not giving myself time to question my decision, I grabbed the knob and pulled the door open. Ryan stood on the other side dressed in his usual hoodie and jeans. My brain glitched at seeing him, and when he looked at me, my heart almost stopped.

Minutes passed before I regained composure. "This is straight out of a romance novel." I laughed.

His face was anything but humored. It was the most serious I'd seen him. My smile fell, and I realized he was probably here to tell me he never wanted to see me again. I didn't blame him for needing closure. I dropped my gaze to the floor, afraid for him to speak.

"Raven," he choked, and in an instant I was in his arms and

his face was a breath in front of mine. His brown eyes were brimstone, and I was so surprised I didn't know what to say.

He brushed a strand of hair away from my face and brought his lips so close I could feel his breath. "Are you going to say the safe word?" he asked.

Safe word? A light bulb flicked on in my brain. This was him asking permission. He was asking me if I wanted him to stop. A sob tore from my throat as I crashed my lips to his, claiming his mouth so thoroughly that we were the same soul.

I kissed him with everything I had in my being, and he kissed me back with the same intensity. His hands came up to grip my face before he slid one around to the back of my neck, holding me firmly in place. I balled my fist in the gray cotton of his hoodie as he scoured my mouth with his tongue like he was staking claim to every inch.

He pulled back, and I stared into his eyes, searching for the words he had yet to speak. His thumb brushed my cheek, and before I knew it, I was wrapped in the tightest hug I'd ever had. I didn't dare to hope because I wasn't sure what any of it meant.

Once he loosened his arms, he took my hand and guided me to the balcony. He plucked a blanket from the sofa as he pulled open the french door. Outside, he wrapped the blanket around my shoulders against the light breeze and we sat opposite each other.

He looked out over the buildings below, toward the few downtown skyscrapers the city had. I didn't know how to say sorry for killing his father. That wasn't a typical thing people had to apologize for. So instead I said, "I've missed you," as a tear slid from the corner of my eye.

He didn't look at me. "Raven, I...I know you won't forgive my violations of your boundaries and privacy easily, but—"

My head snapped up from where my gaze was resting on my hands in my lap. "What?" I interjected.

Ryan continued, his eyes still fixed on the horizon. "My father wasn't lying. I did hire a private investigator to look into your past."

"Ryan..." I began.

He held up his hand. "No, let me finish. The night I texted you as Zander, you thought I was following you. It wasn't me watching you. It had to have been Dad, or someone he paid."

I sat in silence, watching his jaw clench as he spoke. "After getting to know you more that night I had to see you. I'd only seen the photo on your website and couldn't wait any longer. I'd been thinking about you from the moment I heard your voice. So I found your address and watched your apartment. You went to the market, and I followed you. I noticed you were spooked over something. Maybe you sensed me, but I still couldn't get rid of the uneasy feeling that something else was going on. By then, a part of me had become a bit obsessed."

"A bit?" I scoffed, a hint of laughter in my voice.

He smirked. "Maybe more than a bit. So after that, I contacted Dad's guy. I wanted to know everything about you, but more than that, I wanted to make sure you were safe. I'm guessing that's what tipped Dad off, even though Rick didn't break confidence and tell him what I was doing. Dad had eyes everywhere, even on his PI."

Ryan finally looked over to me. "But that's not all, Raven. I had a friend tap into your security systems. I watched you for weeks after you told me you were assaulted and one of them was still out there. But more so because I was crazy for you. Here's the shitty part, though." His demeanor changed from apologetic to determined as he pierced me with his stare. "I would do it again. I don't regret it for a single fucking minute because all of it led me to being there when he came back."

"Earlier that day, Rick called me and sent over all the files he had uncovered—the police files, but also files about Dad following you. The police records were all I got through before I saw a man, who turned out to be my piece of shit father, walk into your office on the security feed. I drove as fast as I could to you, to save you from whatever was happening, but you didn't need saving. It turned out you were the one that saved me."

Tears were openly streaming down my face. "Ryan, I don't fault you for any of that. Everything I said in front of him was to protect you."

"Exactly my point," he gestured. "You saved me then, but you've been saving me from the beginning. You saved me from an isolated future. You saved me from living in his shadow. As long as he existed in the world, I would have hidden myself because I never lived up to what he thought I should be. Most importantly you taught me that I'm capable of love and worthy of it too after never really having it before. I love you, Raven."

I leaped from the chair and crashed into his lap, straddling his thighs. This kiss was different. This kiss was two souls becoming one as I held his face and he wrapped his arms around me.

When I pulled back, he was crying, too. "And I love you, Ryan. I won't apologize for what happened or what I did. The fucked-up thing is that I liked it. The monster inside me enjoyed taking them both out of this world. That's what I've fought for years after the attack all those years ago. But you showed me things too. You showed me there's more to life than work and living for everyone else. I need to live for myself and what I want, too. What I want more than my business, more than success, more than anything is you. I want you."

He smiled the brightest grin I'd ever seen on his lips as I wiped his tears with my thumbs. "I want you, too. I want to wake up to you, make you breakfast, do life with you." His voice changed to sexy Zander. "I want to make you scream when I bury myself inside you. I want to hear both of my names on your lips as you lose yourself beneath my touch. I want to give you control and make every desire you have come true as you turn me into a whimpering mess at your feet. Every single day, I want that."

Heat flushed my body at his perfect words. I loved him, and he loved me. He leaned forward and kissed the tip of my nose.

"So your birth name is Leah?" he asked.

I nodded. "I wanted a fresh start after everything happened, and I didn't want any of my past tied to my future. So I changed my name. You aren't the only one with more than one moniker even though I left one of mine in the past."

He smirked. "Eh, Raven fits you better."

I squealed as he scooped me up into his arms and stood, setting me on my feet. As he led me through the apartment to the bedroom, I couldn't help but tease him. "You know you did that all wrong, right?"

"Did what wrong?"

I laughed. "Haven't you learned anything from narrating romance novels? They normally talk first before he kisses her. You kissed me as soon as you got here."

He pushed me onto the bed, undoing his belt with one hand and tearing it from the loops. "Baby, we've never been normal. We'll make our own fucked-up romance novel."

EPILOGUE

RYAN

With the Anubis mask fixed in place, I slinked past the glass door of Raven's business. My boots thudded down the hall to the room at the end, and I slowly turned the knob. The door swung open to reveal a dark, empty office, the only light coming from the glow of the city beyond the windows. Confusion swirled as I stepped inside and looked around. I was right on time, but she wasn't here. My eyes landed on the spot that had been soaked in my father's blood six months ago.

Good fucking riddance. In the six months since the motherfucker had been dead, I had worked through things with my mom. All of the hurt hadn't been erased, but we talked every now and then. Without his controlling hand, Mom was free to show her love for me. Something she hadn't ever been able to do. It would take time on my end, but I was trying.

My phone buzzed in my pocket and I pulled it out to see a voice message from Raven, a rare occurrence. I was the one who typically sent voice messages because she loved my voice so much. I knew immediately she'd gone rogue from the plan we never got to enact on Halloween. Of course she did. She loved surprising me and being in charge when I was the one who was supposed to be in control.

Smirking, I tapped play.

"Hello darling," her seductive voice came through the speaker. "Small change of plans. Here's what you're going to do. You're going to come find me, and when you do, you can have me. You can have me anyway you like. Oh and baby, here's some motivation."

Raven's moans filled the room, and I could hear the sounds of her fingers in her pussy. Goddamn, this woman is getting me at my own game. I had always been attracted to her voice, but she'd never voice-kinked me like this before.

I was already aroused, but as soon as I heard her sweet moans I was fucking steel. I hurried back to the elevator, smiling at the fact that I paid attention to everything this woman said. I knew exactly where she was.

She'd mentioned a few months ago that she wanted to be fucked in other parts of her building after we thoroughly wore out every surface in her office. I jammed the button for the basement.

When the doors opened to the dim loading dock, it took my eyes a second to adjust to the darkness from the bright elevator. I walked into the large area, surveying for any nook she could be hiding in. Most of the basement was an open concrete floor, but to the right there were dozens of pallets at least twelve feet tall.

I walked through the maze of plastic wrapped towers until I came to the end of the basement. I rounded the corner of the last pallet beside the concrete wall and was greeted with a sight that almost brought me to my knees.

Raven was perched on a small table that looked like it came from her office. It definitely didn't belong in this dingy basement. She wore a black masquerade mask over her eyes and nose, her hair a stream of obsidian over her shoulders. Legs spread wide and heels propped on the table, she'd pulled her black lace lingerie to the side and was rubbing her fingers up and down her pussy.

Suddenly thankful for the tiny sliver of light streaming from the other side of the room, I crossed my arms over my chest, my rolled-up cuffs stretching over my forearms.

"What do we have here?" I asked in the Zander voice I knew would make her the wettest. "This wasn't part of the plan, baby. I was supposed to find you working in your office like a good girl, but here you are being exceptionally bad."

A corner of her mouth turned up into a mischievous grin. "You love it when I'm bad for you. I have to admit that was fast. I didn't expect you so soon," she hurled at me.

My laugh sounded eerie in the large space. "What you failed to remember, Ms. Lovelace, is that I listen and take note of everything you say."

I lunged for her, only to be speared in the stomach with her heel. I let out a growl and grabbed her ankle.

"He's so eager." She yanked free from my grasp and set her foot back on the table and brought her soaked fingers up in offering. "Clean my fingers, baby."

Without a thought I seized her wrist and drew her middle and ring fingers into my mouth. The mere taste of her had my cock trying to burst from my slacks. I devoured her fingers like it was the last time I would get to savor her.

She pulled her hand away and ripped open my shirt, buttons flying and scattering on the table and floor. Reaching for my pants, she undid my belt and jerked down the zipper. She thought she had taken control of this interaction, but I wasn't in the mood to be her obedient boy tonight.

I reached out, wrapping my hand around her throat and bringing my face so close the mask brushed her skin. Her eyes went wide in surprise, and I dropped my voice to the lowest register I could manage. "I'm in charge tonight. I'm going to use you for what you are, a pussy to fuck. Your body is for my pleasure, and I'm going to enjoy every second of ruining you. Understood?"

She nodded, but that didn't satisfy me.

"I've told you countless times to use your fucking words."

"Yes. I understand," she said, breathless as my fingers dug into the sides of her throat.

I dipped my head to the side, bringing the mask next to her ear. "Say my name, baby. Say you're mine to use how I please."

She whimpered at my words. "I'm yours, Zander. Use me. Take what you need," she panted.

With that she freed the beast inside me that I didn't let out often. I released her neck and whipped my belt from my jeans. "Put your wrists together," I commanded.

She didn't hesitate, and I wound the belt around her outstretched hands, securing the buckle tight enough she couldn't escape the bind. I pushed my pants and boxers down my thighs, my cock springing free. She tracked every movement and looked at me hungrily, my tip already dripping for her.

I grabbed her hands and slammed them into the wall above her head with one hand as I fisted my cock with the other. I rubbed the head up and down her soaked pussy before positioning myself at her entrance. I looked into her heavy-lidded eyes as I rammed into her, losing myself in her sweet body as I had so many times before.

It would never be enough. No matter how many times I had her, it wouldn't satiate the fire always burning inside me for the perfect woman beneath me. I thrusted fast, picking up a rhythm as she cried out.

"Fuck, Zander…" she moaned. "Can I? I need to, please," she moaned as my own release built on the horizon.

Her begging was never something I could withstand. When she begged, I always gave in. I reached down between us and circled her clit with my thumb as I picked up my pace. Pressure built at the base of my spine as she came undone, screaming so loudly I let her wrists go and slipped my hand over her mouth.

"Fuck, baby. Fuck." I moaned as she clenched around me. I spilled inside her as her pussy fluttered, claiming her with every drop.

I ripped off the mask and set it beside her on the table, then unbuckled her wrists. Dropping my forehead down to hers, I reached up and cupped her cheek with my hand. When our breathing returned to normal, I dropped a kiss on her lips.

"I love you," I said, wiping her damp hair out of her face.

She smiled up at me. "I love you, too," she answered as her face grew mischievous. "So is this a good time to ask you to move in?"

I threw my head back and laughed. "You can ask me anything, anytime, and I'll probably say yes."

Kissing her once more as she giggled, I slid out of her and buttoned myself back up. I scooped her off the table and led her to the elevator. We stepped on, and she nestled herself into my arms and looked up at me, her emerald eyes shining against the black mask.

"You had your fun tonight, but the next time you're going to have to be a good boy and beg for it."

I pulled her closer. "Anything for you, baby."

THE END

AUTHOR'S NOTE

Moniker was born from a love of narration and voice work. Voice actors are some of the most talented artists—their dedication and hard work to bring our favorite characters to life are both inspiring and galvanizing. To listen to narration is to be immersed in stories in a different way, a way that will incite a unique adoration for words.

ACKNOWLEDGMENTS

There's so much to write here. First and foremost, I want to thank you, the reader. *Moniker* was written on a whim and my gut told me to drop everything for it. Thank you for taking a chance on it and me. The reason I write is for myself, but also readers. Whether it's one person or many people, I want my stories to provide an escape while also evoking emotion and reactions—even if the reaction is squealing at something the love interest said.

Nina, my insanely talented PA, I couldn't have done this without you. You've talked me off a ledge so many times, and made sure I could lean on you when I needed to. Now, you're so much more than someone to help with my author things— an irreplaceable friend.

To my bog witch authors, E, Sky, Torrence, Maeve, M.M., and Phoebe, you keep me sane with your chaos. When I need to laugh, to the chat, I go. Thank you for making me smile every single day.

Courtney, your loyalty and unwavering love have gotten me through my darkest days. From phone calls, texts, and sitting on video calls while I write, you always make sure I have what I need. Thank you for being a steadfast friend.

To Cassie, thank you for your constant excitement about all of my ideas, and for reading them before anyone else. Your feedback and comments spark my brain in the right direction, and my stories are stronger because of you. Our love of books bonded us in the beginning, but you still show up years later.

Laura Maddie, my stories exist because of you. Without your encouragement and insistence, I wouldn't have written the first word. You said I could do it, and I'm not one to back down from a challenge. I did it. Thank you for pushing me.

Jordy and Mary, I'm the person I am today because of you.

To my sister, keep reading and chasing your dreams. Thank you to my husband for being my green flag and always waiting nearby to catch me when I stumble. To the rest of my family and friends, thank you for loving me.

To everyone who has been on my teams, and those who have supported me online, thank you for your dedication and lifting me up.

And again to my readers, thank you for spending time with my words.

ABOUT THE AUTHOR

Wrenna King is a legal professional turned romantic story weaver. A serial reader from a young age, she later found a passion for writing and a desire to give readers "all the feels". She lives in the Southeast with her husband and doggos.

www.ingramcontent.com/pod-product-compliance
Lightning Source LLC
Chambersburg PA
CBHW031954150726
47990CB00005B/1710